The Accidental
Apprentice

The Accidental Apprentice

VIKAS SWARUP

**SIMON &
SCHUSTER**

London · New York · Sydney · Toronto · New Delhi

A CBS COMPANY

First published in Great Britain by Simon & Schuster UK Ltd, 2013
A CBS COMPANY

1 3 5 7 9 10 8 6 4 2

Simon & Schuster UK Ltd
1st Floor
222 Gray's Inn Road
London WC1X 8HB

www.simonandschuster.co.uk

Simon & Schuster Australia, Sydney
Simon & Schuster India, New Delhi

A CIP catalogue record for this book
is available from the British Library

HB ISBN: 978-1-47111-315-4
TPB ISBN: 978-1-47111-316-1
EBOOK ISBN: 978-1-47111-318-5
INDIA PB ISBN: 978-1-47112-824-0

Typeset by M Rules
Printed and bound in India by Replika Press Pvt. Ltd.

For Aditya and Varun
who heard my first stories

Contents

Prologue

In life you never get what you deserve: you get what you negotiate.

That was the first lesson he taught me.

For the last three days I have been putting that guidance into practice, negotiating frantically with my prosecutors and persecutors in a desperate bid to stave off the death penalty, which they all believe I deserve.

Outside the lockup, the press are circling like vultures. The news channels cannot get enough of me, holding me up as a cautionary tale of what happens when greed and gullibility collide to create the blood-speckled train wreck called culpable homicide of the first degree. They keep recycling that police mugshot taken after my arrest. Sunlight TV has even dug up a grainy class photograph of me in school in Nainital, sitting stiffly in the front row next to Mrs Saunders, our Grade 8 teacher. But Nainital seems a world away now, a never-never land of lush mountains and silvery lakes, where, once upon a time, my youthful optimism had tricked me into believing that the future was limitless and the human spirit indomitable.

I want to hope, to dream, to have faith again, but the soulless weight of reality keeps crushing me down. I feel as if I am living a nightmare, trapped in a deep, dark well of endless despair, from which there is no way out.

As I sit in my sweltering, windowless jail cell, my thoughts keep straying to that fateful day when it all began. Though it was more than six months ago, I can still recall every detail with an unwavering clarity as if it were yesterday. In my mind's eye, I can see myself walking towards the Hanuman Temple in Connaught Place on that cold grey afternoon . . .

It is Friday, 10 December, and traffic on Baba Kharak Singh Marg is the usual chaotic snarl of heat and noise. The road is jammed with lumbering buses, honking cars, whining scooters and spluttering auto-rickshaws. The sky is cloudless but the sun is invisible behind that toxic cocktail of smog that smothers the city every winter.

I am wearing a grey cardigan over a demure, sky-blue salvar kameez, having prudently changed from my work uniform. It is a routine I follow every Friday, slipping out of the showroom during the lunch hour to make the short walk across the marketplace to the ancient temple dedicated to the monkey god, Hanuman.

Most people go to temples to pray; I go to expiate. I have still not forgiven myself for Alka's death. Part of me will always think what happened to her was my fault. Since that horrific tragedy, God is my only refuge. And I have a special bond with Goddess Durga, who also has a shrine inside the Hanuman Mandir.

Lauren Lockwood, my American friend, is perpetually fascinated by the fact that we have 330 million gods. 'Jeez, you Hindus sure like to hedge your bets,' she says. That's probably an exaggeration, but every temple worth its salt does have shrines to at least half a dozen deities.

Each of these deities has some special powers. Goddess Durga is the Invincible One who can redeem situations of utmost distress. After Alka's death, when my life was a dark tunnel of sorrow, pain and regret, She gave me strength. She is always with me whenever I need her.

The temple is unusually crowded for a Friday afternoon and I am caught up in the ceaseless scrum of devotees jostling to get to the sanctum sanctorum. The marble floor feels cool under my bare feet and the air is heavy with the intoxicating blend of sweat, sandalwood, flowers and incense.

I get into the ladies' queue, which is considerably shorter and manage to make my communion with Durga Ma in less than ten minutes.

Having finished my *darshan*, I am about to go down the stairs when a hand drops on my shoulder. I whirl around and discover a man gazing at me intently.

When an unknown adult male accosts a young woman in Delhi, the instinctive thing to do is to reach for that bottle of pepper spray one always keeps handy. But the stranger looking at me is no street loafer. He is an elderly man, dressed in an off-white silk kurta pyjama, with a white pashmina shawl draped casually across his shoulders. Fair and tall, he has an aquiline nose, a hard, resolute mouth and a head crowned by a shock of backswept, snowy-white hair. A vermilion tika adorns his forehead. His fingers are loaded with rings glinting with diamonds and emeralds. But it is his penetrating brown eyes that unsettle me. They seem to search me with a directness I find slightly intimidating. This is a man who likes to be in control.

'Could I have a word with you?' he asks in a clipped tone.

'What do you want?' I respond curtly, less acerbic than I would normally have been out of respect for his age.

'My name is Vinay Mohan Acharya,' he says evenly. 'I am the owner of Acharya Business Consortium. Have you heard of the ABC Group of Companies?'

My eyebrows arch in acknowledgement. The ABC Group is well known as one of India's largest conglomerates, making everything from toothpaste to turbines.

'I have a proposition for you,' he continues. 'Something that will change your life for ever. Will you give me ten minutes to explain?'

I have heard these words before. From pesky insurance peddlers and door-to-door detergent salesmen. And they always make me wary. 'I don't have ten minutes,' I say. 'I have to return to work.'

'Just hear me out,' he persists.

'What is it? Say it.'

'I would like to give you a chance to become the CEO of the ABC Group of Companies. I am offering you the opportunity of heading a business empire worth ten billion dollars.'

Now I know he's not to be trusted. He sounds just like

a confidence trickster, no different from those ubiquitous hawkers on Janpath trying to flog shoddy Rexine belts and packs of cheap handkerchiefs. I wait for that half-smile that will tell me he is kidding, but his face remains impassive.

'I'm not interested,' I say firmly, and begin descending the stairs. He follows me.

'You mean to say you are turning down the offer of the century, more money than you will ever see in seven life-times?' His tone is sharp, cutting like a whip.

'Look, Mr Acharya, or whoever you are. I don't know what your game is, but I'm not interested in playing it. So please stop pestering me,' I say, as I retrieve my Bata slippers from the old lady at the temple entrance who safeguards unattended footwear for a small tip.

'I know you probably think this is all a joke,' he declares, slipping into a pair of brown sandals.

'Well, isn't it?'

'I've never been more serious in my life.'

'Then you must be from a TV prank show. I suppose the moment I say yes you will show me the secret camera that's following you around.'

'You expect a man of my stature to be doing silly TV shows?'

'Well, isn't it silly to be offering your business empire to random strangers? It makes me doubt if you are even who you say you are.'

'Good point.' He nods. 'A little scepticism is always healthy.' He reaches into his kurta's pocket and retrieves a black leather wallet. Extracting a business card, he offers it to me. 'Perhaps this might convince you.'

I examine it cursorily. It does look impressive, made of some kind of semitransparent plastic, with an embossed logo of the ABC Group and 'VINAY MOHAN ACHARYA, CHAIRMAN' etched below it in bold, black letters.

'Anyone can get these printed for a few hundred rupees,' I say, returning his card.

He pulls out another piece of plastic from his wallet and holds it up. 'How about this one?'

It is an all-black American Express Centurion card, with 'VINAY MOHAN ACHARYA' engraved at the bottom. I have encountered this rare species just once before, when a flashy builder from Noida used it to pay for a 60-inch Sony LX-900 TV costing almost 400,000 rupees. 'It still doesn't change anything.' I shrug. 'How do I know this isn't a forgery?'

By now we have crossed the temple's forecourt and are in proximity of the road. 'That's my car,' he says, pointing out a shiny vehicle parked alongside the kerb. A chauffeur is in the driver's seat, wearing a peaked cap and a starched white uniform. An armed guard in military fatigues scrambles out of the front seat and stiffens to attention. Acharya flicks a finger and he opens the rear door with alacrity. His zealous servility does not seem fake; it looks like it has been honed by years of unquestioning subservience. The car, I note admiringly, is a silver Mercedes-Benz CLS-500, with a price tag of over nine million rupees.

'Just give me a second,' Acharya says, and ducks inside the car. He removes a magazine from the rear seat and hands it to me. 'I had kept this as a last resort. If this won't convince you, nothing will.'

It is the December 2008 issue of *Business Times*. A man's portrait is on the cover, with the blazing headline, 'BUSINESSMAN OF THE YEAR'. I glance at the face on the cover and then at the man standing in front of me. They are identical. There is no mistaking the distinctive, back-swept, silvery hair, the curved nose or the piercing brown eyes. I am indeed in the presence of industrialist Vinay Mohan Acharya. 'Okay,' I concede. 'So you are Mr Acharya. What do you want from me?'

'I already told you. I want to make you my CEO.'

'And you expect me to believe you?'

'Then give me ten minutes and I will *make* you believe me. Can we sit down somewhere and talk?'

I look at my watch. There are still twenty minutes of my lunch break left. 'We could go to the Coffee House,' I say, indicating the rundown building on the opposite side of the road that serves as the social hub of the chattering classes.

'I would have preferred the Lobby Lounge at the Shangri La,' he says with the reluctant air of a man accepting a poor choice. 'Do you mind if a colleague of mine also joins us?'

Even as he says this, a man materialises out of the crowd of pedestrians like a ghost and stands by his side. He is much younger, probably in his early thirties, and dressed casually in a dark-blue Reebok tracksuit. Just under six feet, he has the sinewy, wiry frame of an athlete. I take in his crew-cut hair, small, ferret-like eyes and thin, cruel mouth. His nose is slightly out of joint, as though it has been broken once, providing the only memorable accent in an otherwise unremarkable face. I reckon he must have been shadowing Acharya all this while. Even now his gimlet eyes dart constantly from side to side, scanning the surroundings like a professional bodyguard, before fixing on me.

'This is Rana, my right-hand man,' Acharya says, introducing him. I nod politely, withering under his icy stare.

'Should we go?' Rana asks. He has a weathered, raspy voice, like dry leaves rustling along the ground. Without waiting for my reply, he begins leading the way to the underpass.

The heavy smell of frying dosas and roasting coffee assails my senses the moment I step through the eatery's swinging door. It has all the ambience of a hospital cafeteria. I can see Acharya wrinkling his nose, already regretting the decision to come here. This being lunch hour, the place is packed. 'Minimum twenty minutes' wait, please,' the manager informs us.

I observe Rana slip him a folded hundred-rupee note and instantly a corner table is readied for us. Acharya and his flunkey sit down on one side, and I take the lone seat opposite them. Rana brusquely orders three filter coffees and then Acharya takes over. He looks me in the eye, his gaze steady. 'Let me be frank with you. This is like a blind bet for me. So, before I explain my proposal to you, would you tell me a little bit about yourself?'

'Well, there's nothing much to tell.'

'You could begin with your name.'

'I'm Sapna. Sapna Sinha.'

'Sapna.' He rolls the word around on his tongue, before nodding in apparent satisfaction. 'Good name. How old are you, Sapna, if you don't mind me asking?'

'Twenty-three.'

'And what do you do? Are you a student?'

'I did my graduation from Kumaun University in Nainital. Now I'm working as a sales assistant at Gulati & Sons. They have a showroom in Connaught Place for electronics and home appliances.'

'I've been there. Isn't it close to here?'

'Yes. In B-Block.'

'And how long have you been working there?'

'Just over a year.'

'What about your family?'

'I live with my mother, and Neha, my younger sister. She's doing her BA from Kamala Nehru College.'

'What about your father?'

'He passed away, a year and a half ago.'

'Oh, I'm sorry to hear that. So are you the breadwinner in the family now?'

I nod.

'If you don't mind telling me, how much do you earn in a month?'

'With my sales commission, around eighteen thousand rupees.'

'That's all? Then shouldn't you be jumping at the chance to lead a multimillion-dollar company and acquire a fortune?'

'Look, Mr Acharya, I'm still quite confused about your offer. I mean, first of all, why do you need a CEO?'

'Why? Because I'm sixty-eight years old and not getting any younger. God made the human body like a machine with built-in obsolescence. I'm about to reach my expiry date. But, before I go, I want to ensure an orderly transition at the organisation I have nurtured for forty years. I want to ensure that I am followed by someone who believes in the same values that I do.'

'But why me? Why not your own son or daughter?'

'Well, for one, I don't have a family any more. My wife and daughter died in a plane crash eighteen years ago.'

'Oh! Then what about someone from your company?'

'I've searched far and wide within the company. I couldn't find anyone remotely suitable. My executives are good implementers, excellent subordinates, but I don't see the traits of a great leader in any of them.'

'And what do you see in me? I don't know a thing about running a business. I'm not even an MBA.'

'These degrees are simply a piece of paper. They don't teach you how to lead people, only how to manage stuff. That's why I didn't go to a management institute to pick my CEO. I came to a temple.'

'You've still not answered my question. Why me?'

'There was something in your eyes, a sparkle that I'd never seen anywhere before.' He searches my eyes for confirmation before glancing away. 'I have always been an observer of people,' he continues, looking around the hall, at the middle-class shoppers and office workers sitting on the other tables. 'And, of all the people I observed in the temple, you seemed the most focused. Call it intuition, psychic sense, whatever you want, but something told me that you could be the one. You alone had the compelling mix of determination and desperation I was looking for.'

'I thought desperation was a negative virtue.'

He shakes his head. 'Happy people don't make good

CEOs. Contentment breeds laziness. It is aspiration that drives achievement. I want people with hunger. Hunger that is born in the desert of dissatisfaction. You seem to have that want, that hunger.'

I am getting caught up in his sweeping statements and grand assumptions. But the logic behind his rhetoric still eludes me. 'Do you always take decisions based on whims?'

'Never underestimate the power of intuition. Eleven years ago, I bought a troubled factory in Romania called Iancu Steel. It was losing money every day. All my experts advised me against the purchase. They said I was throwing good money after bad. But I remained firm in my decision. I was attracted to the factory only because of its name. Iancu means "God is Gracious". Today, fifty-three per cent of our steel revenues come from that factory in Romania. God is indeed gracious.'

'So you do believe in God?'

'Isn't this proof enough?' He points at the vermilion mark on his forehead. 'The main reason I came to a temple to select my successor is because I wanted a devout like me. We are living in Kalyug, the dark age, full of sin and corruption. Religion is no longer in fashion. The youngsters working for me are consumed by consumption. They've probably not visited a temple to pray in years. I'm not saying they are all atheists, but their god is money, first and foremost. But you . . .' He nods at me approvingly. 'You seem to be just the pious, God-fearing candidate I was looking for.'

'Okay, I get it. You act on whims, and your latest whim tells you that I'm the chosen one. Now tell me: what's the catch?'

'There is no catch. But there are some terms and conditions. You will have to pass a few tests.'

'Tests?'

'Don't worry: I'm not taking you back to school. A school simply tests your memory. But life tests your character. My seven tests are rites of passage, designed to gauge your mettle and potential as a CEO.'

'Why seven?'

'In my forty years of running a business, I have learnt one thing: a company is only as good as the person who runs it. And I have whittled down the traits of a successful CEO to seven basic attributes. So each of the seven tests will focus on one of those seven traits.'

'And what exactly will I have to do to pass those tests?'

'Nothing that you wouldn't do in your daily life. I will not ask you to steal or kill or do anything illegal. In fact, you won't even be aware of the tests.'

'What do you mean?'

'My tests will come from the textbook of life. Doesn't life test us every day? Don't we make choices every day? I will simply evaluate your choices, your responses to life's daily challenges. That will reveal the stuff you are made of.'

'And what if I fail any of those tests?'

'Well, then I will have to look for someone else. But my gut instinct tells me you won't fail. It almost seems destined. The biggest lottery ticket of all time will be yours.'

'In that case my decision is quite clear. I'm not interested in your offer.'

He seems astounded. 'But why?'

'I don't believe in lottery tickets.'

'But you believe in God. And sometimes God gives you much more than you ask for.'

'I'm not that greedy,' I say, rising from the table. 'Thank you, Mr Acharya. It was nice meeting you, but I really must get back to the showroom now.'

'Sit!' he orders me. There is steel in his voice. I swallow hard and sit down like an obedient student.

'Listen, Sapna.' His voice softens. 'There are only two types of people in the world: winners and losers. I am giving you the chance to be a winner. All I ask in return is for you to sign this consent form.' He gestures to Rana, who produces a printed sheet of paper from the inside pocket of his tracksuit and lays it in front of me.

Since Alka's death, I've developed a sixth sense about some things, a little warning bell that goes off in my head whenever a situation is not quite right. That bell is ringing as I pick up the form. It is short, just five sentences:

1. The signer hereby agrees to be considered for the post of CEO of the ABC Group of Companies.
2. The signer hereby permits the ABC Group to perform necessary checks and procedures to assess the signer's suitability for the job.
3. The signer is not permitted to terminate the agreement mid-way, while the necessary checks and procedures are still being conducted.
4. The signer agrees to maintain complete confidentiality of this agreement by not discussing it with any third party.
5. In consideration of the above, the signer has received a non-refundable advance of ₹100,000.

'This only talks of one lakh rupees,' I observe. 'Didn't I hear you mention the figure of ten billion dollars?'

'The one lakh is simply to participate in the tests. If you fail, you get to keep the money. And, if you pass, you get the job. I assure you the CEO's salary will have many more zeroes.'

By now the warning bell is clanging like a fire alarm. I know that this is a swindle, and that Acharya has tried this ploy before. 'Tell me, how many people have you got to sign this form so far?'

'You are candidate number seven.' Acharya exhales. 'But I know in my heart that you will be the last one. My quest is over.'

'So is my time.' I stand up decisively. 'I have no intention of signing this form or participating in any test.'

Rana responds by laying a stack of thousand–rupee notes on the table. They look crisp and new, straight from a bank. He is baiting me, but I am not tempted. 'You think you can buy me with your money?'

'Well, this is a negotiation, after all,' Acharya insists. 'Remember, in business as in life, you never get what you deserve: you only get what you negotiate.'

'I don't negotiate with people I hardly know. What if this is some kind of trap?'

'The only trap is that of low expectations. Look, I understand your reservations,' Acharya says soothingly, leaning forward on his elbows. 'But you need to take a less bleak view of human nature, Sapna. I sincerely and genuinely want to make you my CEO.'

'Do you have any idea how ridiculous this conversation

sounds? Such things happen only in movies and books, not in real life.'

'Well, I am real and you are real and my offer is real. A man like me does not waste time in tomfoolery.'

'I am sure you can find other candidates who would be more than willing to accept your offer. I am not interested.'

'You are making a big mistake.' Acharya wags a finger at me. 'Perhaps the greatest mistake of your life. But I will not pressurise you. Take my card, and, if you change your mind within the next forty-eight hours, call me. The offer will still be valid.' He pushes a business card across the table, Rana watching me like a hawk.

I take it, smile tightly at them, and then, without as much as a backward glance, head for the door.

My mind is spinning faster than a CD as I hurry towards B-Block. The overwhelming feeling I have is one of relief, as though I had escaped from some grave danger by the skin of my teeth. I look over my shoulder periodically to make sure the duo are not following me. The more I reflect on what has just transpired, the more convinced I am that Acharya is either a devious shark or a raving lunatic. And I want no truck with either category.

I breathe easy only once I return to the safety of the showroom, to my air-conditioned world of plasma TVs, frost-free refrigerators and fuzzy-logic washing machines. Banishing Acharya and his crazy offer from my mind, I change back into my work uniform, and begin the habit-ual hunt for prospective buyers. Afternoons are generally a sluggish period for sales and there aren't too many customers vying for attention. I try to interest a puzzled-looking shopper with a potbelly in the latest full-HD camcorder from Samsung, but he seems more interested in my legs sticking out of the short red skirt. Whoever designed this risqué costume (and the finger of suspicion has always pointed at Raja Gulati, the owner's wastrel son) meant to make us salesgirls look like air hostesses. Except, as my colleague Prachi says, 'We get the propositions, but not the pay.'

To be honest, I don't have to contend with as many lecherous advances as the other three salesgirls. They are the ones who look like flight attendants, with their coif-fured hair, impeccable makeup and glowing skins. I look like an advertisement for Fair and Lovely cream with my awkward smile and a complexion that is described in mat-rimonial ads as 'wheatish', a polite way of saying 'not fair'. I was always the ugly duckling of the family. My two younger sisters, Alka and Neha, got their milky white complexions from Ma. I inherited my father's darker skin. And, in this part of the world, skin colour is destiny.

Only when I started working at the showroom did I discover that being dark and plain-looking also has its advantages. Wealthy women customers get intimidated by competition and can't stand it when other beautiful women are around. They feel more comfortable with me. And, since most family purchase decisions are made by women, I invariably reach my monthly sales targets faster than everyone else.

Another thing I've learnt is never to judge customers by their appearance. They come in all shapes, sizes and dresses. Like the middle-aged man who walks into the

showroom just after 3 p.m. dressed incongruously in a
turban and dhoti. He looks like a bodybuilder, with a
huge upper body, thick arms and a handlebar moustache
he has teased and twirled into a work of art. He wanders
through the aisles like a lost child, overwhelmed by the
shop's glitter. Finding the other salesgirls sniggering at his
rustic dress and manners, he latches onto me. Within ten
minutes I have extracted his entire life story. His name is
Kuldip Singh and he is the patriarch of a prosperous agri-
cultural family from a village called Chandangarh, located
in the Karnal district of Haryana, approximately 140 kilometres from Delhi. His eighteen-year-old daughter Babli
is getting married next week and he has come to the capital to buy goods for her dowry.

It is another matter that his knowledge of machines
extends only to tractors and tube wells. He has never seen
a microwave oven in his life, and thinks the LG, 15-kg,
top-loading washer is an ingenious device for churning
lassi! He also wants to bargain with me for the price of
things. I try to explain to him that all items in the showroom have a fixed price, but he refuses to accept it.

'*Dekh chhori*. Look here, girl,' he drawls in his home-
spun vernacular. 'We have a saying in our Haryana.
However stubborn a goat may be, in the end it has to
yield milk.'

He is so insistent that eventually I have to prevail upon
the manager to offer him a 5 per cent discount, and he
ends up buying a truckload worth of goods, including a
42-inch plasma TV, a three-door fridge, a washing
machine, a DVD player and a music system. The other
salesgirls look on in hushed awe as he pulls out a thick

wad of thousand-rupee notes to pay for his buying spree. Their country bumpkin has turned out to be a shopaholic baron. And I have notched up yet another sales record!

The rest of the day passes in a blur. I leave the showroom as usual at 8.15 p.m. and board the metro, as always, from Rajiv Chowk station.

The forty-five-minute journey takes me to Rohini, a sprawling middle-class suburb in northwest Delhi. Reputed to be the second biggest residential colony in Asia, it is a cheap, ugly tentacle of the capital, crammed with dismal, unimaginative concrete apartment blocks and chaotic markets.

I disembark at Rithala, the last stop on the Red Line. From here it is a twenty-minute walk to the LIG Colony in Pocket B-2, Sector 11, where I live. Of all the housing societies in Rohini, mine is the most melancholy. The name itself – LIG, shorthand for 'Lower Income Group' – is like a slap in the face. Built by the Delhi Development Authority in the 1980s, the four red-brick tower blocks look like a clump of brick kiln chimneys, their disfigured exteriors and defaced interiors bearing the telltale signs of shoddy government construction. Nevertheless, I am thankful to be living here. After Papa's death we wouldn't have been able to afford even these dreary 2-BHK flats which command rents in excess of twelve thousand a month. Luckily, we don't have to pay any rent for B-29, our second-floor apartment, because it belongs to Mr Dinesh Sinha, Papa's well-heeled younger brother. Deenu Uncle took pity on us and has allowed us to reside here for free. Well, it's not completely free. Once in a while I am obligated to take his moronic sons Rolu and Golu out to a fancy dinner. It beats me why they have to eat out at my expense when their father owns three tandoori restaurants himself.

The first thing you see on entering our flat is a framed black-and-white photo of Papa in the small foyer where we keep the fridge. Decorated with a garland of brittle roses, it shows him as a young man, not yet burdened by the responsibilities of a teacher with three grown-up daughters. The photographer has been kind to him, smoothing away some of the premature worry lines carved into his forehead. But he couldn't touch up the forbidding scowl that was fixed permanently around Papa's mouth.

Our modest drawing-cum-dining room is dominated by a colour blow-up of Alka on the centre wall. Wearing an outrageous red hat, she is posing like the ladies of Royal Ascot. Her head is tilted back slightly, her dark eyes are opened wide and her lips are puckered in a goofy smile. That is how I will always remember her: beautiful, young and carefree. Every time I see this picture, I can feel the room ringing with her infectious laughter. '*Didi! Didi! Kamaal ho gaya!* Something amazing happened today!' I can hear her eager voice greeting me, ready to spill the details of yet another silly prank she dreamt up in school.

Below the photo is a faded green sofa set with embroidered white dust covers, a couple of straight-back bamboo chairs with worn-out cushions, and an old Videocon TV perched on the sideboard where we store crockery and cutlery. To the left of this arrangement is a dining table made of recycled teakwood, which I picked up dirt cheap from an embassy auction, complemented by four matching chairs.

Going through a bead curtain, you enter the first bedroom, which belongs to Ma. It has a bed, surrounded by two wooden almirahs for clothes and a metal filing cabinet that is nowadays used mainly for storing her medicines. Ma's health was always frail; the sudden deaths of her youngest daughter and husband devastated her completely. She just withdrew into a shell, becoming distant and quiet, neglecting to eat and no longer caring about her appearance. The more she retreated from the world, the more disease took over her body. She now suffers from chronic diabetes, hypertension, arthritis and asthma, requiring regular trips to the government hospital. Looking at her gaunt body and silver hair, it is hard to believe she is only forty-seven.

The other bedroom is shared between Neha and myself. My younger sister has only one goal in life: to be famous. She has plastered the walls of our small room with posters of singers, models and film stars. One day she hopes to be as rich and successful as they. Blessed with a pretty face, an hourglass figure and flawless skin, Neha is shrewdly aware of the economic potential of hitting the gene jackpot, and is prepared to exploit her beauty to get what she wants. It helps that she is also a trained singer with a sound base of Indian music and a great natural voice.

All the boys in the neighbourhood have a crush on Neha, but she wouldn't give them the time of day. She has already summed up her future in three letters: B-I-G. And it doesn't include anyone belonging to the L-I-G.

She spends her days hanging out with her richie-rich college friends, and her nights writing application letters for participating in reality shows, talent contests and beauty pageants. Neha Sinha is the poster girl for vaulting ambition.

She also has a penchant for mindless consumerism, blindly aping the fashion of the moment. Half my salary every month goes in meeting her constantly evolving needs: skinny jeans, glossy lipsticks, designer handbags, blingy cell-phones . . . The list never ends.

For the last two months she has been pestering me for a laptop. But that is where I have drawn the line. A ₹800 belt is one thing, a ₹30,000 gadget quite another.

'Welcome back, *didi*,' Neha greets me the moment I step into the flat. She even manages to raise a smile instead of the sullen pout that is her default setting whenever I deny her something.

'You know that Acer laptop I've been dying to get?' She gives me that puppy-dog look of hers I know quite well. It usually precedes a new demand.

'Yes,' I respond guardedly.

'Well, they've just discounted it. It's now available for only twenty-two thousand. Surely you can buy it at this price.'

'I can't,' I say firmly. 'It's still way too expensive.'

'Please, *didi*. I'm the only one in my class without a laptop. I promise I won't ask you for anything after this.'

'I'm sorry, Neha, but we just can't afford it. As it is, we're barely making ends meet on my salary.'

'Can't you take a loan from the company?'

'No, I can't.'

'You are being cruel.'

'I'm being realistic. You have to get used to the fact that we are poor, Neha. And life is hard.'

'I'd rather die than live such a life. I'm twenty years old and what have I got to show for it? I've never even seen the inside of a plane.'

'Well, neither have I.'

'Then you should. All my friends go to places like Switzerland and Singapore for their summer holidays. And we can't even afford a hill station in India.'

'We used to live in a hill station, Neha. Anyway, laptops and holidays aren't important. Your number-one priority should be to get good grades.'

'And what will good grades get me? Look where you landed after topping the university.'

Neha has always had this uncanny ability to hurt me, both with her silence and with her words. Even though I have got used to her caustic barbs, this one stings me for its brutal honesty, leaves me speechless. That is when my cell phone rings.

'Hello,' I answer.

It is Deenu Uncle, sounding very unlike himself. 'Sapna, *beti*, I have something important to tell you. I'm afraid it's bad news.'

I brace myself for yet another death in the family. Perhaps of some ailing aunt or distant grandmother. But what he says next is nothing short of a bombshell. 'I need you to vacate the flat within two weeks.'

'What?'

'Yes. I'm very sorry, but my hands are tied. I've just invested in a new restaurant and need cash urgently. So

I've decided to put the Rohini flat out for rent. An agent called me today with a very good offer. In this situation I have no option but to ask you and your family to find another place.'

'But Uncle, how can we find a place so soon?'

'I'll help you find one. Only thing is, now you'll have to start paying rent.'

'If we have to pay rent, we might as well continue to stay here.'

Deenu Uncle thinks about it. 'I suppose that's reasonable,' he agrees reluctantly. 'But you won't be able to afford my flat.'

'How much is this new tenant going to pay you?'

'We have agreed on fourteen thousand per month. That's a full two thousand more than the going rate. And he is to pay me a one-year deposit in advance. If you accept the same terms I have no objection to your continued stay.'

'You mean you want us to pay you an advance of a hundred and sixty-eight thousand?'

'Exactly. Your maths was always quite good.'

'There's no way we can raise so much money, Chacha-ji.'

'Then look for another apartment.' His tone hardens. 'I've to think of my family too. I'm not running a charitable dispensary. As it is, I've allowed you people to stay for free for sixteen months.'

'Didn't Papa also do so much for you? Don't you have any consideration for your deceased brother? You want his family to come on the street? What kind of uncle are you, Chacha-ji?' I try to prick his conscience.

The strategy boomerangs. 'You people are nothing but ungrateful freebooters,' he says, rounding on me. 'And listen, let's cut out all this uncle sweet-talk. From now on, our relationship is strictly that of a landlord and tenant. So either you pay me the full sum within a week, or vacate my flat.'

'At least give us a little more time to arrange the funds,' I implore.

'One week is all you've got. Pay up or leave,' he says, and terminates the call.

I find my hands are trembling with indignation. I take a moment to wish all sorts of lingering painful deaths on Deenu Uncle, before narrating the conversation to the other two occupants of the flat. Ma shakes her head, more in sorrow than in anger. The wickedness of the world is something she has taken for granted.

'I never trusted that man. God is watching everything. One day Deenu will pay for his sins.'

Neha is surprisingly upbeat. 'I say if that swine is throwing us out, let's get out of this dump. It suffocates me to live here.'

'And where will we go?' I counter. 'You think it is child's play to find a new house?'

Before a fresh argument breaks out between us, Mother brings the focus back to more practical issues. 'How are we going to get all this money?' The question looms over us like an ominous cloud.

Papa didn't leave us much. He had raided his pension fund long ago to finance Deenu Uncle's initial foray in the restaurant business. And his modest savings from his teaching job were used up in the establishment costs of moving to a new city. At the time of his death, he had barely ten thousand rupees in his bank account.

Ma has already figured out the answer to the question. She unlocks her cupboard and retrieves two pairs of gold bangles. 'I had kept these for both your weddings. But, if we need to sell them to retain the house, then so be it.' She offers them to me with a wistful sigh.

My heart goes out to Ma. Since Papa's death, this is the third piece of heirloom jewellery she has been forced to part with: first to pay for Neha's education, then to cater for her own medical expenses, and now to save this flat.

A heavy silence hangs over our home as we sit down for dinner. I am haunted by an acute sense of failure, as though I'd let my family down when they needed me most. Never have I felt the lack of money more keenly. For a fleeting moment the vision of all those crisp notes lying on the table of the Coffee House swims into my mind, before I dismiss it as a sick joke. How can a madman like Acharya be taken seriously? Yet he keeps circling my brain like an irritating fly.

To satisfy my curiosity, I sit down at my computer after dinner. It is a decrepit Dell tower unit that I salvaged from the showroom just as they were about to dispose of it to a junk dealer. A dinosaur running on Windows 2000, it nevertheless allows me to surf the Internet, check my emails and use the word processor to tabulate the household expenditure at the end of every month.

I log on to the Internet and type in 'Vinay Mohan Acharya' in the search box. The query instantly registers 1.9 million hits.

The industrialist is all over cyberspace. There are news

reports about his business deals, speculation on his net worth, image galleries capturing his various moods, and YouTube videos of him making speeches at shareholder meetings and international conferences. Over the next half-hour, I learn many new facts about him, such as his passion for cricket, his occasional (and unsuccessful) forays into politics, his bitter rivalry with his twin brother Ajay Krishna Acharya, the owner of Premier Industries, and his active philanthropy. He apparently donates buckets of cash to all manner of charities and has twice been awarded the President's Medal for having the best CSR programme. I also confirm that he had indeed lost his wife and daughter in the crash of a Thai Airways flight from Bangkok to Kathmandu on 31 July 1992, which killed all 113 passengers.

As I trawl through the mire of information about him on the web, Acharya comes across as a complex and conflicted personality. He has admirers hailing him as India's most ethical businessman, and critics decrying his idiosyncrasies, his narcissism and megalomania. But there is no disputing his genius in single-handedly transforming the ABC Group from a startup into India's eighth-largest conglomerate with holdings in steel, cement, textiles, power generation, rayon, aluminium, consumer goods, chemicals, computers, consulting and even films.

My research makes one thing clear: the owner of the ABC Group is neither a raving lunatic nor a devious shark. By rejecting his offer out of hand, did I miss a big opportunity, I wonder, feeling the first pangs of doubt? The very next moment I chide myself for allowing naïve hope to override sound judgement. In this world, you never get something for nothing, I remind myself. If an offer seems too good to be true, it usually is.

Still, I go to bed plagued with the feeling that time is passing me by. That I am stuck in a dead-end job, with a future on permanent hold. There was a time, not so long ago, when the ship of my life had direction and momentum. Now it seems like an aimless, rudderless drift, where one week leads to another, each day is the same and nothing ever changes.

At least my dreams that night are different. Through the confused farrago of fragmented images, I vividly remember sitting in a luxurious private plane and flying over the snow-capped mountains of Switzerland. There is only one little problem: the pilot happens to be the industrialist Vinay Mohan Acharya.

I start the long, treacherous commute to work the next morning with a positive attitude and a clear mind. The metro is less crowded on weekends, but I am extra careful with my handbag, laying a protective hand over it. A gift from my friend Lauren, it is a tan woven purse by Nine West with beige faux snakeskin and looks really classy. Today it also contains the four gold bangles on which depends my family's collective future.

At Inder Lok station, a familiar-looking man with dyed hair and long sideburns, clad in a politician's khadi dress, barges into the compartment. He is trailed by a band of supporters and a posse of gun-toting commandoes who start evicting commuters to make way for the VIP and his entourage. The man, I learn from one of his lackeys, is our local legislator Anwar Noorani, taking his 'weekly metro ride to bond with the common man'. I have read about this gentleman in the newspapers, how he runs a chain of private hospitals allegedly funded by proceeds from an illegal hawala racket. 'If there are any local issues you wish to bring to my attention, please feel free to visit me in my constituency office located behind the Delhi Institute of Technology,' the MLA announces. His hooded, restless eyes flit across the compartment and come to rest on me. 'How are you, sister?' He flashes me a plastic smile. I avert my gaze and pretend to look out of the window. Mercifully, he disembarks at the very next station.

Delhi is a strange city, I reflect. Here, status is not based on whether you wear Armani, drive a Mercedes or quote Jean-Paul Sartre at cocktail parties. Your status is determined by how many rules you can break and how many people you can bully. That distinction alone puts you in the category of VIP.

The showroom is a hive of activity from morning itself. Saturday is our busiest day. Plus, with the Cricket World Cup approaching, our promotion campaign is in full swing. We expect sales of flat-screen TVs to peak during the next two months.

A newlywed couple approach me for advice on buying the right television. They are debating between LCD and plasma. It doesn't take me long to persuade them to go in for the latest Sony LED TV, with the added sweetener of a free electronic toaster in our two-for-one promotion, but it is not my best effort. I am distracted and impatient, waiting for the lunch break. As soon as the clock strikes one, I sneak out through the back door, only to bump into Raja Gulati, Delhi's most obnoxious playboy. For some reason he is lounging in front of Beckett's, an Irish pub just four doors down from the showroom. Dressed in his trademark leather jacket, he is leaning against his Yamaha motorbike, and counting a sheaf of notes. The moment he sees me, he stashes away the cash and beams at me. Short and pudgy, with a stubbly face, a bushy moustache and long hair, Raja's only claim to fame is that his millionaire father is the owner of the showroom. His sole pastime is drinking alcohol and picking up girls. If office gossip is to be believed, he has already had success with one of the salesgirls. These days he keeps making crude passes at Prachi and me. But I'd rather eat live cockroaches than give in to this slimeball's amorous advances.

'Helloo, who do we have here? The Ice Maiden herself!' He gives me a wolfish grin, and pats the seat of his Yamaha. 'Would you like to come with me for a spin?'

'No, thanks,' I respond coldly.

'You have great legs.' His eyes descend my body. 'What time do they open?'

I feel the burn of anger rising in my face, but this is neither the time nor the place for a showdown. 'Why don't you ask your mother?' I retort, and walk past him. He sighs and heads into the pub, probably to drown his disappointment in drink.

Without wasting time, I proceed to Jhaveri Jewellers in N-Block. Prashant Jhaveri, the young owner, used to be Papa's student at one time, and always offers me a fair price. I expect him to quote well over ₹200,000 for the four gold bangles nestling inside my handbag.

At the crossing on Radial Road 6, traffic is held up by some kind of religious procession. There are hundreds of men, women and children draped in saffron-coloured clothes, chanting and dancing to the tune of trumpet and dhol. Cars honk in frustration and pedestrians fume, but the group continues on its merry path, unmindful of the inconvenience and nuisance it is causing. And this is a daily occurrence. Delhi has become a city of rallies and roadblocks.

I am still waiting for the procession to pass when someone pokes me in the side. It is a street urchin in a tattered sweater. He is no more than eight years old, with a dusty face and grimy hair. He says nothing, just holds out a cupped palm in the universal gesture for need. Nothing upsets me more than seeing these child beggars. At an age when they should be in class, they are on the streets, trying to earn a living by exploiting the only working skill they possess: evoking pity. I almost never give alms to them, as it only encourages their begging habit. Worse, it often leads them into more dangerous addictions such as glue, booze and even drugs. What they really need is a lucky break, a supportive environment and a healthy dose of self-respect. Something that Lauren and her RMT Asha Foundation provide.

This particular beggar is not easily fobbed off. 'I haven't eaten in two days. Can you give me some money?' he mumbles, pressing a bony hand into his belly. Looking down into his large, pleading eyes, I just cannot say no. 'I won't give you money,' I tell him, 'but I'll buy you lunch.' His face lights up. There is a roadside hawker next to us selling chhole kulcha for ₹10 a plate. 'Would you like one of these?' I ask him.

'I love kulchas,' he replies, smacking his chapped lips.

I unhook my handbag from my shoulder and open the zip to take out cash. At that very instant, someone swoops at me from behind, snatching the purse from my hands. It all happens so quickly that I don't even catch the thief's face. All I see is a swish of saffron. Before I know it, he has melted into the crowd of devotees. I turn back and find that the beggar boy has also disappeared. I have fallen for the oldest trap in the book.

For a moment I stand motionless, totally stunned by this turn of events. My hands turn cold and my breathing almost stops. '*Nooo!*' I let out an anguished cry and rush headlong into the sea of saffron. I am pummelled and crushed from all sides, but I continue to burrow through the human wall in blind pursuit of the thief.

I do not find the culprit, but, once the procession has passed, I find my handbag lying discarded by the side of the road. I rush to retrieve it. It still has my cell phone and house keys. My ID card and lipstick and sunglasses and pepper spray are intact. Everything is there except the four gold bangles.

I slump down on the side of the road, feeling dizzy and nauseous. My arms grow heavy and limp and my vision turns blurry. When things clear up, I find a policeman squatting next to me. 'Are you all right?' he asks.

'Yes,' I respond weakly. 'Someone stole my purse.'

'Then what is this?' He taps the Nine West in my lap with his baton.

'He – he took away my mother's gold bangles and left the bag behind.'

'Did you see his face? Can you give us the thief's description?'

'No. But don't the police know all the gangs operating in the area? I'm sure you can catch him.' I clutch his arm like a lifeline. 'Please, you must do something. We'll be ruined if I don't get back the bangles. If you want I can even file a report.'

'It won't do you any good. This happens here every day. Unless we have a description we can't do anything. Take my advice. Don't waste your time and ours by registering an FIR. Just be more careful with your belongings next time.' He assists me to my feet, gives me a sympathetic look and walks off, tapping his baton on his palm.

I rummage desperately through the bag once again, hoping against hope to somehow discover those bangles, but miracles happen only in fairytales and films. A huge lump rises at the back of my throat, and tears start streaming down my cheeks as my mind absorbs the full magnitude of the loss. All around me people are laughing, eating, shopping, enjoying the sunshine. None of them can understand my inner torment. As a child I had once lost a favourite doll and cried two full days over it. Now I have lost my mother's most precious jewellery. The thief has taken more than just gold: he has taken away our future.

I am still sobbing on the pavement when my eyes fall on a giant advertising billboard displaying the temperature and time. With a shock I realise it's already past two o'clock. Madan, my obnoxious boss, does not take kindly to employees taking an extended lunch break. Having lost the bangles, I am in danger of losing my job as well.

I break into a run, my three-inch heels hurting and occasionally tripping me up, until I arrive breathless at the showroom – except that the showroom doesn't look the same any more. Loud voices are being raised, bewildered customers are being shepherded out with abject apologies, and the shutter is being hastily pulled down halfway, the equivalent of the flag at half-mast, a sure sign of trouble.

I duck inside the shutter to discover even more bedlam. There is a lot of yelling and swearing. Accusations are flying in the air like paper planes. Everyone seems to be gathered round the cashier's cubicle, including Mr O. P. Gulati himself, our venerable owner, and someone is crying out in agonised pain. I force my way through the crush of errand boys, back-office clerks, delivery-truck drivers and sales staff to discover that the shrieks are emanating from Mr Choubey, our balding, fifty-five-year-old cashier. He is rolling on the floor, being mercilessly beaten by Madan, our manager and the most hated man in the store. 'Namak-haram! You traitorous bastard,' Madan rants, as he punches Choubey in the face and kicks him in the gut. A gruff, abrasive man, Madan has only two passions in life: sucking up to Mr Gulati and getting sadistic pleasure from reprimanding store employees.

'I don't know how it happened. I was away for just twenty minutes for lunch,' the cashier laments, but cannot prevent yet another lacerating blow. I wince in sympathy for him. I have only lost a few gold bangles; Choubey has lost his pride, his dignity.

'What's going on?' I nudge Prachi. She fills me in on what has happened during my absence. Apparently Mr

Gulati made a surprise inspection this afternoon and discovered a shortfall of almost ₹200,000 from the morning shift. Since the cash was under the cashier's direct supervision, Choubey was now being accused of embezzlement.

'I swear on my three children I didn't do it,' the cashier wails.

'Tell me where the money is and I might still spare you,' Mr Gulati says, his bushy eyebrows furrowed like two caterpillars trying to reach each other.

'Madan has already searched me. I don't have the money,' cries Choubey.

'The bastard must have passed it to his accomplice,' Madan theorises. 'I say we hand him over to the police. They'll get the truth out of him in no time. I've been cultivating Goswami, the inspector at the Connaught Place police station, for quite a while. Now is the time to use him.'

'Please don't do this, *sahib*.' Choubey clutches Mr Gulati's feet. 'I have served this shop for thirty years. My wife and children will die without me.'

'Then let them die,' Mr Gulati says spitefully, yanking his leg free. 'Madan, phone that inspector of yours,' he orders.

I don't know Choubey all that well. He is a quiet man who keeps to himself. Our interactions have been limited to the polite exchange of pleasantries, but I have always found him to be conscientious, courteous and diligent. It is inconceivable that he could defraud the company. And even a hardened criminal does not make a false oath on his children. That is when an image pops into my head: of Raja Gulati sitting on his bike, busy counting a sheaf of notes. I know that the senior Gulati doesn't approve of Raja's drinking and womanising. And the rotten son is quite capable of surreptitiously raiding the till to fund his extravagant lifestyle.

'Wait!' I address Madan. 'How do you know Mr Choubey is the culprit?'

Everyone turns to look at me. Madan gives me a murderous glance, but deigns to answer. 'He is the only one with keys to the safe.'

'Isn't it true that the Gulati family also has keys to the safe?'

'What are you suggesting?' Mr O. P. Gulati interrupts me. 'That I have robbed my own shop?'

'I am not saying it was you, sir. But what about Raja?'

There is a collective intake of breath. Even I am amazed at my reckless audacity.

'Are you out of your mind?' Madan goes into an apoplectic fit. 'Raja-*babu* didn't even come to the shop today.'

'But I saw him outside the showroom an hour ago, counting a sheaf of notes.'

I can see that Mr O. P. Gulati is troubled by this news. He wrings his hands nervously, biting on his bottom lip, as he weighs up the possibilities. Eventually, paternal affection prevails over his doubts. 'How dare you make such a scurrilous accusation against my son?' he lambastes me, eyes glittering with anger. 'One more word and I will dismiss you on the spot.'

I turn silent, knowing that no amount of argument can overcome a father's blind love.

*

Half an hour later a police jeep arrives bearing Inspector Goswami, a tall, beefy-looking officer, who has been getting a 35 per cent discount from us on all his electronic purchases. He catches hold of the accountant as a butcher grabs a chicken. Choubey goes without protest, without making a scene, as though he has accepted his fate. I watch this travesty of justice unfold before my eyes with a helpless rage. Choubey had been branded a thief simply because he was weak and powerless. And Raja Gulati had got away with embezzlement because he was rich and pedigreed. I feel so nauseated, I want to puke. My entire body shudders with loathing for Raja and his father. I know what happened to Choubey today can quite easily happen to me tomorrow. And, like Choubey, I wouldn't be able to do anything about it. There are only two choices available to the powerless of this world: either accept the abuse or walk away, only to suffer the same abuse from some other powerful person.

Acharya was right. The world is indeed divided into winners and losers. People like the Gulatis are the winners and folk like Choubey and me the losers.

Life pivots on a few key moments. This is one of them. Slowly but surely a knot of resolve hardens inside my stomach. I open my handbag and fish out the visiting card Acharya has given me. That little warning bell inside my head begins trilling again, but I am past caring. A loser has got nothing to lose. I take a deep breath, and then dial the number on the card from my cell phone.

A carefully modulated female voice answers the phone. 'You have reached the ABC Group. How may I assist you?'

'I would like to speak to Mr Vinay Mohan Acharya.'

'May I know who is calling?'

'Sapna Sinha.'

I expect her to ask 'Sapna who?' and be passed around a dozen departments, but instead she says, 'Please hold on, ma'am,' and almost immediately Acharya comes on the line, as though he was waiting for my call.

'I'm glad you called,' he says.

'I've decided to accept your offer.'

'Good,' he says simply. There is no triumphal sniggering or I-told-you-so gloating. 'Meet me in my office at six p.m. sharp. The address is on the business card.'

'But my work doesn't get over until—' I begin, only to be cut off by Acharya. 'Six p.m.,' he repeats, and that's the end of the conversation.

I look at the address on the card. The ABC Group's headquarters are at Kyoko Chambers on Barakhamba Road, not far from Connaught Place. I look at the time. It is 3.15 p.m. I have less than three hours to prepare for the meeting that could change my life.

Madan, our tyrant boss, is notorious for not allowing employees to leave before time. And, today being Saturday, permission to leave early is ruled out – unless I can come up with a plausible excuse.

At 5.30 p.m. I approach Madan with a despondent look. 'Sir, my sister just called. My mother's had another asthma attack. I need to take her to the hospital. Can I leave right now?'

The manager scrunches up his face like he just smelled something bad. 'We are already short of a cashier. I cannot be short of a salesgirl too.'

'But if something happens to Ma . . .' I let the implication hang in the air. In the Indian pantheon, Mother is
the highest ideal, next only to God. Even Madan dare not
risk the opprobrium of rendering an employee mother-
less. 'Go, then,' he says resignedly, caving in to my
emotional blackmail.

Ten minutes later I am sitting in an auto-rickshaw, on
my way to Barakhamba Road. I am still wearing my
office uniform of white blouse and red skirt, having
decided against the comfortable but casual salvar kameez.
I am going for a business meeting after all, not a family
reunion.

Kyoko Chambers turns out to be an impressive fifteen-
storey building with an all-glass façade. The security there
is like that of a government facility. There are private
guards patrolling the entrance and I have to put my bag
through a screening machine to go inside. The foyer
resembles an elegant hotel lobby, with an enormous crystal chandelier under which sits a huge bronze sculpture of
Nandi the Bull, the ABC Group's corporate symbol. A
tall man, dressed in a dark suit and red tie, is waiting for
me at the reception. It takes me a moment to recognise
him as Rana, Acharya's right-hand man.

'Why so much security?' I enquire.

'It is necessary. There are rivals keen to steal our
secrets,' he responds curtly, and escorts me to an elevator,
which whisks us soundlessly to the fifteenth floor.

I step into a dramatic atrium with Roman columns, a
20-foot waterfall, and a glass-domed ceiling refracting the
dusk spreading in the evening sky. Rana leads me past

mahogany double doors into a brightly lit room that looks to be a front office. The place is all marble and mosaic. The walls are painted a mottled gold and the gilded décor is reminiscent of an opulent Parisian salon, with large murals, thick-pile carpeting and bronze statuary. Another sculpture of Nandi the Bull, this one gold-plated, guards the entrance to Acharya's private suite.

I am surprised to see a blonde white woman sitting behind the desk.

'This is Jennifer, Mr Acharya's private secretary,' Rana says by way of introduction.

'You must be Sapna,' she says, standing up and offering her hand. Her accent is just like Lauren's, so I assume she is American. Probably in her late twenties. The first thing I notice about her is her height: she must be at least five foot ten, towering over me like a telephone pole. Her startlingly blue eyes are framed behind rectangular, clear glasses, and her shoulder-length, fluffy blonde hair is magazine-ready. In her stylish blue blazer, worn over a cream-coloured buttoned shirt and grey trousers, she looks like a cross between a well-groomed CNN newsreader and a high-class hooker.

She appraises me like a mistress confronted by the wife. Her cool, sweeping glance is half curious, half condescending. I take an instant, instinctual dislike to her.

The wall clock shows the time as 5.58 p.m. I cool my heels for another two minutes till a buzzer sounds on Jennifer's desk. 'Mr Acharya will see you now.' She gives me a thin smile and ushers me into his private chamber.

The sanctum sanctorum is even more impressive, with a boardroom table, bookcases filled with books, and a wall-mounted big-screen TV displaying the market rates of stocks. The furniture looks solid, the carpets expensive.

My eyes are drawn to the massive golden head of a woman watching over the boardroom table. From her large bulging eyes, I recognise it as one of those monumental fibreglass sculptures of Ravinder Reddy I had seen in the National Gallery. The original oil paintings on the mahogany-covered walls also seem familiar. There are horses by Husain, cows by Manjit Bawa, and a cubist rendition of a nude, which might have been painted by Picasso himself. If Acharya's aim in calling me to his office was to overawe me, he has succeeded admirably.

He himself sits on a thronelike chair behind an antique, horseshoe-shaped desk, overlooking a large bay window. In his pinstripe suit, with a pink silk handkerchief jutting out of his breast pocket, he looks every inch the corporate tycoon he is. If further proof is needed, it is provided by the wall behind him, which is covered with framed professional photographs of him hobnobbing with all manner of international luminaries from Pope John Paul II and the Dalai Lama to Bill Clinton and Nelson Mandela. I cannot shake off the feeling of being in a cosy private museum, Acharya's memorial to himself.

'So how do you like my office?' he asks, gesturing that I should sit down.

'It's very nice.' I nod, sinking into a plush leather chair opposite him. Only then do I notice the wooden plaque on his desk. It bears the inscription: 'CLEAR VISION, DETERMINATION, DISCIPLINE & HARD WORK'.

'These are the core values which guide our endeavours

in the ABC Group.' He taps the plaque. 'I would expect you to hold the same values when you become its CEO.'

'You mean *if* I become CEO.'

'That depends entirely on you. As chairman, my task is simply to select the right person and set the right direction. I am convinced you are the best person for this company. But you must also feel the same way. Remember, the first step to achieve success is that you must really want it.' He drops his eyelids, as though recollecting something, and quotes a verse in perfect Sanskrit: '*Kaama maya evayam purusha iti. Sa Yatha kaamo bhavati tat kratur bhavati. Yat kratur bhavati tat karma kurute. Yat karma kurte tad abhisam padyate.*'

I am familiar with the verse. It is from the Brihadaranyaka Upanishad. 'You are what your deep, driving desire is. As your desire is, so is your will. As your will is, so is your deed. As your deed is, so is your destiny.'

'I've never really believed in destiny,' I respond.

'But destiny may believe in you,' he rejoins.

'Then let's get this over with. I suppose you'll need me to sign that undertaking.'

'That's right. Let me call Rana.' He presses a buzzer and Rana enters the room, bearing a leather folder. He sits down next to me and hands me a sheet of paper. It's the same form I had seen last time.

'Before you sign it, I need to know if you have discussed my offer with anyone,' Acharya says.

'No,' I reply. 'I haven't spoken to anyone about this.'

'Not even with your mother and sister?'

'No. But why all this secrecy?'

'Well, as you can see, my methods are a bit … ah, unconventional. I don't want my shareholders getting needlessly twitchy. Complete confidentiality is a necessity when going about such things. You must not utter a word about our arrangement to anyone.'

'I won't.' I nod. 'And what's this clause about not being allowed to terminate the contract mid-period?'

'It simply means that the contract remains in force till all seven tests have been completed. You cannot quit in between.'

'But what if I fail any of those tests?'

'Then I terminate the contract, not you.'

'Please sign at the bottom,' Rana says, offering me a pen.

'Before I sign, I also want something.'

Acharya frowns. 'What?'

'I want double.'

'What do you mean?'

'According to this contract, you are to pay me a sum of one lakh rupees to participate in the tests. I am asking for two lakhs.'

'And what makes you think I will agree to your demand?'

'In life you don't get what you deserve: you only get what you negotiate. Isn't this what you told me in the Coffee House? Well, I'm only following your advice. I'm negotiating with you.'

'Touché!' Acharya claps grudgingly. 'You are a fast learner. But in order to negotiate you need to have leverage of some kind. Do you have a choice in this case?'

'I could ask you the same question. Do you have a choice? A better candidate?'

'I like your spunk.' Acharya nods. 'But why do you need so much money?'

'I have some urgent family commitments.'

Acharya gazes out of the bay window, brooding over my demand. From his vantage point, like an eagle on his perch, he can see Lutyens's Delhi spread out below him. There is something magical and mystical about seeing a city from a high-rise, far from the soot and dust of the concrete jungle, the heat and noise of the road. I crane my neck to catch a view of the capital. All I can see is a shimmering ribbon of glitter draped across the horizon, blurring the boundary between earth and sky.

After a few tension-filled minutes, Acharya finally looks up and nods as if arriving at a decision. 'Rana, give her two lakhs.'

Rana gives me a dirty look and exits the room.

I turn to Acharya. 'Can I ask you a question?'

'By all means.'

'Why didn't you consider Rana for the job you are offering me? After all, he is your trusted confidant.'

'For the same reason that I don't take investment tips from my barber,' he says, leaning back in his chair and fiddling with a crystal Ganesha paperweight. 'To use a cricketing analogy, Rana is a good all-rounder, but would make a poor captain. He doesn't have the mindset of a leader. He can never sit here.' He taps his chair. 'But you can, provided you succeed in my seven tests.'

'Your tests are making me apprehensive.'

'Don't be. My tests are not so much about passing or failing, as about discovering yourself. Through each of the seven tests you will gain practical wisdom of running a business in the real world.'

'It reminds me of those ancient tales of kings who set tests for their children to decide who amongst them should inherit the crown.'

'My inspiration is more modern. I despise the feudal culture of inheritance. Of spoilt rich kids getting everything handed to them through hereditary succession. I am a self-made man and I have created a culture of achievement in the ABC Group. You have to fight for your dreams, earn your place in the company.'

Running a company was never my dream, I feel like telling him, when Rana returns. He plunks down a manila envelope in front of me. 'There is two lakhs inside. Check the cash.'

I open the envelope to discover it bulging with thousand-rupee notes. Counting the lot seems like a rude thing to do. 'I trust Mr Acharya,' I declare, and sign the form with a flourish.

Rana picks up the document and puts it back in the leather folder.

'When will the tests begin?' I enquire, stuffing the envelope inside my purse.

'They have already begun,' Acharya says cryptically.

Before I can probe any further, the intercom on his desk buzzes. He stares at it for a moment, before depressing a red button. 'Sir, the party from Hong Kong is on its way up,' Jennifer's perky voice comes through the speakerphone.

Acharya nods and then looks up at me. 'Good luck,' he says, signalling that the meeting is over.

Five minutes later I am back on the street, pondering over the strangeness of all that has just happened. There is more money in my purse than I have ever possessed in my life and it fills me with a bizarre combination of elation and trepidation. I can already sense the shadowy hand of fate tapping my shoulder, as if warning me that I have made a Faustian pact, and now I must be prepared for the consequences.

The first thing I do after leaving Acharya's office is proceed to Hanuman Mandir to express my gratitude to Goddess Durga. She alone can help me navigate the treacherous currents of life that lie ahead.

After visiting the temple, I take a short detour to a shop in G-Block, before catching the metro. Tonight I don't go all the way to Rithala. I get down at Pitampura, and take an auto-rickshaw to Deenu Uncle's residence. Despite being a wealthy restaurateur, he still lives in a rundown, two-storey house adjacent to a fetid, refuse-clogged canal.

My aunt Manju Chachi, a lazy, overweight woman with a puzzling fondness for sleeveless blouses, opens the door. 'Hello, Sapna,' she greets me sleepily. Deenu Uncle is lounging in the living room, clad in just a vest and pyjamas, thanks to an electric heater going full blast. He has a chubby face, broad shoulders and a nonexistent neck, giving him the mien of a washed-up wrestler. I glance around the room, at the garish red sofa seats, lumpy and fraying at the edges, the haphazard collection of family photos on the mantel, the cobwebs in the corners. The room smells of dust and neglect. Having always seen Deenu Uncle through the tinted lens of a family member, I hadn't realised how cheap and tawdry he really is.

'If you have come to beg me to allow you to stay in the Rohini flat, you are wasting your time,' he begins the moment I sit down. 'Unless you can come up with the money, be prepared to move in two weeks.'

For all his faults, my father was a man of uncompromising principles. His younger brother has none. Deenu is a fast-talking, opportunistic shyster without scruples of any kind. He routinely cheats on his taxes, and probably on his fat wife as well.

'I have brought the full amount,' I inform him, and count out ₹168,000.

He seems more shocked than pleased. 'How did you manage to raise so much money so quickly?' he says and flashes me a sly grin. 'Did you rob a bank?'

'None of your business, landlord,' I respond tartly, shutting him up. 'And, since we are now paying tenants, we expect you to draw up a proper rental agreement, repair the seepage in the bathroom wall, fix the leaking sink in the kitchen, and give the apartment a fresh coat of paint.'

He gapes at me like a startled monkey. I have never ever spoken to him like this. But, then, it is not I speaking. It is the power of all that money in my hand, giving me a voice, giving me a spine. With a smug smirk of triumph I swagger out of Deenu's house and hail another auto-rickshaw.

By the time I reach home, it is past 7.30 p.m. Mother is in the kitchen, preparing dinner, and Neha is sprawled on the sofa, watching a musical talent contest on Zee TV.

'How much did the jeweller give you?' Ma wants to know at once. 'Was it enough?'

'Enough to pay off our shameless uncle,' I reply. 'We can now stay here safely for a year.'

'And what will happen after one year?'

'We'll deal with it when the time comes.' I drop my handbag on the dining table and flop down next to Neha.

She is so engrossed in the show, she hardly notices me or the shopping bag at my feet. On screen, a willowy contestant is belting out a popular song from the film *Dabangg.* 'I can sing much better than you,' Neha mocks her, 'and I certainly look much better.'

'Stop talking to the TV and see what I've got for you,' I instruct her.

Neha turns around and her eyes open wide when she sees what I have withdrawn from the shopping bag: a brand-new Acer laptop.

'*Didi!*' she squeals in delight, and hugs me tightly. 'You're the greatest.'

Grabbing the laptop from my hands, she begins fiddling with it like a child given a new toy, her face flushed with excitement. Mother gently squeezes my shoulder. 'Your father would have been so proud of you,' she says, dabbing at her eyes. 'I have never seen Neha so happy.'

Who will make *me* happy? I feel like asking her, before surrendering to the occasion. For a brief while I am enveloped in the warm glow of family love and every-thing seems rosy and full of promise. Such moments come rarely these days, and disappear all too quickly. Before long, Ma will grow distant again; Neha will become her

usual bitchy self. And despair, heartache and pain, my
daily companions, will return to haunt me.

But today at least I can keep them at bay. My mind is
still buzzing with all the possibilities unleashed by
Acharya's offer, and the house is too small to think in. So
I head down to the garden just outside the colony gate. It
is not really a garden, just a patch of earth contained by
a low brick wall, with a few shrubs and fruit trees scattered around. During the day the neighbourhood kids use
it for their cricket matches, causing quite a racket, but at
this time of night it is deserted and silent. I park myself on
one of the wooden benches. The night air is nippy and
the ground is damp beneath my feet. I draw my woollen
shawl more tightly around my shoulders, hugging the
warmth closer.

I have been sitting for less than a minute when Kishore
Kumar begins to serenade me with a song from the film
Amar Akbar Anthony:

> My name is Anthony Gonzalves.
> I am alone in the world.
> My heart is empty, my home is also empty,
> In which will live someone very lucky.
> Whenever she thinks of me, she should come visit
> Palace of Beauty, Love Lane, house number 420!

I feel a warmth in my face, as if a faint flush of crimson
has crept into my cheeks. I know that the legendary
singer has not returned from the dead. And neither does
he live in house number 420. The melodious voice
belongs to Karan Kant, resident of apartment B-35.

Karan moved into the LIG Colony a month after we did. Over the last fifteen months he has become much more than a neighbour to me. He is an orphan with no family, and works as a call-centre agent in Indus Mobile, India's third-largest cellular service operator. Though he is twenty-five years old, his boyish looks make him appear five years younger. With his above-average height, perfectly sculpted body, chiselled, clean-shaven face and curly hair, he is easily the most handsome man in Rohini, if not in Delhi. Add to that his crinkly smile and dreamy eyes and it's enough to make schoolgirls swoon. Not just schoolgirls, but even the menopausal housewives in our colony are smitten by him. They find one excuse or another to come to the balcony in the evenings just to catch a glimpse of him returning from work. But Karan seems to have eyes only for me. I do not know what he sees in me. Perhaps he regards me as a kindred spirit. We are both high-potential underachievers, bruised by life, buffeted by fate. Of all the people in the colony, he has chosen me to be his confidante. We are each other's sounding board, staunchest supporter and most honest critic.

It is still too early to give a name to our relationship. Suffice it to say that he is my soulmate, my strength, my rock. Sometimes I look upon him as a brother; at other times as a trusted companion; and once in a while – dare I say it? – as a boyfriend. There is always the vulnerable note of courtship in his actions, though he tries to hide his feelings behind a flippant exterior and acts of buffoonery. He is a hugely talented mimicry artist who can impersonate the voice of just about anyone, from the actor Shahrukh Khan to the cricketer Sachin Tendulkar.

For all his droll playfulness, there is an undercurrent of sadness in his eyes. I have often caught him looking at me with a tortured, haunted expression. At times like these I can almost touch the raw loneliness in his heart, and I bleed in sympathy. He is a true clown, making others laugh while crying silently inside.

'Why so serious, Madam-ji?' he says as he plonks down next to me.

'It's been a really crazy day.' I exhale.

'Did you (a) win a lottery, (b) get robbed, (c) get a job offer or (d) meet a celebrity?' He is mimicking Amitabh Bachchan asking a question on *Who Wants to Be a Millionaire?*.

'All of the above,' I reply.

He narrows his eyes. 'Then would you like to phone a friend?'

It seems he has read my mind. So much has happened in the last twenty-four hours that I can't keep it bottled up any more. I need to talk it over with someone, get it off my chest. And I can't think of anyone better than Karan. I am mindful of Acharya's stern admonition about maintaining strict confidentiality, but, if I can trust anyone to keep a secret, it is the man sitting next to me. I gaze into his soulful eyes and feel the world come to a standstill. 'You won't believe what I'm about to tell you.'

I tell him everything, starting with that chance encounter with Acharya in the temple to Deenu Uncle's phone call, the theft of the bangles, the scene in the showroom with Choubey and the final meeting with

Acharya in his office resulting in the unexpected windfall of two lakh rupees in hard cash.

Karan listens to me in rapt attention. Then he lets out a long, low whistle. 'Boy, this is a story for my grandchildren!'

'So you think Acharya is serious about making me his CEO?'

He chuckles. 'Are you nuts? This is a scam if I ever saw one. Nobody suddenly offers a complete stranger a ten-billion-dollar company on a platter.'

'But I researched Acharya. He looks to be above board.'

'So does every conman before he gets caught. Big Bull Harshad Mehta was hailed as a financial wizard before he brought down the entire stock market.'

'But what can Acharya hope to get from me? I don't have any money to invest in his company.'

'Maybe he has a thing for dusky beauties.'

'He doesn't seem like a lecher. And I'm no Bipasha Basu.'

'Is there any chance at all that you might be his long-lost illegitimate daughter?'

'Don't be facetious. This is not a Bollywood film.'

'But I can already visualise the scene.' Karan holds up his hands like a director framing a shot. 'He calls you to his house late at night. You don't find him there, but you discover his wife lying in a pool of blood. She has been shot dead. And the gun that killed her has your fingerprints on it. Then you realise that all this was part of an ingenious plan to get rid of his wife and pin the murder on you.'

Before his hyperactive imagination conjures up yet

another gruesome scenario, I cut him off. 'Acharya doesn't have a wife. End of conspiracy.'

'Then there must be some other devious design. It is common knowledge that Acharya loathes his twin brother Ajay Krishna Acharya. Premier Industries is the ABC Group's biggest competitor. What if Acharya is making you a pawn to get to his twin?'

'Acharya didn't utter a word about his brother. And what am I, a stupid fool who will willingly become someone's pawn?'

'I'm not blaming you. It is a basic rule of human nature that the promise of unexpected wealth short-circuits both intelligence and common sense. That is why we have all these Ponzi schemes, chit-fund scams, timber-plantation frauds. I see it happen every day in the call centre, with gullible customers sucked into dubious deals floated by fly-by-night telemarketers who always manage to fly the coop before the cops show up.'

'There's also something called taking a risk. Only those who risk going too far can possibly find out how far they can go.'

'Did Acharya say this?'

'It was T. S. Eliot. And *I'm* not even the one taking the risk here: Acharya is. He's the one betting on me. How could I pass up the opportunity of a lifetime? For the first time, I sense a glimmer of hope about my future.'

'Ha!' he reacts dismissively. 'Hope is a recreational drug, giving you an artificial high based on a dosage of unrealistic expectations. What you need is a reality check.'

'And what you need is a dose of sunshine. Why do you always have to be so negative?'

'Because I care for you, and I have a bad feeling about this, Sapna. You should never have taken Acharya's money.'

'I had no choice.'

'I just hope you don't end up regretting it. There's bound to be a quid pro quo. And yet you know nothing about his so-called seven tests. What do they entail? How will they happen? When will they happen?'

'Yes, I'm also a bit apprehensive about the tests.'

'Let me tell you a little fable, Sapna. Once upon a time, there was a man who was desperate to be taller. So he prayed to God for twenty years and God finally granted his wish. But there was a condition. God said "I can make you taller, but, for every inch I add, five years will be deducted from your life." The man agreed. So God made him three inches taller – and the man died instantly. Moral of the story: never enter into a deal without know-ing all the facts.'

'I have no intention of taking any tests. I'll promptly fail the first one. And get to keep the two lakhs. End of story.'

'If only it were that simple. A man like Acharya must have thought about this very carefully before he approached you.'

Karan's morbid, unrelenting cynicism grows on me like a fungus. By the time I sit down with Ma and Neha for dinner, I am convinced that signing that contract with Acharya was the worst mistake of my life.

Whenever I am disturbed, I turn to poetry for solace. So, after dinner, I take out the secret black diary in which I have been jotting down my thoughts and feelings since

I was nine. As I flick through its well-thumbed pages, my eyes settle on a short poem titled 'Tomorrow'. It is dated 14 April 1999, when I was a callow, eleven-year-old schoolgirl. Perhaps because it was penned in a happier, simpler time, it is just the tonic I need. This is what I wrote:

> Hope is a shining sun
> That brightens every morrow.
> Love is a mighty wind
> That blows away the sorrow.
> The future is an empty road
> And I'm not afraid of tomorrow.

The First Test

Love in the Time of Khap

'Welcome, sir, would you like to take a look at our range of big-screen TVs? We have some fantastic offers at the moment.' I smile at the customer with all the ingratiating enthusiasm of a presenter on the Home Shop channel.

It is Saturday, 18 December. A week has passed since my rendezvous with Acharya and my mind has been full of worry. All my life I never feared examinations, but just thinking about Acharya's tests causes a weird roiling in the pit of my stomach. Mainly because I know nothing about them, and the uncertainty is stressing me out. On top of this, the showroom has become a madhouse. World Cup fervour is reaching fever pitch and our TV sales are going through the roof. This morning a frisson of excitement went through the employees when we were told that Bollywood actress Priya Capoorr will visit the store two weeks from now. She is the brand ambassador for

Sinotron Corporation and will be promoting their latest TV models.

There have been some other developments as well. We have a new cashier called Arjun Soni, a fat slob who constantly flips peanuts into his mouth and answers questions with questions. Neelam, one of the salesgirls, is quitting next month to get married. The boy is a Non-resident Indian from Stockholm. She is excited about going to Sweden, a country about which I know next to nothing.

In the afternoon the manager calls me to his cubicle. 'Sapna, I was just checking your sales figures. You are top of the list again,' he beams at me. His forced, yellow, toothy grin reminds me of an old Hindi film villain called Jeevan, putting me instantly on my guard. Madan smiles only when he wants to coax a favour out of an employee, like requiring us to stay overtime or come to work on a Sunday.

'You remember Mr Kuldip Singh, the man who bought a truckload of goods last week?' he continues.

'You mean that farmer from Haryana?'

'Yes, yes.' Madan nods. 'Well, he called today to say that no one in his household knows how to operate any of those appliances. Now he wants someone from the shop to come to his village and explain all the operating instructions. You understand?'

'Yes, so why don't you send one of the sales boys?'

'That's the problem,' Madan sighs. 'He wants only you. Apparently you impressed him no end. So here's the deal. We want you to go to his village tomorrow, and show him how the TV and the washing machine and the music system and DVD player work. We'll bear all your travel costs and, on top, you'll receive five hundred rupees for expenses.'

'I'm not wasting my Sunday just for five hundred rupees.'

'Think of it as easy money. I've found out that it takes just three hours to Chandangarh village. You could easily go in the morning and return by evening. Is it okay with you?'

'It's not okay. How can you ask a single woman to go all alone to a remote village?'

'I understand, I understand.' Madan waggles his head. 'But Gulati *sahib* will consider this a personal favour. Please, just this once,' he pleads.

'I can't go this Sunday,' I say with a grave shake of the head. 'It is Alka's birthday.'

'Who is Alka?'

'My sister, who died two years ago.'

'Why do the dead have to interfere with the affairs of the living?' he mutters under his breath, before nodding resignedly. '*Theek hai*. Can you at least go on Monday?'

'Yes, that should be possible. But I'll not stay longer than a few hours in that village. At what time will the taxi report to my house on Monday?'

'Taxi? Who do you think you are? Priya Capoorr? You'll take a bus, understand?'

I feel like telling him to go take a hike but there's only so far you can push Madan and I think I've pushed him close enough today.

If ever I get to become the CEO of the ABC Group, the first thing I'll do is buy up Gulati & Sons, and make

Madan the office sweeper. For now, however, I simply nod and swallow my pride.

An air of deep unsettling gloom hangs over the house. The cruel and mocking stillness of fate. Today is Alka's birthday. She would have been seventeen today. Mother dabs at her eyes. I have a lump in my throat that refuses to go away. The mood of homage and penitence wraps me in its suffocating embrace.

There has not been a single day in the last two years when I have not thought of Alka. The dead don't die. They simply transform into phantoms, hovering about in the air, preying on our thoughts, invading our dreams. Alka's absence haunts me every day, but more so today. There's something particularly damning about being alive on your dead sister's birthday.

As I sit staring at her photograph, consumed by survivor's guilt, memories of our time in Nainital come rushing back to me.

We used to live in Number 17, a large, four-bedroom house on the campus of Windsor Academy, an all-boys residential school, where Papa was the senior teacher for mathematics. Built in the 1870s, the school is like a Victorian fortress sprawling over a hundred acres of land, complete with crenellated turrets, stone parapet spires and angels and gargoyles embedded in the Gothic façade of the main building. Perched atop a low green hill, it is surrounded by mist-clad mountains and oak, pine and deodar forests. From our house we could even see the eye-shaped Naini lake, glimmering darkly.

Papa had a long association with the Academy,

beginning his teaching career in 1983 and working there continuously for more than twenty-five years. We were a middle-class family, leading a quiet, middle-class existence. The atmosphere in our house was one of discipline, responsibility and few extravagances. In many ways it was an idyllic life of peaceful solitude and diligent study, punctuated by summer storms, lazy boating trips on the lake and winter excursions to our ancestral home in Hardoi.

Though we grew up together in the same house, we three sisters had very different personalities and approaches to life. I was the shy, bookish nerd. Neha was the snobbish show-off. And Alka was the free spirit who marched to her own tune. She had a great sense of humour and found joy in even the smallest things. She was boisterous, vivacious, spontaneous, outrageous, even bordering on rash at times. But the moment she flashed her impish smile and said, '*Kamaal ho gaya!*' all was forgiven. She was the apple of my eye, the life of the party, the heart of our family.

We were schooled in an environment of regimented duty, where rules were more important than feelings. Alka, Neha and I attended St Theresa's Convent, an exclusive English-medium boarding school for girls run by Catholic nuns. We three were non-fee-paying day girls, a privilege afforded to us by virtue of Papa's employment at Windsor Academy, which had a reciprocal arrangement with the Convent. Sister Agnes, our tyrannical principal, had very clear ideas on the things we were allowed to do as girls, what we could not do and what we must never do. At home, our father enforced the same strict code of conduct, including an eight p.m. curfew. Without discipline, there is only anarchy, Papa used to say. Being a mathematics teacher, he had reduced his world to the binary of black and white, good and bad. There was no allowance for grey in his universe.

He had also mapped out the futures of all three of his daughters. I, the studious one, was to become a civil servant; Neha, the beautiful one, was to pursue a career as a TV journalist; and Alka, the compassionate one, was to be a doctor.

Like an obedient daughter, I did what Father expected of me. I excelled at school and then joined the BA course at Kumaun University. Even though my subject was English literature, I read up everything that I could lay my hands on. From the life cycle of a moth to the fuel cycle of a nuclear power plant, from black holes to brown clouds to cloud computing, I hoovered up every bit of arcane information to hone my general knowledge, which is essential for success in the civil services exam.

My father's most important rule inevitably had to do with boys. A few years ago, a fellow teacher, Mr Ghildayal, had been singed by his eighteen-year-old daughter Mamta's secret romance with the school head boy, which had resulted in an unexpected pregnancy, and Papa was petrified by the prospect of a similar scandal attaching itself to his family. 'If I catch any of my daughters even so much as looking at a boy on campus, I'll take off her hide,' he would threaten us. But he couldn't prevent the boys from looking at us, or, rather, at Neha and Alka. They were the prettiest girls on a hormone-filled campus, where every day brought a new sexual awakening to some tormented soul. The boys were mostly spoilt rich kids from places like Delhi, Mumbai and Kolkata who had been banished by their parents, and were intent on making full use of their new freedom. Windsor Academy prided itself on being an academic utopia. In actual fact, it was a den of corruption and degradation. All kinds of pornographic materials and alcoholic drinks circulated freely on campus. There were even dark whispers of drug abuse and prostitute visits.

I was too engrossed in my studies to notice boys. Neha treated them with utter contempt. She had concluded quite early on that Nainital was not the place where she wanted to spend the rest of her life, and avoided the locals like the plague. That left our youngest sister Alka. She was an adolescent schoolgirl, trying to deal with the changes in her body. Even though she was growing up physically, emotionally she was just a kid who still believed in the tooth fairy. For me, boys were an avoidable distraction; for Neha, they were a passing amusement; but for Alka they were a seductive puzzle viewed through the rose-tinted glasses of the Mills & Boon romances she was addicted to. Papa's stern admonitions did little to wean her away from her fascination with the bubblegum fantasy world of dashing heroes and damsels in distress. Given her innocent, carefree manner and utter disdain for authority, it was only a question of time before some predatory Romeo swept her off her feet.

It happened sooner than I expected. I had my first inkling that something was cooking on the occasion of Alka's fifteenth birthday.

Papa didn't believe in birthday celebrations, considering them to be on a par with Valentine's Day, a Western import to promote crass commercialism. The one allowance he made to our generation was permitting Neha and me to distribute candies to the class on our birthdays. Only Alka, being the pampered one, was allowed to host her own birthday parties. They were also modest affairs consisting of cake, a few of her school friends and an inexpensive gift, usually a book.

Alka's fifteenth birthday had the obligatory cake and cookies, the usual fun and games. But, besides her typical exuberance, this time she exuded an earthy sexuality heretofore hidden. That night, while inspecting her presents, I found a bottle of Poison perfume by Christian Dior tossed casually among her clothes.

'Wow! Lucky girl!' I rolled my eyes. 'Now who in Nainital can afford a gift like this?'

With a disarming smile and a shrug, Alka tried to make light of it. '*Kamaal ho gaya, didi!* Rakhi the miser suddenly became generous.'

I knew she was lying. Rakhi Rawat was her classmate in St Theresa's. Last year she had given Alka a plastic treasure chest costing fifty rupees on her birthday. There was no way she would gift her an imported perfume costing three thousand.

There were other signals, too. Throughout the two-week Christmas holiday, when the Academy was closed, I caught Alka writing furtive letters, which she would drop stealthily into the red postbox that stood just outside the school's main gate. When I confronted her, she said they were for a pen friend in Brazil. Even more worryingly, her grades dropped a little. She began suffering from insomnia, lost her appetite.

I got conclusive proof the day the Academy reopened. Returning from the library in the evening, I heard muffled sounds coming from behind the deserted school gym. As I edged closer, I saw a girl and a boy locked in a passionate embrace under an oak tree. The girl had her hands on the boy's shoulders and he was kissing her on the lips. They broke up the moment they detected my presence. The boy turned and sprinted down the hill, disappearing into a thicket of pine trees. I couldn't catch his face, but his green blazer and grey trousers were a dead giveaway: it was the school uniform. The girl tried to avert her face and scramble past me, but I caught her hand. It was Alka.

We went for a long walk that night. She refused to tell me the boy's name or any other detail about him, other than that he was the coolest guy on the planet and the son of a very rich Delhi-based businessman. 'I am in love, *didi*,' she kept harping, even breaking into a corny love song.

'You don't fall in love when you're fifteen, Alka,' I counselled her. 'This is simply infatuation. The boy is trying to take advantage of you.'

'Love doesn't have an age limit, *didi*,' she retorted. 'It happens when it happens. And it lasts a lifetime. You'll see when I marry him.'

'And what will Papa say when he finds out about your little romance?'

'He won't find out. I know you will keep my secret, *didi*. You are the only person I trust with my life.'

'Then you have to trust me when I tell you that what

you are doing is not only irresponsibly wrong, it is incredibly stupid as well.'

Despite using every argument, every threat, bluster and influence, I could not persuade Alka to end her liaison. She was as obstinate and headstrong as I was insistent and persuasive. Eventually we reached a compromise of sorts. I extracted a promise from her that she would temporarily suspend her relationship with the boy. In return, I would not tattle about this to anyone, least of all Papa.

Though I trusted Alka, I started monitoring her discreetly from that day, even rummaging through her things when she was not in her room. Two weeks went by without further incident, and then one night I discovered a small package she had secreted inside the toe of her shoe. It was a rolled-up manila envelope. Inside it was a clear plastic packet containing a brown powder-like substance. It looked like a sachet of brown sugar, but I had seen enough films to know it was high-grade heroin.

I called Alka into my room and closed the door. 'How did this come into your possession?' I asked her coldly, holding aloft the sachet.

'Where did you find it?' she asked in fearful agitation.

'Answer my question. Who gave it to you?' I repeated sternly.

'My boyfriend,' she replied with downcast eyes.

'I thought you had broken off from him.'

'I tried to but I can't,' she moaned. 'He's my oxygen. I'll die without him. And he'll die without me. He almost cut his wrist the day I told him I won't see him any more.'

'It only goes to show that he is a sicko, besides being a drug dealer.'

'He's not a drug dealer. And I am not doing drugs. We tried it just once. And that, too, only as an experiment.'

'An experiment that might make you an addict, even end up taking your life.'

'Why do you have to take everything so seriously, *didi*?'

'Nothing can be more serious than drugs, Alka. You betrayed my trust. The water has now passed over my head. I'll have to report this to Papa.'

'No, *didi*,' she said vehemently, clutching my arm. 'I swear I'll kill myself if you breathe a word about this to Papa.'

'Drugs will kill you before that, Alka,' I said and brushed her aside.

Papa was engrossed in a newspaper when I barged into his study. 'Your daughter Alka has started doing drugs. Please deal with her,' I said without preamble, dropping the plastic sachet in his lap like a discarded banana peel.

That night there was the mother of all showdowns in the house. Papa was notorious in the Academy for his strict ethics and discipline. I consider myself lucky that I inherited only his dark skin, not his dark temper. Papa always believed he was meant for higher things, that teaching school kids was beneath him. And he took out his frustration on them. Stories were still circulating about the time he flogged a student who had made the mistake of bringing a bootlegged copy of *Playboy* to class, until the boy was reduced to a quivering mass of lacerated flesh. The students used to cower in his presence. His tests could reduce anyone to tears. The school was aware of his combustible emotional state, but tolerated it because he was quite simply an outstanding maths teacher, perhaps the best in the country. He could do calculations faster than a computer, solve any equation, prove any theorem.

What he didn't know was how to deal with the stresses and anxieties of a fifteen-year-old teenager. I thought he would have a heart-to-heart chat with Alka, instil some sense into her through the sheer moral force of his personality. Instead, their confrontation quickly degenerated into a street brawl, full of belligerent theatrics, yelling and screaming.

'I can have you sent to jail for possessing drugs,' Papa said, trying to frighten Alka.

'Then send me,' Alka gave him right back. 'I will be happier there than in this prison called home.'

Many things were said in the heat of the moment that shouldn't have been said. Father accused Alka of being a spoilt brat who was a blot on the family's name. Alka labelled him a bully: 'Your expectations are unrealistic, your tests impossible.' The unkindest cut came when she denounced him as a coward. 'The entire school laughs at you behind your back. You are nothing but a perverse, pathetic loser, undeserving of any respect,' she shrieked.

It was as if a volcano had erupted. 'How dare you!' Papa thundered, blood rushing to his face as he suddenly sprang to his feet. 'How *dare* you!' he repeated, and slapped her across the cheek, knocking her to the floor.

Ma, Neha and I stared in stunned horror. This was the first time Papa had raised his hand on any of his daughters.

Alka picked herself up from the floor. There was a great red welt on her cheek and a scratch on her arm. Her dark eyes glittered with an incandescent fury that would have melted rock. She looked at all of us, before settling on me. I felt a laser beam of pure, unrestrained loathing boring into my soul. 'I hate you, I hate all of you,' she hissed through clenched teeth. Then she ran to her bedroom and bolted the door from the inside. I pleaded with her to listen to me, tried desperately to get her to open the door, but she stubbornly refused.

I deserved her hate. I deserved everything she threw at me that night.

'Let her rot in her room,' Papa said disdainfully. 'Our overindulgence has brought matters to this pass.'

None of us had dinner that night.

The next day was 26 January. India's Republic Day. The school wore a transformed look with bunting in saffron, green and white strung all around the campus. The tricolour fluttered proudly from the tall poles in the sports field. I could hear the students rehearsing patriotic songs from early in the morning, their hearty voices adding to the festive fervour. Alka, however, had still not emerged from her room and I was getting just a little worried. I knocked on her door several times but there was no response. So I crept in from the back garden. The first thing I noticed was that the window of her bedroom was open. My instant reaction was that Alka had run away. In the background I could hear the hum of 'Hum Honge Kamyab' being sung by the boys in the open assembly area: 'We shall overcome ... We shall overcome ... We shall overcome some day ...'

I parted the heavy window curtain a crack and a shaft of sunlight spanned the dim penumbra of the room. In its piercing beam I saw a sight that chilled me to the bone. Alka was dangling from the ceiling fan, with her head hanging to one side. There was a yellow dupatta knotted around her neck. The small wooden chair in her room lay upturned on the floor.

I felt a wave of dizziness assail me. 'Papa!' I screamed and stumbled back away from the window.

> We'll walk hand in hand, we'll walk hand in hand,
> We'll walk hand in hand someday;
> Oh, deep in my heart, I do believe,
> We'll walk hand in hand someday.

I remember everything else happening in slow motion through a veil of tears. Papa kicking open Alka's door, gasping and writhing like a man on fire. Mother climbing up onto the bed and holding Alka's limp body to take the strain off the piece of cloth she was hanging from. Neha fetching a knife with which we cut her down.

> We are not afraid, we are not afraid,
> We are not afraid today;
> Oh, deep in my heart, I do believe,
> We are not afraid today.

It was too late. Life had already ebbed away from my beautiful sister. We laid her on the bed and untied the yellow headscarf from her neck. I had never seen it before. Her face was pale in repose. Her bare feet were tinged bluish purple, due to all the blood pooling there – a coloration known as postmortem staining or hypostasis.

Another thoroughly useless piece of information I had picked up for my general-knowledge bank. In her right hand, she clutched a piece of paper. I gently pried it from her cold fingers. Written in her charming, childlike scrawl was the inscription, 'Love never dies. It just acquires a new form.' I recalled it as the tagline of a Hindi film we had seen recently on TV, a modern-day tragedy. Then there was a final line: 'I forgive you all.'

I cradled my dead sister in my arms, shoulders hunched, as I succumbed to the cruel reality that our paths would never cross again on earth. Her heart was almost too big for this world. In life, she had touched us all with her radiant presence, her kindness and her grace. And even in death she had chosen to forgive us. As Sister Agnes used to remind us about Jesus, Alka had redeemed us through her blood. We never fully understood her, and now she was gone for ever, making us feel so small.

> The truth shall make us free, the truth shall make us
> free,
> The truth shall make us free someday;
> Oh, deep in my heart, I do believe,
> The truth shall make us free someday.

The police came, and an ambulance, which took away Alka's body. Neighbours gathered and spoke in sombre tones about the inevitability of fate. The headmaster also arrived, having cut short his Republic Day speech. He seemed more concerned at the disruption in the day's programme than at our loss. Mother and Neha took no note of him. They were busy wailing. I did not cry. I just sat there like an immobile rock, my face frozen in a twisted rictus of absolute shock mixed with overwhelming pain. The final image of my dead sister seared into my memory for ever.

We shall live in peace, we shall live in peace,
We shall live in peace someday;
Oh, deep in my heart, I do believe,
We shall live in peace someday.

There was no peace. There was only guilt in the stunned aftermath of the tragedy. First came the nightmares, when I'd wake up in the middle of the night covered in sweat and gasping for breath. Then came the panic attacks, caused by the festering wounds of memory. Reality became a psychedelic film, full of jittering cuts and freeze-frames of Alka's dead body swinging in the breeze. Matters reached such a point that I couldn't look at a ceiling fan without suffering a gag reflex. The sight of any piece of yellow cloth gave Ma anxiety attacks.

Alka's ghost stalked us every hour of every day. House Number 17 was drenched in her smell, filled with her presence. Every little thing in her room reminded us of her. Every old photograph prompted a new bout of self-flagellation. Eventually we couldn't take it any longer. Since history could not be altered, we decided to change geography.

It was Neha who suggested the move. 'Let's go someplace far away from Nainital. I'll die if we stay here.' Papa accepted the suggestion almost with relief. The taint of scandal that he had always been so careful to avoid had spread far beyond the campus, tarnishing his career and eroding his self-esteem. Even he longed to be free of the daily humiliation he faced in the censorious stares of his fellow teachers and the sniggering malice of his students. So we locked up our belongings in four trunks and left the cold comfort of Nainital for the warm humid air of Delhi, 320 kilometres away.

Liberated from the incestuous claustrophobia of small-time Nainital, we sought to rebuild our lives by grafting onto the coarse anonymity of the metropolis. Alka's death had taught me the meaning of life, how fragile it is, and how blithely we take it for granted. I woke up many mornings with the chilling certainty that this very day might be my last on earth. And, once you start living with the consciousness of death, it brings urgency, intensity and focus to life. It teaches you to live a less trivial existence, impels you to seek the greatest possible value for your actions. I started donating blood regularly to the Red Cross. After my first donation I learnt that my blood type was one of the rarest ones, known as the Bombay blood group. Only four people in a million have it. Now, if ever there is an emergency requirement, the Red Cross rings me, sends a car to fetch me. I am its most prized donor.

I also used to volunteer at the Blind School, till I got the job at Gulati & Sons. Now I have free time only on Sundays, and I utilise it to teach English to a group of slum kids who live near our colony. Which means very soon, Suresh, Chunnu, Raju and Aarti will be knocking on my door.

As the flood of memories abates, I start hunting for *The Simple English Reader*, which I use as an informal textbook for my small class. It turns out the book is with Neha, being used as a coaster for the glass of Diet Coke she is gulping down with great gusto. She does not seem weighed down by the occasion of Alka's birthday. Far from feeling gloomy, she is positively bubbling with excitement. 'Just read this, *didi!*' She thrusts a letter in my hands.

It is from the organisers of *Popstar No. 1*, a popular musical talent show she has auditioned for. Out of 500,000 candidates, she has been selected for the final audition in Mumbai, where twenty of the best singers will be chosen for the actual contest on TV. Four top music directors will be the 'musical gurus' judging the show.

'This is the chance I have been waiting for all my life. *Bas*, I'm going to be a star now, you'll see, *didi*,' she squeals.

I give Neha a wan smile, marvelling at the beauty of chance, the tricks of fate. Alka dazzles me again from the centre wall. Perhaps she is orchestrating all this from wherever she is, still redeeming us, giving us second chances. I look into her warm sparkling eyes. '*Kamaal ho gaya!* It's incredible!' I can almost hear her lilting voice ringing in the room.

The dead don't die. As long as we remember them, they remain alive in our hearts.

It is a crisp Monday morning and there is a chill in the air, with the temperature hovering around ten degrees centigrade. It is the sort of weather that makes you wish you were still curled up in bed. Instead, I am at the Maharana Pratap Inter-State Bus Terminal at Kashmiri Gate, which everybody refers to simply as ISBT. The place is teeming with people from all walks of life – executives, students, pilgrims and tourists – about to embark on journeys to destinations all over north India. My destination is Karnal, as there is no direct bus from Delhi to Mr Kuldip Singh's village of Chandangarh.

I have chosen to dress conservatively in an off-white salvar kameez with a fully draped dupatta, which is hardly visible under the collar of my dark-grey overcoat. A small handbag contains all that I need for the trip: some savouries and salted snacks, a Bisleri bottle and a yellowing paperback of poems by Anna Akhmatova.

At platform number 18, I am pleasantly surprised to discover that my bus is a brand-new Volvo, with reclining seats and adjustable armrests. I have a window seat, next to a young lady in jeans and a bob cut who looks to be my age. She's not pretty in a conventional sense, with her boyish crop and square face, yet she seems oddly familiar. I feel like talking to her, but she is totally engrossed in texting on her cell phone. Not wanting to intrude, I also bury my face in the paperback the moment the bus departs at 09.00 sharp.

It is slow going while we are in the city, but once we are onto the stretch of the Grand Trunk Road, the Volvo picks up speed. The four-lane highway snakes like a black ribbon through the sparse, flat landscape dotted with small farms, brick kilns and patches of urban sprawl. The ride is so smooth it almost lulls me to sleep.

Eventually, the woman sitting next to me tires of her

phone. That is when I turn to her. 'Pardon me, but have we met before?'

She smiles. 'I don't think so, but you might have seen me on TV.'

'Are you an actress?'

'I'm an investigative reporter for Sunlight TV.'

'Of course,' I respond in slow recognition. I don't watch Sunlight TV all that often, but the news channel is well known for its daring exposés ('Like the sunlight which enters a dark room and brightens it, we uncover hidden facts,' goes the channel's tagline).

'Hi! I'm Shalini Grover.' She extends her hand, and I gladly accept it.

I learn that Shalini is on her way to Panipat to cover a story about an honour killing that took place six months ago. She tells me that a young couple – Mahender and Ragini – were murdered by their respective parents and thrown into an irrigation canal simply for defying the taboo against love marriages between members of the same subcaste.

'Honour killings in India?' I raise my eyebrows. 'I thought this kind of thing happened in tribal Afghanistan.'

'Haven't you heard of *khap panchayats*?' she asks.

I shake my head. Once my civil service aspirations went out of the window, I had stopped honing my general knowledge.

'*Khap panchayats* are social structures in Haryana, U.P. and Rajasthan who dole out their own form of rough justice. These caste-based councils consider themselves guardians of a medieval morality and one of their priorities is to prevent love marriages between members of the same *gotra* or subcaste. Young couples defying their *fatwas* have been ostracised, beaten up, forced to live like brother and sister, and even killed. They are worse than kangaroo courts.'

'Yes, but how can parents kill their own child?'

'They can, when honour is seen as more important than the life of a son or daughter. These *khaps* have had too much of a free run. They are composed of murdering goons, intent only on perpetuating a feudal and patriarchal order. Even the Supreme Court has asked for them to be stamped out ruthlessly.'

'You said the couple were murdered six months ago. So what's the interest now?'

'There are many Raginis in our villages, but their stories are unseen and unheard. I want to highlight the terrifying oppression that an ordinary village girl faces in rural India if she chooses love over fear.'

Hearing her speak so impassionedly, I begin to experience that dull, leaden sensation I used to get in school whenever the teacher asked me a question I did not know the answer to. Somehow my eyes always seem to skim over the grisly stories of battered wives, burnt brides and raped schoolgirls in our newspapers.

To change the subject I look around the bus. 'Where's your camera crew?'

'I don't have one,' Shalini replies. 'This is just a research trip, for background.'

'But what if a TV journalist like you suddenly comes across an unexpected story?'

'Then this becomes my camera.' She waves her cell phone. 'It has a twelve-megapixel CMOS sensor that allows me to shoot 640-by-480 video at 30 f.p.s. What's more, I can stream directly from my cell simply by connecting over the Internet to our dedicated website.'

Now she is speaking my kind of language. We get into an animated discussion on the merits of the latest smartphones. A little while later the conversation shifts to Hindi films. By the time Panipat arrives, we have settled into a comfortable rapport with each other.

'Well, good luck,' I wish Shalini as she prepares to disembark. We exchange telephone numbers, promising to remain in touch, but it is one of those casual promises fellow travellers make to each other in full knowledge that their paths may never cross again.

After Panipat the road is congested and plagued with traffic snarls till the bus reaches Karnal. With its bustling markets and luxury apartments set amid lush greenery, Karnal has the air of a prosperous provincial centre. I have no time to explore the town or check out the hollow silver-bead jewellery it is famous for, as I have to catch another bus to Chandangarh, forty kilometres away. This time the vehicle is a rusty old Ashok Leyland and the road is a rutted dirt-and-gravel track, full of potholes. The jarring one-hour ride to Chandangarh makes me nauseous and headachy. But, at the stroke of noon, I am in Mr Kuldip Singh's village.

The big man himself is waiting at the bus stop. 'Come, come, *beti*,' he says by way of welcome. 'Your arrival has filled my heart with happiness.' He is dressed in his usual shirt and dhoti and his handlebar moustache is magnificent as ever. We get into his chauffeured Toyota Innova and drive off, trailing a cloud of dust behind us.

'Have you ever been to a village?' Kuldip Singh asks me.

I shake my head. Having been a city girl all my life, I have caught only fleeting glimpses of villages from train and bus windows. My idea of rural life is still anchored in the idyllic villages depicted in Bollywood films, where beautiful maidens sing racy folk songs in lush green fields and people live happy, uncomplicated communal lives. This is the first time I've set foot in an actual village.

'Chandangarh village has three thousand inhabitants,' he informs me.

'That's less than a tenth of the number of people in Sector 11 of Rohini alone,' I remark.

'I still don't understand how you city people can live in multistoreyed buildings, hanging between earth and sky,' he chuckles. 'We villagers cannot imagine living in a place where we don't have a roof over our heads and solid ground under our feet. This is what we call land, what we call home. Home is our land. Land is our home.'

We drive past a series of farms, fully equipped with tractors, tube wells and threshers. Even the road is not all dirt: there are sections paved with granite bits. A farmer waves at us as we pass him on his scooter.

'So when exactly did your village get electricity?' I enquire.

He looks at me with a slightly cross expression. 'Don't you know that Haryana was the first state in the whole of India to give electricity to each and every village, way back in 1970? And every village is now connected with metalled roads. The only thing our village doesn't have is a hospital, and that might also come in a few years.'

I catch a glimpse of a temple spire peeking out between the trees and electric power lines in the distance. 'That is Amba Temple, dedicated to Goddess Durga,' Kuldip Singh says. 'She is our village deity.' My respect for Chandangarh goes up a notch as I dip my head in obeisance.

Kuldip Singh's house, it turns out, is located quite close to the temple. A pucca brick-and-cement construction, it is a rambling ancestral compound with plenty of rooms. I enter through a sunlit courtyard where a group of *halwais* are busy making sweetmeats. In the left corner is the kitchen, where another set of male cooks are cooking in large pots over an open fire. The women, dressed in glittering Punjabi suits, are huddled on a charpoy. They give me coy, curious glances. The entire house is suffused with the festive atmosphere of a traditional wedding.

'When is the wedding?' I ask my host.

'Just tomorrow. In fact, you should attend it as our honoured guest. Why are you in such a hurry to leave today itself?'

'Work,' I say matter-of-factly, as if it required no further explanation.

I am conducted into a large, whitewashed room, with just a bed and a dresser. An army of servants then serves me an elaborate vegetarian lunch in a steel *thali* with six different kinds of dishes. It all tastes finger-licking delicious. The missi roti is the best I have ever eaten. I wash it all down with a couple of glasses of sweet lassi.

The job I have come for begins after lunch. A Mahindra Scorpio arrives outside the house and a man wearing a black sweater over a white shirt and black trousers steps down. He seems to be in his mid-forties, with a stocky build, a clean-shaven face and squinty eyes. 'This is Badan Singh-ji,' Kuldip Singh says, introducing him, and begins leading the way to the rear of the house, where the cowsheds are located. There are more than a dozen cows and buffaloes masticating their cud. Detached from the cowsheds is a hut made of brick, but with a thatched roof. Inside the hut, stored alongside bales of hay, are all his purchases from the store. A fluorescent rod glows brightly overhead, providing the only illumination in the rather gloomy room. The appliances have been opened and displayed neatly. A long extension cord runs from an electrical outlet, pooling at the base of the television.

'I understand head nor tail of these newfangled machines,' my host says sheepishly, grinning. 'Even Chhotan, our local electrician, has no clue how to operate the clothes washer. So we had to trouble you. Please explain their operation to Badan Singh-ji. I have to attend to the decorators now.'

He exits the hut, leaving me alone with Badan Singh. The air inside the shack feels oppressive, thick, permeated by the odour of hay, and I cannot breathe for a moment.

'You came from Delhi?' Badan Singh asks.

'Yes,' I reply.

'All these goods will eventually come to our house, so I thought it best I came here myself. I drove from Batauli village, about thirty kilometres from here. Our house is just across the canal.'

'Are you the father of the groom?' I ask.

He looks at me askance. 'I *am* the groom. Do I look old to you?'

'No, no,' I say quickly, kicking myself for this blunder.

'I have called my workers. Now you just tell us how to hook up and run the gadgets. Chhotan, Nanhey,' he hollers and immediately two men appear. From their dusty clothes, deferential air, nervous expressions and low-slung tool belts, I guess them to be electrician and plumber respectively.

'Should we begin with the TV?' I insert the plug of the Samsung 42C430 into the extension cord. The plasma screen comes alive, snowing softly to the sound of static.

'I know everything about TVs,' the electrician declares. 'I am the cable operator for the village. It's the washing machine that I find complicated. Can you show us how to use it first?'

'Sure.' I shrug and plug in the Whirlpool washer. The moment I press the start button, the tube light above me begins stuttering. 'What's wrong?'

'Kuldip Singh-ji still has the old electricity meter, which cannot handle too much load,' Badan Singh sniggers. 'There's no problem in our house. We can run four ACs simultaneously.'

'Voltage is bound to be an issue in the villages. You must run all these appliances with voltage stabilisers,' I say, yanking out the plug.

Over the next hour, I explain to them the programme cycles on the washing machine, the functions on the music system, the HDMI connection between the DVD player and the television, the correct settings on the fridge. Badan Singh and his two minions keep nodding, but I doubt that they understand everything. Throughout my briefing they maintain the slightly dazed, sheepish expression of men who are unable to deal with the fact that a woman knows more about electronics than they.

By 2.30 p.m. I am done. I want to leave instantly. There is nothing holding me back in this hick village, but my return bus to Karnal is only available at 4 p.m.

Kuldip Singh is still trying to persuade me to stay the night. 'Babli is my only daughter. Her wedding will be an affair to remember,' he says proudly as he escorts me back to the guestroom. 'Are you sure you don't want to participate in the festivities?'

'Positive,' I reply. 'If you don't mind, I'll just rest for an hour and then your driver can take me back to the bus stop.'

I lock the room, take off my coat, and lie down on the bed for a short nap. Outside, the women are singing what sounds like a rousing wedding song. It makes me drowsy.

I am woken up by muffled sounds coming from somewhere close to the room. I sit up and look around. It is only then that I notice the wooden door on the far side of the room. The sound is coming from behind it.

I hear a latch being pulled down and the door opens a crack. A young girl peeps out. She has a delicate, beautiful face, with big, almond eyes, shapely pink lips and thick black hair. '*Didi, didi,*' she whispers to me, 'Can you do me a favour?' There is the furtive look of a caged animal about her.

'Yes,' I react cautiously, getting down from the bed. As I approach her I notice a dark bruise on her left cheek, like an angry rose blooming on her fair skin. She is alarmingly pale and her eyes are all red and puffy; I can tell she has been crying.

'Can you post this for me, please?' She holds out a folded piece of paper.

'Who are you?' I ask.

'I'm Babli,' she says.

'Oh, so you are the one getting married?'

She nods.

'Well, congratulations on your wedding.'

She doesn't reply, but the infinitely sad expression in her eyes conveys more than words.

'Babli? What are you still doing in your room?' I hear a woman's voice call her from the other side.

'I know you are going back today. If you could just put this in an envelope, affix a five-rupee stamp and drop it into the nearest letterbox, I will be eternally grateful. I've written the address on the top. Will you do this for me?'

'With pleasure,' I reply, taking the folded piece of paper from her hennaed hands.

'Please don't forget to post this, *didi*. It's very important to me,' she says plaintively. Then, like a turtle withdrawing into its shell, she pulls her head back, latching the door shut once again.

I am still trying to absorb the shock of this unexpected encounter, when there is a knock on my door. 'Are you awake, *beti*?' I hear Kuldip Singh's voice. Outside, his driver is tooting the Innova's horn. It is time for my four o'clock bus to Karnal.

With a last, lingering look at the locked door, as if bidding farewell to a loved one, I put on my coat and walk out of the room. Kuldip Singh is waiting outside with a big box of laddoos, which he thrusts into my hands. 'Since you cannot stay for the wedding, at least enjoy these sweets.' He grins. I thank him profusely, make my goodbyes and get into the Innova.

As the vehicle speeds away from the house, I cannot stop thinking of Babli. There is something about her that reminds me of Alka. Her sorrowful, resigned look raises troubling questions about this wedding. This much is clear: that an eighteen-year-old girl is being married off to a much older man, probably against her will. But such marriages happen all the time in the country. There is nothing I can do about it. I am simply a passer-by. I have no right to trespass into a family's private affairs.

Almost involuntarily, I insert a hand into my coat pocket and withdraw the piece of paper Babli has given me. It is addressed to someone called Sunil Chaudhary who lives in Vaishali, Sector 4, Ghaziabad, and I cannot resist taking a peek at it. I discover a note penned in a schoolgirl's shaky handwriting on rule-lined paper ripped from a notebook. This is what it says in chaste Hindi:

My dear darling Sunil

They are marrying me off tomorrow.
Marriage is supposed to be about two people loving each other and devoting their lives to each other. But this marriage is about oppression and suppression, because, for my family, prestige is more important than my happiness.
I am being sold to Badan Singh. For Father it is a business transaction. For Mother it is a means to get rid of me. No one in this house has any regard for my feelings. Everybody's heart has turned to stone.
Forgive me for not being able to contact you during the

last three months. After they sent you away from here, I have been kept imprisoned in the house, not allowed to step out even for a minute. But tonight I will be free.

I just want you to know that I was always yours and will always remain yours. If not in this life, then surely the next.

Yours
Babli

My hands turn cold as I read the missive. It is not a love letter: it is a suicide note, eerily reminiscent of the note Alka wrote before hanging herself.

I know that Babli is not making empty threats. She will go through with the act. I have seen that look in her eyes, the look of a girl who has lost all hope. *Tonight I will be free.* It sends a shiver down my back.

The bus to Karnal is waiting for its last passengers when we reach the bus stop. 'We just made it.' The driver wipes his forehead in relief. 'Hurry, madam.' He scrambles to open the door, but I remain sitting inside the van, my mind a whirlpool of indecision and anxiety.

It would be the easiest thing to board the bus and forget about Babli and this village. I can choose to post her letter or shred it into pieces and discard it on the footpath like a used bus ticket. But something keeps holding me back. I know it is guilt, preying on my mind like a vulture. Suddenly a vision swims before my eyes of a dead body hanging from a ceiling fan with a yellow piece of cloth. When the body swings left, I see that it is Alka. And when it swings right it is Babli. I close my eyes, but the scene keeps repeating again and again, like a demented slide show I cannot look away from. The searing images are overlaid with a silent scream of agony that fills my senses. It echoes like thunder, reverberating from every pore of my body. When it dies, I open my eyes, and immediately feel like throwing up.

'What's the matter, madam?' The driver looks at me, concerned.

'Nothing,' I reply, as the cobwebs of uncertainty begin clearing from my mind. 'Take me back to the house.'

'Back to the house?' The driver does a double-take.

'Yes. I am not going to Karnal. I am going back to Kuldip Singh's house. I think I will attend the wedding after all.'

'Yes, madam,' the driver says with an exaggerated roll of his eyes, and begins reversing the vehicle.

Fifteen minutes later I am back in the house. Kuldip Singh greets me with surprised delight. '*Yeh hui na bat.* I'm so glad you decided to come back. Tonight you will see what a Haryana wedding celebration really looks like.'

I am desperate to communicate with Babli, but the ladies of the house insist that I join their *sangeet* ceremony. So I sit in the front row and pretend to enjoy the songs and dances being performed in the courtyard to the rhythmic beat of a dholak and spoon. The bride is supposed to be present during the ladies' *sangeet*, but even after three hours there is no sign of Babli. I make a polite enquiry with Kuldip Singh's wife, a plump and stern-looking woman.

'Babli has gone to the beauty parlour,' she tells me.

'Your village even has a beauty parlour?'

'What did you think?' she smirks, eyes alight with a tri-umphant glow. 'We are not as backward as you city people think.'

It is almost 7.30 p.m. by the time Babli returns, escorted by three older women. As she is crossing the courtyard, our eyes meet for an instant. I can see that she is startled to see me, and a look of fear passes over her face. I smile reassuringly at her, trying to convey that her secret is safe with me. I sense an answer in her glance, as though we have just made a silent pact.

The beauty parlour has done a good enough job on her. The puffiness around her eyes is gone and the bruise on her cheek has been expertly covered up with makeup. Her hair has been swept into an elaborate bun and her skin shines with a faux glimmer. Dressed in a magenta salvar kameez and matching chunni, she looks like a glowing bride rather than the distraught teenager of the afternoon. It is only the wistful sadness in her eyes that tells me this is all an act.

After a communal dinner featuring such mouthwatering delights as mooli ke paranthe, kadhi pakoras, jeera chawal and besan pinni, I am ready for bed. Kuldip Singh offers to put me up in a deluxe room in an adjoining house, but I tell him I prefer the guestroom in which I had stayed earlier.

Once I am inside the room, with the door securely locked, I tiptoe to the other door and put my ear against it, trying to listen in. I can hear muffled sobs coming from within, and a couple of women talking. Babli is obviously not alone.

I return to bed, turn off the light and wait patiently for

Babli's chaperones to doze off. But a wedding house is like a hospital's emergency ward, plagued by constant interruptions. Someone is always coming in or going out. Add to that creaking floorboards, mooing cows, howling dogs, clanking chains, clanging pans and a running tap, and it is enough to turn me into a cranky nervous wreck.

I remain lying in bed, staring at the dark ceiling, trying to get used to the unfamiliar surroundings. At 2 a.m., I get up and peek through the curtains. A deep silence hangs over the courtyard. Not a soul stirs in the compound. The house has finally gone to sleep.

I tiptoe back to Babli's door. I know she will still be awake, her mind wound tight like mine. 'Babli! Babli!' I whisper urgently. 'I want to talk to you.'

Nothing happens for a couple of minutes. Just when I am about to give up, I hear a little scraping sound. It is the latch being carefully pulled down. Then the door opens a few inches, and Babli eases into my room, wearing a silk night suit. In the pale moonlight she looks like a fragile porcelain doll. She shivers momentarily, as a cold breeze blows in from my open window. I hastily draw back the curtains, plunging the room into darkness.

The air between us is awkward at first, heavy with our unsaid thoughts. I am ready to listen, but Babli is not yet ready to share. She is silent, guarded.

'I had a sister called Alka,' I disclose. 'She committed suicide when she was just fifteen.'

'Why?' Babli asks.

'She was in love with a boy who was a drug addict. We tried to make her break off from him.'

'Is that why you came back? To make me break off from Sunil?'

'No. I came back to tell you that life is very precious. And that we have no right to take life, whether it is someone else's or our own.'

'Tell that to my father and mother, who have taken away my life.'

'We all get upset with our parents from time to time. But they always have our best interests at heart.'

'Are you married?' she asks me.

'No,' I reply.

'Then how will you understand my pain? Tomorrow is not my wedding: it is my funeral.'

'I know you don't want to marry Badan Singh. Then why don't you tell this to your father?'

'He's the one who has got me into this situation. I love Sunil. If I am not able to marry him, I am going to die. Tonight.'

'What are you going to do?'

'Consume a whole bottle of pesticide spray. And when I go up I'm going to ask God, Why can't we girls live our lives like we want to? Why can't I marry the man who loves me, the man I love?'

'Did Sunil speak to your parents about wanting to marry you?'

'Of course he did. And my father turned him down. We were going to elope but Bao-ji found out and reported the matter to the *khap*. *Bas*, the sky fell upon us. The *khap* decreed that because Sunil's *gotra* is related to my subcaste, marriage between us would be like a marriage between a brother and a sister. From that day I was confined to the house. And Sunil was hounded out of the village, with the threat that if he ever comes back he will be killed. Tell me, *didi*, did we commit any crime? Why are we made to feel like criminals?'

'Who is this Badan Singh?'

'He is a dirty old man who has always lusted after me. I am convinced he had bribed the head of the *khap panchayat* to give a verdict against Sunil.'

'Do you have Sunil's number?'

'No. And I don't even have a cell phone. The *khap* has banned cell phones for unmarried girls in our village. I live in a prison, not a house, *didi*.'

I nod with a sympathetic grimace. Alka had said the same thing.

'At times I feel that the biggest curse is to be born a girl,' she continues. 'The struggle begins even before we are born, and continues till our death. My only wish is to be born a boy in my next life.'

'Don't be so pessimistic. What if I were to somehow stop this wedding?'

'How will you do that?'

'I can't tell you right now. But I swear to you on my dead sister's memory I will not allow this travesty of a marriage to take place.'

'Even God cannot stop this wedding now. Only my death will.'

Her voice has begun to acquire a definite note of hysteria. I catch her hand and hold it. 'Promise me, Babli, that you won't do anything rash tonight. In fact, I want you to bring me that bottle of pesticide.'

Babli does not speak for a long time, as though she is

churning that thought over and over in her head, wrestling with her destiny. Then she ducks under my bed and withdraws a plastic bottle bristling with warning labels: 'DANGEROUS POISON', 'KEEP OUT OF REACH OF CHILDREN', 'CAN KILL IF SWALLOWED'. I had no idea my bedroom was serving as her secret storage facility.

'My life is now in your hands, *didi.*' She hands me the bottle with a pleading, plaintive expression. Then, as silently as she entered my room, she returns to her own.

As I hold the bottle of pesticide in my hands, I am overcome with a powerful feeling of *déjà vu*. I have been down this trail so many times before, in my mind, in my dreams. What if? That question has dogged me since Alka's suicide. What if I had not tattled about Alka to Papa? I could not save Alka, but perhaps I can save Babli. This is a moment of grace, a chance at redemption. I won't be doing this for Babli. I will be doing it for myself.

There is only one problem. I have made her a promise but I have no clue how I am going to fulfil it. It is one thing to try to right an old wrong, but how do I conjure up a happy ending from a situation that has all the makings of a tragedy?

I can only hope that tomorrow will bring the answer.

Chandangarh is a village of early risers. Even before the sun has pushed its way past the horizon, the villagers are out and about, drawing water from the well, milking cows or going for their daily ablutions, like me.

The concept of *en suite* bathroom does not exist in Kuldip Singh's house. The communal toilets are located at the western end of the compound, and they are all

Indian style. I also have to carry an overflowing *lota*, since the toilet tap generates air, not water. This is what I detest about village life. The poor sanitation. Every winter Papa used to take us to Hardoi, his ancestral town, where grandfather had a sprawling house with a mango grove. But my only memory of that house is of the hole in the ground that used to be the squat latrine. And I used to have nightmares of a disembodied hand rising from that orifice, grabbing me and taking me down to the pile of shit.

After a quick, cold bath, I seek out Kuldip Singh. He is sprawled on a charpoy in a corner of the courtyard, getting a massage from a thin-looking masseuse with knobbly fingers.

In the centre of the courtyard, workers are constructing the *mandap*, where the wedding ceremony will be solemnised tonight.

I hang around my room till the massage is complete and Kuldip Singh has put his vest back on. 'Can I have a word with you?' I ask, puffs of air condensing in front of my face.

'*Bilkul*, of course,' he says expansively. 'Come, sit with me here.' He pats the charpoy.

I sit down at the edge and broach the subject gingerly. 'I learnt yesterday that Babli's groom is Badan Singh-ji . . .'

'Yes. Badan Singh is the pride of our community. He even owns a rice mill. Babli will live like a queen.'

'But don't you think the age difference between them is a bit much?'

'Who said so, eh?' He suddenly tenses up. 'Has Babli been speaking to you?'

'No . . . no. I was just curious, that's all.'

'A man's age is not important. As they say in our village, "*Joban lugai ka bees ya tees, ar bael chaley nou saal. Mard aur ghora kadey no ho burha, agar milley khurak.*" A woman remains youthful only till she is twenty or thirty; an ox remains active for nine years; but a man and a horse, if given a good diet, never get old.'

'I just hope Babli is as happy with this marriage as you are.'

'Of course she *is*,' he says, stressing 'is'. 'You know how girls are. She is sad to be leaving our family. But then a girl is *paraya dhan*, someone else's wealth. One day she has to leave the father's house and go to her husband's. You'll also get married someday. If you want I can suggest some good-looking guys from the village.'

'No, thanks,' I say, rising from the charpoy.

'Where are you going now?'

'I want to visit the Amba Temple.'

'You can go in the Innova.'

'I'd rather walk and get some fresh air.'

I saunter out of the house, dressed in the same clothes as yesterday. Once I am some distance away, I take out my cell phone and punch in Karan's number.

'Where are you?' he wants to know.

'In Chandangarh village in Haryana.'

'What are you doing there?'

'It's a long story. For now, I need you to locate someone for me.'

'Who? Your twin brother who got lost in the stampede during the Kumbh Mela?'

For Karan everything is a joke. But for me it is a matter

of someone's life or death. 'It is a man called Sunil Chaudhary, who lives in Ghaziabad.' I read out Sunil's address. 'I want you to give me his cell phone number.'

'Hold on,' Karan says. A couple of minutes later he tells me, 'You are lucky. Sunil Chaudhary has an Indus mobile. Note down the number.'

I call up Sunil, only to be confronted with the wall of a prerecorded message. 'The Indus Mobile number you are trying to reach is currently switched off. Please try after sometime,' says a female voice. I keep calling his number at two-minute intervals, but fail to get through even once.

When you are desperately trying to reach someone, the most frustrating thing in the world is a phone that refuses to perform its primary task. Every time I try Sunil, I encounter the woman's faintly gloating voice, making me want to smack her.

Finally I dial Madan's cell phone number, informing him I won't be able to come to the office today. 'I'm still stuck in Chandangarh village, with a severe case of diarrhoea.'

'What did you eat?' he demands.

'Whatever Kuldip Singh gave me. Oh, my stomach is hurting so bad.' I throw in a throaty groan for effect. 'You should never have sent me here.'

'Look, I'm really sorry. It's okay. You get some rest and take *pudin hara*. I'll reimburse its cost.'

I savour the rare pleasure of hearing a guilty undertone in Madan's supercilious voice. Feeling self-righteous and smug, I head for the Amba Temple, which is only a stone's throw away. It stands at the edge of a small pond, and contains an ancient statue of an eight-armed Durga. I bow my head before the goddess, asking for strength to fight the battle on Babli's behalf.

Fortified by Durga Ma's blessings, I set out to seize the day. The men are already heading out to the fields or the nearby mills for work; the women are busy making cow-dung patties for cooking fuel.

As I am leaving the temple precincts, I come across a jeep with a red beacon and a golden inscription on the number plate stating 'BLOCK DEVELOPMENT OFFICER'.

The BDO, I know, is an important functionary responsible for formulation and implementation of various government schemes. My eyes light up at this unexpected good fortune. If there is one entity that can get Babli out of this unholy mess, it is the government.

The BDO turns out to be a middle-aged, turbaned Sikh called Inderjit Singh, sporting an unkempt beard flecked with grey. I tell him about Babli's plight and seek to enlist his help in resolving the situation.

He listens to me sympathetically. 'Look, I don't know about Babli and Sunil, but there have been several instances of the local *khap* creating trouble for couples who go against the diktats of the community. In one instance they had the boy forced to drink urine; in another they had him paraded naked through the village.'

'Then shouldn't you be doing something to stop these inhuman acts?'

He shakes his head slowly. 'I cannot do anything in the matter. No one can fight the *khap*.'

'Even when you know what they are doing is criminal and wrong?'

'Yes. I know some of their pronouncements are anti-poor and anti-women in character,' he says candidly. 'But to meddle with the local social hierarchy is to invite trouble.'

'If you won't help me, who will?'

'Try and understand this is a village, not India Gate, where you can hold protest marches and candlelight vigils. There are no social activists here who can challenge the *khap*. The men are indifferent, the women cowed down.'

'I'm not cowed down. I'll challenge the *khap*. Who is the head of the *khap panchayat*?'

'It is Sultan Singh. And that is his house.' He points out a redbrick house in the distance. 'But, if you think you can reason with him, you are being foolhardy.'

'Perhaps I am. But, as a famous Hindi proverb says, now that I have decided to put my head into the mortar, why fear the pounder?'

'Well, then, good luck to you,' the BDO says, and drives off in his jeep.

It takes me a fifteen-minute walk to reach my next destination. Sultan Singh is a wizened old man with the impressively patrician air of an old zamindar. He meets me on the porch of his decaying *haveli*, wearing a black waistcoat and carrying a cane in his gnarled hands. 'Yes, what do you want?' he says gruffly, gazing at me with the suspicious eye of a girls' hostel warden.

'You are the venerable head of the *khap panchayat*, and the flag bearer of its principles. So I thought I would meet you directly to seek justice for Babli.'

'Babli? Who is Babli?'

'Kuldip Singh's daughter.'

'Ah, that *chhori*,' he says, with a portentous pause. '*Wa to aafat ki pudiya sai.* She is nothing but trouble.'

'You know she loves Sunil. Then why are you condemning her to this loveless marriage with Badan Singh?'

'Don't you know that Babli is from Jorwal *gotra* and Sunil from Jaipal *gotra*? In our village, people from these two subcastes have had a relationship of brotherhood for centuries. So a marriage between these two *gotras* cannot be sanctioned.'

'Who cares about *gotras* in this day and age? I don't even *know* my *gotra*.'

'I pity your parents. They didn't teach you anything about our glorious heritage and traditions.'

'There was a time when *sati* was also supposed to be part of Hindu tradition. Widows used to be burnt alive on their husbands' funeral pyres. Hounding people who are in love and killing them is no less reprehensible.'

'Who says we kill people?' he says heatedly, almost poking me in the face with his cane. 'This is a canard spread by the lower castes. Our *khap* has played a positive role in banning dowry and liquor consumption in the village.'

'But you have banned Sunil from entering the village. And now Babli is threatening to commit suicide.'

'Then let her die. No one will shed any tears for her. A dishonourable girl is a blot on a family,' he says unapologetically.

'So love has no value for you?'

'These modern whims of the heart have no place in tradition. *Khap* is an institution, a very honourable one.

Don't interfere with our traditions. Go and tell Babli that what cannot be changed must be endured.'

'Tell me, Sultan Singh-ji, how many women are members of your *khap panchayat*?'

'None.'

'So women have no role but to listen to your diktats?'

'Our dictates are based on reason and logic. A marriage between Babli and Sunil amounts to incest. How can we permit such an abomination?'

'But the Hindu Marriage Act recognises such unions.'

He laughs. 'This is my village. Here my writ runs, not the government of India's.'

Listening to him fills me with utter revulsion. Sometimes I feel that there's no country in the world with so much wasted love as ours. Instead of uniting lovers who dare to dream across the barriers of caste and class, the forces of orthodoxy and tradition separate them, hurt them, torture them, starve them, murder them, constantly finding new and horrifying ways of squelching love. I have still to fathom which is the greater existential horror: the lost humanity of fathers who dismember their own sons and daughters out of a perverse shame, or the reckless chivalry of star-crossed lovers who prefer death to separation. All I know is that I will not allow Babli's name to be added to this unfortunate list, come what may.

I take my leave from Sultan Singh and continue walking past the fields and fallows. The scenery looks quite different from the quaint, peaceful haven depicted in Yash Chopra films. Instead of lush, sunny fields of yellow and green, the landscape is uniformly brown. Instead of cheerful villagers, I see only sullen men and women, working their fields. The old-timers sit on their charpoys, smoking hookahs, while toddlers play in the dirt.

This part of the village is considerably less prosperous. The houses here are mostly mud huts with thatched roofs. The women glare at me for no apparent reason and no one offers me as much as a glass of water.

Suddenly I come across Chhotan, the electrician, riding a scooter. 'What are you doing here?' he asks.

'Nothing. Just out for a stroll.'

He dismounts from his scooter and begins walking with me. It is from him that I learn that the village is a hotbed of communalism and caste warfare. 'There are thirteen different castes in Chandangarh,' he tells me. 'Upper castes, like Kuldip Singh, make up nearly half the village; the rest are Harijans and other lower castes, like mine.'

'And where is the police station located?'

'Why? Do you have to report something?'

'No. I'm just curious.'

'On the eastern side, at the edge of the village, just before the river.'

'I would love to see the river.'

'I am going that side. If you want, I can give you a ride.'

A minute later, I am riding pillion through the dirt tracks of the village. People watch me curiously, as though they have never seen a woman sitting on a scooter before.

The bumpy scooter ride takes me past the village school where students are lazing under a neem tree. 'The teachers in the school are like gods,' Chhotan says wryly, 'believed to exist but never seen.' The village market is a conglomeration of a few kirana shops, some hardware stores, roadside shacks selling vegetables, Maggi noodles and boiled eggs, a video parlour stocking the latest Bollywood blockbusters and even an Internet facility. Slowly, but surely, progress seems to be coming to Chandangarh.

Swaying and jolting, I finally reach the rugged riverside. Chhotan drops me near a suspension bridge and takes off. The waters of the Yamuna glimmer silver and brown beneath me. This being the dry winter season, the river has contracted, exposing its sandbars.

It doesn't take me long to locate the police station. It is just a one-room brick house with a gated courtyard. Sub-Inspector Inder Varma, the officer in charge, looks like one of those cops in Hindi films: paan-chewing, pot-bellied, probably thoroughly corrupt as well. He hears me out and then laughs. 'Who are you, some kind of social worker?'

'It's not important who I am. I am reporting to you a forced marriage.'

'How do I know it is a forced marriage? Where is the girl? Why does she not lodge a complaint personally?'

'I told you, they have kept her imprisoned in the house.'

'Then get her out. Bring her here. Let her show me proof that she is above the age of eighteen. And I will take action.'

'You promise?'

'Look, madam, my duty is to uphold the law. But the law requires me to verify that the girl is an adult. If you can bring Babli here, I promise to get her justice.'

For the first time a ray of hope enters my heart. The

dour figure of SI Inder Varma could turn out to be Babli's unlikely saviour.

As I leave the police station, I try Sunil's number once again. My luck seems to be running at the moment, as I do get through this time. 'Hello?' a guarded voice responds.

I introduce myself and then ask him the million-dollar question. 'Sunil, do you still love Babli?'

'Of course I do,' he says.

'Then why don't you marry her?'

'Ha!' He gives a bitter laugh. 'Don't you know what the *khap* did to me? Three months ago, they humiliated me by parading me through the village with a shoe in my mouth. Then they forced me out of the village, threatening to kill not just me but also Babli if I ever return.'

'Well, now they have gone a step further. They are marrying Babli off to Badan Singh tonight.'

'No!' He lets out a wail which cackles over the line like static.

'Listen, Sunil. If you can come to the village right now, we can still prevent this wedding. I've spoken to the police; they will help you and Babli.'

'I wish you had told me this yesterday.'

'I kept trying your number but it was switched off. It's still not too late. It'll take you just a couple of hours to get here from Ghaziabad.'

'Yes, but right now I'm in Chennai, two thousand kilometres away.'

'Oh, no!'

'Don't worry, I'll take a plane. I'll come as fast as I can. I'll do anything for Babli.'

'Good. I'll wait for you. Just call me on this number when you reach Chandangarh.'

'Thanks,' he says and, after a moment's hesitation, adds '*didi*', instantly forging a relationship with me.

Even before I have finished the call, the outline of a plan has begun to take shape in my mind. The first thing I need for the plan to work is a getaway car.

'Is there any place I can rent a car?' I ask a villager crossing the bridge.

He looks at me as if I were from outer space. Obviously, the last thing to expect in a village like Chandangarh is a car-rental service.

'Do you know anyone who owns a motorcycle at least?'

He nods. 'Babban Sheikh mechanic has a Hero Honda.'

'How do I get in touch with him?'

'Come, I will take you to his garage,' he says. 'It's in Uttar Pradesh, on the other side of the river.'

We cross the bridge and I find myself in a Muslim colony. There is a small cluster of houses, and a gaggle of shops. A few bearded worshippers are milling around an old mosque.

The garage is little more than a tin shack. Babban Sheikh is a short, muscular-looking man in his mid-forties, with a pockmarked face and watchful eyes. Dressed in greasy overalls, he is attending to a broken-down Bajaj Pulsar when I arrive. He also has a helper, a boy of fifteen or sixteen, dressed similarly but with his hair dyed a light brown, who is busy tuning a Kawasaki Ninja.

'Er ... Babban Bhai, can I have a word with you?' I address the older man.

Babban Sheikh puts down the spark plug he is cleaning, wipes his hands on a rag and looks up. 'Yes, madam, what can I do for you?'

'I am told you own a Hero Honda.'

'Yes, that's right.'

'Well, there is this wedding tonight and . . .'

He hears my plan and then shakes his head. 'We run an honourable business here. We are not gangsters who spirit away young brides. I cannot help you.'

'A girl's future depends on this,' I implore, but he is unmoved.

The young helper seems more sympathetic. 'This lady is right, Abbu,' he intercedes, revealing that he is Babban's son. 'We should stop that wedding. I know Salim Ilyasi would. He saved Priya Capoorr just as she was being married off to that scoundrel Prakash Puri in *Love in Bangkok*.'

The father would have none of it. 'So you have started watching films again, eh? Don't you know Imam *sahib* has imposed a complete ban on watching Hindi movies and listening to their dirty songs?'

'I know, Abbu, but what to do. I just can't control myself the moment a new Salim Ilyasi movie is released.'

'These films are the root cause of all the ills in our society. You see one more film and I will report you personally to Imam *sahib*. Then you will spend the rest of your days cleaning carpets in the mosque,' Babban admonishes his son before noticing that I am listening in. 'What are you still doing here?' He turns on me. 'You've wasted enough of our time. Now be on your way.'

Dejected, I slowly trudge back to the bridge, feeling the day's disappointments press down on me like a giant thumb. The sun is at its peak, but my heart is at its lowest ebb, sinking with remorse at having failed Babli.

Just as I am crossing the bridge, a motorcycle sputters to a stop near me. It is the Kawasaki Ninja, being driven by the young mechanic. 'I am sorry for my *abbajan*'s outburst. I will help you,' he says with a ready smile.

'And what about your father?'

'He thinks I am out delivering this bike to the customer. You don't worry about him. I know how to handle him. But how will we handle the girl's father? What if he chases me?'

'Well, then you will just have to be faster. And I will pay you for your trouble.'

'No, I will not take any money for this,' he declares, aping the studied nonchalance of Salim Ilyasi. 'To protect *muhabbat* – love – Aslam Sheikh will even give his life.'

The young mechanic offers to drop me back to Kuldip Singh's house, and I accept gratefully. This time the villagers stare at me with open-jawed astonishment, wondering who this woman is, riding pillion on a scooter one minute, and a motorcycle the next.

I get dropped off a little distance away from Kuldip Singh's house, not wanting to arouse his suspicion. But it turns out to be a needless precaution. Word of my indiscretions has already reached the household. The patriarch is in a foul mood and lashes out at me the moment I step in through the door. 'We called you here to tell us how to operate a washing machine, not wash our dirty linen in public. Sultan Singh has told me everything. Please leave immediately. There is no place in our house for a troublemaker like you.'

'Kuldip Singh-ji, you are misunderstanding me,' I say, trying to reason with him. 'Babli will never go through with this marriage. She'll rather die than accept Badan Singh as her husband.'

'Come what may, she will marry Badan Singh. And, if she wants to die, she'll die in her husband's house, not ours.'

'What kind of father are you, willing to sacrifice your daughter for the sake of a regressive custom?'

'Enough!' he bellows. 'Get out of my house this very instant or I will have you thrown out.'

'I will leave, but not alone. Babli will also leave with me.'

'Have you lost your mind completely? Babli is my daughter. She will do what I tell her to do.'

'Then why don't you ask her?' I challenge him.

He accepts the challenge readily. 'Let's settle this right now,' he says, and calls out, 'Babli's mother! Bring our daughter here.'

Babli enters the courtyard, trembling like a leaf, held tight by her mother. She stares at her feet, unable even to meet my gaze. Kuldip Singh jerks a thumb at me. 'Tell me, Babli, do you want to go with this woman?'

Babli shakes her head slowly. Then, bursting into tears, she covers her eyes and runs back to her room.

'There, you got your answer.' Kuldip Singh twirls his moustache, smirking like an evil magician. 'Now get out.'

'I don't know whether to despise you or pity you,' I say as a parting shot, and walk out of his house.

I make my way back to the Amba Temple, my crisis headquarters. The next five hours are the longest of my life. I keep trying Sunil but his cell appears to be switched off once again. Despondency looms over me like a dark shadow across my heart. I wish Karan were here to comfort me, lift my spirits. The temple priest offers me some fruit. I sit with him on the stoop, watching the afternoon fade.

As the dusk settles in, the air begins to vibrate with the cacophony of a wedding brass band. There are multiple trumpets blaring, and a nasal singer crooning '*Aaj mere yaar ki shaadi hai*' ('Today is my friend's wedding') to the noisy accompaniment of trombones, tuba, saxophones and dhol. It is Badan Singh's *baraat*, on its way to Kuldip Singh's house, which is lit up with twinkling lights.

That is when my cell phone beeps with an incoming message. It is from Sunil, informing me he has reached the village. I SMS him back to come straight to the temple.

Sunil Chaudhary impresses me on first sight. He is a young, presentable man of twenty-four, with a gentle face and soulful eyes. An engineering graduate, currently working for a software firm in Noida, he is a bit shy, a bit awkward and unsure of himself, but there is no mistaking his love for Babli. I know he will do anything to make her happy, anything to keep her safe.

'I flew down from Chennai and took a taxi all the way from Delhi. I just saw a wedding procession enter Babli's house. Am I too late?' he blurts out, his face a mask of worry and fear.

'We'll find out soon enough. Come with me.'

I explain my plan to Sunil as we hurry towards our destination. We stop in our tracks on seeing uniformed men patrolling outside Kuldip Singh's house, before realising that they are not armed guards but members of the brass band. Their work over, they are now relaxing, waiting for the dinner to commence. We peep in through the open door. Babli and Badan Singh are seated under the *mandap* with a priest lighting the sacred fire in the centre. The wedding is about to commence. In Hindi films this is the moment when the hero enters and declares, '*Yeh shaadi nahin ho sakti*' ('This wedding cannot be solemnised'). He can do so because he has the full protection of the direc-tor. In real life, if Sunil were to try this stunt, he would be instantly lynched.

Aslam Sheikh is lurking in the shadows of the nearby alley, his motorcycle growling softly, primed for flight. He smiles and gives me a thumbs-up sign. I introduce him to Sunil and then make my way stealthily towards the back of the house.

I reach the cowsheds without any difficulty. The cows and buffaloes are busy chewing cud, supremely unmind-ful of the noisy wedding celebrations going on next door.

The storage hut is in darkness when I enter it. I hit the light switch and bright white light floods the room, reflecting off the glazed surfaces of the appliances that are exactly where I had left them. I plug in the TV and turn it on. Then I do the same for the DVD player, the music system and the fridge. The tube light begins flickering alarmingly, unable to withstand the load. The moment I switch on the washing machine, it emits a soft pop and shuts off. Simultaneously the entire house is plunged into pitch darkness, just as I anticipated.

I leave the hut and race back to the alley, where Aslam is waiting on his motorcycle.

Moments later, the drowsing band members are startled into wakefulness by the Kawasaki Ninja that zooms past them down the road with four people on it, including a runaway bride. We can hear voices shouting behind us and some people giving chase, but they are on foot and we are on a 250cc bike.

Sunil, Babli and I hold on to each other and to dear life as Aslam expertly navigates the rutted lanes of the village. The cold winter air bites and whips my face like a studded glove. Mercifully, we reach the police station in just five minutes. Aslam drops us off, makes a theatrical bow, and zooms away, his mission accomplished.

Babli and Sunil embrace each other like there is no tomorrow. 'The moment the lights went out and someone grabbed my arm, I knew it was you,' Babli says, tears streaming down her face, smudging her makeup. But she still looks radiant in her flaming red lehenga and brocade blouse. Sunil gently wipes her tears with his fingers. I expect them to break into a filmy love song any second.

However, when we enter the police station, we find SI Inder Varma singing a different tune entirely. 'What you have done is very wrong. I will book you for unlawful confinement. You have spirited away a girl,' he threatens Sunil.

'You said bring the girl. Well, I have brought the girl,' I interject, before turning to the bride. 'Babli, why don't you tell him?'

'Yes. *Didi* and Sunil have saved me from a forced marriage,' Babli says defiantly. Sunil's presence has infused her with a new boldness. 'I don't want to marry Badan Singh. I only want to marry Sunil.'

'Listen, this is not a marriage registrar's office. This is a police station,' Varma admonishes, wagging a finger in her face. 'First of all, show me proof that you are above eighteen years of age.'

'Proof? You can see my high school mark sheet. It lists my date of birth.'

'Then produce it. Do you have it with you?'

'How can I have it with me? I am coming straight from a *mandap*, not a school.'

'Then there is nothing I can do. I am going to treat this as a case of kidnapping of a minor girl. Ram Kumar,' he calls out to his head constable. 'Take this boy into custody. Call the girl's father. Tell him to come and take away his daughter. And also inform Sultan Singh-ji.'

'You can't do this,' I cry. 'This is gross injustice. We trusted you.'

He grins through his paan-stained teeth. 'Never trust a policeman.'

'If you call my father, God will not spare you,' Babli says, tears streaming down her face again.

'Inside this police station *I* am God.'

'Look, Inspector *sahib*,' I try again. 'This is a simple case of a boy and a girl deeply in love, both adults, who want to marry. Instead of threatening them, you should be helping them.'

'Nothing is simple in life, and definitely not in marriage,' he says. 'You keep out of it, otherwise I'll also put you in with the boy as an accomplice to kidnapping.'

All our pleas fall on deaf ears. This wanton abuse of

authority fills me with disgust. I feel the impotent rage of the powerless, denied their rights by an arrogant, arbitrary dictator. That is when I remember Shalini Grover. Taking advantage of the inspector's preoccupation with Sunil and Babli, I scurry into the ladies' toilet and quickly dial the investigative reporter on my cell phone. 'Shalini,' I whisper to her, 'you were investigating the case of a couple murdered on the diktats of a *khap*. I'm at Chandangarh police station, where a young couple might be murdered right now for going against the *khap*. Can you come here immediately? Only you can save them.'

'I'm still in Panipat,' Shalini says, pouring cold water on my hopes. 'There's no way I can reach Chandangarh quickly enough.'

By the time I leave the toilet, Ram Kumar has already made his calls. An Innova screeches to a halt outside the police station and Kuldip Singh strides in, accompanied by Badan Singh and a posse of half a dozen male family members, all carrying rifles. He gives me a withering look and goes straight to the inspector. I see some cash exchanging hands and realise that for SI Varma this was a business opportunity.

Having paid off the inspector, Kuldip Singh grabs Babli by her hand. 'Come with me this very instant. Even a whore does not bring the kind of shame you have brought upon our family.'

Babli somehow frees herself from her father's grip and ducks under the inspector's wooden desk. As Kuldip Singh bends down to catch her, she entwines herself with one of the legs of the table. 'I will not go. You will have to cut me down if you want to take me,' she cries.

'Then we will cut you down, bitch, and throw the pieces in the Yamuna,' Badan Singh declares as he, too, joins Kuldip Singh in trying to pull Babli away.

'I must say the girl has *dum*,' says the head constable, as he squats on the floor to get a better view of the tussle.

'Help her,' I urge Ram Kumar, when Sultan Singh walks into the room. The head of the *khap panchayat* is interested only in Sunil. 'So you have dared to come back?' he asks with a theatrical swish of the cane in his hands. 'Now we'll show you what happens to those who violate our sacred traditions.'

He has not come alone: there are at least fifty of his supporters who surround the police station, chanting, 'Death to those who defy the *khap*!' It is a lynch mob that will have no hesitation in tearing Sunil, Babli and me from limb to limb. Like those mindless zombies in B-grade horror movies, they cannot be stopped, they can only be appeased.

From this point on, events proceed with the inevitability of a Greek tragedy. Babli is finally pulled out from under the table. She screams and claws at the floor, as Badan Singh and Kuldip Singh drag her towards the door. The inspector hands over Sunil to the lumpens of the *khap*. 'Go and do whatever you want with him. I'm washing my hands of this entire mess.'

Sultan Singh twirls his cane in glee. 'We'll finish him off right now.'

'Take my advice and do it on the other side of the river. Then it will fall under the jurisdiction of Bhojpura *thana*, and will become the U.P. police's headache,' the inspector advises chillingly.

'Sunil!' Babli cries, making a last-ditch effort to break free from her father's grasp.

'Babli!' Sunil tries to reach for her, as he is bundled into a blanket and kicked repeatedly by Sultan Singh's goons. The inspector and his constables watch all this with a calm detachment, as though this were a roadside *tamasha*. I feel like retching.

It is Ram Kumar, the head constable, who brings the focus on me. 'What about her, sir?' he asks, jerking his head at me. 'She looks like a real troublemaker to me.'

The inspector sighs, his manner implying that he considers me a needless complication he has to deal with. 'What exactly is your interest in this whole affair? Are you Babli's teacher or Sunil's sister?'

'Neither,' I reply. 'I am just a public-spirited citizen trying to help them.'

'I don't know too many public-spirited salesgirls. You seem more like one of those nosy journalist types. Which newspaper do you belong to? Is it *Punjab Kesari* or is it *Jag Bani*?'

'I am not a journalist. I'm only—'

Varma cuts me off. 'Do you know what we do to troublesome journalists? We encounter them.' Then, just like that, he slaps me.

I am more stunned than insulted. This is the first time in my life someone has slapped me. 'How can you . . .?' I begin, blood rising in my cheeks, when he raises his hand again. 'Shut your trap or worse will follow. Ram Kumar, take her into custody.'

'On what charge?' I demand.

'Oh, there is no dearth of charges. We could recover

drugs from your handbag, book you for criminal conspiracy, arrest you for a hate crime, or even indict you for
prostitution.'

My body literally goes limp as I hear these words. Just
as my vision begins to turn grey and blackness surrounds
me from all sides, the deafening silence in my head is
broken by the sound of distant sirens, several of them,
coming closer and closer. It seems like the Prime Minister's motorcade is passing by the village.

The convoy comes to a stop directly in front of the
police station. There is the sound of car doors opening and
then an important-looking politician wearing a bandgala
troops in from the door accompanied by half a dozen uniformed police officers and bureaucrats in wrinkle-free
suits.

A mystified Sub-Inspector Inder Varma snaps to attention. Head Constable Ram Kumar is too flustered even to
salute, seemingly overwhelmed by the sight of so much
top brass in one room.

'Arrest them,' the politician directs, and a police officer
wearing a national emblem with a silver star on his
epaulettes produces a pair of handcuffs.

'What – what h–happened, sir?' Inder Varma stammers
as the handcuffs are closed on his wrists.

'Are you aware of the live spectacle that has been going
on the Sunlight TV channel for the last half-hour?'
another senior police officer blasts him. The three stars on
his epaulettes identify him as a Deputy Inspector General
of Police. 'The whole country has seen you terrorising an
innocent boy and girl, allowing the *khap* to take the law
into its own hands, and browbeating a good Samaritan by

framing false charges against her. You are a blot on the police force.'

'Live coverage? Sunlight? But sir, there are no TV cameras here.' Varma quickly looks left and right.

The DIG walks up to me and gently withdraws the cell phone that is peeping out from the top pocket of my coat, with the camera facing outwards. 'I don't think we need the live broadcast any more.' He switches it off, before returning it to me.

Varma's eyes pop out as the penny finally drops. I flash him a cheeky smirk. Once I realised Shalini was not going to make it, I decided to become an undercover journalist myself. Using my cell phone, I started secretly recording all that was happening in the police station, with the video feed going directly to Sunlight TV's website.

What follows next is reminiscent of the scripted ending of a Bollywood movie. SI Inder Varma and Head Constable Ram Kumar are taken into custody. The frenzied crowd outside is *lathi* – charged and dispersed. Sultan Singh runs for cover with his tail between his legs. And Kuldip Singh has an instant change of heart, deciding that the best match for Babli will be Sunil.

As I watch the joyous bride and groom perform the seven rounds around the sacred fire that night, I cannot resist looking up at the sky. I wink at Alka, and whisper, '*Kamaal ho gaya.* Something amazing happened today!'

I arrive back in Delhi the next morning, driven in Kuldip Singh's Toyota Innova all the way to my residence. After a quick shower and change of clothes, I'm off to work and the daily grind.

'You don't look sick at all.' Madan eyes me suspiciously the moment I step into the showroom.

'Thanks to *pudin hara*.'

After all that has happened yesterday, the return to the humdrum world of dishwashers and microwaves feels like a weary plod. But I'd rather sell TVs than risk getting slapped by a psycho cop.

That afternoon I get a call from Shalini Grover. 'Hats off, Sapna. You really pulled it off. You were incredible,' she gushes.

'I couldn't have done it without you,' I reply. 'It was you who taught me how to log onto the Sunlight TV website.'

'Look, I also do a column in the *Daily Times*. For my next column, I want to do a feature on you. You are an inspiration to Indian women.'

'No,' I say firmly. 'I don't want my fifteen minutes of fame. It'll only make people jealous, and goons from the *khap panchayat* may make me a target.'

'Yes, that is a danger,' Shalini admits. 'How about if I do the piece without using your real name?'

'That should be okay,' I say doubtfully, still not fully reconciled to the idea.

'What name should I use for you?'

'How about Nisha?'

'Sounds good. But why Nisha?'

'Don't you see? It's a perfect anagram for Sinha!'

Two days later I get a call from Rana. 'Mr Acharya wants to see you today. Come to the office at six p.m. Don't be late.'

A knot of apprehension forms in my gut. I get so flustered I can't even think of a new excuse. So I just go with the old one when I approach Madan in his manager's cubicle. 'Sir, my mother has had a relapse. I have to rush her to hospital again.'

Madan throws up his hands in exasperation. 'This is getting tiresome. Why don't you put your mother permanently in hospital? If you have to leave early every other day, I will be forced to terminate your employment.'

'Look, I'll put in extra hours next week. But I have to go right now.'

This mollifies the manager somewhat and his threatening attitude turns to sullen acceptance. At 5.45 p.m., I am on my way to Kyoko Chambers once again.

Rana meets me in the lobby and Jennifer ushers me into Acharya's office promptly at six.

'Congratulations!' The businessman greets me with a warm smile.

'Congratulations on what?'

'On passing the first test.'

'What test?'

'The test of leadership.'

'I'm afraid this is making no sense to me.'

'Look at this.' Acharya picks up the newspaper lying on his desk. It is today's issue of the *Daily Times*. He jabs a finger at Shalini's article titled 'LOVE IN THE TIME OF KHAP'. 'Have you seen this piece?'

I nod.

'I know you are the heroine of this story.'

'What makes you say that? The article is about a call-centre operator called Nisha.'

'There's no need to pretend with me. The DIG who visited you in Chandangarh police station is the son of an old friend of mine. He's told me everything. And I've also spoken to Sunil and Babli.'

'How did you even know I went to Chandangarh?'

'I found out from the showroom. Look, Sapna, it's not important how I know. What's important is that you passed the first test. If you wanted to, you could have walked away from it all, left Babli to her fate. But you chose to take responsibility for doing what was right. You decided to fight an injustice even when the odds were stacked against you. In my book, that qualifies you as a leader.'

'I didn't know this was a test set by you.'

'Not by me: by life. What did I tell you? That life tests us every day by forcing us to make choices. You made the right choices in that village. You showed real leadership.' He drops the newspaper in his lap and rubs the top of his forehead. 'Leadership is the one competency that cannot be learnt in management school. A manager is trained to do things right; a leader does the right things. It is not a matter of training and preparation, but one of instinct and conscience.'

'Look, Mr Acharya, just because I helped Babli, it doesn't mean I've become a great leader. I'm just an ordinary salesgirl.'

'That's precisely the point. A leader doesn't have to be the smartest, strongest or prettiest. I'd rather have a less-than-brilliant leader as my CEO than a genius but gutless plodder, because leadership is the most important factor for a business to succeed. Just as machines need maintenance and products need marketing, employees need direction. It is the leader who provides that direction, who encourages and inspires ordinary people to do extra-ordinary tasks. For this the leader has to walk the talk. To paraphrase Thomas Jefferson, in matters of style, a leader swims with the current; but, in matters of principle, he stands like a rock. You stood like a rock in Chandangarh. I'm not just proud of you, Sapna, I'm proud to be your mentor.'

I have not heard such words of praise and appreciation outside of university. It makes me acutely self-conscious. 'Well . . . I don't know what to say.'

'Don't say anything, just do. Continue to follow your conscience, and you will pass the remaining tests with flying colours.'

I have to remind myself that this is all a game to Acharya. Neither have I become a leader, nor is he my mentor. He is simply a bored rich man, using me as a toy for his enjoyment. And I am obliged to play along because I had taken ₹200,000 from him. So I look up at him and flash him a grateful smile. A two-lakh smile.

That night I share the latest development with Karan at our garden rendezvous. 'Acharya said I've passed the first test. I'm now a certified leader.'

'Ha!' he laughs. 'He thinks we are certified numb-skulls. He had nothing to do with what happened in that village, yet he is taking credit for it. Anyway, stuff Acharya! I'm proud of you for what you did for Babli and Sunil.'

'Do you think they will live happily ever after?'

'I don't know. But, thanks to you, they will at least live.' He gazes off into the distance. There is a curious tension in his features; the line of his jaw is tight. Then he releases a half-smile. 'Actually, there is only one class of people that lives happily ever after.'

'And who are they?'

'The dead.'

The Second Test

Diamonds and Rust

It is 11 a.m. on Friday, 31 December, the last day of the year, and a mile-long queue has already formed outside the showroom. In a country where five hundred gather routinely to watch a street brawl, it is only natural for five thousand to turn up to ogle a celebrity.

Yes, today is the big day when Priya Capoorr graces our showroom as the brand ambassador for Sinotron TVs.

Two days ago, a pushy woman named Rosie Mascarenhas, the actress's PR manager, came to the store to select an 'attendant' for Ms Capoorr. The requirements were very specific. 'It has to be a girl. She must be able to speak excellent English. And she must have a soft voice and good manners.' All four salesgirls were paraded before her and she chose me. I will undoubtedly provide the best contrast to Ms Capoorr's fair complexion, allowing her to shine more brightly. The change in my status from 'flight attendant' to just 'attendant' is deeply galling, but the entire store is behaving as though I have won a lottery. 'So you'll get to spend some quality time with a star. How lucky, *yaar*,' Prachi moons. 'Who knows, she might even offer you a bit part in her next movie.'

I enjoy watching Hindi films, but I'm not a great fan of Priya Capoorr. She has no real talent; she's just a glamour doll whose only claim to fame is that she is the scion of one of Bollywood's most enduring dynasties. And this mindless celebrity worship nauseates me. I don't envy celebrities: I pity them. They are abnormal human beings, sad clowns dancing to entertain others, condemned to live their lives in a fishbowl, ogled by their legions of fans.

The fans are even more pathetic. These vapid, starstruck fools who blindly follow celebrities, seduced by the fake intimacy of their tweets, need to have their heads examined. Take Swati, our store clerk, for instance. She says she feels closer to Priya Capoorr than to her own mother!

Most celebrities are so insecure that they take super-stition to a whole new level. Priya Capoorr herself is a perfect example. The name she was born with was Priyanka. When her debut film bombed, she shortened her name to Priya, on the advice of an astrologer. Then she changed her surname from Kapoor to Capoor. And finally, on the urging of her numerologist, she added another 'r', so that now to pronounce her name you need to purr like a cat. That is not all. If the rumours doing the rounds in Tinsel Town are to be believed, she has had more cosmetic surgery than Pamela Anderson, getting her lips stuffed with collagen, her bust size increased and her nose tucked. As a result, she looks like a freaky, plastic

Barbie, older than her twenty-six years. Nevertheless, she has given three superhits in a row and is now ranked among the top four heroines in Bollywood.

Her visitation is scheduled at twelve noon, and we have been working round the clock to get everything ready. The entire store has been decorated with balloons and streamers. Advertising posters for Sinotron TVs adorn every wall. A makeshift stage has been created on one side of the main display hall, against a giant backdrop of the actress's face, while dance anthems from her hit films blare from loudspeakers, creating a disco-like mood.

At 11.30 a.m., the front door is opened and the crowd are allowed to come in and settle down. Within seconds, every inch of space in the main hall, the foyer and aisles is filled with people. Their anticipation and eagerness is palpable. 'Priya! Priya! Priya!' someone begins chanting. Pretty soon others join in, heightening the atmosphere to a fever pitch.

Priya Capoorr arrives fashionably late at 1.30 p.m., an hour and a half behind schedule. She doesn't come alone. There's a whole entourage with her consisting of six burly bodyguards, PR manager, makeup man and even a hair-dresser. She comes in through the rear entrance, and is whisked into the back office, which has been cleaned up and converted into a holding area. Our owner, Mr Gulati, and his son Raja are there to personally welcome her, together with a Chinese-looking man named Robert Lee, the marketing head of Sinotron Corporation.

I have to admit that in real life Priya looks just as glamorous as she does in films, only a bit shorter. Her light-brown hair is styled into ringlets that frame her oval face and cascade down her shoulders in soft, somewhat rebellious waves. Years of squinting, grimacing, simpering and smirking on screen has turned the corners of her doe-shaped eyes into a predator's steely stare, unsettling and intense. Dressed in a white ruffled shirt and a brown jacket, complemented by skin-hugging jeans, leather boots and a Birkin handbag, she carries herself with the cocksure confidence of an imperious diva who knows exactly her own worth. Raja Gulati almost goes down on his knees in his attempt to offer her a bouquet of roses.

'Thank you,' she mouths, wearing the blank smile of a woman at a party she can't wait to leave.

Within minutes of her arrival, the entry to the back office gets jammed with employees craning their necks to catch a glimpse of the actress. They stand in awe, heady with the thrill of seeing a movie star in the flesh. Normally, I would be the last person to get flustered by the idea of being in the presence of a celebrity, but, seeing the way the others are behaving, I find it difficult not to get caught up in the drama of it all.

The bodyguards eventually shoo away everyone from the holding area, leaving Priya Capoorr with just her PR manager, makeup man, hairdresser and me. They sit around a work table. I stand deferentially in the back-ground, ready to offer tea, soft drinks and sandwiches, which are all at hand.

'The tournament is less than four months away and you have still not identified the team,' I overhear Priya tell Rosie Mascarenhas. My ears prick up. The Cricket World Cup is less than two months away, so she is probably refer-ring to the Indian Premier League, which begins in April.

'I'm working on it,' the PR lady says.

'I don't care which team, but I simply have to be seen at the IPL.'

The actress takes no notice of me as the makeup man applies a powder puff to her forehead. For her, I am just part of the scenery. Witnessing her lording it over me (and everyone else, for that matter), I am filled with the same burning indignation that I felt in Chandangarh village. There was a caste system back there, but there is a caste system at work in Bollywood, too. A system that confers undue advantage on a privileged few – the sons and daughters of film stars and producers, who piggyback their way to fame and fortune without often having either looks or talent. People like Priya Capoorr are born with golden spoons in their mouths, destined for success even before they have learnt to walk. She never had to slave like an extra, dancing in geometric formations on a beach with a group of scantily clad girls, as the hero and heroine cavorted in the sea. She knew she would commence her career as a heroine and then inevitably become a star. But for every Priya Capoorr there are thousands of aspiring actors who land on the shores of Mumbai every day and never get a lucky break. No one has ever broken out of the ranks of faceless extras to become a famous star, with the possible exception of Salim Ilyasi. And even he had the financial muscle of industrialist Ram Mohammad Thomas behind him.

In fact, at one time Priya had a torrid romance with Salim Ilyasi, which had sparked rumours that they might soon marry. But then she found greener pastures in the form of Rocky M, son of billionaire coal baron Laxman

Mudaliar. The two of them have been going steady for the past couple of years, and there are reports that Rocky has already proposed to her. If this is true, Priya has not only secured her present, she has also shrewdly insured her future.

Once her makeup is done, she opens her Birkin handbag and extracts a diamond ring, which she slips on the ring finger of her left hand. I can see that it is loose: it does not grip the finger very well. Priya adjusts it a couple of times, keeping it centre. It is clear she wants to flaunt it. And why not? I've never seen a diamond this big. It must be at least four carats, probably more. Under the harsh strip light, it sparkles like a brilliant star in a sea of gold, its dazzling radiance casting a rainbow of colours in my eyes.

Rosie Mascarenhas raises a finger. 'Are you sure you want to wear this here?'

'Yes,' says Priya. 'It's high time.'

'People will talk. The media will go into a frenzy. They'll come after you like a pack of hungry dogs thrown an unexpected bone.'

'I know how to handle dogs.'

'I'm not very comfortable in this setting. I'd rather we did an exclusive with *Filmfare* on the engagement.'

'I don't want any further discussion on this. I'll do it the way I want to do it,' she says, raising her voice just enough to let the PR manager know who is calling the shots here.

The hairdresser, a northeastern girl with small, doleful eyes, gently touches up Priya's curls. The actress takes a final look in the mirror held up by the makeup man, and then rises from the chair. 'Okay, let's get this over and done with.'

Just as she is about to head into the main hall, Raja Gulati comes running in and asks her to wait. 'Sorry, madam, we're having some trouble with our PA system. It will take another ten minutes to repair.'

I can see Priya getting impatient. 'Why didn't they keep a backup ready?' she grumbles. To while away the time, she pulls out her BlackBerry and begins texting. But her heart is not in it. She puts it down after a while, looking visibly bored.

'Are you on Twitter?' I ask her, just to break the silence.

She looks up, as if noticing me for the first time. Rosie hurriedly introduces me. 'This is Sapna, one of the sales-girls in the store.'

Priya eyeballs me from top to bottom, sizing me up. 'No, I'm not on Twitter, and I don't want to be on Twitter,' she answers, fluttering her hands in a theatrical manner. 'You see, I am a star and a star by definition has to be mysterious and distant. Too much familiarity kills the mystique. A successful brand must be unique and exclusive and I am a brand now, am I not?'

It is a rhetorical question; she doesn't expect me to answer. I answer nonetheless. 'Salim Ilyasi says the same thing in the new biography out on him. Have you read it?'

'I don't read,' she says flatly. 'I hardly have the time, and, quite honestly, books bore me. Why waste a week reading a book, when you can watch its film version in two hours? And these days we are making a lot of films based on books.'

'What did you think of *Slumdog Millionaire*?'

'I thought it was quite good. But, just because a white man made the film, our people got jealous.'

Even as she makes these unguarded revelations, her face does not soften one bit. She is merely indulging me, not inviting me to get closer. 'Which was the last film of mine you saw?' she asks me suddenly.

I think about it. The last film I saw with Priya in it was *Murder in Mumbai* and it was execrable. I couldn't even sit through it. 'It was *City of Dust*,' I lie.

She raises her perfectly plucked eyebrows. 'That came out two years ago.'

'Yes, but I saw it on cable just a couple of days ago.'

'And what did you think of it?'

'It was good, quite good. You essayed a rather non-glamorous role, for a change.'

She nods, becoming more animated. 'Yes. It was a real challenge playing a simple village girl, but I pulled it off. I almost got the National Award for it.'

'I must say I was a bit confused by the ending.'

Her cold stare tells me I am treading new waters. 'And what exactly did you not get about the ending?' she asks frostily.

'Well, almost the entire film is a sensitive, postmodern critique of materialist culture, but then near the end we suddenly get this over-the-top dance number with you in harem pants. I found it a bit jarring, that's all.'

She flicks me a sardonic look. 'You just didn't get it, did you?'

I gaze at her blankly.

'You said you watched the film two nights ago, right?'

I nod.

'I recommend you mull over it for five more days.'

'Beg your pardon?'

'You see, this movie was meant for the elites, not the masses. People like you need to analyse it for at least a week to understand it fully. That's how long it normally takes for the tube light in your brain to switch on.'

A surge of anger flares within me. 'People like you—' That phrase rankles like an egregious insult that cannot stand unchallenged. But Rosie Mascarenhas is already giving me a warning glare to shut up. 'Why don't you serve us some tea?' she interjects.

'Yes, tea would be nice,' Priya agrees, seconding the idea, putting me in my place even more firmly, telling me that she is the celebrity, and I am merely an attendant. People like me serve tea, and people like her drink it. I pass her the cup, with self-pity oozing from every pore of my being.

She does not deign to speak another word to me after that. In any case, the PA system is soon fixed and she goes into the hall. I follow her, watching from the back rows.

She gives an accomplished performance, launching into a practised spiel about the superior features of Sinotron TVs, modelling in front of their top-of-the-line flagship units and posing for the shutterbugs.

When the Q&A session commences, the reporters show scant gratitude for Sinotron's hospitality. They have no interest in plasma TVs and LED panels. Their eyes are fixated on Priya's ring finger, and there is only one question on their lips: 'Is this your engagement ring?'

'Yes, it is,' Priya answers, proudly showing off the

ornament to a chorus of groans and sighs from the male members of the audience and mesmerised stares from the females.

'How many carats?'

She holds up five fingers, drawing oohs and ahs all round.

'When are you getting married to Rocky M?'

'We're in no hurry. Certainly not for the next two years.'

'How expensive is the ring?'

'Priceless.'

With a final flourish she brings the session to an end, having floored reporters and audience alike. I marvel at her business acumen, how she has managed to extract acres of coverage for Brand Priya Capoorr, even from a boring product launch.

When she re-enters the holding room, she has the satisfied smirk of a woman who has got what she wanted.

'So what are you doing for New Year's Eve?' she asks me, perhaps her way of making up for the sharp words she had said to me earlier.

'Nothing,' I reply. 'For me, December the thirty-first is like any other day.'

'Well, it's not,' she argues. 'It is the end of one year and the beginning of another. A new year buries the old and ushers in new dreams, new hopes and new aspirations.' She says this with such glib, cheery sincerity, it sounds like a dialogue from one of her films.

I feel like telling her that a new year does not bury the detritus of the past. There will be the same slow iteration of our lingering sorrows and old regrets in the new year as well. Instead, I ask her, 'So what will *you* be doing tonight?'

'Oh, Rocky is throwing a big bash at the Regency and I'll be partying all night long. In fact, you are welcome to join us. Come around eleven thirty or so. You'll get to see how the other half parties.'

It looks like one of those spur-of-the-moment offers she might already be regretting. Rosie Mascarenhas is sufficiently alarmed by it to go into a spasm of coughing. In any event, I have no intention of suffering through another round of the other half's patronising condescension.

'Thanks for the invite.' I smile at Priya. 'But I just remembered I'd promised an American friend of mine to come to her New Year party in Mehrauli.'

By now Rosie and her team have finished gathering the odds and ends they had left behind. The PR manager looks around the holding room for a final time before announcing, 'I think we are ready to go.'

Priya continues to gaze at me, as if I were a new plaything she is reluctant to part with. 'Don't you want an autograph before I leave?'

The question is so unexpected, that I am taken aback. 'Of course,' I mumble.

'Where's your autograph book?'

I don't have an autograph book. I don't even have anything I can *use* as an autograph book. My eyes dart around the holding room in panic, my mind a flustered flurry. I can see only thick ledger books lining the shelves, arranged year-wise. And then I notice a slim volume lying on a top shelf. I pull it out and dust off its leather cover.

It is a blank photo album, its thick pages coil-bound with frosted plastic covers. It is perfect!

I remove the plastic cover from a middle page and place it before Priya, who is already poised with a pen. 'To Sapna with love, Priya Capoorr,' she scribbles on the page in an expansive scrawl. Just then, there is a commotion at the door. I turn around to find a fan trying to barge into the holding room. There is a bit of a scuffle with the bodyguards, but nothing serious.

Priya shuts the album and offers it to me. 'Here, better keep this someplace safe.'

I see Raja Gulati entering the room and hastily deposit it back on the top shelf. 'Thank you, Priya-ji, you were amazing,' he says, preening like a greasy showman. This time Priya does not smile at him. She barely acknowledges our presence as she gets into her limousine. With a polite but dismissive wave, she pulls up her tinted windows and the car drives off.

'I thought tinted windows were banned in Delhi.' I turn to Raja Gulati.

'For you and me,' he replies, still gazing at the corner the vehicle disappeared around. 'Not for superstars like the one we just saw.'

I return to the shop floor, only to be mobbed like a rock star by the other salesgirls. 'Tell us, what did you talk to Priya about?' asks a breathless Prachi.

'Was there a call from Rocky M?' Neelam tugs at my arm.

'Did she give you any makeup tips?' Jyoti wants to know.

The entire store basks in the reflected glow of the

celebrity visit, but the euphoria lasts only for an hour – because, at 3 p.m., the actress is back at Gulati & Sons, angry and distraught.

It turns out she cannot find her five-carat engagement ring. It slipped from her finger and she is convinced it must have dropped somewhere in the store. She instructs us to turn out all the customers and down the shutters. Then, over the next hour, she makes us scour every inch of the store. We look below the floorboards, under desks and chairs, behind TVs and washing machines, in toilet bowls and wastepaper baskets, but do not find the missing ring.

The police are summoned, led by the same Inspector Goswami who had dealt with our former accountant Choubey. 'It is obvious to me that one of you has the ring,' he declares ominously, going around the store, scrutinising our faces as if we were in an identification parade in a police station. 'It's still not too late to fess up,' he continues, his voice taking on the patient tone of an admonishing father sharing some critical piece of wisdom. 'Miss Capoorr will not press charges if you return the ring.'

Finding himself up against a wall of silence, he turns to the actress. 'Priya-ji, do you suspect anyone in particular?'

Priya also scans the circus of employees, her eyes cold and hard. When she comes to me, she pauses, trying to read my face. My heart is beating so fast, I'm sure everyone can hear it out loud. Then she lifts a manicured finger at me. 'This is the girl who spent maximum time with me. I am sure she knows where's my ring. Check her bag!'

I gape at her, slack-jawed in disbelief. A police constable moves to take my Nine West bag from my hands. I am too stunned to protest. Besides, to protest would be a tacit admission of guilt. So I allow the policeman to open my bag and upturn it on the table, spilling its contents. I watch in agonised suspense as he sifts through my personal belongings, like a customs officer inspecting a smuggler's luggage. Needless to say, the ring is not found among the keys, cards, clips, tissues, used tickets, receipts, lip balm, pepper spray and cell phone that tumble out.

Priya is still not finished with me. 'Search her,' she orders, as though she were the inspector. She is exercising the most obvious prerogative of celebrity: power. Even before I can squeak out a word, I am herded into the ladies' toilet by a woman constable with tattooed arms, who asks me to strip.

'What?'

'You heard me, take off your clothes,' she growls, pushing me roughly against the wall, her hot breath on my face. She is exercising the most obvious prerogative of power: licence to misbehave.

'Take your hands off me. There's no way I'm stripping. You can't force me to.'

'I can even force you to eat shit, understood?' She suddenly grabs me by the hair and pushes my head down into the toilet bowl, inches away from the water. A wave of pure terror washes over me, convincing me of her brute might, cowing me into submission.

The next few moments are the most humiliating of my life as the policewoman rips off my shirt and skirt and prods and pokes inside my bra and knickers. I close my eyes and wish the earth would open up and swallow me whole.

Two minutes later, when I emerge from the toilet, my pride is in tatters, but my probity is still intact. 'She doesn't have the ring,' the constable sighs.

The actress is inconsolable. 'That ring is worth two crores – twenty *million* rupees! If it is not found, my fiancé will kill me. Just keep on looking till you find it.'

'We will, madam, we will.' Raja Gulati's comforting assurance is as solemn as it is fake.

The moment Priya Capoorr leaves, the showroom shutters are opened and normal operation resumes, but everything has changed for me. The sideways glances from the store employees, varying between pitying and gloating, are simply unbearable. In the space of a few hours, I have gone from rock star to robbery suspect.

Just before closing time, Prachi and Neelam get into a huddle with me. 'Whatever happened to you, *yaar*, wasn't good,' says Prachi, trying to soothe my hurt feelings. 'These spoilt film stars think they can accuse whoever they want.'

'I am never going to see another film of hers,' Neelam declares. 'And, if I ever get the opportunity, I'll gouge out that bitch's eyes.'

'Let's not be hypocritical, Neelam,' Prachi interjects. 'You are saying this today, but I bet you if you were to find yourself in a room with Priya tomorrow, you are not going to gouge out her eyes: you'll ask her for her autograph.'

That is when I remember the autograph Priya has

given me. In the tumultuous aftermath of the ring's disappearance, I'd clean forgotten about it.

When no one is looking, I slip into the back office and take down the album from the top shelf where I had deposited it. 'To Sapna with love'. The inscription sears my consciousness with the scorch of a branding iron. It is a badge of my humiliation. With the bitter gall rising in my throat, I rip off the page, tear it into small pieces and throw the lot in a nearby wastepaper basket.

As I am about to close the album, I hear a metallic jangling from it. Intrigued, I examine the volume again, and recoil in horror. Because lodged in the narrow space in between the metal coils is Priya's five-carat diamond ring. How it slipped from her finger and got deposited into the album's spine I have no idea. There was probably a one-in-a-billion chance of such a thing happening, but happen it did.

Even as I struggle to come to terms with this new situation, my mind is rapidly analysing the options available to me. One, I could let the ring lie in the album and pretend I never found it. Two, I could take the ring to Raja Gulati, tell him how I found it, and ask him to return it to Priya. The trouble with both these options is that they don't absolve me completely from perceived guilt. There will always be the lingering doubt in people's minds that I probably hid the ring in the album and chickened out at the last minute.

That is when a third option strikes me. I could myself take the ring to Priya, tell her how I discovered it and bring closure to this sorry chapter.

Even before I can think this through, I hear

approaching footsteps. Almost instinctively I pocket the ring, just as Madan barges into the room. 'What are you doing here?' he barks.

'Nothing. I just came to see if I had left my pen here.'

'I don't see any pen lying around.'

'I must have forgotten it somewhere else then,' I say and quickly leave the room, my heart thudding.

As I sit in the metro going home, my cheeks are still burning with shame. My mind keeps playing the scene in the toilet over and over, till I distract myself by taking out the ring. I twirl it in my fingers, captivated by its sparkling facets. It is a round solitaire that seems to pulse with a hidden energy, glowing with iridescent fire. Priya had estimated its value at two crores. The sheer value of the piece makes my mouth dry. I'd have to work for almost a hundred years to earn an equivalent amount in salary. I slyly look left and right. The compartment is mostly deserted, the New Year party crowd yet to show up. With trembling hands, I slip the ring onto my middle finger. It fits me perfectly. I admire it for a moment, then, feeling like a thief caught cold in the night, hastily remove it and put it back inside my bag.

I am restless in the flat, consumed by a nervous energy. Neha is already out celebrating with her college friends, and Ma is reclining in bed, staring blankly at the ceiling. She has retreated so far into the quagmire of her grief, the end of the year doesn't even register with her. I feel a stab of guilt leaving her all alone as I change and hurry out of the flat at 10 p.m.

I catch the metro to Dhaula Kuan. It's a complicated

route, requiring me to change three lines. From Dhaula Kuan I take an auto to Bhikaji Cama Place, where the Grand Regency is located.

The doorman flicks a wary eye at my denim jeans and defiantly unfashionable grey sweater as I step into the hotel. I take a moment to admire the polished splendour of the lobby before striding towards the front desk. The receptionist is noticeably cold to me. I see in her eyes the same condescending look that my fellow salesgirls reserve for window shoppers. She has perhaps gauged from my clothes and general air of awkward unfamiliarity that I am not someone who has weekly lunches at the hotel's Polo Lounge. 'I am here to see Ms Priya Capoorr,' I announce, hoping this will impress her.

'I'm sorry, ma'am,' she replies instantly. 'We have no guest by that name staying here.'

'I meant the film actress.'

'Same answer.'

'Perhaps you don't understand. Ms Capoorr has personally invited me to the party her boyfriend is throwing tonight.'

'I told you she is not staying here. But, if you want, you can try the Regency Ballroom downstairs, ma'am.'

On reaching the ballroom foyer, I am stopped by an even more officious registration clerk. She moves her finger down a typed guest list on her desk and shakes her head. 'I'm sorry, your name is not on this list.'

'Look, you can ask Rosie Mascarenhas. Priya invited me personally. If you just allow me to go in for a second, I'll clarify everything.'

She eyes me with her fist pressing against her chin, as

though she can see right through me. 'I'm sorry, this is a private, invitation-only event. Without an invite I cannot let you in.'

'Okay, can you at least send word to her that Sapna Sinha is waiting outside?'

'I can't do that, and I can't allow you to wait here. I suggest you leave now or I will have to call security.'

It is impossible to reason with her. And I have no way of reaching Priya. The wall of inaccessibility erected around the actress just cannot be breached. After fifteen minutes of fruitless effort, I storm out of the hotel, frustrated and irritated. I catch the first auto I can find and tell the driver to take me straight to Lauren's place in Mehrauli. Ideally, I should have gone back to Dhaula Kuan and taken the metro, but I am still smarting from the registration clerk's slight. And, when you have a two-crore rock in your pocket, you don't think twice before indulging in a hundred-rupee auto ride.

Right now, I need the balm of friendship and no one can provide it better than Lauren. In just eighteen short months she has become a cherished part of my life. Our bond was forged in the crucible of tragedy. She was the one who witnessed Papa's accident and brought him to the hospital.

When we first arrived in New Delhi in March 2009, Papa rented a small flat in RK Puram, and we tried to build a new life around the nucleus of South Delhi. I applied for the MA English course in Jawaharlal Nehru University, Neha the BA course in Kamala Nehru. For a while it looked as if we had succeeded in overcoming the ordeal of the past, but it was an illusion. Papa just wasn't the person he used to be. Gone was the swagger and arrogance of old. He had become a trembling morass of regret and self-pity. In fact, within one month of relocating to Delhi, his right hand, the one he had used to slap Alka, developed a mild form of paralysis. He did find a job as a maths teacher in a school in Vasant Kunj, but he couldn't teach any more. Guilt had made him hollow from inside. He was virtually sleepwalking through life. And he died the only way a sleepwalker can die: in a senseless hit-and-run accident.

Delhi has more cars than Mumbai, Kolkata and Chennai combined, which means there is a greater chance of meeting with an accident on Delhi roads than in any other city in India. If a Blue Line bus won't get you, a BMW surely will. My father was killed by a speeding truck just outside the Deer Park in South Delhi, close to midnight on 8 June 2009. He was trying to cross the road, when the truck knocked him over and ran over him. What he was doing at the Deer Park, so far away from home, so late at night, we have not been able to figure out to this day. And neither has the murderous truck driver been caught.

Lauren happened to be driving out of the nearby Indian Institute of Technology at almost the same time, as her then boyfriend was a professor in the Chemical Engineering Department. She saw Papa lying on the side of the road in a pool of blood. Several cars passed by the busy crossing but not one stopped to help Papa. It was Lauren who loaded our profusely bleeding father into her Maruti 800 and took him to the emergency ward of

Moolchand Hospital. Apparently, Papa was conscious for a while, but the only thing Lauren heard him mumbling was what sounded like '*hiran*' – 'deer' in Hindi. Perhaps he was trying to convey what he was doing at the Deer Park. We never got a chance to query Papa about it, as he went into a coma shortly after being brought to the hospital. He remained in the ICU for three days, but did not regain consciousness. On 12 June, he passed away.

Alka's death had devastated us psychologically; Papa's death devastated us financially as well. He was the sole breadwinner in the family. With his death, the burden fell on me, the eldest daughter. It completely changed the trajectory of my life. I had to quit studies and start looking for a job.

Though Papa wanted me to become a civil servant, my dream growing up was always to be a writer. So I applied for the post of assistant to the editor in a leading publishing house. To my surprise, I got the job. The editor was more impressed with my amateur poetry collection than with my first-class first degree in English Literature. But the pay they offered was a mere ₹9,000, even less than what a government peon gets these days. Reluctantly, I had to put paycheque before passion.

After a series of temping jobs, I finally found more permanent employment at Gulati & Sons. From an aspiring writer I became a sales clerk. It was painful making the transition from Tennyson to televisions, Fitzgerald to fridges. But the plan was to use this as a stopgap job till I found something better, more suited to my tastes. It's been over a year now, and I have yet to find that something better.

Lauren is the only person I can discuss literature and poetry with. A postgraduate from Vassar, she has an intellectual wit and a passion for the arts. Whenever we meet for coffee to swap thoughts and book recommendations, the fourteen-year difference in our ages just melts away. She says that, like Columbus with America, she came to India by mistake. 'For my PhD thesis, I had an opportunity to do a field study on a grant,' she told me. 'I chose to do the study in Nepal, but my air ticket was via India. I initially planned to transit for just two days. I've been here now for fifteen years. And I don't think I'll ever go back. I'm completely under the spell of this amazing country, which only adds, which never subtracts.'

The house Lauren lives in is as interesting as she is. Located close to the Qutub Minar, it is an old, half-ruined *haveli* that used to be the residence of the nawab of some princely state. Even though the plaster is crumbling, the antiquated furniture stained and scuffed, and the carpets so threadbare you can see right through to the floorboards, the place has character. The magnificent crystal chandeliers and lofty ceilings attest to its former splendour. And Lauren has spruced up the front walkway garden and covered the paved patio with bougainvilleas and jasmine to create a warm and welcoming ambience. It is a safe haven for anyone who enters its trellised front gate, especially the homeless and abused children who are the primary focus of the RMT Asha Foundation, Lauren's charity, which she started eight years ago with funds provided by the billionaire industrialist Ram Mohammad Thomas, himself a former street kid. Today, the Foundation supports more than a thousand children, providing them with shelter, education and a loving environment where they can grow up with dignity and pride. Above all, infusing them with hope – *asha*.

Despite being the host of a New Year party, Lauren is dressed in her usual no-nonsense style. Her dirty-blonde hair is tied sternly back. She wears an embroidered phulkari shawl over her white kurti and denim jeans and her trademark kolhapuri slippers. Her exuberant hazel eyes light up when they see me. She greets me on the steps of the patio with a warm hug and a kiss on both cheeks.

Inside the spacious drawing room there is a crackling fire and beer on tap. There are close to forty guests, mostly Indian, with a sprinkling of foreigners. The women wear big bindis, the men sport straggly beards. All are dressed uniformly in cotton Fabindia kurtas, faded jeans and cloth sling bags. They are part of what is referred to as the jho-lawala or NGO crowd. They are the passionate advocates at environmental meetings, the colourful presence at social development forums, the audacious hecklers at official press conferences and the placard-wielding protesters at global summits.

'Meet James Atlee,' Lauren says, introducing me to a tall Britisher with shaggy blond hair and striking blue eyes. From the way James slides a proprietary arm around her waist, I surmise he is her current boyfriend. I am envious of the way Western women find love so easily. James is Lauren's third boyfriend in eighteen months, proof also that they fall out of love equally quickly.

'So, are you also trying to save the world?' I ask him.

'That's Lauren's field.' He smiles. 'I'm just trying to save some companies.'

'Meaning?'

'Meaning that I'm a brand consultant.'

'I've never met a brand consultant before.'

'We are the chaps who help organisations build, manage, change or revive their brand image. In simple terms, we help create a company's unique identity, at times even its name and logo.'

I nod my head in impressed agreement. 'So where do you work? London?'

'I used to, but now I live in New Delhi. I'm on a one-year contract with Indus Mobile, helping redesign their corporate image. They're flush with money, and are planning a major expansion.'

'Oh, a friend of mine works at Indus, Karan Kant. Do you know him?'

'What does he do?'

'He's a call-centre agent.'

'In that case I wouldn't have met him. I deal only with top management, Mr Swapan Karak, the owner, in particular.'

After chatting with James, I move on to the other guests. A bearded, bespectacled man accosts me, waving a brochure for the RMT Asha Foundation in my face. 'Do you also work for Lauren?'

'No. She's a friend.'

'Then tell me, how is she able to afford this magnificent place?'

'Pardon me?'

'According to this brochure, she is a trustee of the

Foundation. But the first rule for a trustee is that she cannot derive any benefit from the trust. I can smell the stink of corruption coming from the Foundation.'

His own breath stinks of too much whisky. I excuse myself politely and walk away from him. A drunk I can tolerate, but not an ingrate abusing the hospitality of this house.

I make idle conversation with a couple of other guests but I'm only going through the motions. I do not have anything in common with these people. And small talk bores me. Besides, something is making me uneasy. I know it is the ring secreted in my handbag. 'I'm not feeling too well,' I say, making my apologies to Lauren. 'Perhaps I should go home. Can you call me an auto?'

She is understanding, as usual. 'I wouldn't advise taking an auto at this time of night. I'll get Shantanu to drop you.'

Shantanu is Lauren's devoted chauffeur, who has been with her for the last eight years. A thin, lanky man in his forties, he takes me home in Lauren's battered Maruti 800 of 1999 vintage. As we are passing through Hauz Khas, the sky suddenly lights up with fireworks, signifying that midnight is upon us.

'Happy New Year, madam!' Shantanu says, glancing in the rear-view mirror.

'To you too. May all your dreams come true in the New Year.'

'Don't waste your wishes on me. I have stopped dreaming dreams.'

'Why?'

'If you keep a dream for a long time, it gets rust. And

nothing is more dangerous than rusted dreams. It poisons the heart.'

'What was your dream?'

'To own my own garage. But it will never happen. I will never earn enough money to afford it. That garage is rusted now. Like my brain.' His voice catches in his throat, choked by the bitter juice of disappointment and defeat.

For a second I am tempted to take out the ring and gift it to Shantanu right then and there. He can buy ten garages with it. But the little bell in my head is going, 'No! No! No!' warning me that the ring does not belong to me. And I have never really lived by the dictum of 'finders keepers'. I am simply a trustee of the ring. And the first rule for a trustee is that she cannot derive any benefit from the trust.

In the first golden light of the New Year, I examine the ring again. Like a magic spell that has worn off, it does nothing for me this time. I look deep into its facets, but it remains just a shiny piece of rock. I am tempted to show the ring to Neha, sleeping peacefully in her bed, before junking the idea. It is a guilty secret that I dare not share with anyone, not even Karan.

Various impossible plans flash through my brain. I can throw the ring into the Yamuna River, à la *Titanic*. I can sell it to a shady jeweller and give the proceeds to Lauren's charity. I can smuggle it into Madan's pocket and frame him for robbery. All I know is that I don't want to return it to Priya Capoorr. The actress has lost her right to it after the way she treated me.

Rosie Mascarenhas calls the store four times during the day, enquiring if we were able to locate the ring. Madan cannot keep up the pretence any longer. 'No, madam,' he informs her, 'we have not found it, and I don't think we will find it.'

On Monday, 3 January, I do something audacious. I actually wear the ring when going to work in the metro. It is an act of calculated defiance. I rotate my wrist, bite my nails, wave my hand, to let the rush-hour crowd know I'm wearing a two-crore bauble. I want them to notice the size and sparkle of the diamond, to hear their oohs and aahs, but I get no reaction at all. No one takes the slightest notice of me or the diamond on my finger. That is when it hits me. People don't realise I am wearing a diamond. They think it's a cheap cubic zirconia ring, the type you can pick up in Janpath for a few hundred rupees. They know that someone with a real diamond does not travel in the metro. A bitter smile crosses my lips at the irony of it all. Even if I wear a real diamond, people will think it is a fake. And, even if Priya Capoorr wears a fake diamond, people will think it is real. We never really see things as they are. Just as beauty lies in the eyes of the beholder, value lies in the beholder's mind.

Rosie Mascarenhas calls again today, but rather half heartedly. By the middle of the week she stops calling entirely. To all intents and purposes, Priya is resigned to the ring's loss; it is mine to keep for ever. But the longer I keep the ring, the more it oppresses me. The diamond has become kryptonite, sapping my strength, giving me the blues. I can sense that the time has come to part with it.

I manage to obtain Rosie Mascarenhas's number from Madan's telephone book and call the PR manager in Mumbai. 'I think I may have found the ring.'

'I don't believe it!' she gasps. 'I'm flying to Delhi straightaway to get it.'

'Not you. I will give it only to your boss.'

'Now that's not—'

'Listen.' I cut her short. 'Either Priya comes to my house at seven a.m. tomorrow, or the ring goes into the Yamuna. The choice is yours.'

At 6.45 a.m. on 7 January, a black BMW pulls up at the gate of the LIG Colony. Priya Capoorr has arrived fifteen minutes early. Most of the residents are still asleep, including Neha. The actress who steps into my drawing room is very different from the one who visited the store. Instead of the preening diva, I see a distressed fiancée, devastated by loss. She has come alone, without her makeup man and hairdresser and PR manager. She is nervous and jittery, biting her nails in suspense, fumbling with the cell phone in her hand as she sits on the sofa. She looks as if she has been crying: her face is blotchy and tear-streaked. Her hair is a mess. It is obvious she has fallen off the wagon. No wonder the guard at the front gate did not even recognise her.

'Is it true you have my ring?' she asks me in a trembling voice.

'Yes,' I reply. 'I found it on the same day you visited the store, lodged inside the album you had autographed.'

'Can I . . . can I see it, please?'

I produce the ring and pass it to her. She examines it,

tests it on her finger, and then gives a satisfied nod. 'Yes, this is my ring.' She quickly pockets it and stands up.

'Won't you stay a little longer?'

'No,' she says, glancing around the room for the first time. As she takes in the peeling paint and faded decor, I see her face melt into that same mask of scorn and disgust I had once seen on a suited businessman in the metro when a baby puked on him while being burped.

'At least have a cup of tea.'

'I have no time. I'm catching the first flight back to Mumbai,' she says, and begins to head for the door. Then she stops, turns back. 'Before I go, can I ask you something?'

'Sure.'

'Why did you return it? It is a very expensive ring. You could have kept it if you wanted to.'

'I couldn't have kept it. I am not really into diamonds.'

'Then how come it took you so long to return it?' she demands. 'Do you have any idea how much you made me suffer?' The grateful tone is gone. She has reverted to her mean, bossy ways.

'What to do, madam?' I sigh. 'You see, people like us, our tube light takes a week to switch on.'

A week later, Acharya invites me to his office once again. For a change he is more considerate, fixing the meeting at 1.30 p.m., so that I can visit him during the lunch break.

'Well done, Sapna!' he says. 'I am glad to see that you have passed the second test. The test of integrity.'

'Integrity? How?'

'By returning the diamond ring to Priya Capoorr.'

My head spins. There is no way he could have known about the return of the ring. It was between me, the actress and the walls of our drawing room.

'But how did you know about that ring?'

'I have my ways.'

'Are you keeping me under some kind of surveillance?'

'Of course not. It is really quite simple. You know that ABC Corporation also produces films. Priya Capoorr is the heroine in my production company's latest film. She mentioned the story of the ring to her makeup man, who, in turn, told the director, who told the producer, who told me.'

I have no way of knowing if he is telling the truth or just testing to see how gullible I am. Either way, I decide to stick to the facts. 'I should have returned the ring the very first day. I got no pleasure keeping it for a week.'

'Integrity means much more than just honesty, Sapna. The real test of integrity is to be honest even when no one is looking. You proved you have a solid sense of right and wrong. Remember, a good leader must have an exemplary character. Only then can he or she inspire trust. Nothing damages an organisation more than the dishonesty of its employees. And, if the CEO himself is crooked, heaven help that company.'

He beckons me to his side. 'Come here; look down on the street below. What do you see?'

I gaze down from the bay window. Barakhamba Road is crawling with traffic. 'I see hundreds of cars and people.'

'Yes. From up here you can see their heads, but you cannot know what is inside those heads.' He sighs as though he's been through an ordeal. 'People have become adept at masking their true natures. An expert conman can easily cheat his way through the integrity test we give at pre-employment screenings, even fool a polygraph.'

'So how do you know you are hiring an honest person?'

'That is the biggest challenge for a CEO. There is no software, no device that can reveal a person's true feelings with hundred per cent accuracy. I have always gone with my gut instincts, surrounding myself with people who I believe are dependable and loyal. But occasionally even I slip up.'

'What do you mean?'

'We have a mole in the system. Someone who has been leaking confidential information about the company to our rivals.'

'That's terrible!'

'Don't worry, we'll find the traitor eventually. I don't want you to lose sleep over it. You need to prepare for the third test.'

'What's that going to be about?'

'How would I know? It is life that deals the card, you who play the hand. I am merely the croupier who announces the results. Goodbye for now.'

Later, I grab Karan's arm and lean into his ear, my voice taking on the exaggerated conspiratorial whisper of someone about to share a grave secret. 'There's a traitor in ABC Corporation who has been passing confidential company information to Acharya's rivals.'

'Aha!' he exclaims. 'So the plot thickens!'

We are sitting on one of the benches in the garden outside the colony, surrounded by the cool of the night. I am seeing him after a full week. 'I wonder why he told me such a sensitive thing.'

'I'll tell you why. Because this is all a scheme to draw you in, make you trust him. He's playing some kind of warped, sick mind game with you.'

'I know that too. But he sounded so sincere, I almost felt like believing him.'

'Then you must be extra careful. Wake up to the lies of the enemy, Sapna. Wake up before you get sucked into the abyss.'

'I am awake and alert. It was you who was sleeping when Priya Capoorr visited my house.'

'What? Priya Capoorr came to the LIG Colony?'

'Yes, sir. For once I was able to put a superstar in her place.' I narrate the episode with the actress to Karan.

'This is incredible. So you actually returned her two-crore diamond, huh?'

'Yes. Diamonds are not my best friend. You are.'

The Third Test

Locked Dreams

'Now repeat after me: C-O-L-D, cold, meaning *thanda*; T-A-L-L, tall, meaning *lamba*.'

'C-O-L-D, cold, *yani thanda*; T-A-L-L, tall, *yani lamba*,' the students chorus, before breaking into scattered giggles.

It is the Sunday English class, being conducted in the drawing room of our flat. Sitting in front of me are Chunnu, Raju, Aarti and Suresh. They are all between the ages of ten and twelve, and live in the nearby MCD Slum Colony. Chunnu is the son of Sohan Lal, who is employed as a gardener in the Japanese Park. Raju's father, Tilak Raj, is a ward boy in the government hospital in Sector 17. And Aarti and Suresh are children of Kalawati, a single mother who works as a part-time maid in several houses in the LIG Colony, though not in ours. I cannot afford to keep a servant on my salary.

It was Kalawati who roped me into becoming an English teacher six months ago. 'Aarti and Suresh go to the government school, but there they teach everything in Hindi. Unless they learn a little English, how will they get a good job?' she agonised, before clutching my hands. 'Their future is in your hands, *didi*. Please help them.' Unable to hold off her incessant pleas, I agreed to these weekly English lessons for her children. Pretty soon Raju and Chunnu also joined.

I actually enjoy teaching these kids. They may not have all the opportunities, but they do have ambition and motivation. Their dreams have not been corrupted by fate and circumstance. Their destinies are no longer fettered by the morass of caste and class. There is a spark in their eyes and hope on their faces, which will let them reach higher stations in life than their parents.

As I am about to conclude today's lesson, my cell phone rings. It is Lauren. 'Sapna, my dear, I've just received an anonymous tip-off about an illegal lock factory functioning from the MCD Slum Colony in Rohini. Isn't that close to where you live?'

'Yeah. The colony is almost in our backyard.'

'I'm told this factory employs more than twenty children in extremely dangerous conditions.'

'That's shocking!'

'Isn't it? Listen, I want you to do me a favour. I want you to make some discreet enquiries with the folks in the MCD Colony to find out if this tip-off is genuine. Can you do this for me?' Her voice has a desperate, pleading edge to it.

'Don't worry. I'll get back to you today itself.'

I put away the phone and turn to the children. 'Is there some kind of lock-making factory in the slum?'

'Yes, *didi.*' Suresh nods. 'It's run by Anees Mirza.'

'Who is Anees Mirza?'

'He is a mafia don. The entire colony is scared of him.'

'Can you show me this factory?'

Suresh begins scratching his head. 'Mother has given me strict instructions not to go near that place. If she catches me—'

'I'll take you, *didi,*' Chunnu says. 'It's right next to my house. They even offered me a job, promising eighty rupees per day, but I said no. I prefer to go to school.'

'Well done, Chunnu.'

When I convey this to Lauren, she is immediately distraught. 'We need to rescue those kids a.s.a.p. I cannot wait a minute longer.'

'Shouldn't we inform the authorities?'

'Only after I've checked out the place myself. I'm coming to Rohini right now. Can you arrange a local guide?'

'He's right here with me,' I say.

An hour later Lauren and I are following Chunnu as he leads us through the maze of dingy alleyways of the slum colony. It is better than some of the other slums I have seen. Instead of temporary shacks made of corrugated iron, tarpaulin, cardboard and plastic bags, most of the houses are made of brick and cement, even though they are small and cramped. The outer roads of the slum are relatively clean, but, as we go inside, the putrid smell of human waste permeates every space. We notice overflowing drains, and garbage piled at the kerbs. A haze of kerosene smoke hangs in the air, casting a grimy pall over the surroundings.

Chunnu takes us past little eateries and vendors selling groceries, till we reach the effluent drain that marks the northern boundary of the slum. The houses on the opposite side of the *nala* are bigger and better. Chunnu points out a two-storey duplex painted in pale yellow. 'That is the factory. But don't tell anyone I brought you here,' he says, and then scampers back to his house, a one-room shack at the very edge of the slum colony.

I approach the nondescript building with the hesitant steps of a bomb-disposal expert. Lauren, on the contrary, is raring to go.

'Okay, here's the plan,' she says. 'We're lost. And we're trying to get directions to the Delhi College of Engineering.' She knocks on the front door and waits. After an uncomfortable delay the metal door swings open and standing in front of us is a little boy of about ten, dressed in just a dirty vest and shorts. He stares at Lauren as if he's never seen a white woman before. 'Hello, *munna*, may we speak to your father?' Lauren asks in perfect Hindi.

For a moment the kid is shocked into silence. He did not expect a foreigner, and certainly not a foreigner speaking in Hindi. 'Anees Bhai has gone out. He will come back after one hour,' he responds.

'Then we'll just wait for him,' says Lauren, and, without waiting for his reply, pushes her way inside, pulling me along.

The sight that meets my eyes is one that I will never forget. There are approximately thirty kids packed into a long, low, stifling room. The floor is made of cheap cement; the walls are filthy. There are just a couple of tube lights providing illumination, and there is no ventilation.

My ears are assaulted by the sounds of hammers beating metal into submission and noisy power tools whirring and roaring in the background. My eyes begin to smart from the heavy, toxic fumes that swirl in the air like flying snakes.

The children, who are all between the ages of eight and fourteen, are engaged in various activities, ranging from working on hand presses to polishing, electroplating and spray-painting. Not one of them has any protective gear. They glance up briefly when Lauren and I enter, and then go back to whatever they were doing. There are no adults in the room.

'It's worse than I thought,' Lauren whispers. 'This is a sweatshop run by child labour alone.' She pulls out her cell phone and begins taking pictures.

'Hey, what are you doing?' A tall boy, who looks like the team leader, drops his spray-painting gun and stares at us belligerently.

'Relax,' says Lauren. 'I am not a labour inspector.'

'But Boss told us not to allow anyone to take pictures.'

'That does not apply to us.'

'Who are you?' he demands, eyeing us suspiciously.

'We are importers from America. And we have come to see the quality of your locks to see if we want to buy them,' Lauren says without batting an eyelid, intimidating him into a wary acceptance of our presence.

'What's your name?' I ask him.

'Guddu,' he replies.

'Tell me, till what time do you all work?'

'It depends on Anees Bhai. Sometimes till eight, some-times till ten at night.'

'How long have you been doing this, Guddu?'

'For five years. Ever since Anees Bhai came from Aligarh and opened the factory. I have become such an expert lock and key maker, now I can open any lock within a minute.'

I observe the young kids operating hand presses to cut different components of locks. What I notice instantly is that many of the children have bandages on their fingers. 'These poor kids often lose the tips of their fingers in accidents caused from sheer exhaustion,' Lauren explains, her eyes clouding up with tears.

I move on to stand beside a kid working on the buffing machine used for polishing locks. He is covered in black emery powder, making him look like a coal miner. As he bends over the rotating machine, barely ten inches from the bobs, I can see that he is inhaling the emery powder, causing him to go into periodic bouts of coughing. Even I have to clamp my nose and mouth to prevent breathing the fine metal dust. 'Many of these children will develop respiratory disorders, asthma and tuberculosis,' Lauren grieves.

Another boy has what seem like rashes on his back. As I trace a gentle finger over the skin, I discover them to be a lattice of angry welt marks. 'How did you get these?' I ask him.

He does not answer, but the boy next to him does. 'Radhua got punished by Anees Bhai. Boss does not like any boy making too many mistakes and on top of that coming late to work.'

I shudder in revulsion. 'The man's a sadistic monster,' I whisper to Lauren. 'Let's go before he returns.'

'Okay, I think we have seen enough,' Lauren announces loudly, stashing away her phone. 'We're leaving.'

We have reached the door when Guddu shouts. 'Wait!'

'Yes?' Lauren turns slowly on her heels.

'You never told us your name. If Boss asks me who came, what should I tell him?'

Lauren thinks about it for a moment. 'You tell him that Ma Barker had come to visit from New York.'

'Ma . . . what??'

'She's Ma.' Lauren points at me. 'And I'm Barker.'

'Wasn't Ma Barker a notorious crime lord?' I ask Lauren as we hurry back to my flat. 'I seem to remember a Boney M song about her.'

'That song was "Ma Baker",' Lauren explains. 'But it's the same lady. They changed the name because "Baker" sounded better. But even her crime was minor compared to what this man Anees has done,' she continues, her voice suffused with anger. 'Her gang merely stole money. This man has stolen the future of those kids.'

'So what's our next step?'

'We report this to the local subdivisional magistrate. He's the one who will organise a raid party to rescue those kids and close down the factory. Let's go there right away.'

'But today is Sunday. The office will be closed.'

'Damn, I completely forgot. I guess we'll have to go there first thing tomorrow morning.'

At 9 a.m. on Monday, we are at the SDM's office. It looks like a typical government office with whitewashed walls

adorned with portraits of national leaders, utilitarian furniture and ledgers and files stacked up everywhere. There
are crowds milling outside the building, but the atmosphere inside is one of sheer lethargy. Lauren's presence,
however, elicits a flutter of interest from a middle-aged
clerk called Keemti Lal, a jowly man with a toothbrush
moustache and grizzled sideburns. 'Yes, madam, how can
I help you? Do you need to get a property registered?'

'I have come to report an illegal workshop employing
child labour. When can the SDM see us?'

'I'm afraid SDM *sahib* doesn't come before ten thirty.
But you can discuss with me.'

For the next half-hour we patiently explain what we
saw inside the workshop, the illegal nature of the operation and the health hazards to the children and the general
environment. Lauren has even printed out the pictures she
had taken with her cell phone. The clerk gets us to submit
a written report and sign various forms. I begin to chafe
at all this bureaucracy. Filing a simple complaint seems to
require more paperwork than applying for a bank loan.

'This is a very serious matter,' Lauren stresses. 'I hope
you will take immediate action to rescue those poor children.'

Keemti Lal nods gravely. 'Absolutely, madam. But we
will have to follow the laid-down procedure in such cases.
A notice will need to be served, followed by an enquiry,
which can lead to an appeal. All this will take time.
However, things can be speeded up if . . .'

He leaves the sentence hanging, but from the expectant
look on his weasel-like face we can gauge his intention.
He is asking us for a bribe.

I am aghast. 'What kind of man are you, trying to enrich yourself at the expense of innocent children?' I upbraid the clerk.

Lauren, however, simply purses her lips and nods. With a philosophical detachment she opens her wallet and counts out five thousand-rupee notes. 'Will this be enough?'

'Oh, madam, you are embarrassing me,' Keemti Lal says ingratiatingly, even as he accepts the money, stuffing it into his shirt's top pocket. 'Rest assured that I will apprise SDM *sahib* as soon as he comes. *Namaste.*' He folds his hands. My hands itch to pummel that smirk off his ugly face.

As we step out of the building, I cannot help remarking to Lauren, 'I didn't expect you to grease the palms of that swine so easily.'

'For me the paramount consideration is saving those children. If it takes a little speed money, I don't mind.'

'We seem to have become a nation of bribe givers and bribe takers.' I shake my head in dismay.

'If it makes you feel any good, let me tell you there's bribery in America too.'

'Really?'

'Yes. Except we have refined it into a fine art. And we call it lobbying.'

It is 26 January, India's Republic Day. For the nation, it marks the birth anniversary of India's Constitution. But for me and my family it marks Alka's death anniversary.

Outside, patriotic songs are blaring from loudspeakers. Inside our flat the mood is sombre and contemplative.

Today we are all emotional refugees, seeking sanctuary from our collective pain. Ma, steeped in religion, takes shelter in the Bhagwad Gita, the holy scripture. Neha hides behind her MP3 player, ears plugged out to some thumping dance beat. I try to divert myself by reading a book, but it is impossible to concentrate. So I sit in front of the TV, doodling on a paper tissue and watching the live coverage of the Republic Day parade. It is a foggy morning and the sky is grey, yet thousands of spectators are braving the cold to cheer the marching contingents and mechanised columns as they make their way from Raisina Hill to the Red Fort. A succession of tableaux showcase our military might and cultural diversity. There are tanks and missiles, intercut with Sufi traditions of Bihar and festival dances from Sikkim.

'Why are you wasting your time watching this song and dance?' a voice reprimands me from the door. I turn around to see Nirmala Ben enter the flat.

Nirmala Ben lives in B-25, three flats removed from ours, on the same floor. She is a thin, diminutive woman, in her early sixties, with quick, darting eyes that take in everything around her at once. Her greying hair is pulled tightly behind her head in a small bun. As usual, she is dressed in a simple white sari, and plain slippers.

Nirmala Ben's life story mirrors our own struggles. Before marriage she was Nirmala Mukherjee, a Bengali from Kolkata with a passion for Rabindra Sangeet, the songs of Tagore. When she was twenty-four, she fell in love with a Gujarati accountant named Hasmukh Shah. Despite opposition from her family, she married him and moved with him to Surat. They had just one child, a boy named Sumit. Unfortunately, her husband passed away of a sudden heart attack in 1985. After that, all her hopes were centred on her son. Her heart swelled with pride when Sumit joined the Indian Army and got commissioned into the Rajputana Rifles. He was posted in Assam and Delhi before being sent to Kashmir. It was there that he attained martyrdom on 13 June 1999, bravely fighting the enemy on the icy slopes of the Drass sector during the Kargil War.

After Sumit's death, Nirmala Ben moved to Delhi. Her flat is a shrine to her son, full of framed pictures of the dashing officer who was posthumously awarded the Maha Vir Chakra, the nation's second highest wartime gallantry award. But, alongside mementoes of her son, you can also see miniature spinning wheels and busts of Mahatma Gandhi. One bookcase is full of Gandhi's *Collected Works*, running into ninety volumes. 'I was completely devastated by Sumit's death,' she told me once. 'I grieved for almost two years, till I discovered Mohandas Karamchand Gandhi. I started reading everything that he had written. It was Bapu who opened my eyes to the true meaning of truth, nonviolence and self-sacrifice.' Since then, Nirmala Ben has devoted her life to Gandhi and the advancement of his principles. From communal harmony to cow protection, she is there to lend her voice and her helping hands to every public campaign.

Every now and then the residents of the colony are treated to little sermons by her on fighting injustice, loving your enemies and overcoming evil with good. She is antiwar, she is antiglobalisation, but most of all she is anticorruption. 'My son was not killed by the enemy's bullets,' she never tires of saying. 'He was killed by corruption. The guns they gave him were defective, his bulletproof vest was substandard, and, when he died, they even made money on his coffin. I tell you, corruption is the cancer eating our country from within.'

Throughout the day she maintains a cacophony of insults, invectives and admonitions directed at India's political class. But behind that crusty exterior lies a heart of gold. Ben means sister in Gujarati and she is truly the colony's elder sister, kind, selfless and generous to a fault. We've lost count of the number of times we've been treated to delicious khandvi, dhokla and rasagullas from her kitchen.

It was almost destined that, of all the people in the colony, Nirmala Ben would forge the closest bond with Susheela Sinha, my mother. Both share the traumatic experience of losing their husbands and a child. The Gandhian's headstrong ways and sharp tongue are a perfect foil for Ma's soft demeanour and earthy common sense.

A by-product of this poignant friendship is that Nirmala Ben has more or less adopted me as her daughter, always making sure I'm eating healthily, not overexerting, and getting enough sleep.

She sits down next to me, takes off her round glasses and begins polishing them with the *pallu* of her sari. 'I was also watching TV in my flat, but it became too depressing,' she says.

'How can you find the Republic Day parade depressing?'

'I was not watching the parade, but the news. It was

only about corruption: the 2G scam in telecom, mining scam in Karnataka, land scam in U.P., sugar scam in Kerala. And if that's not enough you have doctors striking in Patna, Naxals killing ten security men in Chhattisgarh, and onions hitting fifty rupees a kilo. What is happening to our country?'

'That is why I've stopped watching the news,' I say in a lighter vein.

'That is the real problem in our country. Youngsters like you just don't want to engage with the nation. *Arrey*, you have to take the bull by the horns. Then only will we be able to get to the bottom of all these scams.'

'Hasn't the government already appointed committees to look into them?'

'Hmph!' she snorts. 'That is the only thing the government does, appoint a committee, which gives its report after five years. By then fifteen other scams take place. We don't need committees: we need courage. Courage to expose the real people behind these scams. Courage to unmask Atlas.'

I know what Nirmala Ben is referring to. The news these days is full of stories about Atlas Investments, a front company that is alleged to be behind most scams in the country. Except no one seems to know the real identity behind Atlas. And the government claims it has no easy way of finding out.

'Anyway, let's not spoil our mood by talking about scams,' I say, to divert her.

'On the contrary, we must *only* talk about scams. That is how the public will get educated to fight against corruption. I have been reading up on the subject, making notes. See how much research I've done on Atlas.' She produces a notebook, its pages filled in pencil with her dense handwriting. The pencil itself is on its last legs, sharpened so much that it is now just a stump, an inch long. But Nirmala Ben is like that, reluctant to waste or throw away even the smallest thing. Her apartment is cluttered with all kinds of knick-knacks. Except most of them don't belong to her. On occasion I have discovered our own spoons and forks in her kitchen. She has this weird habit of picking up little items from homes and shops that she visits – a nail cutter here, a pen there. Even things that she has no use for, like a cricket ball or a cig-arette lighter. In the colony, we speak in hushed whispers about her condition. In psychological parlance, it is called kleptomania – the irresistible urge to steal items that you don't really need and that usually have little value. Nirmala Ben is quite possibly the world's only Gandhian kleptomaniac.

As we continue chatting, it is obvious that she is sorely exercised about the matter of the elusive Atlas. 'One day we are told that Atlas is based in Switzerland; the next day we are told it is in Monaco; the third day it is supposed to be in Mauritius; and the fourth day in Cyprus. *Arrey*, do we need an atlas to locate this Atlas?' she asks with a rhetorical sneer.

'But what can we ordinary citizens do?'

'We have to launch a fight. Corruption must be stopped. What this country needs is a second Gandhian revolution.'

'And how do we launch that revolution?'

'I don't know. Bapu will show me the way. He always

does.' She looks up at the wall clock and reluctantly gets up. 'I must be getting back now. It is time for my noon prayer.'

Only after she has left do I discover that my ballpoint pen, the one I was doodling with, has vanished!

At 6 p.m. the doorbell rings and Neha tells me that there are two strangers at the door, wanting to see me.

I meet them in the drawing room. They are both in their mid-thirties. One is a short, swarthy, clean-shaven man wearing a woollen knitted cap. He has the shifty look of a fixer outside a government office. The other is a totally bald guy, taller and beefier, with the dangerous air of a seasoned convict who has just stepped out of Tihar jail.

'Are you Sapna Sinha?' the short guy asks.

I nod. 'What is this all about?'

'It is about the complaint that you and your American friend lodged against Mirza Metal Works two days ago.'

'Are you Anees Mirza's men?'

'Yes and no. We are simply trying to resolve the situation.' He leans forward, adopting the conciliatory tone of a hostage negotiator. 'Madam, we have come to request you to withdraw the complaint.'

'And allow those poor children to suffer?'

'Who says those children are suffering? Look, this is not bonded labour. The children come to us voluntarily. And we pay them a good wage.'

'But employment of children under fourteen is illegal.'

'Forget the law. Look at reality. If these children don't work for us, they will work somewhere else. If they don't make locks they will make bricks or carpets or bangles. Worse, they will steal or beg. At least we provide them an honourable livelihood, allow them to eat *izzat ki roti*.'

'I find nothing honourable in making children work twelve hours a day in hazardous conditions. They should be in school instead.'

'They don't want to go to school. They want to earn, to help their families.'

'That's because no one has given them the chance.'

'So will *you* give them a chance, adopt all of them?'

'My friend Lauren will. She runs a charity called RMT Asha Foundation.'

'I will say once again, with folded hands, please reconsider your decision. You have picked the wrong person to tangle with. Anees Bhai is not an unreasonable man, but he can be quite vindictive.'

'Are you threatening me?'

'No, no. We don't threaten decent citizens like you. Consider this a friendly piece of advice. *Achha*, we shall go now.'

The short man gets up, his thick lips parted in a leery grin. The bald man continues to sit, reluctant to leave. 'Come on, Joginder,' his partner says. 'We shouldn't overstay our welcome.'

Joginder eases his bulk off the sofa. He stands up and flexes his biceps, as though giving a bodybuilding demonstration. Then he passes a hand over his bald pate and throws me a vicious glare. My fingers tighten into clenched fists as I watch the duo exit the door. Together they make a perfect team of determined bullies, one guy the talker, the other the enforcer.

I find that my entire body is shaking, from anger or from fear I don't know. Perhaps it is a combination of both. Right now it is difficult to think past the bitter taste of bile in the back of my throat.

Ma and Neha emerge from behind the bead curtain and surround me. It appears they were surreptitiously listening to the entire conversation. Mother is already hysterical. '*Beti*, go right now and withdraw that complaint. Otherwise yet another calamity will befall our family,' she frets with a mother's instinctive premonition of the future.

'Why do you always have to behave like Rani of Jhansi, *didi*?' Neha says, her voice thick with insinuation. 'You know I have to go to Mumbai to participate in the contest. Nothing is more important for our family's future. Yet you start meddling in other people's business.'

'How can you be so selfish, Neha?' I let it rip. 'You have no concern for those thirty children working like bonded labour?'

'No, I don't,' she insists. 'It's a job for the police, not respectable girls like us.'

'Neha is absolutely right, *beti*,' Ma chimes in. 'Do whatever it takes, but I don't want these *goondas* entering our house again.'

'It's pointless talking with both of you.' I throw up my hands and storm out of the house.

I have always had a pathological, visceral hatred of bullies, people who use their power, authority or size to pick on those weaker and smaller. Most bullies think they are strong but they are actually sick, gutless wimps who will back down if confronted forcefully enough. I learnt this important lesson early on in my life.

There was a time when I was being bullied by a group of classmates in St Theresa's. They called themselves the Spice Girls, even though their names were Amrita, Brinda and Chavi, and the only music they were capable of was cruelty and abuse. They were my nemesis, my oppressors. They were bigger than me in size but much weaker in intellect. They bullied me all through Grade 5 and the first six months of Grade 6. My only crime was that I invariably topped the class and I was independent, unlike the other girls, who all had their coteries and cliques. They would torment and tease me incessantly, in the corridors, in the playground, during breaks. Being ridiculed became part of my daily life, making me feel as small as humanly possible. My textbooks were stolen, my exercise books defaced. Chairs were pulled out from under me as I was about to sit down, and doors were slammed in my face. I was once locked out in the toilet; on another occasion my hair was almost set on fire.

It made me loathe myself, gave me a victim mentality. I began flirting with the idea of self-harm, planning my suicide every weekend, fantasising about my death. Till one day I decided to end it all. I made up my mind. I would kill myself, but before that I would kill my three tormentors.

That day I went to school with a kitchen knife in my satchel. During the lunch break I made my way to a deserted classroom on the third floor, where the Spice Girls were bound to ambush me. Sure enough, they followed me into the room and began calling me ugly names. I listened quietly to their verbal tirade for a minute, and then whipped out the kitchen knife from my skirt pocket. 'Enough, bitches,' I growled, baring my teeth, rolling my eyes and making my voice as raspy and inhuman as that of Linda Blair in *The Exorcist*. 'One more word and I will cut out your tongues.'

Then, like a panther springing upon its prey, I caught Amrita, the leader of the gang, by the throat, my fingers digging hard into her voice box, almost choking her. The other two girls held their breaths as, slowly and deliberately, I began sawing off a lock of her hair with the knife in my free hand, impelled by some atavistic force buried deep inside me. Not a squeak emerged from any of them. The only sound I could hear was of the adrenaline pumping through my veins, the blood singing through my muscles, sounding like the stirring hum of battle. It was as exhilarating as it was terrifying.

Just then the school bell rang, announcing the end of the lunch break. It was as if a spell had been broken. The three girls screamed in unison and bolted out of the classroom as if it were on fire, leaving me stranded with a knife in one hand and a clump of hair in the other. I knew they would rush straight to Sister Agnes. I expected the tyrannical principal to march in any minute to announce that she was rusticating me from school. I would give her a mocking smile, and then plunge the knife into my abdomen, *hara-kiri* style, a violent suicide in tranquil Nainital.

I waited for a long time, but no one came, neither the principal nor any teacher. Slowly, I returned the knife to my skirt pocket and walked back to class, where the history period was about to begin. The Spice Girls shrank into their seats the moment I entered the classroom, and pretended to look elsewhere. I learnt later that they did not make any complaint against me. They nicknamed me 'Psycho', but I was never bullied after that.

The encounter with Anees Mirza's goons has brought that long-lost memory rushing back to me, generating those same emotions. I am still heaving with fury when I bump into Karan on the ground floor.

'I saw two rather unsavoury types asking directions to your flat,' he says. 'Is everything okay?'

'It's not,' I reply and tell him about the illegal workshop.

'How dare they threaten you! How dare they!' Karan snaps, his face contorting with rage. 'If they even so much as set foot inside the colony again, you let me know. I'll fix those bastards.'

'I am not so worried about myself. But what if they start harassing Neha?'

'Look, I'll get you a panic button tomorrow.'

'What's that?'

'It's a small electronic device that, when pressed, sends a soundless signal to alert someone else about an emergency situation. In this case, the signal will come to me and I'll come instantly to the rescue, like Superman.'

The more I listen to him, the more I thank Durga Ma for giving me such a wonderful neighbour. There is nothing more reassuring than a friend who just simply refuses to be rattled, who can always be relied upon, who is always there when you need him.

'Is there something special in your diet that makes you so brave?' I rib him.

'Yeah, right,' he grins. 'The trick is to consume plenty of liquid courage.'

'And what drink is that?'

'Just another name for alcohol!'

A week passes, and there are no further visits from the goon squad. Gradually the incident begins to fade from my mind, taking with it all my restless nights. In any event, with Karan's panic button inside my purse, I feel much safer.

Thursday, 3 February, is stocktaking day and, as usual, it extends well beyond closing time. I am able to leave the store only at 10.15 p.m. The moment I disembark at Rithala metro station, a young street hawker gets after me. 'I have the perfect thing that you need,' he says, displaying a kitchen knife with a wooden handle bearing the logo of a company called KK Thermoware. I take a good look at him. Dressed in torn trousers and a filthy, tattered sweater several sizes too big for him, he doesn't look a tad over ten. He has the sickly, anaemic look of a fever patient. On top of that he has a runny nose, repeatedly wiping snot on his sleeve. But this does not prevent him from breaking into a ditty in Hindi extolling the virtues of his knife:

It can cut and carve and slice and dice,
The stainless steel blade is really nice.
For a husband who wants to please his wife,
There's nothing more perfect than a KK Knife!

'Look, you don't seem too well,' I tell him. 'Why don't you go home now?'

'I can't go home till I sell all my knives. I've just one left now. Buy it. It's only a hundred rupees.'

'I don't need a knife. I've got plenty at home,' I say as I head into Rammurti Passi Marg.

He continues to pester me. 'Okay, just for you, I'll reduce the price. Only fifty rupees.'

'No.'

'How about twenty?'

'Still not interested.'

'Okay, last price. Ten rupees.'

'I told you I don't want a knife.'

'*Didi*, I haven't eaten since afternoon. I'll sell it to you for just five rupees. You won't find a better bargain in all of Delhi. Please buy it now at least.'

His pleading face is impossible to resist. I take the knife from him and offer him a ten-rupee note. 'Keep the change. And now go and get some rest.'

He almost snatches the note from my hand, and scampers away into the gloom.

I insert the knife inside my purse and quicken my steps as I approach the Swarn Jayanti Park, better known as the Japanese Park, a huge green lung with manicured gardens, boating lakes, floating fountains and jogging trails. While it is a haven for fitness enthusiasts and families during the day, it is a rather unsafe area at night. Last year a woman was murdered near Gate Number 1, and a noted criminal was shot dead inside the park in a police encounter earlier this year.

I have just crossed the park's Gate Number 2 when all of a sudden three young men jump down from the boundary wall. With their half-open shirts and long hair, they look like those unruly, unemployed youths who can be found all over the country, loitering at chai shops, hassling girls, whistling raucously from the front stalls of cinema halls. In Nainital we used to have a term for them – '*chavanni chhap*', worth a quarter of a rupee only. But the damage they are capable of inflicting on people and property is considerably more. What makes me even more apprehensive is the fact that the stretch I am walking through is dimly lit and deserted. There are no other pedestrians in sight. My hand immediately dips into the handbag in a conditioned reflex, fingers curling around the panic button. I am pretty sure Karan is out of its range, but I press it nevertheless.

My apprehension turns out to be justified, as the three youths begin dogging my footsteps. I increase my pace and they do the same. In just a few long, determined strides they are abreast of me, flanking me on all sides. '*Jaaneman*, why are you in such a hurry? Have a look at us as well,' the ruffian directly behind me says, tapping my shoulder. He seems to be the leader of the pack, with sharp malignant eyes and a thin, wispy moustache.

I respond by whipping out the can of pepper spray and whirling around on my heels. 'You take one more step and I'll make all of you blind,' I hiss, pepper spray poised at eye level.

The startled ruffian recoils a step, but his partner to my immediate right lashes out with his fists in a lightning-quick move. I feel a whiplash on my forearm and the can pops out of my hands like a wet bar of soap.

'Ha!' The ruffian leader roars with laughter. 'If you are carrying any other weapons, we would like to see them. Come on, hand over your purse.'

The wolfish expressions on their faces tell me they

want more than just my purse. It is the first time in my life I feel physically, mortally threatened. My breathing becomes shallow. A cold knot of fear coils nauseatingly in the pit of my stomach. That is when I remember the knife I have just purchased.

The handbag held in my left hand is already open. I can see the knife, its steel blade glinting dully under the yellow street light. In a flash I pull it out with my right hand, while simultaneously discarding the purse on the footpath.

'Stay back!' I shriek, whirling around in a full circle, shredding the air with my knife. 'I'll cut the bastard who tries to come near me.'

Worryingly, the thugs show no sign of being intimidated. They do step back a few feet, but continue to regard me with an amused contempt.

'I said leave me alone, or I will cut down each one of you,' I threaten again, tightening my grip on the knife's handle.

'You think you can scare us with your little knife?' the leader taunts me. 'Then you should see this.' He takes out a silver gun from the back of his trousers and aims it in my face.

'Drop the knife,' the baddy on my right snarls.

There's something very deflating about being confronted with a loaded gun. I comply. The knife clatters to the ground with the clinking sound of coins rattling in a pocket. The youth on my right picks it up gingerly from its tip, like a forensic investigator handling a murder weapon at a crime scene. 'It's really sharp,' he observes, before dropping it into my handbag.

'Let's go inside the park, baby,' the ruffian leader smirks. I refuse to budge. I know the moment I step inside the dark park, something very bad will happen to me.

I squint at the faces of my tormentors, trying to discern features, scars, tattoos, any identifying characteristics that I would be able to pass along to the police when they ask, before it dawns on me that I may never be able to go to the police. They will kill me after they rape me. As this sickening realisation sinks in, I am overcome with an almost unbearable sense of sadness. What will happen to Neha and Ma after I am gone? How will they manage all alone?

The thug leans over and shoves the gun in my face, imprinting a *bindi* on my forehead. 'Didn't you hear what I said? Are you deaf?'

'Please, please let me go.' I make a noise that sounds like a whimper, my heart almost stopping.

'How can we let you go? You are so beautiful,' he says, the harsh tone fading away. He looks at his two cohorts. 'What do you say? It's time to enjoy.' They all laugh. It is their gloating that makes me nauseous, fills me with pure, undiluted hatred. A policeman has slapped me, another has pushed my head inside a toilet bowl, and now these three ruffians are planning to gang-rape me. What am I? An animal to be kicked around? A plaything to be abused? Just because I happen to be a woman? Something snaps inside me at that very instant, like a rubber band that has been stretched too far. I don't care if I get shot and diced but I will not take this lying down. Pulsing with that same primal rage with which I confronted the Spice Girls, I lash out with my right leg, kicking the leader as hard as

I can in his groin. He drops to the ground like a felled
tree, doubling up in pain. The memory of that afternoon
in the deserted classroom floods my brain and I begin
raining blows on the other two, hitting, kicking, clawing,
scratching. There is a white-hot fire burning inside me,
consuming me. I hate these bastards, I hate them more
than anything in the world. Heat is rising in my cheeks
and my heart is pounding like a drum. Red fills my
vision, blinding me completely. Everything in me wants
to strangle, to gouge, to just kill, kill, kill.

My unexpected counterattack works for a while, but
the force of numbers is against me. Before I can land a
knockout blow, the ruffian leader is already returning to
action. Through the corner of my eye I can see him lifting his head. He raises the butt of his gun and swings it at
me. Pain ripples across my stomach and I stumble and fall
down. Another thug kicks me in the back.

Within minutes they have dragged me into the under-
brush of the Japanese Park. Pinning me to the ground, the
leader proceeds to take out a shiny metallic switchblade
from his worn-out trousers. It flicks open to reveal a thin,
ugly-looking knife with a ten-inch blade. 'If you want to
scare someone then don't use a kitchen knife. Use a
Rampuri *chaku*, like mine.' He grins and slides the knife
over my body; eventually, it comes to rest against my
neck. His fetid breath is hot against my skin.

I struggle against my captor, trying to free myself, when
he puts a finger against his lips. 'Be quiet.' His voice slithers and climbs into my ear. 'Or I'll have to kill you.'

With no emotion in his dead eyes, he rakes my cheek
with the tip of the knife, the steel blade digging into my

flesh. One little push and it will break the skin, disfiguring me permanently. I feel my entire body heating up, as though I were on fire. It rages through my bloodstream, making me tremble with the insane anticipation of death. I just want it to end, and I pray to God to let me die quickly, preferably with the revolver. Just one little bullet through the brain. I don't want him to cut me up piece by piece, to slash, slash and slash with his knife till I am a whimpering mass of blood and bones, a pathetic heap of twitching muscles and jerking limbs. I don't think I will be able to bear so much pain.

'Leave her!' A voice suddenly rings out in the darkness. It is a booming baritone that resonates like thunder across the park. The ruffians look around and then at each other, completely nonplussed. The leader removes the knife and crouches like a dog, trying to suss out the intruder.

'This is the police,' the voice booms again, reminiscent of the instructions relayed through loudspeakers during a police raid. It instantly galvanises my captors into flight. They scatter and run like headless chickens into the Japanese Park, disappearing into the darkness.

Jut then, a figure emerges from the gloom of the park. I was expecting a police inspector, but it turns out to be Karan. I've never felt more relief in my life than at that climactic moment.

He runs to me and helps me get on my feet. I cling tightly to him, my body still shuddering with fear. He whispers my name and I whisper back to him. I hug him closer, feeling his warmth, my breasts grinding into his chest. Locked in that position, I feel a strange new flower blooming in my heart, filling me with a sensual rush.

Almost involuntarily, I start kissing him. It starts with his chin, moves to his cheek and eventually to his lips. I am desperate, and grateful, and muddled, only dimly aware of what I am doing, yet greedily filling the emptiness of my life with his smell, his taste, his life breath.

Karan stiffens, and I can sense an almost imperceptible flinch – one that makes my heart run cold. He gently untangles himself from me and shines a penlight in my face, checking to see there are no bruises. 'Do you need to see a doctor?' he asks, his practical concern restoring some sanity to the situation.

'No . . . no,' I reply, my breathing still ragged. 'I'm fine. Just check if my handbag is around.'

He scours the nearby area, only to confirm what I already feared. The ruffians have made off with my Nine West. 'Was there a lot of money in it?'

'Not really. The most expensive item was my cell phone.'

'Don't worry. I'll get you a brand new one from Indus.'

'How . . . how did you find me?'

'It was the signal from the panic button. You were not in the house so I knew you must be returning from work. I raced as fast as I could towards the station. But then I heard voices near the Japanese Park and decided to investigate.'

'You arrived just in time. What might have happened if—'

'Don't even think about it any more. Let's go straight to the police. Those bastards must be caught.'

'No.' I shake my head vehemently. 'I don't have the strength to face an interrogation. And I know the police will never find those thugs. Just take me home, okay?'

'If that is what you want.' He shrugs.

'Do me another favour,' I say. 'Don't mention a word about this to Ma and Neha.'

'They are bound to be Anees Mirza's men,' says Lauren, when I tell her about the incident the next day.

'But we have no proof.'

'It's too much of a coincidence. I find it despicable, the way Mirza has been allowed to roam free all this while.'

'Any progress on our complaint?'

'Nope,' she says. 'I think Keemti Lal took us for a royal ride. He's done precious little to investigate that workshop. Those poor children are still suffering. I've tried to meet the SDM several times but I keep getting fobbed off. I tried going to the police but they tell me to go to the SDM's office. I just don't know what to do.' There is a depth of despondency in her voice.

'I know what to do. We'll go again to the SDM's office. One last time.'

The next morning I accompany Lauren to the SDM's office on my way to the showroom. The place is extremely crowded and we are told the SDM won't be able to see us. '*Sahib* is very busy. No chance today,' the office peon informs us.

I am equally unbending. 'You tell your boss that we are not leaving till he sees us. Even if it means we have to camp here for a week.'

The bluster works. An hour later we are summoned

into the SDM's presence. He appears to be a vague man, an impression reinforced by his bland, almost featureless face, and peculiar habit of leaving his sentences dangling, as though he expects the listener to finish them for him.

'Yes, that complaint of yours . . .' he begins before lapsing into silence.

'Well, did you check out that factory?' Lauren demands. 'I even gave documentary evidence.'

'These things take a lot of time, a lot of time. It is not possible to . . .'

'How long are we expected to wait?'

'It is a process, you have to understand. We cannot just . . .'

'But those children are suffering every day.'

'They are not suffering. They are earning a living. Just as you are. Just as I am. Should we stop them from . . .?'

'Employment of children in hazardous industries is prohibited, isn't it?'

'What is hazardous? The air we are breathing in this city is also hazardous. Does this mean . . .?'

'So should we just leave those children at the mercy of Anees Mirza?'

'Anees Mirza is not a bad man *per se*. He is . . .'

It is like having a one-way conversation with a brick wall. Lauren is seething as we step out of the bureaucrat's office. 'I've done my math. Keemti Lal took a small bribe from me. This man has taken a much bigger bribe from Anees Mirza.'

It is hard not to agree with her. The stench of corruption hangs over the place like a pall. There are deals being cut on every table. I glimpse Keemti Lal sitting on his corner desk, engrossed in conversation with an elderly gentleman, doubtless extracting yet another bribe. I studiously avoid eye contact with him. That is when my gaze falls on a poster stuck to the bulletin board outside the office. It is about the Right to Information Act.

'Hey.' I nudge Lauren. 'There's one option open to us. Let's use the RTI.'

'How will that help?'

'Under the Right to Information Act, a public authority is required to provide information on any matter requested by the applicant within thirty days or less,' I read out from the poster. 'So let's file an RTI application with the SDM asking to know what happened to our complaint. At least it will put some pressure on him.'

Lauren is sceptical. 'I doubt the SDM can be galvanised into action by a paper application.'

'Look, there's no harm in trying. And it costs just twenty-five rupees.'

I pick up an RTI form from the counter and fill out the application, asking for a status report on our complaint and adding, for good measure, how Anees Mirza had tried to intimidate me by sending his goons. Then I bid goodbye to Lauren and catch the metro to Connaught Place.

Today is Neelam's last day in the office. She is getting married next week. And immediately after that she leaves for Sweden. She seems more excited about her first foreign trip than her first wedding.

'What about you, Sapna?' she asks me. 'When are you planning to get married?'

'You know what they say about marriage. It happens when it has to happen.'

'But have you found your Mr Right yet?'

I do not reply, but her question brings back memories of that night I kissed Karan. His taste still lingers on my lips; his scent still hovers in the air around me. But there is an awkward distance between us now, as though I have crossed some kind of invisible boundary, a *lakshman rekha*. I feel hurt, almost betrayed, by his aloofness that night. It has left me confused and bewildered. Does he not like me any more? Does he have a secret girlfriend? Is he just very shy? Or am I unfairly rushing to judgement of someone who was probably as over-whelmed by the situation as I was? There are so many questions that burn within me. But I dare not ask him because I fear his answer. All I know is that I don't want to lose Karan. I need time to think and work this all out, figure out his true feelings about me, feelings that he keeps hidden deep inside him, locked away in some dark black box.

I'll find the key to that box eventually. And till then I'll lock my dreams inside my heart, where no one can steal them.

A fortnight later the Cricket World Cup starts and everything else takes a back seat. Like the rest of the country, I too get caught up in the hoopla surrounding the Indian team's victory over Bangladesh in the opening match.

Another week goes by. By now I have almost forgotten about my RTI application when out of the blue I get a call on the office number. It is the SDM himself. 'Madam, I just wanted to let you know that . . .' he begins, and then stops abruptly.

'That what?'

'That today we raided the illegal lock factory and . . .'

'And what?'

'And we closed it down. We rescued thirty-five children. They will all receive . . .'

'Receive what, for god's sake?'

'Educational rehabilitation to the tune of twenty thousand rupees each as provided under the Child Labour Act. Is there anything else . . .?'

'Nothing,' I say and put down the receiver, unable to believe the news. It seems too good to be true. But the evening newspapers carry the story of Mirza Metal Works being sealed. There are even photos of Anees Mirza being led away by the police like a common criminal, his face veiled by a headscarf.

Lauren is over the moon. 'Hail to the RTI!' she whoops. 'I was always told that information is power. Now I've seen it too. Today we begin to shape the future for each of those thirty-five kids.'

'Yes,' I concur. 'Today we unlock their dreams.'

'Why didn't you tell me your cell phone number had changed?' Acharya launches into a complaint the moment I step into his office. It is Thursday, 3 March, and I have been summoned, as usual, at barely an hour's notice.

'My old Nokia got stolen,' I explain. 'I've got an Indus Mobile phone now.'

'That's the same as mine. At least it won't cost me now when I call you. Make sure Rana has your new number. It is important that you remain accessible to me at all times.'

A ripple of irritation runs through me. I have half a mind to tell him he doesn't own me, when he breaks into a smile. 'Anyway, I called you to congratulate you on passing the third test.'

'And what exactly was this test?'

'The test of courage. The way you stood up for those kids, the way you withstood the threat from Anees Mirza, the mafia boss, refusing to back down till his illegal workshop was closed, can only be described as courageous.'

I spring to my feet. 'That's it. I'm not participating in your tests any longer.'

He looks up sharply. 'Why? What's the matter?'

'You denied that you are keeping me under surveillance. But there's absolutely no way you could have known about my run-in with Anees Mirza. I didn't even tell anyone in the showroom.'

'But you did file an application under the Right to Information, and I got the story from here,' he says, holding up a magazine.

I take it from his hands. It is the February issue of a publication called *RTI News*, brought out by an NGO called Resurgent India, and on page 32 there is an article expounding how my timely RTI intervention helped save thirty-five children from hazardous employment. It is unnerving how the industrialist manages to get hold of every little bit of information concerning me.

'To chart out a course of action, and follow it to the end, requires a leader to show a great deal of courage,' Acharya continues. 'And I'm not referring to the physical courage a soldier needs for combat, but the moral courage to always do the proper thing regardless of the consequences. Remember, courage is not the absence of fear: it is the ability to act *in spite* of fear and overwhelming opposition.'

'I still don't get how courage applies to a corporation.'

'It's simple.' Acharya smiles. 'The most common fear in a CEO is the fear of failure. A good leader has learnt to conquer this fear. He or she takes calculated risks boldly, knowing that the greatest fear is not taking the wrong action, but not taking action at all. That is the fear of regret, the regret of not having tried.'

I nod. It brings to mind a quote of Kierkegaard I read once: 'To dare is to lose one's footing momentarily. To not dare is to lose oneself.'

'We should never allow fear to limit ourselves. To face a challenge with courage is the true test of leadership. Leadership without courage is like a racing car without an accelerator. It can sputter about for ages but will never cross the finish line.' His voice drops a little low, and a tinge of bitterness creeps into it. 'Of course, sometimes even with the best racing car you can fail to cross the finish line, if you have a saboteur in your midst.'

I seize on his cutting allusion. 'This reminds me, any further news on that mole in the company?'

'No,' he sighs. 'But last week we lost yet another tender to the Premier Group to supply technology for the national ID card.'

'So the mole is obviously someone supplying information to the Premier Group.'

'Correct. That has always been the way my brother Ajay Krishna Acharya has operated. Subterfuge, duplicity and chicanery come naturally to him.'

'I hope you find the traitor, whoever he is,' I commiserate.

'That I will,' he says grimly.

I glance at my watch. It's almost 2 p.m. 'I'd better go.' I rise from the chair. 'I should also tell you that I won't be around for the rest of the month.'

He looks up. 'Are you going somewhere?'

'To Mumbai. My sister Neha has been selected for the final audition of *Popstar No. 1* and I will be accompanying her. I've already taken leave for a fortnight.'

'In that case, good luck to your sister. And to you too.'

'Why me?'

'Who knows? There may be another test in store for you.'

'Have you considered one possibility?' Karan asks me when I narrate my latest meeting with Acharya to him.

'What?'

'That those boys who attacked you outside the Japanese Park might not be Anees Mirza's men.'

'Then who sent them?'

'My hunch is they were hired by Acharya. Just so that he could give you the certificate of courage.'

The suggestion is so horrific that I am startled into silence.

'Why don't you just quit this nonsense, stop seeing that warped bastard?'

With a determined thrust of my chin, I take his hand in mine. 'You have yourself a deal. If this turns out to be Acharya's handiwork, I am not going to have anything to do with him. Ever.'

The Fourth Test

The Blindness of Fame

Suddenly there is a hush in the air. The sky blushes with the opalescent tints of the dying day as the red ball of the sun begins to slowly sink into the ocean, silhouetting the fishermen's boats bobbing on golden water. In the far distance the ramparts of skyscrapers and high-rise condominiums stand out in clear relief. The incessant clamour of the world is stilled, with not even a wispy breath of wind. It is just the gentle waves lapping at my feet, the sand getting into my toes, the shrill cries of the gulls circling overhead, and the crisp tang of salt in my nostrils.

For someone like me, who has never dipped her toes in an ocean before, it is an exhilarating feeling of pure transcendence. The mountains of Nainital evoked in me a spiritual experience, a sense of endurance and time-lessness. The frothy ocean of Mumbai conveys a feeling of boundless freedom, much like the city itself. Delhi seems like a bastion of conservatism compared with the relaxed promiscuity of Mumbai. There are lovers necking unabashedly behind me on Chowpatty Beach, oblivious to the tittering onlookers. The fashionably forward girls have no qualms about flashing their cleavage and their bellybuttons to the world. And even the beggars who besiege tourists at the Gateway of India aren't the least bit embarrassed to show off their dance moves in public.

Neha and I arrived here less than twenty-four hours ago and already we are under Mumbai's spell. People say Mumbai is about money, as Delhi is about power, but that's not entirely true. Mumbai is ultimately about opportunity, a brash city of big dreams and rough ambition, which wears its heart on its sleeve. This is also a city of hyperbole, where everything is bigger, higher, faster. For those who live here, Mumbai is its own country. But, for the rest of India, it is a Siren, singing an irresistibly enticing song of glamour, glory and gold.

Neha is completely seduced by it. She can sniff her destiny in Mumbai's humid air. This is the city she was born to rule. And her ticket to success is *Popstar No. 1*, the singing talent contest that has brought us here.

We landed at VT station last evening by train from Delhi and were whisked away to Colaba, at the southern tip of the city. That is where we received our first shock. The accommodation provided us by the organisers was a dilapidated primary school. The classrooms have been converted into dormitories and we were put up in one with seven other outstation contestants and their chaperones. Neha was horrified at the thought of sharing a

room with a bunch of strangers and having to use communal toilets. She was probably expecting to be put up at
the Taj.

Today was an off day, for sightseeing. And we saw
everything, from the Hanging Gardens to Marine Drive
to Haji Ali. We passed by the slums of Dharavi and the
skyscrapers of Nariman Point. We travelled in the jam-
packed local trains where the crush of sweaty bodies
pressing in from all sides was almost overwhelming. We
peeped into the chawls – the tenements offering cheap,
basic accommodation – which were full of men in vests
who leaned casually on their balconies and watched street
life below. We had vada pav in Prabhadevi and bhel puri
in Juhu. And now we are in Chowpatty, the last stop
before heading back to Colaba.

The sheer size of Mumbai is breathtaking. It really is
maximum city, where the rich and the poor, the worldly
and the saintly, jostle each other every day, chasing that
same elusive dream of making it big.

Now the denizens of the city have been joined by forty
new contenders, the contestants of *Popstar No. 1*, all of
them between the ages of sixteen and twenty-two, each
one of them lured by the promise of overnight success
and instant fame.

That night I get my first introduction to the seven in our
dormitory.

Gaurav Karmahe is from Jharkhand, a state made
famous by M. S. Dhoni, the captain of the Indian cricket
team. A third-year student of mechanical engineering at
IIT-Kharagpur, he claims that singing is in his blood. 'You

just hear me sing, and you'll think Mohammad Rafi has been reincarnated in me,' he asserts.

Anita Patel is a bespectacled home-science student from Bhavnagar in Gujarat. Her spokesman is her father, a shrewd businessman with a calculative mind and a tendency to deal in big figures. 'When Anita wins the contest, she will get a recording contract and forty lakhs cash,' he says. 'I have decided to plough the forty lakhs into a fixed-income fund. At the end of twenty years we will get a minimum of two crores plus free life insurance. Not a bad investment, eh?'

Javed Ansari, the sixteen-year-old son of a rickshaw puller from Lucknow, exudes a boyish charm and a cocky confidence. 'I have been singing since I was five. It is my destiny that has brought me to Mumbai,' he tells me. 'I don't care if I win or not, but I am not going back to Lucknow after this. This is the city where I have to make my mark. And make my mark I will. Nothing can stop me.'

Eighteen-year-old Koyal Yadav is another child prodigy from the backwaters of Bihar. 'She started singing when she was just two years old. That is why we named her Koyal – cuckoo,' her mother says proudly. 'Her father is himself a well-known harmonium player who works with a Bhojpuri musical troupe. My daughter's kismat is very strong. I can sense something big in store for her.'

Jasbeer Deol is the only Sikh in the competition. He is a strapping teenager whose father runs a prosperous business in Ludhiana making woollen blankets. 'What made you decide to become a singer?' I ask him. 'Wouldn't you have done quite well in the family business?'

'I don't want money,' he answers frankly. 'I want recognition.'

'And why is that so?'

'See, my father has slaved for the last thirty years to earn his wealth. But even then his photo did not appear in the newspaper even once. I sang for just three minutes to win the regional audition and the very next day my photo was splashed in the local papers. What does this show? That it's better to be famous than rich.'

According to the rooming list given to us, there is another girl in the dormitory, nineteen-year-old Mercy, with no surname. I discover her hiding behind the curtain, a silver crucifix dangling from her neck. Dressed in a cheap cotton sari, she is frail-looking, with frizzy hair, crooked teeth and a face disfigured by leucoderma. The blotchy white patches give her skin an unhealthy pallor, as if it were made of wax that is slowly melting away.

'Where are you from?' I query her gently.

'Goa,' she replies, staring fixedly at her feet encased in worn-out rubber slippers.

'Who has come with you? Your father?'

'I don't have anyone,' she replies, shrinking in on herself, as if trying to make herself smaller than she already is.

Before I can probe her further, I am waylaid by Nisar Malik, a handsome seventeen year old, who has come all the way from Pahalgam in Kashmir. '*Didda*, would you lend me twenty rupees?'

'Why?' I raise my eyebrows. 'Don't you have any money?'

'No.' He shakes his head. 'I left my house three days

ago with just a hundred rupees in my pocket. Now I
don't even have a twenty-five-paise coin on me. Don't
worry, I'll return it to you with interest once I win.'

I reluctantly part with a twenty-rupee note. 'What
made you participate in the contest?'

'Just one thing – the desire for fame,' he says with
mournful earnestness. 'I don't want to live a life of
anonymity, *didda*. I'd rather die tomorrow as a famous
person than live a hundred years in obscurity.'

Hearing the painful convictions of these contestants,
the way they boast without irony, gets me thinking. What
is it that makes people so desperate to be famous? Why
this perpetual clawing for recognition, this obsession to be
noticed, to stand out from the crowd? I think it's a kind
of sickness, a virus in the blood, circulated by television.
And the infection has spread far and wide, from Kashmir
to Kanyakumari. Fame is no longer seen as a by-product
of talent, but as an end in itself. Everyone wants to
become an instant celebrity. And being on TV is the
quickest way to achieve this. That is why we have contestants willing to do just about anything to get on a
reality show. They will eat cockroaches, abuse their parents, have sex, get married, announce divorce and even
give birth on camera. Anything that can possibly be done
in real life is now being packaged as a reality show. And
the envelope is constantly being pushed. We now have a
show based on past-life regression, as if this life weren't
exciting enough.

I find reality TV as morbidly fascinating as watching a
car accident: you want to avert your eyes, but you cannot
help but be captured by what is taking place.

Neha is not thinking such thoughts. She is busy check-ing out the competition. 'If the rest of the field is like these idiots' – she flicks a contemptuous look around the room – 'I'll win hands down.'

I admire her steely self-confidence. But I also worry how she will handle failure. As with other TV contests, the winner of *Popstar No. 1* will be chosen ultimately by audience vote. And, as our politicians have learnt time and again, there is nothing more fickle than a voter.

The show begins in earnest the next day. We are all taken to Mehboob Studio in Bandra where the forty contestants are formally introduced to each other.

The set is retro chic, made to look like a classy night-club of the kind that used to be quite common in Hindi movies of the 1970s. Painted with a dark palette of red-dish brown, deep mauve and blue, it features a black, grooved, circular rotating stage modelled like a record from the 78-r.p.m. era. The *noir* atmosphere is accentu-ated by the dramatic lighting, hazy reds and purples that bathe the stage in a dreamlike glow. There are more than two hundred people in the studio audience, consisting of members of the general public and friends and relatives of the contestants.

The producer-cum-director is a tall, gangly hipster who looks like a reggae musician with his goatee and dreads. A Syrian Christian from Kerala, he goes by the name of Mathew George. Dressed in scuffed jeans and sneakers, he explains the ground rules to the contestants like a coach prepping a new team. 'The first thing you all must know is that *Popstar No. 1* is not a musical talent show. It is an entertainment show, a cross between *Bigg Boss* and *Indian Idol*. So I don't want just your songs: I also want your life, with all its messiness, sorrows, uncertainties, with all its beauty and ugliness. I want your tears, I want your fears. I want catfights, scandals, lovers' tiffs. I want your dark secrets, your dirty laundry. I want everything that you have within yourself to come screaming out, announcing to the world why you and only you deserve to become Popstar No. 1, and how you will stop at nothing to get there. Remember, the world only worships number one. It has no place for the number twos. History is severe upon the vanquished. So rise up, fight and claim your crown.'

He pauses and looks around at the contestants huddled backstage, some nervously biting their nails or tapping their feet. 'Do you get it?'

I don't know about the others, but Neha certainly got it. 'This is it, this is it, *didi*.' She grips my hand. 'I can feel it in my bones that I'm going to be the number one.'

'So do the thirty-nine others,' I sigh.

A short while later the judges troop in. They are the four 'Musical Gurus'. Heavily built Bashir Ahmad is the Bollywood music director *du jour*, having given music for a number of hit films as part of the Bashir–Omar duo. He also has a regrettable knack for self-promotion. Rohit Kalra is a well-known lyricist and ghazal singer, who had tried his hand at acting, and failed. Though now comfortably middle-aged, he still has a certain dissolute charm, emphasised by his long and rakish mane of hair. Udita Sapru provides the glam quotient, a nubile singer with a sultry voice who was herself discovered three years ago through a talent contest called *Song of Life*. And lastly there is Vinayak Raoji Wagh, wearing his trademark dark glasses. In his late fifties, Raoji is a regular fixture on singing talent contests. Regarded as a living legend, he is Bollywood's only blind musician, composer and singer. His pockmarked face is a vestige of a childhood disease, but the striking scar raked below his left eye is a legacy of the grisly incident that took away his vision. A deranged female fan attacked him with a knife at a concert six years ago, and almost gouged out his eyes. She then committed suicide by plunging the same knife into her own neck. Raoji lost his vision but not his spirit. He has continued to score music for films and is on track to be listed in *Guinness World Records* as the world's most prolific blind composer.

Once the gurus have taken their seats on the judges' podium, Mathew George explains the format of the contest. 'All forty contestants will be divided into four teams of ten, each mentored by a musical guru. Over the next two weeks we will have the direct elimination rounds, to select the twenty best contestants. And then the voting rounds will commence on live TV, allowing the public to choose, by the end of the year, the singer who will be crowned Popstar No. 1.'

He snaps his fingers and the houselights dim. A single spotlight flares up on the stage. Simultaneously the orchestra launches into the show's overture. 'Now I want each one of you to come here and perform a song of your choice, on the basis of which the judges will finalise the four teams.'

This is what I have been waiting for, a chance to see

if these pompous airheads have any singing ability at all. So I settle down with the rest of the audience as, one by one, the contestants take the stage in a predetermined order.

There's something transformative about being on stage in front of a crowd. I marvel at the curious alchemy by which these nobodies from dusty *mofussil* towns transmute into preening vocalists in the blink of an eye. The moment they stand in the spotlight and hold the mike in their hands, their entire body language changes. They are no longer engineers and farmers, students and salesgirls: they rise above their ordinariness to become performers on stage, the TV cameras endowing them with an instant halo of stardom.

Over the next three hours, I hear thirty-seven of them belt out all manner of songs to the accompaniment of a full orchestra. My impressions are decidedly mixed. Some clearly are trained singers who can hold a tune. And there are others with no musical talent at all. Their singing is so flat, it makes me wonder if they paid their way through the audition.

Then comes Neha's turn. She sings the title number from *City of Dust*. The judges – Raoji in particular – nod their heads, impressed as much by her vocal prowess as her stage command. She is easily the best so far, a rare combination of a good voice, a pretty face and a regal presence.

Neha is followed by Javed. The rickshaw-puller's son surprises everyone with his polished performance. He chooses a popular anthem from *Love in Bangkok* and almost immediately has the crowd screaming its approval and the judges tapping their feet in synchronised rhythm with the cadence of his rich baritone.

Neha begins to chafe as she is forced to acknowledge a competitor with 'star quality' that is superior to hers.

The crowd is still chanting 'Javed! Javed!' when, rising above the din, comes the delicate thread of an unearthly melody. It is the last contestant, the waiflike Mercy. Though her body is frail and slender, the sound that emerges from her lips is akin to a torrent of water flowing across parched desert sands. Her voice swells like a prayer, touching the deepest parts of my soul, transporting me to a celestial place of deep calm and bliss. The hall falls silent. It is the rapt silence of a crowd that knows it has stumbled onto something greater than itself, an experience that is special, almost magical.

I can see that the gurus are mesmerised by the unique timbre of her voice, but George is shaking his head in slow negation. Mercy doesn't stand a ghost of a chance of being crowned Popstar No.1. She may have the voice of a goddess, but she has the personality of a potted plant.

Having listened to all the singers, the judges go into a huddle. The contestants are on tenterhooks, like jittery high school students awaiting their board exam results. Everyone, it seems, wants to be in either Bashir Ahmad's team or Raoji's. They are the music directors who can give a new singer a much-needed break in films.

When the results are finally declared, there is gloom in some quarters and jubilation in others. Javed has been chosen by Bashir Ahmad to be a part of his team. Mercy goes to Udita, Nisar Malik, the Kashmiri, to Rohit Kalra. And my sister is taken under the wings of the blind Raoji.

Neha is ecstatic. 'I can't believe I will be learning from a musician of Raoji's calibre.'

The next day the veteran music director invites all ten of his team members to his palatial, three-storey bungalow in Juhu, where he has his own private recording studio. A lifelong bachelor, Raoji lives all alone with an ancient manservant who looks half-blind himself. The recording studio is ultra-modern, complete with banks of synthe-sisers. Pretty soon an impromptu rehearsal commences. Someone begins playing a harmonium, another picks up a guitar. I begin to feel like a groupie at a backstage party as the strains of ragas fill the air.

Raoji patiently hears everyone and singles out Neha for special praise. 'I can sense the presence of goddess Saraswati in your voice. You will go very far, my girl.'

Neha bends down and touches his feet. 'I want to be your disciple and imbibe all the knowledge you possess, Guru-ji.'

'So you shall. But don't forget my *gurudakshina*,' he laughs, referring to the tradition of repaying one's teacher after the completion of study.

I know blind people have a sixth sense, but the way Raoji says it, tilting his head and looking straight at Neha, for a moment it feels as if he could actually see her.

That night, Mercy seeks me out at dinnertime. 'Tell your sister to be careful of Raoji,' she says cryptically.

'Do you know something that we don't know?' I press her.

She bites her lip and does not answer.

*

Once the teams have been formed, the eliminations begin
in that same tired and predictable format I have seen on
countless reality contests. In every session four singers are
chosen, one from each group. They are asked to perform
a song selected by their own guru. Then the other judges
critique the performance, and the weakest among them is
eliminated. It is the equivalent of sudden death; there is
no second chance for the eliminated.

Pankaj Rane, a twenty-two-year-old medical repre-
sentative from Nagpur with limited talent and even less
personality, is the first to be shown the door. He breaks
down, starts wailing inconsolably. The cameras zoom in
on his tear-streaked face. I can see Mathew George grinning. This is exactly what he wants.

It makes me sad for these young contestants and their
blind ambition. The show will embrace just one winner.
The rest it will chew on and spit out, leaving behind the
burned rubble of vandalised hopes and broken dreams.
These wannabes who have come with stars in their eyes
will suddenly find themselves on the footpath, forgotten
and all alone.

George is right. This is not a talent show. It is a trashy
reality competition.

Two days later, Raoji sends his car to fetch Neha for a
rehearsal session. I decide to tag along. We arrive at his
residence to discover that we are the only ones; he has not
invited any of the remaining seven team members.

'Why this favour just for Neha?' I enquire gently once
we are settled into his recording studio.

'Your sister will sail through the elimination rounds,' he

answers. 'Now I need to start grooming her for the second phase, when the entire country will be voting. If Neha chooses the right songs, she has every chance of becoming Popstar No. 1.'

This is exactly what Neha wants to hear. 'Which songs do you recommend, Guru-ji?' She flutters her eyelashes at the blind musician, sounding like an overeager schoolgirl desperate for approval.

'Let's begin with the classical "Kuhu Kuhu Bole Koyaliya" – "The Cuckoo Goes Coo Coo".'

I recall this as a really obscure song from the 1958 film *Swarna Sundari*. To my surprise, Neha knows it. She launches into the song with her usual gusto, but her voice falters, fails to catch the high notes.

Raoji beats his fist against his palm and cries, 'No! No! No!'

Neha stops in mid-bar. 'What happened, Guru-ji?'

'This song is beyond you,' he says flatly. 'It is one of the most difficult songs to master because its four verses are based on four different ragas. Only an extremely versatile vocalist can negotiate the transitions between these ragas without creating a break or going off-note. You are not in that class at the moment. But with constant practice you will be.'

Having administered the putdown, he softens. 'Okay, let's try a lighter number. How about that Udita Sapru song "It's Raining"?'

Neha brightens. 'That's one of my favourite numbers,' she says. This time she takes charge from the beginning, crooning her way through the catchy and mostly up-tempo beat, her voice climbing effortlessly up and down the scales.

Raoji claps when she finishes. 'Wah! That was perfect! Now come and stand before me. I want to see you.'

Neha moves towards him hesitantly. 'But ... but you cannot see, sir.'

'A blind man does not see with his eyes, but with his hands,' he says and begins gently tracing his fingertips over Neha's face, as if memorising every dip and curve. A frisson of unease goes off in my stomach as his palm continues to roam, moving down to her neck, going lower and lower till it is almost to the swell of her bosom.

Neha's breath is trapped in her throat, her body frozen in place. She sees me about to intervene and raises a warning hand at me. I have to grip the armrest and clamp my lips to stop myself from shattering that terrifying silence. A moment later, Raoji withdraws his hand. 'I have now seen you,' he declares. 'You are as beautiful as your voice.'

Neha winks at me, the corners of her mouth tilted in predatory amusement.

Later, as we are being driven back to Colaba by Raoji's driver, Neha bursts into hysterical, uncontrollable laughter. 'How pathetic was that?'

'It's no laughing matter,' I say sternly. 'He was definitely trying to paw you.'

'It's all right, *didi*.' Neha dismisses my fears with a haughty hand. 'Let's not make this out to be the casting couch. That poor blind man just wanted a little human contact. I really pity him. Imagine having to fumble through your life in complete darkness, with no colour, no shape, no hope.' She shudders as though the thought itself made her sick. 'I'd sooner die than live such a life.'

'Something about Raoji doesn't seem right to me,' I persist. 'From now on you shouldn't allow him to come near you.'

'On the contrary, I must stay close to him,' Neha asserts. 'It's not often that you get a chance to help a blind man. And his blessings certainly won't harm my prospects of winning the contest.'

I can only shake my head at her calculative insouciance, knowing that I have a doubly difficult task on my hands. Not only do I have to save Neha from Raoji, I have to save my sister from herself.

The rest of the week passes in a whirl of rehearsals, performances, wardrobe changes and photoshoots. Those who are eliminated pretend to smile through their tears. The survivors thank their good fortune and trade words of encouragement.

I don't have much to do: I'm simply a cheerleader for Neha. With all the free time on my hands, my thoughts stray invariably to Karan. We speak on the phone almost every other day. 'When are you coming back?' he asks. 'I'm suffering from an acute deficiency of Vitamin-S.' Whenever I hear his low, smooth voice my pulse quickens. Memories of that night I kissed him come flooding back to me. The only poetry I write these days comes from moments of unspeakable emotion, when my pen begins to bleed with the unbearable agony of separation and the raw pain of longing. Is it a response to all the mushy love songs I have been hearing the contestants sing? Or am I really falling in love? Karan is funny. He's smart. He's gorgeous. He's the perfect man for me. But the closer I get to him, the more I feel like he's keeping something from me. And my traitor's mind begins to whisper its poisonous doubts, creating that sudden sinking feeling in my gut. Am I good enough for him? Just because we spend hours in conversation, it doesn't mean he's in love with me. If he were, wouldn't he have responded to my kiss?

To take my mind off this troublesome fancy, I begin spending time with Mercy. Of all the contestants, she intrigues me the most. Her swooping soprano and mellow contralto are burned into my ears. But, beyond her voice, it is her eyes that speak to me. They always seem to be on the verge of tears, as though there were a perpetually bubbling fountain of sadness inside her heart.

She is a loner, forever trying to avoid company. Whenever I see her sitting all alone, it reminds me of a whipped dog cowering in a corner.

'Why did you decide to come on this show?' I ask her one night. 'To become Popstar No. 1 you need looks more than voice.'

Even though she is good at hiding her true feelings, I manage to get through her defences this time. 'I came to see Raoji,' she blurts out.

I am taken aback. 'Came to see Raoji? What kind of strange reason is that?'

Bit by bit the story tumbles out of her, and I learn the ugly truth about Raoji. Mercy's elder sister, Gracie Fernandez, was an aspiring singer who came to Mumbai eight years ago from Goa. Raoji became her mentor and began training her. Soon he forced her into a physical relationship. But, the moment Gracie became pregnant with his child, Raoji became an entirely different person. He called her a whore, refused to marry her. Gracie begged him to reconsider, but he disregarded all her pleas. Mercy's sister then made the fatal mistake of threatening to go to the press. Raoji became enraged. He beat her black and blue with his belt, said he would kill her. Gracie suffered a miscarriage and had to remain in hospital for six weeks. When she came out, she was consumed by revenge. It was she who attacked Raoji with a knife during a concert six years ago.

'My sister wasn't mad,' Mercy concludes, tears budding at the corners of her eyes. 'She was left with no other option by this man. The world thinks Gracie committed suicide, but it was actually murder. Raoji forced her to take her own life.'

'Then why didn't these facts come out?'

'Because my sister was a nobody from Goa, and Raoji has money and power. He bribed the police, hushed up everything.'

'So have you come here to kill Raoji, to take revenge?'

'No.' She shivers, holding up her crucifix. 'As Jesus is my witness, I'm not capable of killing a fly. Justice and revenge are best left to God.'

'Then what's the plan?'

'There is no plan. When I heard Raoji was going to be a judge on this show, I decided to enter it. I simply wanted to see the man who destroyed my sister's life. She was my guru; she taught me how to sing. Her dream was to see me win a singing contest. I didn't come on the show to avenge her, simply to honour her.'

'And what about Raoji?'

'He will eventually be judged in Christ's court.'

Listening to this tragic tale, I can't help admire Mercy's forbearance. If I were in her shoes, I don't think I could have looked at Raoji's face without wanting to spit on it. And neither would I have had the patience to wait for God's judgement.

Gracie's story not only moves me, it also strengthens my growing suspicion of the music director. 'From now on you are not to meet Raoji in any circumstance,' I instruct Neha. 'Once a sadist, always a sadist in my book.'

'This is stupid,' Neha fumes. 'He's my guru, for God's sake. And he has called me tonight for a final rehearsal.'

'Tell him you won't come.'

'And miss out on the title of Popstar No. 1? Don't talk nonsense, *didi*. Besides, what can a blind man do to me? I am definitely keeping the appointment.'

'If you must go, then I insist on coming along.'

Raoji meets us on the terrace of his house. It is a cool and breezy night. A full moon shines in the cloudless sky, illuminating the enormous mansion.

Dressed in a silk kurta pyjama, the music director is his usual charming self, but I cannot look at him now without a shudder of loathing for what he did to Mercy's sister.

Neha looks lovely in a soft, pink, crêpe salvar suit she bought yesterday from Crawford Market. The chiffon dupatta alone cost me eight hundred rupees.

Raoji's manservant enters with a tray bearing drinks. I have asked for an orange juice, Neha a Diet Coke. Raoji's preferred poison, I have learnt, is Talisker single-malt whisky. 'Tonight I will give Neha my greatest lesson,' he says somewhat mysteriously, filling his glass with dark golden liquid. 'We are almost at the end of the first stage. Tomorrow is the final elimination round. After that, Neha, you will be unstoppable. Cheers!' He raises his glass in salute and downs the liquor in two swigs.

Neha gets into an involved discussion with Raoji on singing technique. I stroll to the edge of the terrace, rest my elbows on the ornate stone balustrade and look out over the vast conurbation stretching beyond the rippling velvet of the ocean. Mumbai's skyline looks spectacular at night. Glittering, sparkling lights blanket the city, glowing with the luminescence of a mirage. Neon signs blaze softly on the high-rise buildings along the seafront. The markets are alive with the sound of commerce. Cars are still racing on the streets down below. This is truly the city that never sleeps.

The air is bathed in the intoxicating fragrance of a night-blooming jasmine growing in a pot. It mixes with the damp, salty smell of the ocean, making me drowsy. I take another sip of the juice. It tastes a bit funny. Suddenly my head starts aching, my knees go all weak. I feel as if I'm about to vomit and rush into the toilet at the far end of the terrace.

I stumble to the wash basin, where I look into the mirror. My eyes seem unusually heavy-lidded. Waves of sleep assault my mind, one after another. I feel lethargic and nauseous. It takes a superhuman effort to splash water on my face. I try to blink the world in front of me back into focus, but my head refuses to clear. I lean against the wall and try to make sense of what is happening to me.

Raoji must have told his servant to spike my drink, I realise. I can see him now from the window, patting Neha on the back. In my distorted vision he becomes double, then triple, and keeps on multiplying till my mind is filled with the hallucination of a ten-headed Raoji, grinning evilly like the demon Ravan.

'Let's go down to the studio,' I hear, as a distant echo. 'Will you guide me?'

Through blurry pupils I watch Neha take Raoji's arm and lead him towards the staircase. 'Don't!' I want to cry out, gripped by a terrible prescience of imminent danger, but find that I cannot move or speak. It is as if I had been hypnotised, put in a trance. My brain does not feel connected to my body any longer.

I fight off the creeping paralysis and stagger out of the toilet. Raoji and Neha have already gone, leaving behind a bowl of salted cashew nuts.

My head sags down and my body turns so limp, I can barely lift my head. I know I am about to keel over like a hopeless drunk. That is when my eyes fall on the half-empty bottle of Talisker Scotch glinting on the table. I grab it in my hands. It feels as though it weighs a ton. Summoning up all my reserves of energy, I lift it above my head and smash it down on the concrete floor, where it shatters into pieces. The pungent smell of whisky fills the air. I am left with just the stem of the bottle in my hand, with sharp jagged teeth where it broke off. Still wobbling with dizziness, I take a deep breath and plunge the jagged end into my left thigh like a dagger. It goes through the thin fabric of my salvar to pierce the skin. Hot, searing, excruciating pain shoots through my leg, and radiates throughout my body, clearing the fog in my brain in an instant, awakening all my senses.

Ignoring the stabbing agony in my thigh, I hobble down the staircase, tear through the drawing room and burst into the recording studio to discover Neha and Raoji entwined on a couch. The musician has clamped his arms around her waist, pinning her arms at her sides. He is trying to kiss her as she is struggling desperately to wrestle free of his passionate embrace.

'Raoji!' I scream and wrench Neha from his grip.

He lets go of her, heaving like a man about to have a heart attack. Spit is dribbling out of his mouth and the veins on his face are engorged. 'Go, Neha!' he snaps. 'I was only trying to help you. But you are not worthy of my attention.'

I am on fire, burning with indignation. I sweep Neha aside with my hand, and lash out at him with my right leg. The next instant his face contorts in shocked pain as my heel slams into his solar plexus. 'Bitch!' He lets out a strangled groan, clutching at his stomach.

My fury is building up to a crescendo. 'You don't deserve to live, you pig!' I swing a fist at him, but with amazingly quick reflexes he catches my arm in midair. He spins me around, pushing my face into the wall and twisting my arm to breaking point. I writhe in agony. 'I can crush you like a fly,' he hisses into my ear. Then, equally abruptly, he releases me.

'No more rehearsals now!' he says, by way of dismissal. 'Get out of my house, both of you.'

*

Neha is badly shaken by the incident. I can almost feel the shame, horror and revulsion sweeping through her like a desert storm as she sits with me in the taxi taking us back to Colaba. 'He ... he tried to t-touch me,' she says, faltering. 'You were right about him, *didi*.' She buries her face in my lap, dissolving into tears.

'Don't worry. Everything will be all right,' I say soothingly, stroking her hair.

Her hand accidentally grazes my thigh, where she discovers a sticky wet patch on my salvar. The blood is still seeping through the wound.

'Oh my God, you're bleeding, *didi*,' she cries. The throbbing pain, which the adrenaline in my system had dammed up till now, comes searing back. The flesh stings like a touch of acid.

Without a moment's hesitation Neha tears off her brand-new dupatta and fashions it into a bandage, which she wraps around the wound, staunching the flow of blood.

Sitting in the back of that taxi, we discover each other anew. For perhaps the first time in my life, I see Neha in a new light, truly connect with her. I sense the pulsing of the deeper and warmer heart she has kept hidden beneath that narcissistic veneer of self-centredness, shallowness and superficiality.

'I always felt you loved Alka more than me,' Neha says, her voice pained with all the pent-up hurt and bitterness she has accumulated over the years. 'But not any more.'

It is turning out to be a night of surprises, of confessions and revelations. 'I always thought you would do anything for fame,' I respond with equal candidness. 'But not any more.'

We hug each other, like two survivors in a flood drifting on the same log of wood.

Life does not give us the option of choosing a blood relationship, but it always gives us the opportunity to repair it.

Neha continues to cling to me even after we reach the safety of the dormitory. Her forehead feels feverish. Mercy helps me tuck her into bed. As I turn to leave, Neha clutches at my arm. 'Where are you going now, *didi*?'

'To the police station, to lodge a report against Raoji. He tried to drug me, to molest you.'

'No, *didi*.' Neha springs out of bed and bars my way. 'I will not allow you to do that.'

'But why?'

'It will destroy my chances of winning the contest.'

'Are you crazy? You're still thinking of the contest after what he did to you?'

'Look, I'll tell George to change my team after this round. I'll have nothing to do with that swine Raoji any more. But I don't want to miss this chance. I'm almost there. Once I make it to the last twenty, even Raoji won't be able to stop me. Don't take away my only hope, my one dream, *didi*.' She starts sobbing again.

I give in. 'All right. I'll not report Raoji if that's what you want.'

Mercy, who has been overhearing our conversation, is more concerned about the wound on my leg. 'You need to see a doctor, *didi*. If not treated soon, the infected area can become septic.'

She accompanies me to a nearby clinic, where a nurse cleans the wound and disinfects it. Our route passes through a bustling street market. On the way back, we come across an inspector wearing the uniform of Maharashtra Police. He is busy negotiating with a toy vendor, his Rajdoot motorcycle purring like a wildcat on the side of the road.

Mercy tries to propel me gently in the officer's direction. 'We can still go to the police.'

'I can't. I've promised Neha.'

She grips my arm. 'We shouldn't allow Raoji to get away again, *didi*.' Her eyes burn with a dark fire, like black lava from a volcano that has erupted inside her.

I gaze at her, at the toyshop, and an idea flashes across my mind.

'I have a plan,' I whisper to her.

'Tell me,' she whispers back.

There is an electric charge in the air. It is the final round of eliminations. Today the last two singers will be shown the door, leaving the twenty contestants who will fight it out for the coveted crown on live television.

I wait with the rest of the audience, as the tension builds to a peak.

One by one, the judges announce the names of today's contestants. It is like a game of chess; the trick is to anticipate your opponents' move. The judges try to protect their assets, pit their best singers against weaker opponents and checkmate the other teams.

'I nominate Javed,' Bashir Ahmad declares. A ripple of excitement goes through the audience. Javed Ansari is the clear favourite till now. Bashir's move is a queen's gambit.

'I select Sujata Meena,' says Udita Sapru. Sujata is an earthy singer with a throaty voice. She is the equivalent of the horse, the joker in the pack, capable of causing an upset.

'My warrior is Nisar Malik,' says Rohit Kalra. The Kashmiri is not the best singer in his team. He is a pawn who can be sacrificed.

'And I field Neha,' announces Raoji. A gasp escapes from everybody's lips. A face-off between Javed and Neha makes no sense at this preliminary stage. It is like pitting two queens against each other in the opening gambit itself.

The four contestants line up on stage and the elimination round begins.

Bashir Ahmad chooses a powerful love song for Javed, and his protégé delivers it flawlessly, wowing everyone with the range, intensity and raw expressive power of his voice.

Sujata Meena's forte is folk songs, and her guru allows her to sing to her strengths. The Rajasthani ballad that she belts out has the audience entranced, her gutsy, free-wheeling voice a compelling counterpoint to the calculated perfection of Neha's vocal style.

Nisar Malik's rendition of a tragic Kishore Kumar song is also surprisingly impressive, dripping with the melancholy of heartbreak and disappointment.

And then it is Neha's turn. Everybody looks at Raoji expectantly. Neha waits on stage with an angelic smile, but I know she must be having butterflies in her stomach. The only thing that matters to her is winning this contest. And this is the make-or-break moment.

Raoji clears his throat. 'Neha is my best singer, so I will give her a song that showcases her full vocal range.' His face is expressionless under his dark glasses as he tells Neha, '*Beti*, I want you to sing "Kuhu Kuhu Bole Koyaliya".'

I am stunned. The taut grimace that skews Neha's mouth tells me even she wasn't expecting this. Raoji has set a clever trap. Unfortunately, there is no way for my sister to avoid it. She tries bravely to carry the song, but yesterday's ordeal has left her underpowered. Her notes sound a little tired and pinched. Once again, the upper register in the song's most difficult *antara* strains her voice, which sags towards flatness.

The result is a foregone conclusion. In the judges' reckoning, as also in that of the audience, Neha is the weakest singer of the lot. She gets eliminated.

A solemn hush falls over the audience as it comes to grips with the humbling realisation that one of the early favourites has bitten the dust. Neha is stony-faced, accepting the verdict with stoic resignation.

The final elimination round begins almost immediately thereafter, one that pits Mercy against three other singers, all much inferior to her.

Udita Sapru asks Mercy to sing 'Aye Mere Watan Ke Logon' ('O! The People of my Country'), a patriotic song by Lata Mangeshkar, which is revered as the ultimate tribute to the fallen Indian soldiers of the 1962 war with China. Today, Mercy surpasses herself. She breaks through her frozen depths and sings with daring, gifted abandon.

The song acquires wings, as though liberated from its earthly confines. Her lilting voice soars upwards to the heavens, sweeping away the orchestra, the judges, the audience, everything in its path. Imbued with the exquisite agony of loss, the dirge becomes almost like a catharsis, an elegy for her fallen sister. I get goosebumps hearing her notes reach a purity of perfection unmatched in the history of the contest.

The song over, she withdraws into her shell, flushed like an exhausted runner. The judges whisper among themselves, make embarrassed eye contact with the producer. It is clear they are devising strategies to justify eliminating her from the contest.

Bashir Ahmad takes a sip of water from the glass in front of him before announcing his verdict. 'It was a ... er ... good performance. You are obviously talented. But I don't think you are ready for the next level. There is a rawness in your voice which needs polishing.'

Rohit Kalra finds fault with her deadpan expression and her awkwardness. 'Singing is not just about nailing the notes,' he observes. 'It's also about how you convey your message to the audience.'

Raoji discovers an imaginary lapse in concentration in the penultimate stanza. 'That one little blemish spoilt the entire performance for me. But I tell you what: you do a little more *riyaaz* – a little more practice – and no one can stop you from winning next year's contest.'

'Thank you, sir,' Mercy squeaks. 'I need your blessing.'

'I shall deliver it personally,' says Raoji. He leaves the judges' podium and shuffles towards the stage, feeling his way forward with his stick. Mathew George guides him up the steps. Mercy stands with her head bowed as Raoji approaches her. When he is barely ten paces away, she springs to her feet with a silent cry, a knife appearing magically in her right hand. Under the stark red spotlight, the serrated blade seems to be soaked in blood.

A shocked gasp rises from the audience, and reverberates around the hall.

As Mercy arcs the knife at Raoji's chest, the music director instinctively extends his hands to protect himself. Discarding his stick, he leaps down from the stage with a stifled scream, his face a waxlike pastiche of panic.

An even bigger gasp of surprise emanates from the crowd.

'You ... you can *see?*' Bashir Ahmad notes, his jaw dropping open.

'That is true,' I say, clambering onto the stage and grabbing the mike. 'Mercy was not trying to kill Raoji, only to expose him.'

Mercy throws down the plastic toy knife I purchased last night from the street market, her chest heaving with emotion. She falls on her knees, crosses herself and kisses the crucifix around her neck. With tears running down her face, she lifts up her hands in prayer. 'Lord, have mercy on my sister's soul.'

'Raoji is not blind, at least not in both eyes,' I continue. 'He had kept up the pretence so that he could feel up young girls, lure them by sympathy and ultimately exploit them, like he exploited Mercy's sister Gracie, forcing her to kill herself. Last night he tried the same dirty trick with Neha. This evil man deserves to be publicly whipped.'

The crowd roars in approval.

Udita Sapru stands up suddenly. 'I cannot bear to stay in the same room as this monster,' she declares in a shaky voice, and then stalls, as though fighting with herself to continue. 'He ... he ... did this to me, too, when I was a contestant on *Song of Life*.'

The revelation is met with shock, astonishment and ultimately anger by the audience. A couple of men advance threateningly towards Raoji, who cowers in fear.

'Cut it!' Mathew George leaps out from his director's chair. 'I say, what's going on?' he asks no one in particular, struggling to maintain an air of professional calm.

'I should never have agreed to judge this third-rate contest.' Udita flashes a scornful look at him. 'I quit.'

'So do I,' says Bashir Ahmad.

'Me too,' says Rohit Kalra.

They walk out of the studio in a huff, leaving Raoji at the mercy of the hordes swarming at him from all sides.

Half an hour later, I discover Mathew George sitting forlornly on a bench, surveying the ruins of his set vandalised by the frenzied mob.

'What have you done?' the producer-cum-director screams at me. 'Raoji is in hospital with fifty broken bones. And my contest has ended even before it had begun.'

'Don't blame me,' I respond calmly. 'I only gave you what you wanted.'

'Why would I want to destroy my own show?' he cries, tearing at his dreads like a madman.

'You wanted our dirty laundry, our secrets and confessions. Well, I've given you a first-rate scandal. Enjoy.'

*

Neha and I take a train to Delhi the same afternoon. We spend the eighteen-hour journey in near complete silence, absorbed in our own thoughts. Karan's face hovers in my mind like a persistent fever dream. Neha is unnaturally subdued, with a faraway look in her eyes. 'No more singing contests for me,' she tells me. She has seen the true face of the world, at last, and it has shattered her illusions, doused her fiery ambitions of instant stardom.

There is a pleasant surprise in store for us the moment the train pulls into Paharganj station at seven a.m. the next day. Waiting on the platform is Karan Kant, holding an enormous bouquet of yellow carnations. I had informed him of our arrival, briefed him on the fiasco that was *Popstar No. 1*, but I never expected him to meet us at the station itself, and that too with a welcome gift. It melts away the failure and frustrations of Mumbai in an instant, makes me feel truly special.

He looks dashing in a striped polo shirt and khaki chinos. My face flushes and my heart almost lurches out of my throat as I step forward to receive the flowers.

To my utter astonishment, he slides past me and puts the bouquet into Neha's lap. 'Welcome back, Singing Queen.' He beams at her. It's a sweet gesture to cheer her up, but I cannot help feeling a trifle betrayed. A sickly surge of jealousy sours my gut as I watch Neha blush.

Perhaps Karan had anticipated my reaction, for he turns to me an instant later. 'And don't think I've forgotten you, madam.' He grins like a magician at the end of a trick, and whips out a single red rose encased in cellophane. He offers it to me with a grave little half-bow. Finding me still wrapped in confusion, he scratches his head and rolls his eyes. 'You don't like roses? Would you have preferred a steaming cup of tea?' Screwing up his face, he intones throatily, 'Chai! Chai garam!' mimicking the singsong voice of the mobile chai wallahs who stalked our compartment at every stop.

And I know then that he is the same old Karan. The Karan who hides his true feelings behind trite banalities. He remains as frustratingly inscrutable as before. Plus, now he has left me yet another riddle to solve. Is a single red rose worth more than a dozen yellow carnations?

Vinay Mohan Acharya summons me in the evening of the same day.

When I reach his front office on the fifteenth floor, I find a homely-looking South Indian girl sitting on the secretary's desk. 'Hello, Miss Sapna. I'm Revathi Balasubramaniam,' she greets me. Her cheeks dimple as she gives me a timid smile. Before I can even greet her back, the buzzer on her desk rings and I am ushered into the industrialist's presence.

'What happened to Jennifer?' I ask Acharya.

'I fired her,' he grimaces.

'Why?'

'She was the snake in our midst, passing on sensitive company information to the Premier Group.'

'My God!'

'It was Rana who exposed her. He managed to obtain the call records from her personal cell phone. We found plenty of calls to the private number of Ajay Krishna Acharya, the head of Premier Industries. It was especially intriguing to see calls made to my brother on the same night we finalised our quote for the national ID-card software tender.'

'So did you confront her?'

'She denied it, of course. Said someone must have forged the call records to frame her. But every thief denies being a thief.' He gazes pensively out of the bay window at the fading pink sky. 'An enemy I can forgive, but not a traitor,' he resumes in a hollow voice, as though in the grip of a powerful emotion. 'A mistake can be corrected, but, once trust is betrayed, it's gone for ever.'

I nod in silent assent.

'Anyway, I didn't call you here to complain about Jennifer, but to compliment you. You have passed the fourth test with flying colours.'

'And what test was that?'

'The test of foresight.'

'I don't understand. What did I do to show foresight?'

He taps the pile of newspapers lying on his desk. Almost all of them carry the exposé of Raoji on the front page. 'It took a blind man to reveal your strategic foresight. You had an inkling that something was not quite right about Raoji and you made an ingenious plan to unmask that charlatan. Bravo.'

'But how did you know of my role in the matter? None of the papers I have read mentions my name.'

'But they do mention a certain Mercy Fernandez. I got the full story from her. She told me how you were suspicious of Raoji from the beginning. And what you did to save your sister from his clutches.'

'How do you know Mercy?'

'We've just hired her as a voice-dubbing artist in our films division.'

'She'll do very well. She has the voice of an angel.'

'But does she have the vision of a seer? I believe that the only way to prepare for the future is to plan for it. Those who fail to plan, plan to fail. Foresight is the art of reading a situation astutely and anticipating events. It is critical to an organisation's success. Thirty-five years ago I saw my first computer, the Commodore PET, and I knew instinctively that this machine would change the way we do things in our everyday life. That is when I made my initial foray into the computer business. Today ABC Computers controls 32 per cent of the PC hardware market in India.'

He drones on for another fifteen minutes on his favourite topic – himself – but I've already tuned out. His childish vanity does not make me wince as much as his misplaced belief in my abilities. How I wish I had foresight. Then I would never have let Alka take her life.

The world is full of godmen and astrologers who claim to know the future. But no one really does. The future is a mystery that is never revealed to us completely; it can only be glimpsed dimly in our dreams and imagination. Foresight is just a glorified name given to the process of drawing lessons from yesterday's failures and successes to plan for a better tomorrow. It's a process humans have been pursuing since the dawn of history. And it's called survival.

The Fifth Test

The Atlas of Revolution

It seems like a cross between Diwali and Independence Day. There are fireworks going off all over the city and the streets are jammed with slow-moving cars honking in approval, trucks full of boisterous tricolour-waving fans and crowds of pedestrians dancing and shouting 'Long Live India!' and 'Jai Ho!'

Even though it is close to midnight, no one in our colony wants to sleep. Neha and I are also caught up in the excitement of India's victory over Pakistan in the semifinal of the Cricket World Cup, billed as 'the mother of all matches' by the hyperbolic media. All through the evening we were glued to the TV set, on edge until the last over, and then, as the final Pakistani wicket fell, the entire colony erupted in a thunderous celebration of ear-splitting whistles, deafening cheers and riotous applause. Mr J. P. Aggarwal, a cricket-crazy hardware dealer in apartment B-27, immediately trotted off to the market and returned with a big bowl of rasagullas for distribution among his neighbours on the second floor. Even Ma, who finds cricket about as much fun as waxing one's legs, joined in the revelry, unobtrusively slipping a juicy rasagulla into her mouth, ignoring her chronic diabetes and the stern warning of her physician, Dr Mittal, to avoid all sweets.

There is one neighbour, though, who remains entirely aloof from all the hoopla. That is Nirmala Ben in B-25, our resident Gandhian. I find her sitting all alone in her room with a book of Bapu's quotes in her lap, gazing at the wall like a prophet awaiting a revelation.

'Nirmala Ben, what are you doing here when the entire colony is celebrating India's victory?'

'Spare me this madness,' she replies tersely.

'Oh, come on, don't be such a spoilsport. We're all going to the roof to watch the fireworks.'

She reacts as though I have touched a raw nerve. 'Do you have any idea how many crores we waste in these firecrackers? When millions go to sleep on empty stomachs, when thousands of children die for want of medicines, when entire families live on footpaths because they cannot afford a house, it is the height of folly to blow up money in smoke. And this World Cup, what will it get us? Will it remove poverty and illiteracy from our country? Will it stop farmers from committing suicide? The other day Kalawati's son Suresh was telling me he prays every day for India's victory in the World Cup. I pray for good sense to prevail on my countrymen. *Sabko Sanmati De Bhagwan.*'

Taken aback by her outburst, I struggle for a response.

'What is happening in our country these days is truly frightening,' she continues. 'Scam after scam is taking place, all masterminded by Atlas, and no one seems to have any clue as to the identity of the man behind this company. *Arrey*, did this Atlas come from the moon or some other world? Is he invisible like God?'

'They say Atlas is also behind the fake housing-loan scam that the CBI unearthed last week,' I add, recalling the lead item in today's news.

'*Bahut thaigyoo*. Enough is enough,' she declares. 'I cannot just sit back and watch this loot and plunder of national wealth. This isn't what Bapu fought and died for.'

'And what do you propose to do?'

'I was still searching for a way, till a seer from Rishikesh came to see me and illuminated my path.'

'What did he say?'

'"Shake the world gently", he told me.'

'And how do you propose to do that?'

'I will launch a people's revolution. That is the only way of stamping out the cancer of corruption and expos- ing the forces behind Atlas.'

'So are you going to take out a rally or something?'

'No. I will sit on a fast unto death till the government concedes my demand for a thorough probe into Atlas Investments.'

The alarm bell in my head begins ringing instantly. I try to dissuade her. 'Don't do this, Nirmala Ben. A fast unto death is not a one-day token agitation.'

'Who said it was?' she replies, surprised at my remark. 'There are only two results possible when a *satyagrahi* resorts to a fast unto death. Either the government will have to bend, or it will have to remove my dead body. A revolution, after all, demands a martyr.'

'A revolution also needs followers, and an organisation. You have neither.'

'But I have myself.' She smiles as though emphasising the self-evident nature of her statement. 'And if you have yourself you don't need anyone else. It takes just one person to make a difference.' In a soft mellow voice she begins singing, '*Jodi tor dak shune keu na ashe tobe ekla cholo re*' ('If they answer not to thy call, walk alone'), from a Bengali song by Rabindranath Tagore, which was a favourite of Gandhi's.

As her soulful voice fills the room, I am left hoping she will not carry out her pledge to walk alone. Because, however good a singer Mrs Nirmala Mukherjee Shah may be, her lone voice will not be sufficient to shake the world gently.

Friday, 1 April, begins like a normal day of work. My first customer of the morning is an overly polite Sikh businessman with a well-kept beard and moustache. He has almost decided on buying a Panasonic Viera 50-inch plasma TV. 'It's for my son Randeep,' he tells me. 'The boy insists he will watch tomorrow's World Cup final only on a big-screen TV.' I nod sympathetically and begin explaining the merits of an extended warranty to him, when my Indus cell phone buzzes.

I pull the phone out of my skirt pocket and frown at the screen. These days, 70 per cent of calls on my cell are by unsolicited telemarketers and when I see a number I don't recognise I usually don't even bother to answer. The caller ID displays a landline number starting with +22, the code for Mumbai. Intrigued, I press the talk button. 'Hello.'

'Hello, can I speak to Miss Sapna Sinha?' says a familiar-sounding voice on the other end.

'This is Sapna.'

'Sapna-ji, I am Salim Ilyasi, calling you from Mumbai.'

Of course! How could I forget that deep, masculine voice, which has seduced millions of filmgoers. Salim Ilyasi is the reigning King of Bollywood and the heartthrob of practically every young girl in India. That the superstar would deign to speak to me out of the blue sounds strange, but so many strange things have been happening to me lately that nothing truly surprises me any longer.

'Congratulations! You have been selected as Indus Mobile's lucky customer of the month. Which means you will be having an exclusive dinner with me on Sunday, the tenth of April, at the Maurya Sheraton in Delhi. Do we have a date?'

Salim Ilyasi wants to have dinner with me. *Me?* A tidal wave of euphoria surges through my body, sweeping away every rational thought in my head. I have always fancied myself as a hardboiled realist, immune to the cult of celebrity. But in that extravagant moment my brain collapses into a quivering mass of jelly. Which contest was Indus running? How did I manage to win it? All such mundane considerations go out of the window as I regress into adolescent schoolgirl fantasies of hero worship. 'Y-yes,' I blabber, feeling a flush spreading over my skin. 'I . . . I . . . would love that.'

'Now that's what I call funtaastik,' he exults, repeating an expression he made famous in *Love in Bangkok*. 'But there is one problem. How will I recognise you?'

'I . . . I will wear something distinctive.'

'Yes. Do that. My favourite colour is yellow. Do you have something in yellow?'

I think quickly, rotating through my meagre salvar suit collection in my head. 'Er . . . I don't think I have a yellow outfit, but I can buy one.'

'No need to do that. I'll tell you what. You wear whatever you want. Just attach a little yellow Post-it at the top.'

'Post-it?'

'Yes, with the letters A–P–R–I–L–F–O–O–L imprinted on it. You got that?'

It is only then that I get it. 'Karan Kant, it is you, isn't it?'

A hearty chuckle emanates from the other end of the line. 'Fooled you, didn't I?'

I can almost picture him rolling on the floor, clutching his belly with laughter. My own naïveté, my utter credulousness, makes me cringe.

'I'm going to kill you!' I scream at Karan.

'Now that won't be so funtaastik,' he says by way of a parting repartee before ending the call.

As I stash away my cell phone, I find my first customer of the day scurrying towards the exit. 'Hey, Mr Singh! Where are you off to?' I call out to him.

He pauses momentarily and gives me the derisive, pitying look that a sane person gives a lunatic. Then he bolts out the door.

*

Karan has a twinkle in his eyes when I encounter him in the colony's courtyard later that evening.

'You cheat!' I punch him playfully in the ribs. 'Your impersonation of Salim Ilyasi was so spot on, I didn't think for a second it could be someone else.'

'Well, if it's any consolation to you, I tried the same prank with ten other Indus customers. They didn't catch on either. We had a good laugh in the call centre over my April Fool joke.'

'But how could you fake the Mumbai number? That's what made me believe the call was genuine.'

'It's called spoofing. Since we control the network, we can make any number appear on our customers' caller IDs.'

Just then Neha wanders in. 'What are you doing here?' she addresses Karan. 'They are looking for you all over the place.'

'Who?' asks Karan.

'The police. There's an inspector with two constables.'

'What?' he croaks, his face tight with worry.

'Why would the police be looking for you?' I wonder, my voice dripping with concern.

'I have no idea. There ... there is bound to be some kind of mistake.'

'Anyway, you better go and sort it out,' says Neha. 'They are banging on your door, about to break it down.'

'No!' Karan lets out an anguished scream. 'Don't allow them to enter my room.' He charges up the stairs, two at a time, loping with an athlete's long strides. Neha and I follow him in hot pursuit.

I am completely exhausted by the time we wheeze onto the tiny landing of the third floor. Karan turns the corner, beyond which lies apartment B–35, and freezes. There is no one in the corridor.

'Looks like the police have already gone inside,' says Neha.

'Oh, no!' Karan murmurs, stepping back into the shadows, and pressing his back against the wall.

'Don't you want to check?' I ask, prodding him.

With uncertain steps he approaches his door. Only then does he see the poster stuck just below the peephole. It shows a jester holding up a placard which reads, 'HAPPY APRIL FOOLS' DAY!'

'Gotcha!' Neha lets out a triumphant whoop as Karan begins scratching his head in embarrassed chagrin. 'Two can play at a game.' She gives him a meaningful glance before hurrying down the stairs.

'Neha Sinha, you'll pay for this,' Karan growls in the voice of Prakash Puri, the famous villain, and scrambles behind her, giving chase.

I watch this little byplay in amused, tolerant silence. Karan must have called Neha as well, pretending to be Salim Ilyasi, I realise. She has now got her own back. Then why does it feel as if the April Fool joke was on me?

The sun that rises on 2 April is a special one, carrying with it the hopes of a billion Indians. India is playing Sri Lanka in tonight's Cricket World Cup final, and the entire country is praying for the team's victory.

Cricket is the only subject of conversation in the

showroom. There is a feeling of surging excitement and expectation in the air. Such is the craze for the match that half the staff have taken leave to watch it.

Just after lunch, Madan summons me to his cubicle. 'I need a favour,' he says with a grin.

'What is it now?' I ask. 'Are you planning to send me to yet another village?'

'No, no, nothing like that. Someone has just ordered a Sony KDL-65. I need you to do an urgent HVD.'

HVD is store code for high-value delivery. It is the policy of Gulati & Sons that for any delivery above ₹200,000, a sales employee has to personally accompany the item to ensure that it has been delivered safely and obtain the customer's signature on a pre-installation checklist.

'You know I don't do deliveries,' I grumble. 'Why don't you send one of the boys?'

'Two of them are out and the remaining are on leave. Please, it'll take you just thirty minutes, and I can throw in a bonus.'

'What bonus?'

'After the delivery you can go home, watch the final.'

The offer is certainly tempting. 'What's the delivery address?'

He consults the order sheet. 'It says Plot Number 133-C, Poorvi Marg, Vasant Vihar.'

'What's the name of the customer?'

'That's not been told to me. Apparently it's a birthday gift for someone and they want to keep it hush-hush.'

'Fine,' I say. 'I'll do it.'

*

Ten minutes later I am sitting in the front seat of the delivery vehicle, a battered Bajaj Tempo, driven by Sharad, one of our oldest drivers. The forty-minute ride to the delivery address is bumpy, noisy and hot, the vehicle's air conditioning having long since conked out.

Vasant Vihar, in southwest Delhi, is reputed to be one of the most expensive residential areas in the world, and only millionaires can afford to live there. When we reach the delivery address, however, we discover that we have arrived at the residence of a billionaire.

A team of guards in blazers and sunglasses, equipped with walkie-talkies and earpiece microphones, stop us outside high automated gates bristling with security-camera systems. Our order sheet is carefully examined before we are allowed to proceed to the guard post, where there are further checks. The Tempo is scanned for hidden bombs and Sharad has to open his bonnet and boot for inspection. Finally, the gates are opened and we enter the grounds.

In the distance I can see a sprawling mansion of the kind showcased in Bollywood films, set on acres of land. To reach it we have to go through a long, curving drive-way with manicured hedges. Along the way I catch a glimpse of a couple of vicious-looking Dobermans teth-ered to a tree trunk. They begin to strain at their leashes the moment they see the Tempo. All this security makes me uncomfortable. It also makes me curious about the identity of the owner. The marble nameplate on the out-side wall mentioned only the name of the house: 'Prarthana' – 'Prayer' in Hindi.

The main residence itself is a grand, gaudy structure,

with Corinthian columns, Palladian windows and cascades of flowering bougainvillea pouring over French balconies. A liveried orderly opens a carved bronze door and I step into an opulent drawing room with gilded furniture, fine Persian carpets and even a grand piano.

'There you are.' A man rises from a sofa. 'Welcome to Prarthana.'

It is Vinay Mohan Acharya. 'What are *you* doing here?' I ask in astonishment.

'Receiving delivery of the TV set I ordered,' he deadpans. That is when I realise I have arrived at the industrialist's residence.

'So is it your birthday?'

'No. The TV was just an excuse to get you here.'

'What is it now? Which new test have I passed – or failed?' I ask peevishly.

'It's not about any test this time,' he replies. 'I called you here because I want you to attend a rather important business meeting I am about to have.'

'With whom?'

'You'll find out soon enough,' he says, and dismisses Sharad. 'You can leave. I'll have Miss Sinha dropped.'

For the next fifteen minutes he takes me on a guided tour of the property. I see the indoor swimming pool, the full-fledged gymnasium and the temple with statues of deities in gold and ivory. There are rooms upon rooms full of incredible antiques from all over the world and a magnificent art collection, including a mural in the dining room designed by Tyeb Mehta. Liveried servants hover about, ready to cater to every whim and need a guest may have.

'How many rooms does this place have?' I am curious to know as we enter the study.

'I've never counted, but, if you add all the servants' quarters on the edge of the compound, it must be close to fifty.'

The study is equally opulent, a high-ceilinged room with oak panelling, hardwood flooring and a mini-library full of leather-bound, antique-looking books. The double French glass doors overlook a lush, landscaped garden with marble fountains and travertine statues.

I have just sunk into a luxurious, high-backed chair when an intercom buzzes. It's the security at the gate, informing him that his visitor has arrived.

'Send him through,' Acharya says.

'I've never seen so much security at a private residence,' I observe wryly.

'Delhi is an unsafe city. We need to deter strangers trying to enter the compound.'

'Nobody takes such precautions simply to deter strangers.'

'It's not public knowledge, but there have been two attempts on my life. And I have a strong suspicion both were masterminded by the person who is about to meet me. He is more dangerous than a poisonous snake.'

'Then why are you meeting him?'

'He has asked for this meeting.'

'At least tell me the name of this mystery person.'

'It is my twin brother, Ajay Krishna Acharya, or AK, as he likes to call himself. The owner of Premier Industries.'

An electric current darts through my body, making me

leap out of my chair. 'In that case I will not attend this meeting,' I announce.

'Why?'

'I don't think it's a good idea to involve me in your corporate rivalry,' I reply, Karan's words ringing in my ears: 'Acharya will use you as a pawn to get to his brother.'

Acharya presses his fingertips to his temples, his face suddenly slack. It is clear he did not anticipate this reaction from me. ' "Know your enemy" is the first rule of strategy and of business,' he says. 'I wanted you to get acquainted with the ABC Group's biggest enemy. The man who tried to infiltrate my organisation. The man who has been trying desperately for the last thirty years to destroy me.'

Just then the doorbell rings. I can hear the sound of the front door being opened.

'Quick!' He herds me towards the connecting door. 'If you don't want to attend the meeting, at least observe it.'

Before I know it, I have been shooed into the adjacent room, which I discover to be the master bedroom. It is dominated by a majestic mahogany bed with an ornately carved headboard and rich purple bed linen. The left wall features a massive oval mirror made of black onyx stone. The right wall has a portrait of a stern old man with a walrus moustache, dressed in the style of the 1940s, probably Acharya's father. On a side table immediately below it sits a collection of family photographs.

I am both apprehensive and uneasy as I drag an upholstered chair from the foot of the bed and sit down facing the connecting door, which Acharya has left open a crack to allow me to see what's going on.

The man who walks into the study looks like a duplicate of Acharya – same height, same build, same physical features. It is uncanny to see two men in one room looking like mirror images of each other, with the same piercing brown eyes, aquiline nose and firm mouth. The only real thing to distinguish them is their hair. AK keeps a trimmed French beard and his slicked-back, jet-black hair is obviously dyed. In contrast to Acharya, he seems to be a bit of a dandy, dressed all in black – a silk shirt, tight trousers and pointy shoes. His tanned face looks freshly Botoxed, or embalmed, depending upon one's taste. The overall effect is that of an effete and ageing playboy, an old man trying hard to look young.

He settles down into the chair opposite Acharya, who summons a servant. 'What will you have, AK?'

'A martini on the rocks,' says his twin. Even his voice is eerily similar to Acharya's.

'I'm sorry, I don't serve alcohol in the house.'

'You're still the same old prude, aren't you? Well, then get me a *nimbu paani.*'

While Acharya is busy instructing the servant, AK takes out a cigar from his chest pocket and lights it. Stretching his legs, he blows cigar smoke towards the ceiling.

Acharya frowns at him. 'I'm afraid you cannot smoke in here. Prarthana is a no-smoking zone.'

'Then what do you keep this for?' AK points scornfully at the marble ashtray on the centre table. He stubs out his cigar in a quick, brutal movement and exhales a last time.

'So what did you want to talk to me about?' asks Acharya.

'About the ABC Group. How badly it is doing.'

'We are doing quite well, thank you.'

'Is that so? I'm told your first-quarter results are going to be quite disappointing: revenues down 8.52 per cent in January and 4.7 per cent in February.'

'First-quarter results haven't been announced yet. Where did you get these figures?'

'I have my sources.'

'Is it the same mole who has been feeding you our secret information, allowing you to underbid us on the national ID-card software tender by one rupee?'

AK ignores the comment. 'The bad news doesn't just end there. You have virtually no new revenue, no cash from financing activities, and your overheads are continuing to mount because of your obstinate refusal to lay off workers.'

'Did you come here to teach me how to run my business?'

'No. I came here to drill some sense into you. The writing is on the wall, whether you read it or not. Face it: you've lost your touch, Vinay Mohan. The ABC Group has been beaten by the Premier Group on seven consecutive bids. Your stake deal with Nippon Steel is in jeopardy. Your proposed buyout of Clemantis Windpower is likely to be rejected by stockholders.'

'You are reading too much business gossip. Come to the point, AK,' Acharya says testily.

'Well, the point is this. I know that the ABC Group is facing a cash crunch and is negotiating to renew its line of credit with bankers. I can provide you with that cash.'

'Sorry, we're not releasing any new stock.'

'I don't want to buy your shares: I want to buy your company, lock, stock and barrel. Sell out to me. I am prepared to make a reasonable offer for the ABC Group, as much as five billion dollars.'

'Never!' Acharya almost springs out of his chair. 'I know how you do business, AK. You are a godless thug who buys companies only to suck them dry. I will never allow the ABC Group to be run by scum like you.'

'Calm down, Vinay. It's strictly business, nothing personal.'

The atmosphere has become so electric, I can almost see the sparks flying between the two. For the first time in my life I am witnessing the cut and thrust of the business world. How deals are made and rejected. Acharya and his twin are genetic copies of each other, yet vastly different. One is a freewheeling tyrant who rules by instinct and conviction, the other a cunning opportunist who profits through deceit and guile. It's like watching two bulls lock horns, their contrasting personalities clashing like storm clouds, the room reverberating with the thunder of their mutual animus.

AK has still not given up. 'Listen to me, brother,' he says, leaning forward on his haunches and speaking in his most suave voice. 'We are united by ties of blood. We have both faced personal tragedies. You lost your wife and daughter. My only son committed suicide. Why can't we bury the hatchet? United we stand, divided you fall.'

'I seem to recall that many years ago you had made a similar plea to our mother. Poor Amma sold out her share, only for you to squander it all on fast women and slow horses.'

'That's old history. You better not bring Mother into the discussion.'

'Then you better not bring the ABC Group into it.'

'If I won't, someone else will. I am told you have been keeping indifferent health lately.'

'Lie. Utter lie!'

'Still, have you considered what will happen to the ABC Group after you are gone?'

'I have a succession plan ready.'

'And who is this successor, if I might ask?'

'Someone who believes in the same values as I do. Someone who will keep the ABC Group safe from predators like you.'

'You don't need a succession plan: you need a *rescue* plan. I still care for our blood ties and my buyout offer will remain on the table. You can either make it happen, or, at the very least, *let* it happen. Otherwise, I promise you, Vinay, you will be left wondering what happened.'

'That is enough.' Acharya raises his voice. 'I suggest you leave now.'

'Fine.' AK gets up and smooths his shirt out. 'The next time I see you will be at your funeral.'

The moment AK departs, Acharya charges into the bedroom, nostrils flaring, jaw set in anger. 'Who does this uncivilised bigot think he is? The King of England?'

I assume the neutral attitude of a judge at a particularly bitter divorce proceeding. 'AK may be an obnoxious jerk, but are the facts and figures he trotted out true? Is the ABC Group really in bad shape?'

'Not at all,' Acharya says vehemently. 'We have been impacted by the continuing global slowdown, as has everyone else. But the situation is not half as bad as made out by AK. Our balance sheet is quite healthy and our debt–equity ratio is less than one. That's why he wants to buy us out.'

'But you rejected his offer out of hand. Was it too low?'

'Let me ask you a question. Would you agree to marry a practised womaniser, a habitual drunk and a thief to boot?'

'Certainly not.'

'Exactly. That is why I will never sell out to the Premier Group, even if they offer me twenty billion. Because it is run by a cabal of cheats, headed by the biggest villain of them all, AK.'

'He also mentioned something about you refusing to lay off workers.'

'I can fire employees for cheating and disloyalty, not for an economic crisis they didn't create. Before you fire an employee you have to think of the social costs, not just the economic benefits. Take our cement factory in Laos, for example. It's losing money, but not so much that we need to shut operations. People are poor there. If we lay off the workers, their families will starve to death. I can't allow that.'

'And I thought corporations were callous and unscrupulous, driven solely by the need for profit.'

'Traditional corporations are. By its very nature, business is supposed to be about hard-headed economic decisions, with no scope for emotion. It is hard-wired to think only about making the most money possible, with no regard for the public good. I started out doing business like that, before realising it was the wrong way. Now value comes first for me, and profit second.' He pauses and looks at me. 'Do you know who taught me this truth?'

'Your father?'

'No. It was Maya, my daughter. She was wise beyond her years. That is why God took her away when she was just twenty-five.'

I walk to the side table and pick out the photo of a teenaged girl sitting in an armchair, her black, slanted eyes crinkled in a smile. 'Is this her picture?'

'Yes. I miss her every day.'

I search the girl's face for any features similar to mine, but there's not even a superficial resemblance. Acharya certainly didn't pick me because I looked like his daughter. 'Her features don't seem typically Indian,' I observe.

'That's because her mother – my wife – was Japanese.'

'Where did you meet her?'

'In Nagasaki. I went to Japan as a student and lived there for ten years. I fell in love with their culture and a girl named Kyoko.'

I pick up another photo, this one of a slender, gentle-looking woman in a kimono. 'Is this Kyoko?'

He nods. 'She also died in that air crash with Maya.'

He takes the photo frame from my hands and gazes at the picture longingly. 'Japanese women are very similar to Indian women. They are gentle, sincere, kind, and devoted to family. Like Indian wives, they understand hierarchy.'

I take it as a subtle hint to me. I have to understand and obey hierarchy.

As he places the photo back on the table, I observe a teardrop escape the side of his eye. It is the first time he has let down his taciturn exterior to reveal his softer side.

Despite my reservations about this entire project, I cannot help feeling a twinge of sympathy for him. I can see the ravages of loneliness in his weary eyes, imbuing his face with a certain noble sadness. His monumental egoism, I now realise, is actually a form of defence mechanism to hide his vulnerability. He is still a grieving husband and a distraught father. He has succeeded as a businessman, buying up firms and factories, but all his wealth cannot fill the hole in his heart.

He notices me noticing him and looks away, blushing slightly, as if embarrassed at his own sentimentality. 'Now that you have seen AK, can you appreciate why I need to keep him at arm's length?' he asks, evidently to change the subject.

'I must say I found him to be incredibly pushy and rude.'

'The real problem isn't his rudeness: it's his volatility. Have you ever wondered why the symbol of the Premier Group is a charging bull? It's because AK is exactly that, a rampaging bull. He will stop at nothing to get what he wants.'

'Is he really that powerful?'

'It's power that comes from collusion and corruption. Let me share something with you in the strictest confidence. Have you heard of Atlas Investments?'

'Yes, of course. It's the front company behind virtually every scam.'

'Well, I have a strong hunch that AK is the mastermind behind Atlas.'

'What?' My head jerks up sharply. 'That's a pretty strong accusation.'

'Obviously I don't have hard evidence, but I have carefully analysed the patterns of Premier Group's investments in recent times and they seem to match the timelines of the scams. Plus, as you have already seen, he seems to be flush with cash. No prizes for guessing where all this money has come from.'

'Then why isn't action being taken against him?'

'Because everyone is in this together. To bust him we need clinching evidence of payouts into his secret bank accounts.'

'There is an elderly lady in our colony, a Gandhian called Nirmala Ben, who is threatening to start a people's revolution to force the government to reveal the identity of the scamster behind Atlas.'

Acharya waves dismissively. 'Tell her not to waste her efforts on Atlas. The network of payoffs runs so deep, it will require more than a totally transparent analysis of structure ownership to reveal the real culprit. And that's not going to happen in a hurry.'

Just then Rana enters the room carrying a thick folder. He is surprised to see me with Mr Acharya. 'I brought you the Avantha contract for signing, sir,' he tells the industrialist.

'Yes, of course,' says Acharya, as if reminded of something important.

Suddenly I feel awkward, standing in the middle of Acharya's bedroom. 'Can I go now? I would like to catch some of the cricket action at least.'

Acharya gestures to Rana. 'Will you see that she is dropped back to her house?'

With a displeased scowl, Rana leads me down to the

underground garage with space for six cars. There is a BMW, a Mercedes, a Jaguar, a Porsche and, rather incongruously, a Tata Indica.

'What's the Indica doing in this line-up of luxury imported cars?' I ask Rana.

The scowl on his face deepens. 'It happens to be my personal vehicle. I don't like taking lifts in other people's cars,' he says coldly, as he summons a uniformed chauffeur.

Two minutes later, I leave the mansion in a Mercedes-Benz, my first ever luxury ride. Stretching my legs and watching the city go by from the tinted windows of the sedan, I feel instantly energised and uplifted. The plush leather seat, the temperature-controlled environment and the soothing voice of Jagjit Singh filtering through the car stereo have something to do with it. But most of all it is the thought that one day this car might actually be mine.

By the time I return to Rohini it is almost 5 p.m. Coincidentally, Karan enters the gates of the colony at the same moment as I do. He sees me alight from the Mercedes, does a double-take, and assumes the stiff posture of a professional soldier. '*Ba-adab, ba-mulahiza hoshiyar, Mallika-e-Hindustan aa rahi hain.* With respect, pay attention, be alert, the Empress of India is arriving,' he intones, pretending to be a medieval sentry announcing the arrival of a Mughal queen.

'*Takhliya*, dismissed,' I reply with suitable hauteur, before breaking into a chuckle.

'So, is this going to be your usual commute from now on?' He jerks a thumb at the departing Mercedes.

'I wish. Acharya was just getting me dropped back from his residence in Vasant Vihar.'

He rolls his eyes. 'What were you doing in his house?'

'Attending a bizarre meeting,' I say and recount the stormy scene between Acharya and AK.

'So finally AK is in the picture.' Karan exhales. 'What did you make of him?'

'There's obviously some kind of history between the two. "It's strictly business, nothing personal," AK said, but the truth seems to be the exact opposite. What I saw wasn't business: it was strictly personal.'

'For all I care they can both go rot in hell,' Karan says. 'I'm going to watch the match. See you later.'

The courtyard, which is usually bustling with residents, is completely deserted. India is about to bat and the entire colony is glued to its TV sets. As I pass by Nirmala Ben's apartment, I discover a lock hanging on her door, definitely not a good sign.

'Have you seen Nirmala Ben?' I ask Ma, who is pleasantly surprised to see me come home early.

'She came to return the scissors she had borrowed from me, telling me she was going away for a while.'

'Did she tell you where she was going?'

'No, but she behaved a bit strangely, embracing me as though she wasn't going to return again.'

Dhiman Singh, the colony's guard, confirms my fears. Nirmala Ben was seen leaving the colony at 2 p.m. with a small suitcase and a couple of placards. He has no idea where she has gone, but I have. I immediately hail an autorickshaw and tell the driver to take me to Jantar Mantar.

*

Situated on Parliament Street, Jantar Mantar is an astro-
nomical observatory with instruments in masonry built by
Raja Jai Singh II of Jaipur nearly three hundred years ago.
These days it is better known as Delhi's Hyde Park, the
only place where political parties, ordinary citizens and
activist groups are legally allowed to hold a sit-in when
Parliament is in session.

The actual protests take place on Jantar Mantar Road,
a leafy thoroughfare close to Connaught Place, where
people with a grievance converge from all over the country, in the hope of getting a hearing, or at the very least,
some media coverage. I generally avoid this chaotic and
noisy showroom for our democracy, constantly teeming
with slogan-shouting, placard-waving demonstrators.
There are some groups who camp on the pavement for
weeks on end, virtually making it their second home.

Today, the demonstrators are few and far between. There
is a middle-aged couple from Madhya Pradesh, huddled in
their makeshift tent. A handmade placard states that they
are protesting against police inaction in tracing their teenaged daughter Parvati, missing since 6 January. Next to
them is a traders' association demanding that the government impose a blanket ban on the entry of multinational
companies and big corporate houses into retail trade. A
third group consists of a bunch of students from Delhi
University with gas masks, rallying to save the Yamuna
River from pollution. And finally there is a lone woman in
a white sari, sitting on the dusty pavement against the drab
backdrop of a faded bed sheet, which she has fashioned into
a banner. 'INDEFINITE HUNGER STRIKE AGAINST CORRUP-
TION', declares the banner in red ink. In each of her hands

she holds a rectangular placard with wooden handles, one saying 'UNMASK ATLAS' and the other 'SAVE INDIA'.

Her eyes light up the moment she sees me. 'Sapna, *beti*, you have come here to join my protest?'

'No, Nirmala Ben,' I reply. 'I have come to take you home.'

'That I am not doing,' she declares with a firm shake of her head. 'I told you I will only leave this place when the government assures me that they will expose the people behind Atlas. Otherwise this fast will continue until my death.'

'Can you see a single person supporting your fast?' I ask in exasperation. 'You have chosen the worst possible day to protest. Everyone is busy watching cricket.'

'Some friends of mine from the Durga Pooja Association and the Gujarati Samaj have promised to come.'

'Then why aren't they here? Why don't you accept the fact that they don't really care for your cause?'

'It doesn't matter. Once a *satyagrahi* undertakes a fast from conviction, she must stick to her resolve whether there is a chance of her action bearing fruit or not. *Barobar chhe ne?*'

No amount of argument can dissuade Nirmala Ben from abandoning her fast. She is as stubborn as a teenager, reminding me of Alka. Equal parts frustrated and concerned, I sit down beside her, hoping that good sense will prevail upon her in the next few hours.

By 9 p.m. I am beginning to feel the pangs of hunger. I turn to Nirmala Ben. 'Don't you want to eat something?' I ask.

'How can I eat during a hunger fast? You go ahead and

get some food. I will make do with this.' She takes a bottle of mineral water from her suitcase and gulps down a mouthful.

An hour later a police constable wanders into the area. Rat-faced and corpulent, he looks suspiciously at us. 'What's all this?' He taps his baton against the placard in Nirmala Ben's hand.

'It's called a protest,' I reply, the words laced with more sarcasm than I intended.

'Have you taken permission? Where is your permit?'

'I didn't know we needed a permit to protest. We are living in a democracy, after all.'

'Come with me to the Parliament Street police station,' he leers, 'and I will teach you the mechanics of democracy.'

'Look son, we don't intend to cause you any trouble,' Nirmala Ben interjects. 'This is a peaceful protest to make our country a better place.'

'Listen, *budhiya*,' the constable growls. 'This is not your private property where you can hang a banner whenever you want. Now show me your permit or I will forcibly evict you.'

'I will not obtain any permit,' says Nirmala Ben. 'And I will not budge from here.'

'Stupid woman, trying to argue with me?' He gnashes his teeth and raises his stick to strike her, when I rush forward and interpose myself between them.

'Let's resolve this in a civilised way. I will get you the permit tomorrow. Just allow us to stay here tonight. And please accept this little token of our gratitude.' I open my purse and offer him a fifty-rupee note.

He snatches the note from my hands and inserts it into his top pocket. 'Well, all right. I'll spare you tonight because the entire city is engrossed in the World Cup. But pack up and leave tomorrow,' he says sternly, and walks off jauntily.

'Why did you bribe that policeman?' Nirmala Ben berates me. 'This is exactly what I am fighting against.'

'If I had not bribed that bullying cop he would have hit you.'

'Then you should have let him hit me.' She smiles. 'The essence of *satyagraha* is soul force against brute force. That is the only way to wean away such people from the path of hatred and violence.'

I cannot help being drawn in by her loving smile, suffused with kindness and courage. And I realise deep down that we are in this together. I may not believe in her method, but I believe in her cause. And I will walk with her, even if there is no one else who is prepared to follow her.

By now the night has darkened into a sinister black, and I know I have to head home. I do not want to leave Nirmala Ben all alone, but I draw the line when it comes to sleeping on the pavement. Reluctantly, I bid her goodbye and take the last metro back to Rohini.

I am still in the train when I get a call on my cell phone. It is Neha, screaming with joy. '*Didi*, where are you?'

'Why? What's happened?'

'India has just won the World Cup, after twenty-eight years!'

A full brass band greets me when I alight at Rohini. There are horns and trumpets blaring, and a young boy wearing tricolour face paint doing cartwheels. The streets are jammed with cars and people and the sky is exploding with fireworks. It all seems a blur to me. The celebrations feel hollow, because one resident of the colony is missing. The entire nation has cheered for the Indian cricket team as it battled against Sri Lanka, but there is no one supporting a heroic woman, fighting a much more important battle.

Ma is the only one concerned about Nirmala Ben. 'Take me to her, *beti*. I will persuade her to come back.'

'She's not prepared to listen to anyone.'

'Then I will also sit on fast with her.'

'Don't be ridiculous.'

'I've never told this to anyone, but I owe my life to Nirmala Ben.'

I stare back in surprise. 'What are you saying?'

'It's true. Six weeks ago, my blood sugar suddenly dipped very low and I collapsed in the kitchen. But for Nirmala Ben, who took me to the hospital, I might have died that afternoon.'

'And you're telling me all this now?'

'I didn't want Neha and you to be needlessly worried.'

'Why do you always have to be the one carrying the weight of the world on your shoulders?' I mask my worry with mock irritation. 'Sometimes I feel you and Nirmala Ben are identical twins, cut from the same cloth.'

Ma wrings her hands. 'I cannot sleep knowing that I should be with Nirmala.'

Neither can I. The thought of Nirmala Ben lying all alone on the pavement keeps me up all night. I owe her a deeper debt than I thought.

Both Ma and I arise before dawn and take the first metro of the morning to get back on Jantar Mantar Road.

Yesterday's protesters are still asleep, wrapped in blankets inside their temporary tents. This motley group of students, traders and housewives do not inspire much confidence. In fact the entire stretch of the road looks less like a showroom of democracy and more like a museum of the powerless.

Nirmala Ben is the only one up and about. She has already finished her daily ablutions at a nearby public toilet and is singing 'Raghupati Raghav Raja Ram' when we arrive.

'Ben, end this stubbornness and return home with us,' Ma pleads, but she simply smiles.

'How long can you stay like this without food?' Ma tries again.

'As long as I have inner strength. And as long as the government doesn't respond to my demand.'

'But the government doesn't even *know* about your demand,' I cry. 'And what to talk of the government, even the man on the street does not know. A milkman just passed by on his cycle. I asked him if he supported your cause. He said he's never heard of Atlas Investments.'

'If you asked him about corruption he would have given you a different answer. Bapu said that truth is by nature self-evident. As soon as you remove the cobwebs of ignorance that surround it, it shines clear. My *satyagraha* is to wake up the powerless and shame the powerful,' says Nirmala Ben. 'You will see how my protest will swell into a movement that will change the course of history.'

I know then that Nirmala Ben will not return to the colony. Animated by a grand grievance and seduced by the grandiose vision of revolution, she will literally fast to death. But her death will be in vain. The powerless of the world can neither change history nor create it. We are condemned simply to study it.

'Her blood pressure is rising and her heart rate has increased. It's not life-threatening yet, but I don't think she can continue without food much longer. She should call off her fast,' says the doctor as he packs away his stethoscope and holds out his hand for his visitation fee. I hand him a hundred-rupee note and he shortly disappears into his hole-in-the-wall clinic.

It is Wednesday, 6 April, and Nirmala Ben has not had a morsel of food for four days. Even more worryingly, her protest has found no traction at all. She has attracted a few curious onlookers, but beyond that she could be fasting on the moon. Even the police have stopped bothering her, dismissing her as a crank. The fact is, without a brigade of slogan-shouting supporters and placard-wielding followers, her protest doesn't resemble a protest at all: it looks like a homeless woman dumped in a corner of the city.

'Do something, *beti*, or it might be too late,' Ma frets. We have worked out an arrangement between us. Ma remains with Nirmala Ben all day and gives her company. I visit her whenever I can spare some time from the showroom, which is just minutes away.

Nirmala Ben has lost some weight but her crusading zeal and her faith in human nature are intact. 'People will come, eventually,' she says, still hopeful.

No one comes, of course, but during the lunch break I chance upon Shalini Grover, my friend from Sunlight TV. It turns out that one of the students with the gas masks protesting against pollution in the Yamuna is her nephew.

I look to her for advice. 'How can we get the word out about Nirmala Ben's fast?'

'You have to get TV cameras here,' she says. 'That is the only way to start a chain reaction.'

'Can you come with a camera crew?'

'We are an investigative channel not a general news channel. And even the news guys don't cover a protest unless it is significant.'

'Well, what makes a protest significant?'

'Either the subject should be catchy, or the numbers should be massive. Have you ever wondered why a thousand journalists cover the glamorous models strutting down the ramp during India Fashion Week, but I was all alone reporting on farmers' suicides in Vidarbha? Bad news doesn't sell. Nirmala Ben's fast against a nebulous front company just isn't sexy enough. But, if she were to get the women of Delhi to organise a SlutWalk kind of protest march, like the one which took place a couple of days ago in Toronto, it would instantly attract eyeballs and become a media event.'

'Atlas Investments is only a symbol. Her real target is high-level corruption.'

'Don't make me yawn. No one gives a damn for corruption in this country. Half the middle class indulges in bribery and the other half just isn't bothered to come out on the streets and do something about it.'

'Don't you think you are being a bit unfair on the middle class?' I protest.

'I'm simply expressing a harsh truth. The middle class doesn't care about anything – we neither vote nor fight elections – so nobody cares about the middle class.'

The next day also brings no new supporters to the cause. The only change in the situation is that Nirmala Ben's health deteriorates even further. 'Her pulse rate is eighty-eight and her blood pressure is a hundred and fifty by ninety. Urgent medical attention might be needed in the next twenty-four to forty-eight hours. Please keep an ambulance on standby,' says the doctor as he completes her medical examination.

Nirmala Ben has lost over three kilos in the last six days. Her complexion has turned darker because of dehydration, and her face has acquired a dangerous gauntness, emphasised by dark circles under her eyes. She no longer has the strength to sit up all day. Most of the time she is curled up on a sheet. But her mind is still lucid and sharp.

'Nirmala Ben, please end this madness,' I implore her. 'Let's just accept that we failed this time. You have to live to fight another day.'

'No,' she says firmly. 'Now only my dead body will leave this place.' Her terrifying fixity of purpose chills me.

Vinay Mohan Acharya comes visiting at noontime. He claims he heard a brief mention about Nirmala Ben's fast on Sunlight TV. 'Is this the people's revolution you were promising me?' He gazes at the Gandhian lying all alone. 'But where are the people?'

'Nirmala Ben is dying.' I wring my hands. 'And no one seems to care.'

'I told you she would be wasting her time on Atlas.' He lets out a derisive snort. 'I, too, tried to be an agent of change, but to usher in a revolution in this country is impossible. History tells us that for a revolution to succeed you need one of two things: either a ruling figure who is universally hated or an opposition figure who is universally liked. In India we have neither. We Indians have neither too much hate nor too much love for anyone.'

'Is there nothing we can do to galvanise people in support of her cause?'

'Forget it. People can be galvanised into action only on an issue that touches their heart. And removing corruption, I am sorry to say, is still not an emotive issue with people. They feel it is too pervasive to be removed.'

The industrialist leaves after delivering his homily, but I am not prepared to accept defeat so easily. Back in the showroom, I rack my brains for a solution. I know it is time for a new approach. People will not come on their own to support an unknown woman with no organisational backup. It is a cardinal rule of marketing that you have to build presence in the consumers' minds before you can get them to buy your product. This is what advertising is all about. But how do you market a protest?

That is when my eyes fall on a giant billboard towering over Jantar Mantar. It shows actress Priya Capoorr, her face glowing brightly, holding up a tube of Amla herbal skin cream. The answer comes to me in a flash: Nirmala Ben, too, needs celebrity endorsement.

I still have the number for Rosie Mascarenhas, the PR manager for the actress. I call her up and explain my proposal. 'Do you think Priya will agree to say a few words in support of Nirmala Ben's fast? It's for a noble cause.'

The PR lady is not amused. 'You have some nerve calling me after the way you behaved with Priya,' she admonishes, before adding, 'Who's heard of this Nirmala Ben? We never associate ourselves with unknown brands.'

Undeterred, I switch to Plan B, and turn to Karan. 'If Priya Capoorr won't support Nirmala Ben's fast, then Salim Ilyasi will.'

'But how do we get in touch with him? I don't have his secretary's number.'

'You *are* Salim Ilyasi. Remember the prank you pulled on me on April Fools' Day? I want you to do the same for Nirmala Ben.'

'I don't get you.'

'I want you to record a message in the voice of Salim Ilyasi, asking people to come to Nirmala Ben's fast, and send it out to Indus customers as an MMS message.'

'Hold on! You want me to go to jail? What if Salim sues me?'

'We'll not use Salim Ilyasi's name. If someone's voice sounds just like his, it's not our fault, is it?'

'And what about the company? If my boss finds out I've sent this bulk MMS for free, I'll get fired.'

'I know there is a risk, but this is our only chance. Otherwise, Nirmala Ben dies.'

Karan takes a little convincing, but, once he's on board, he gives it his all. I have already prepared a text, and Karan records it perfectly, his voice an exact clone of Salim Ilyasi's. Even he is impressed at his uncanny mimicry. 'The

hundred million subscribers of Indus are in for a real surprise,' he grins.

Three hours later, my cell phone beeps with an incoming message from a Mumbai number. I click it open to be
instantly captivated by Salim Ilyasi's deep baritone.
'Friends, our country is going through trying times,' the
superstar says. 'Scam after scam has shaken the confidence
of the people. We cannot remain helpless bystanders any
more. I have therefore decided to join Nirmala Ben's
courageous fight against corruption. I will be there to
support her at Jantar Mantar on Saturday, the ninth of
April. So should you. Together we can make India a
better place. So do come. It will be funtaastik.'

I call up Karan. 'It's superb! But I am just a little bit
worried about the Mumbai number you used. Is it Salim
Ilyasi's actual phone?'

'Are you nuts? I'd be arrested if I did that.'

'Then whose number is it?'

'It's a nonexistent number, but, if you change the last
digit from zero to one, you will get connected.'

'To whom?'

'The Andheri Mental Hospital!'

The plan works better than I could ever imagine. The
fake Salim Ilyasi MMS goes viral. Details of Nirmala Ben's
fast are conveyed through blogs, Twitter, Facebook,
MySpace and YouTube, till some kind of critical mass is
reached. People start streaming into the fast venue from
early in the morning of Saturday. They come looking for
Salim Ilyasi but then something curious happens. They
see Nirmala Ben, this frail old lady carrying on without

food for a week, and they stay on, drawn as much to her sheer doggedness as to the prospect of meeting a Bollywood superstar.

By afternoon the crowd has swelled to eight thousand people, maybe more. That is when another interesting thing happens. Almost on its own, a force of active volunteers forms. They begin constructing a proper stage. Somebody sets up a collection bucket and donations start pouring in spontaneously. The owner of a tent house loans us a huge *shamiana*, providing much-needed protection from the harsh sun. Someone brings in a portable generator, another a PA system. A group of local singers and musicians joins Nirmala Ben on stage and the air begins resonating with bhajans and patriotic songs.

Nothing revives a fasting protester more than the sight of cheering throngs. Nirmala Ben is filled with new energy and fresh zeal. She even manages to stand up and give an impassioned speech, calling upon the multitude to launch a new revolution to cleanse the country of corruption. 'You unmask Atlas, and you strike a body blow against corporate collusion,' she declares to sustained applause, her voice pulsating with moral fervour and motherly authority.

After this, it doesn't take long for the media news cycle to begin. Reporters, photographers and TV news crews converge on Jantar Mantar like sharks to fresh blood in the sea.

Once news of the fast gets on primetime television, the rush of people becomes a tide. Within a few hours, Nirmala Ben starts dominating the airwaves, even bettering the cricket carnival of the Indian Premier League, which started a day earlier. Panel discussions are hastily brought together on the subject and everyone who's anyone is airing their views on the fast and decrying corruption in general and Atlas in particular.

Come Sunday, the protest snowballs into an avalanche. Jantar Mantar Road is completely jammed with demonstrators waving the tricolour and singing and dancing to the rhythm of drums, creating a carnival-like atmosphere. More than a hundred people decide to emulate Nirmala Ben's fast unto death, including a ninety-two-year-old veteran freedom fighter willing to forfeit his life if the government doesn't give in. Strangers hug each other and shout slogans hailing Nirmala Ben as a new Gandhi.

The stream of people continues unabated throughout the day. They come by train and bus, on cycles and on foot. They come from distant villages and dusty townships, from swanky shopping malls and air-conditioned offices. There are Gujjar farmers from Haryana, unemployed youths from Noida, school students from RK Puram, housewives from Chittaranjan Park, dairy workers from Jind, clerics from a madrasa in Nangloi, tailors from Ghaziabad, eunuchs from Yusuf Sarai, and call-centre executives from Gurgaon. It's hard to imagine a more disparate and amorphous group, united only by its outrage over the culture of graft and patronage. Each and every one of them has faced corruption in his or her everyday life, from the father forced to make a 'donation' to a private school to gain admission for his son, to the construction worker who has had to bribe a clerk to obtain a ration card. It is a spontaneous coalition of the disaffected and the dispossessed. Nirmala Ben has become

the rallying point for their daily frustrations and unful-
filled aspirations. And 'Unmask Atlas' has become the
rallying cry of an angry nation finally expressing itself.

As I watch the sea of fists pumping in unison, as I hear
the full-throated cries of 'Nirmala Ben *zindabad*!'('Long
live Nirmala Ben!') from the stage, I turn to Karan, standing beside me in a relatively less crowded corner. 'Thank
you.' I squeeze his hand in gratitude. 'Could you have
imagined this spectacle when you sent out that voice
clip?'

'You mean to say I caused all this mayhem?' Karan
looks bemusedly at the jostling multitudes surging to
catch a glimpse of Nirmala Ben.

From the direction of the stage comes the sound of live
drumming followed by high-pitched shrieks.

'Oh, my God!' exclaims Karan. 'Looks like Desi
Nirvana are here.'

'Yes. They are supporting Nirmala Ben by giving a free
concert.'

'Spending a Sunday with the unwashed masses of India
grooving to a rock band is not my idea of fun. But, then,
I might never get this chance again,' he says as he wades
into the milling throng. 'Come, join me.'

'You go,' I tell him. 'Hard rock is not my cup of tea.
Besides, I'm waiting for Dr Motwani of Apollo Hospital.
He's India's most expensive cardiologist. And he's offered
to monitor Nirmala Ben's health condition for free.'

News of the swelling support for the fast even draws
Lauren's boyfriend James Atlee, the brand specialist, to
Jantar Mantar. 'I need to get tips from you,' the English-
man says in quiet amazement. 'You've achieved something

that I could not. You've turned a complete nobody into an international icon.'

'With a little bit of help from Salim Ilyasi.' I wink at him.

'Half my office seems to have come here to lend support to the protest. I even spotted my boss's son a while ago in the crowd.'

'Your boss's son? You mean the owner of Indus Mobile?'

'Yeah. Karak Junior. He's only nineteen or twenty, but a right royal mess, I tell you. He's a complete weirdo, probably on drugs.'

'What's he doing here?'

'That's easy to guess. Everybody's trying to figure out how that Salim Ilyasi MMS got broadcast on the network.'

The alarm bell in my head goes off instantly. I start searching frantically for Karan. It takes me twenty minutes to find him, enjoying an ice lolly from an ice-cream stand.

'Want one?' He grins.

'I just met Lauren's boyfriend James,' I inform him. 'He said he saw your owner's son, Karak Junior, in the crowd.'

'What?' His face turns ashen and his smile evaporates. He dumps the ice lolly in a trash can and wrings his hands in a nervous tic. 'I'm sunk,' he mumbles. 'It means Salim Ilyasi has complained and the company's launched an investigation. Shit!'

'Maybe your boss's son just came to check out the protest.'

'You don't know him,' says Karan. 'He's a crazy son-ofabitch. When he gets after someone, he never lets go.'

'You think you might lose your job?'

'I've covered my tracks pretty well. I just hope my friends in the call centre who know about my mimicry don't spill the beans. I better vamoose now.' He spins around on his heels and takes off without even bothering to say goodbye.

I return to the dais, where Ma is tending to a supine Nirmala Ben. She has turned weaker and painfully thin. Dr Motwani, after examining her, has prohibited her from speaking and exerting herself. He says she won't be able to carry on for more than two days without food. 'All the mass adulation in the world cannot be a substitute for nutrition,' as he put it.

Late in the evening, the government finally sends an emissary to meet Nirmala Ben. He is a lowly deputy secretary from the Ministry of Company Affairs. 'We are making every effort to trace the people behind Atlas,' he says. 'The process is a complicated one. We need some time.'

Nirmala Ben hears him out and then holds up two fingers.

'What does this mean?' the bureaucrat asks, turning to Ma who, willy-nilly, has become Nirmala Ben's unofficial spokesperson.

'It means she can give you two months, that's sixty days,' says mother.

'That won't be sufficient.' The official shakes his head. 'We require minimum eight months to a year.'

Nirmala Ben waves dismissively. 'Then go,' Ma translates. 'We don't have a deal.'

*

Monday arrives and the crowds refuse to go away from Jantar Mantar, throwing the entire traffic in Connaught Place into chaos.

Beyond its political overtones, the fast becomes a cultural phenomenon as well. Gandhi caps disappear from Khadi Bhandar outlets. Nirmala Ben's white sari acquires the status of a fashion statement, featuring in glitzy catwalks. Rohit Kalra, the Bollywood lyricist, launches a bawdy remix with the catchphrase 'My wife's not kissing, because Atlas is still missing', which quickly becomes a rage on YouTube. Citizens' groups all over India begin organising bonfires in which they symbolically burn copies of school atlases.

By the end of Tuesday, there is only one show in the country: the Nirmala Ben show. The Gandhian's face is everywhere: in newspapers, on TV, on billboards, T-shirts, caps and ladies' nails. Just as Amitabh Bachchan is fondly called 'Big B', Nirmala Ben is quickly dubbed 'Big Ben'. Even Priya Capoorr jumps onto the bandwagon. I derive a certain malicious satisfaction in seeing her on Star News, expressing platitudes on how she has always admired Nirmala Ben and wants to join her fast but for the fact that she is presently in Istanbul busy shooting her next film.

Caught up in the heady togetherness of the people's revolution, I find Dr Motwani's latest health bulletin a complete bombshell. Around midnight the cardiologist announces grimly that Nirmala Ben's health has deteriorated considerably and she could even die if not placed on a drip immediately.

Predictably, Nirmala Ben refuses to break her fast or

accept a drip. 'If my son can give his life for his country, then so can I,' she declares gaspingly, struggling for every breath. In a city where life can end too abruptly and too anonymously to be memorialised, the spectacle of a public martyrdom holds a dangerously seductive appeal for her.

News of Nirmala Ben's impending death spreads like wildfire. The movement, which was entirely peaceful till now, turns violent. Irate mobs set fire to buses and government vehicles. Protesters clash with police all over the country. Opposition parties give a call for a nationwide strike.

Faced with an increasingly hostile electorate, and sensing the popular mood, the government tries to seize the initiative, with the Minister for Company Affairs himself giving a written assurance to Nirmala Ben that he will get Atlas investigated and its true identity revealed within sixty days. 'It is not a capitulation,' he declares to the assembled reporters. 'It is pragmatism based on a clear sense of the nation's interest.'

At 12.01 p.m. on Wednesday, 13 April, Nirmala Ben ends her fast on live television by accepting a glass of juice from a schoolgirl, and a loud cheer goes up all around the country.

She is taken to Apollo Hospital immediately, trailed by a legion of devoted followers and a small army of doctors. Ma and I are saddled with the task of winding up the protest and taking her personal belongings back to the LIG Colony.

That evening, while rearranging her things in B-25, I open her battered suitcase, the one she took to Jantar Mantar. It contains the bed sheet she used for her banner and a couple of her plain sarees, but lurking underneath the clothes are plenty of handkerchiefs, spoons, plates, glasses, hair bands, bangles, lighters and pens. There's even a doctor's stethoscope and a men's Titan watch. Stuff that couldn't conceivably belong to her.

I can only shake my head at the discovery. It tells me her kleptomania has not been cured by her fast.

Big Ben has become a new national icon. But she still has her old habits.

When Acharya calls me to his office on Thursday evening, I'm almost expecting it.

'It's something to do with Nirmala Ben's fast, isn't it?' I blurt out the moment Revathi ushers me into his private office.

'Correct. You've passed the fifth test, the test of resourcefulness, by showing you can be a good problem solver. To make Nirmala Ben's fast succeed you even navigated the messy terrain of mass politics. That's no mean achievement.'

'It certainly wasn't easy.'

'That's precisely the point. Resourcefulness is the ability to act effectively and imaginatively, especially in difficult situations. A CEO is above all a master strategist. A chess player who has mastered all the moves of his opponent. Leaders who are resourceful make things happen when the chips are down and the situation looks bleak. They are able to operate in the most lean conditions. They never give up. If the wall is too high to scale, they find a way around it.'

'Whatever I did, I did for Nirmala Ben. I just couldn't allow her to die.'

'You also had the foresight to know that Nirmala Ben

was channelling public anger against corruption into its most visible symbol, Atlas. And you made people believe that what Nirmala Ben was doing was worth supporting. The same strategy you used today to build an obscure Gandhian into a popular hero, you can use tomorrow to build a product into a brand. It could be your most valuable business secret when you become CEO of the ABC Group.'

'Well, I guess I got lucky.' I smile.

'Luck had nothing to do with it. You even managed to persuade Salim Ilyasi to endorse Nirmala Ben's fast. I received a voice message from the actor on my phone. How on earth did you engineer that?'

'Now that's a business secret I dare not reveal!'

Karan has been avoiding me for the last three days. Whenever I see him he has the preoccupied look of a student cramming for his final exam, with no idle moments to lose. So, when he saunters into the garden that evening, I do not know what to expect.

First, I tell him about my meeting with Acharya.

'Five down, two to go, eh?' he remarks.

'Look, you know and I know Acharya is leading me up the garden path. I have as much chance of running a ten-billion-dollar company as I have of winning the Miss World crown.'

'I would take issue with the Miss World part, but that's not important. What's important is that you must remain one step ahead of Acharya.'

'And what about you? Is the company still conducting an investigation into the Salim Ilyasi MMS?'

'That was the number-one item on the agenda of Mr Swapan Karak, the owner of Indus,' he responds gravely.

'Did he find out about you?' I ask with my heart thudding.

'I escaped!' he grins. 'Mr Swapan Karak has no inkling I was behind the MMS. The investigation ended today. It has come to the conclusion that the MMS was "a socially useful prank" perpetrated by a group of rogue hackers.'

I let out a sigh of relief. 'Phew! That was a close call. You've no idea how guilty I felt these last four days.'

He pats me gently on the back. 'I can imagine. That's why I was sorely tempted to send you another MMS, this time in the voice of Aamir Khan in *Three Idiots*.'

'Saying what?'

'Just three words. All izz well.'

The Sixth Test

150 Grams of Sacrifice

The LIG Colony runs, like the rest of middle-class India, on an intricate web of ties, relationships, obligations and favours. Everyone knows someone who knows someone. Mr Gupta, in A-49, for instance, is friends with a computer expert who meets the entire IT needs of the residents. Mr J. P. Aggarwal, in B-27, is the go-to man for all hardware-related requirements. Mrs Lalita, in C-18, is the busybody with a unique talent for spotting bargains, especially on clothes. Nirmala Ben, in B-25, is everyone's elder sister (since upgraded to universal leader). And Dr Dheeraj Mittal, in D-58, acts as the colony's resident physician.

Every three months we use our connection with Dr Mittal to get Ma's checkup done in the MCD government hospital in Sector 17, where Dr Mittal works as a nephrologist. He can easily afford to live in a much swankier apartment building but he prefers the LIG

Colony because of its convenience. In his Ford Fiesta he can zip across to the hospital in less than ten minutes.

My relationship with hospitals is like that of a battered wife who keeps returning to her abusive husband. I hate to visit them. A trip to the government hospital is enough to make an atheist out of a believer. You see so much pain and suffering that it prompts the question: how can a merciful God permit disease? Yet I cannot do without them. Hospitals are the boats that move damaged souls across the river of human sickness. They provide a quarterly certificate of reassurance that all is well with Ma and the world.

By now it has become a settled routine. I take Ma to the government hospital early on a Sunday morning. They take Ma's blood and urine. She is tested for B_{12} deficiency, iron deficiency and anaemia. A chest X-ray is done as well as an eye exam. Then Dr Mittal himself holds a consultation with us, armed with reports of CBC, FBS, PPBS, serum creatinine and urine culture. He gives her a good lecture on maintaining a sugar-free diet and taking her medicines regularly before renewing her prescription: glibenclamide for her diabetes, salbutamol inhalers for her asthma, diclofenac 50 mg for her arthritis and telmisartan 40 mg for her hypertension. 'Your mother is fine.' He usually makes a thumbs-up sign at me. 'Bring her back after three months.'

The last three-month period ended at the beginning of April. At that time we were all preoccupied with Nirmala Ben's historic fast. But the very first Sunday after that I am at the government hospital with Ma.

It is a cloudless sunny day outside but inside the

hospital it is gloomy and grey. Most of the tube lights are fused, and it is only the sunlight streaming through the two casement windows at either end that illuminates the reception area. The walls wear the faded, neglected look of a place that has seen better days. The air reeks of sweat, loud with people. A young mother in a blue sari is squatting in a corner, wailing inconsolably. There are long queues in front of the registration counter. It takes three hours just to get a hospital card for those without clout or connections.

As I traverse the corridors to the nephrology department, the sour, chemical smell of the hospital invades my nostrils, making me quicken my steps. Dr Mittal's office, on the third floor, is equally crowded. Most are elderly patients with chronic conditions, settled uneasily into the hard, plastic chairs inside the waiting room. Some of them give Ma curious glances, perhaps jogging their memories to check where they have seen her. Those who succeed will recognise her as the unknown woman by Nirmala Ben's side in TV coverage of the fast.

As usual, the duty nurse allows us to jump the queue, and ten minutes later we are face to face with Dr Dheeraj Mittal. A short man in his mid-forties, Dr Mittal has the slightly unkempt look of a forgetful professor with his shaggy dark hair and rimless eyeglasses. But he more than makes up for it with his pleasant bedside manner and deep medical knowledge. He exudes confidence and competence. 'Welcome, Maa-ji,' he greets Mother. 'I am told you have also become quite a celebrity, thanks to Nirmala Ben.'

'Nirmala Ben is lucky,' Ma says wryly. 'She doesn't have to endure these endless trips to the hospital.'

'If only you could maintain a constant weight you would also be spared these check-ups. But, every time I see you, your weight decreases a little.'

'What to do?' Ma sighs. 'Nirmala Ben is hale and hearty even after fasting for two weeks. I eat thrice a day and yet just cannot seem to put on any weight.'

Dr Mittal glances at me. 'Are you aware that two months ago Maa-ji collapsed in the house, due to hypo-glycaemia?'

'Ma never told me, Doctor. I learnt about it only now.'

'That is why we need to examine her more thoroughly this time,' says Dr Mittal as he begins scribbling on his pad.

He orders a battery of new tests: Hba1C, fructosamine, 1.5-anhydroglucitol, microalbumin, CMP, BUN, cystatin C, C-peptide – it is the first warning sign that this checkup is not proceeding according to script.

The tests take a full day and the results a full week. As usual they go directly to Dr Mittal. I have always found it strange that test results are shown to the doctor first, as though patients cannot be trusted with analysis of their own bodies.

That is what adds to the mystique of the medical pro-fession. Doctors and car mechanics have something in common. Both work under the hood and we have no accurate way of knowing what's happening down there, in the innards of the human body or the core of a car engine. Just as a perfectly good car can stall suddenly, our bodies can betray us in a myriad ways. So when Dr Mittal summons me to the hospital at 11 a.m. on Sunday, 24

April, I enter his office with the trepidation of a marginal student about to receive her report card.

'Is everything all right with Ma, Doctor?' I ask the moment I settle down in the chair opposite him.

The sombre expression on his face makes my chest start to tighten up. 'I have always believed in full disclosure with my patients,' he begins. 'That is why—'

'Please don't tell me it's cancer,' I interrupt him plaintively.

'No, it's not cancer,' he says.

'Thank God.' I exhale.

'No need to thank God just yet. Your mother has ESRD, which is just as bad.'

'ESRD? What's that?'

'End-stage renal disease, also known as chronic kidney failure. Diabetes and hypertension are the most common causes of ESRD, and your mother has both. These are diseases that affect the blood vessels and they impair the kidneys' ability to filter blood and regulate fluids in the body. In end stage kidney failure, the kidneys function at less than fifteen per cent of their normal capacity.'

I am shocked. 'But . . . but she looks fine. There must be some mistake.'

'The test results are in front of me and they don't lie.' He picks up a printout and begins reeling off figures: 'Haemoglobin six grams, fasting blood sugar eighty, PPBS a hundred and ten, serum creatinine 7.5 milligram, urine shows protein of three-plus and sugar is also three-plus.' He takes off his eyeglasses and scratches his brow. 'If these aren't indicators of ESRD, then what are they?'

'Then how come we are discovering this now?'

'Kidney disease is a silent killer, proceeding stealthily over many years, with no signs or symptoms the patient can recognise. When detected late, as in your mother's case, it can be fatal.'

Fatal. The word sends a chill up my spine.

'The only way to treat ESRD is with dialysis or transplantation,' he presses on. 'Permanent dialysis you won't be able to afford. So there's only one option left to you.'

'What's that?'

'A kidney transplant. Your mother needs a new kidney and quickly.'

'And how much is a new kidney going to cost?'

'Nothing.'

'Nothing? How come?'

'Because it will be yours. Or your sister's.'

'I . . . I don't understand.'

'Under the Human Organ Transplantation Act of 1994, only living, related donors are permitted to provide organs to a patient. This includes father, mother, brother and sister.'

'Donating blood is one thing. But how can a living person donate an organ like the kidney?'

'It's called living-donor kidney transplantation. You see, the advantage of the kidney is that it is a paired organ. We have two of them. The second kidney is actually redundant, because it serves no useful purpose. In fact, some say it wastes the resources of the body. So it is possible to remove a kidney from a living person. Reasonably healthy humans can function quite well with one kidney. The only thing is, are you and Neha up to it?'

I am staring at the floor, head hanging down, trying desperately not to throw up. Nodding weakly, I ask, 'How do we go about it?'

'Well, I'll need both you and Neha to come in and give blood tests. If possible, today itself. The good thing is that your mother's blood type is AB positive, which makes her a universal receiver. I'll just have to do a tissue antigen match and crossmatching to determine final compatibility for organ donation.'

'And what if Neha and I are not found compatible?'

'We'll cross that bridge when we come to it, right?' He smiles brightly at me, but it does nothing to lift my mood.

'Thank you, Doctor,' I say, my voice sounding hoarse and unnatural, and exit his office.

The waiting room outside his chamber contains a faded poster showing the main structures of the urinary system. I've never given it a second glance. But today it draws me like a magnet. I study the two dark, bean-shaped organs located one on either side of the spine, just below the rib cage, as though they were coordinates to some long-buried treasure. They look quite small, each no bigger than a clenched fist. Both are covered with a mesh of fibrous tissue, nerves and blood vessels. Both have ureters going into the urinary bladder. To me the left kidney and the right kidney look identical. And there is nothing in the diagram to suggest that one of them is redundant.

By the time I reach home, my mind is thoroughly

confused and spinning with worst-case scenarios. Ma is in the kitchen as usual, preparing lunch. She doesn't even bother to ask me about her test results. She has conditioned herself to believe that death is inevitable and no amount of antibiotics will stop it when her time comes. It is just one last desire, one final hope that keeps her going. 'All I am waiting for is to see my two daughters get married and settled,' she has told Nirmala Ben innumerable times. 'After that I can die in peace.'

Neha is engrossed, as usual, in herself. When I enter our room she is preening before a mirror, imitating Priya Capoorr's iconic pose in *Love in Bangkok*. 'I have decided to apply for the Miss India contest, *didi*,' she informs me. 'A voice may have its ups and downs, but there is no doubting a beautiful face. After all, a rose is a rose is a rose, isn't it?'

'Can you for once think of something else besides beauty pageants and modelling competitions?' I rebuke her. 'Dr Mittal has got Ma's test results and he says she has end-stage renal disease. She needs a new kidney.'

'A new kidney? So where do we buy it from? Big Bazaar?'

'It's not a joke, Neha. You can't buy a kidney: you can only donate it. Dr Mittal has called you and me for a blood test to see if either of us can be a kidney donor for Ma.'

Neha recoils as though I had slapped her. 'Kidney donor? Are you out of your mind, *didi*? There's no way I'm giving my kidney.'

'Fine. Then you go tell Ma that she is about to die.'

At least I shame her into coming with me to the

hospital. We go past the reception, and head straight to the clinical laboratory on the first floor.

The lab nurse is a middle-aged, sour-faced woman in a stiff, starched, white uniform, who has already received her instructions from Dr Mittal. With cold-blooded efficiency she locates a vein in my inner elbow region and is poised to pierce the skin with her hypodermic needle when my cell phone rings. It is the Red Cross, calling to remind me of World Blood Donation Day on 14 June. 'The blood centre is running low again on the Bombay blood group,' the duty clerk informs me. 'Would you care to come in for your quarterly donation? We can even send a car to bring you.'

I marvel at their timing. 'Sorry,' I tell the clerk. 'I am in a hospital right now, about to give blood for my mother. I cannot help you out this time.'

The nurse gives me a disapproving frown and guides the needle into my vein. I have given blood many times before but somehow this feels different. As the dark, crimson liquid begins to fill the syringe, I am filled with a nameless dread, a shape-shifting monster that takes the form of my worst fears. The sample will soon be tested, when it will whisper its secrets, reveal its antigens and antibodies. And I know deep in my gut that this is one test I would be happy to fail.

Neha, who has never given blood before, is fidgety and nervous when her turn comes. She bites her lower lip, clenches her hands and avoids looking at the syringe. The moment the needle enters her skin she begins hyperventilating and complains of feeling weak and dizzy. 'Don't be a drama queen,' the nurse shushes her and continues to draw blood. Neha endures the procedure with gritted teeth, glaring daggers at the nurse, and throws up immediately afterwards.

Once the blood is drawn, there is an agonising three-hour wait for the results before Dr Mittal calls us to his office.

'I have good news,' he says, addressing me. 'The HLA test has yielded a perfect six-of-six match for Neha and a half-match, that is three-of-six match, for you, which is just as good, because the partial rejection can be overcome through the use of immunosuppressive drugs. And the crossmatch for both of you is negative.'

'Negative?' Neha, who has been gripping the seat rest, suddenly unclenches her hand, a quick flicker of relief crossing her face. 'That means we are incompatible with Ma's blood group, isn't it?'

'On the contrary it means that there is perfect compatibility. In this test, we mix white blood cells from the donor with blood from the recipient. If the white blood cells are attacked and die, then the crossmatch is "positive", and it means the recipient's immune system cannot accept the donated organ. But if the crossmatch is "negative", then the donor's antigens are compatible with the recipient's. Both your and Sapna's blood is compatible with Maa-ji's and both of you are capable of donating your kidney. Now it is up to you two sisters to decide who loves Mother more.'

Neha and I look at each other, and then look away. The air in the room grows dense and oppressive, weighed down by the gravity of the situation and the hospital's ominous ambience.

Dr Mittal senses the palpable tension between us. 'I know it is not an easy decision. That is why I want both of you to think about it carefully and come back to me in seventy-two hours. That's three full days.'

We walk home in silence, not knowing what to say or do next. It is a new challenge to both of us, something we have never faced before. The only ground rule we agree on is not to breathe a word about this to Ma.

That night, as I lie in the dark, I can hear Neha tossing and turning in her bed. And I know she is thinking the same thought as me. All our filial love and affection has eventually come down to this bizarre predicament: whom do you care for more – your mother or your kidney?

It is a question I wish no daughter should ever have to answer. For it has the potential of pitting sister against sister, laying bare the hidden weakness of the soul. Every anxiety, every doubt, every foible and pretence waylays me in the street of indecision. Every selfish desire sprouts in the garden of my fear.

I occupy myself by researching ESRD and kidney transplants. The kidney of an adult human, I learn, measures ten to twelve centimetres in length, contains one million nephrons and weighs approximately 150 grams. I trawl the Internet, seeking inspiration from those who have donated kidneys to their loved ones and are still leading happy, healthy lives.

Neha spends her time researching the opposite, marshalling arguments against donation. She holds whispered conversations with me when Ma has gone off to sleep. 'Donating a kidney is not like giving your iPod to a friend,' she says. 'It is a major surgical procedure and carries long-term health risks. After the operation you can forget about playing any more sports or doing physical activity. Besides, I don't even buy the argument that the second kidney is redundant. God forbid, but if something were to happen to me one day, say an accident or some serious disease, the second kidney would come in mighty handy.'

There is some truth to what she says. My research reveals that people with just one kidney tend to suffer from a few problems later in life. Some have high blood pressure, others a condition called proteinuria, which refers to excessive protein in the urine, and a third category has been known to suffer from a reduced glomerular filtration rate, which basically means that the single kidney is no longer as effective in removing wastes from the bloodstream.

'After knowing all this, you still think we should go ahead with kidney donation?' Neha demands.

'We don't have a choice. If Ma doesn't get a new kidney, she dies,' I respond. 'Blood demands a price. Love demands sacrifice.'

'Then you make it,' she says with characteristic bluntness. 'I have to appear for the regionals of the Miss India contest. I can't go looking pale and unhealthy. Besides, you are the eldest in the family.'

Neha has hurt me before; now she is trying to backstab me. I can feel the knife of betrayal twisting up my insides. And it fills me with utter disgust. 'Why? What special favours have you all done me?' I erupt in virtuous anger. 'Where does it say that the eldest has to suffer for everyone else? I gave up my dreams, I cut short my studies, and now you are forcing me to even cut open my body?'

For once Neha is dumbfounded. She takes an involuntary step back, her eyes wide from disbelief. Then a gasp of contrition escapes her lips and she falls down at my feet. 'Forgive me, *didi*,' she cries, clutching my legs. 'I take back my words. After all that you've done for me, how could I be such an ingrate? I don't deserve to live.'

It is enough to make me break out in tears. I raise her up, mumbling, 'We're in this together, stupid.'

We cling to each other, two scared souls trying desperately to gather the courage to do one brave thing.

When the moral instinct for filial love collides with the primal instinct for self-preservation, the first casualty is decision-making. We try to postpone the inevitable by immersing ourselves in the mundane routine of life. I religiously go to my job, Neha to her college. At night, closeted in the same bedroom, we hardly speak to each other, suffocated by our anxieties.

For forty-eight hours we remain in deadlock, tense with uncertainty, torn with irresolution, like a jury unable to agree upon its verdict.

It is Neha who suggests a way out of the impasse on the third morning. 'Let's toss, like they do in cricket. Heads it is me. Tails it will be you. Okay?'

I nod. Perhaps it is the neatest way. Sometimes the big decisions in life have to be left to pure, cold chance.

Neha rummages through her clothes drawer and comes up with an old one rupee-coin, its surface tarnished by time. We gather in the middle of our bedroom, like two duellists about to meet their destiny. Neha shows me both sides, confirming that it is not a trick coin. Then, without further ado, she tosses it up. Though aged and well-worn, the coin catches the sunlight streaming through the open window as it spins in the air. Neha catches it expertly on the downward arc. She slaps it down on the back of her free hand, sheathing it. 'Our decision is sealed. There will be no second chance, agreed?' she asks in a shaky voice.

'Agreed. Heads or tails, it will be God's decision, not ours. Let's resolve to honour it.'

Neha nods. 'I repeat: heads it will be me, tails it will be you.'

'Now remove your hand.' I swallow hard. 'Let's see our fate.'

Slowly, ever so slowly, like a plot twist being revealed on a soap opera, Neha slides away her hand. Sunlight bathes the coin, and the three lion heads from off our national emblem glint at me.

Neha's face crumples with shock. A sob catches in her throat at the terrible finality of the verdict. But she regains her poise equally quickly, displaying the same stoic resolve she showed in Mumbai. 'If it is me, so be it. I will gladly give my kidney to Ma.'

We have finally reached closure, but instead of making me feel better it makes me miserable. I want to hug my sister and tell her, You will do no such thing. I will fulfil my duty as an elder. But what emerges from my throat is a gargled, 'Sorry! Tough luck!'

We are shortly on our way to the hospital for our rendezvous with Dr Mittal. Today being a weekday, the hospital is less crowded. But it has the same smell of blood and antiseptic that makes me want to puke.

As we step onto the landing on the third floor, a dark, swarthy man accosts us. I recognise him as Tilak Raj, who works as a ward boy at the hospital. His son Raju is part of my Sunday English class.

'Madam-ji, can I have a word with you?' he whispers, drawing us into a secluded corner.

'Yes?' I say cautiously.

'I am told your mother needs a new kidney.'

'That is correct. How did you know?'

'I overheard Dr Mittal tell the duty nurse. So how are you arranging the kidney?'

'Neha is donating hers.'

'Tch, tch.' He shakes his head. 'What is this? Such a beautiful girl. You want to kill her future? After donating her kidney she will fade like a wilted flower. Take my advice, don't take this step.'

'Then what can we do? We cannot afford permanent dialysis.'

'There is another way.' He winks.

'Tell me!' Neha almost clutches his arm.

'You can buy a kidney.'

'Buy? But that is illegal,' I remark. 'The Transplantation Act does not allow it.'

'Are you going to look at the law or the future of your sister? You want a kidney, I can get you a kidney, and dirt cheap too.'

'How cheap?' asks Neha.

'You will find out when you go to this address.' He

takes out a slip of paper from his top pocket and passes it to me. It gives the contact particulars of a Dr J. K. Nath, a nephrologist working at the Unity Kidney Institute, a private hospital located in Sector 15 of Rohini.

'Isn't the hospital owned by our local MLA, Anwar Noorani?' I ask, recalling the politician with the dyed hair and long sideburns I once encountered in the metro.

'Exactly.' Tilak Raj nods. 'MLA *sahib* is very helpful. It was he who got me this job here. He'll help your mother too. His hospital specialises in kidney transplants.'

'And what about the cost?'

'Tell Dr Nath I sent you. He will give you a good price.' Tilak Raj smiles knowingly and slinks silently down the stairs.

'I didn't know Tilak Raj was a tout, running an illegal kidney racket,' I muse aloud as I watch his disappearing back.

'I don't care if it's illegal or not, *didi*,' says Neha. 'I would like to meet Dr Nath.'

'I think that would be a mistake. We should first discuss with Dr Mittal.'

'Because it's my kidney, not yours, isn't it?' Neha says with sudden vehemence. In that unguarded moment her mask of bravado slips. She sinks down to the floor and all her pent-up anxiety and frustration comes flooding out in uncontrollable sobs.

I feel a surge of compassion for her, accompanied by a flare of hope. Perhaps a miracle is about to take place. 'I won't go to work today,' I tell Neha. 'Come, let's go meet Dr Nath.'

We step out of the hospital and hail an auto-rickshaw for Sector 15. Thirty rupees and fifteen minutes later, we are at the gates of the Unity Kidney Institute.

From outside, the hospital looks like an office building, with an all-glass façade. Inside, it resembles a hotel lobby, all marble and stone, spotlessly clean.

The reception area has the bustling efficiency of a military cantonment. I am surprised to see quite a few foreigners in the registration queue. A smart young receptionist beams at us. 'Yes, what can I do for you?'

'We are here to meet Dr J. K. Nath,' I say.

'Do you have an appointment?'

'No. Can you get us one?'

Dr Nath sees us after an hour's wait. He is a bald, diminutive man in his early fifties, with a fleshy, clean-shaven face and yellow teeth. Even though he is in his doctor's uniform, there is something about him that reminds me of Keemti Lal, that weaselly clerk in the sub-divisional magistrate's office. He gives us a kindly smile, but the hungry glint in his eye betrays him, makes me wary.

'We were referred to you by Tilak Raj from the government hospital in Sector 17,' I begin hesitantly.

'Good.' He nods. 'It means you need a kidney. Is it for her?' He jerks his thumb at Neha.

'No. It is for our mother. She has ESRD.'

'Well, you've come to the right place. I can arrange a replacement kidney for your mother once I know her blood profile.'

'From a deceased donor?'

'No, a living one. This is the great thing about the

market economy of the twenty-first century. You can buy a kidney as easily as you can buy a car. It's all a matter of demand and supply.'

'But won't that be illegal? I am told only close relatives can donate their kidney.'

'You have obviously not read the 1994 Act fully. There is a clause for altruistic donation under which even unrelated persons can donate their kidney provided they feel emotionally attached to the recipient.'

'But we don't know anyone like that.'

'You leave that to me. I'll find the donor and it will all be perfectly legal. You'll be surprised to see how quickly emotional attachment can be formed once we bring money into the equation.'

'So how much are we looking at?'

'At UKI, we charge a flat rate of six lakhs for a kidney transplant package, all inclusive.'

'Six lakhs? That's way beyond our budget.'

He passes a hand over his bald pate. 'Then you better go somewhere else. Just know that more than a hundred and fifty thousand Indians need a kidney transplant every year, but only three thousand five hundred kidneys are available. That's why it's a bit expensive. And we have enough patients, both from India and abroad, who are willing to pay the price. Six lakhs is a steal. It's less than fifteen thousand dollars. In America you would have to pay more than ten times that for a kidney transplant.'

It is clear that we are dealing with a wheeler-dealer businessman rather than a principled physician. And there is no way we can afford his fancy prices. 'Let's go.' I tug

Neha's arm. 'It's pointless wasting any more time here. Dr Mittal must be waiting for us.'

'No, *didi*,' Neha says with a firm shake of the head. 'Whatever happens, I am not going back to the government hospital.'

I am struck speechless at the sudden, insane idea that takes hold of Neha. She is desperate to buy a kidney, and cost be damned.

Neha takes over the negotiations from then on. 'I'm just a student. Can't you give me a student discount?' she asks Dr Nath, her lips curving into a smile that is simultaneously pleading and teasing.

The doctor is instantly smitten. 'Okay, just for you I will reduce the price by a lakh. How does five lakhs sound to you?'

'That is also way too high.' Neha pouts.

I watch in silence as she trades figures with Dr Nath like an expert haggler. Finally, the kidney specialist throws up his hands. 'What do you think this is, a grocery shop? My last price is two lakhs, and only because I take pity on you. Take it or leave it.'

'We'll take it,' Neha says quickly.

I lean into Neha's ear. 'How the hell are we going to rustle up so much money?' I demand, my voice a furious whisper. 'Even Ma has no more jewellery left.'

'You leave that to me,' she says confidently as she rises to shake Dr Nath's hand. 'Thank you, Doctor. You'll get the money in less than a week.'

'In that case let's begin the preliminary procedures right away. Bring in your mother tomorrow for a blood test,' says the doctor.

As we exit the hospital, Neha momentarily looks up at the heavens, searching the sky. I crane my neck too, squinting at the clouds floating across the blue expanse. I do not know what Neha saw, but I fail to glimpse any sign of a miracle.

Neha reveals her strategy only when we are halfway to the house. 'I have many friends who are stinking rich. They will lend me the money. Two lakhs is chickenfeed for them, probably less than their poodle's monthly food bill.'

I feel like asking her where these friends were when we needed money to retain the flat, but decide against it. Who am I to judge her? After all, it's her kidney at stake. And she can beg, borrow or steal that money for all I care.

There is a big crowd gathered in the courtyard when the auto drops us in front of the LIG Colony. I learn from Dhiman Singh that Mrs Nirmala Mukherjee Shah, our most famous tenant, is leaving B-25 to shift into Gandhi Niketan, a community centre for the practice of Gandhian values, situated in the premium and upscale locality of West End in South Delhi.

The move does not come as a surprise to me. Nirmala Ben is no longer the simple Gandhian with the frugal lifestyle that I used to know. She has acquired the trappings of a well-heeled guru. Her hair is now immaculately made up, her plain chappals have been replaced by designer sandals, and even her trademark sari looks whiter. Nowadays she is constantly surrounded by a retinue of loyal followers, admirers and hangers-on. Even though her flat is just three doors down from ours, her fame has created a distance between us, a chasm too deep to be easily crossed.

'*Arrey*, Sapna *beti*,' she calls out the moment she spots me. 'How have you been?' She embraces me warmly.

'I'm fine. But why are you deserting the colony?'

'*Shoo karoon?* What to do?' she sighs. 'I didn't want to go, but my comrades insist that this place is too small for my daily talks.'

'I'll miss you,' I tell her, genuinely meaning it, too.

'*Arrey*, I am not leaving the city, only going a few kilometres away. You and Susheela must come and visit me whenever you want homemade dhoklas and rasagullas.'

As I watch her get into the back seat of a sleek Hyundai Sonata, I have the distinct feeling that I am seeing her in person for the last time. Henceforth I will be able to meet her only in the pages of the newspaper and on the TV screen.

At least she is using her newfound stardom to touch lives and inspire positive change. Her campaign against high-level graft has continued to gather momentum. There are daily news reports that the noose around Atlas Investments is tightening. Government investigators claim to have secured crucial bits of evidence from Mauritius, igniting a wave of speculation that the names of the individuals behind Atlas will be revealed soon.

Inside our flat, Ma is slumped at the dining table, crying silently. She is disconsolate at Nirmala Ben's departure. 'My best friend in the colony has gone,' she laments. 'I wish I could go away from this world.'

'You are not going anywhere,' I tell her sternly.

'What's the point?' She spreads her hands. 'My two daughters never tell me anything. They treat me like a child, do things behind my back.'

I share a wry glance with Neha. Ma is in one of her periodic bouts of depression, imagining conspiracies everywhere.

'What is it that we have kept from you?' I challenge her.

'I know you and Neha are up to something. Is it something to do with my test results? At least tell me what Dr Mittal said. How much time have I got left?'

I sense the moment has come for full disclosure. 'Dr Mittal said you have a disease called ESRD, in which the kidneys become less effective. That is why you have been feeling tired, losing your appetite, having muscle cramps. What you need is a new kidney. And we are arranging one for you.'

'How? By giving me one of yours?' Ma's hand flies to her lips as she contemplates the horror of that implication. 'May God strike me dead before I cause harm to my children. A mother's job is to give, never to take.'

'It won't be our kidney,' I assure her. 'It will be another donor's.'

'Why rob someone of their kidney for my sake? No one knows how much time they have left in this life. Perhaps my time has come,' she says with the world-weary air of a much older woman. 'No point wasting any more money on surgery and medicines for me.'

Mothers have this awesome ability of instantly humbling their children. All our lives we never thought of Ma as separate from the kitchen. Just because she was a simple housewife from the rustic town of Mainpuri, a Class 8 pass who didn't know Camus and computers and didn't speak English, we never took her seriously, never really tried to understand her. Alka was the one who was closest to her. Papa's attitude towards her was one of haughty superiority, and Neha and I subconsciously imitated it. We relegated Ma to a background presence, someone who kept the house running and kept track of religious occasions and the network of family relationships with distant aunts and even more distant cousins, while we wrestled with more important stuff like quadratic equations and *Hamlet*. Even after Papa's death, it never crossed our minds to try to find out how she was coping. Did she feel lonely or weighed down by the trivia of life? She killed off all her wants and needs for everyone else's. And now, when her life is on the line, she is prepared to sacrifice even that for our sake.

I rush forward and embrace Mother, guilt welling up inside me like a tearless sob. 'You're only forty-seven,' I remind her. 'Your time has not come and neither is it going to come any time soon. You have fulfilled your duty as a mother; now we will fulfil our duty as daughters.'

'Not *we, I*,' Neha interjects. 'I am the one arranging a replacement kidney for you from the best kidney hospital in the city.'

I gape at her in astonishment. It is not just what she said but the way she said it, simultaneously taunting and patronising me.

'But it must cost a lot,' Ma agonises.

'You don't have to worry about money as long as *I* am

there to look after you,' Neha says, directing yet another barb at me.

'My darling daughter!' Ma dabs at her eyes and pulls Neha to her chest.

I feel sequestered, cast out from this family scene, like an uninvited guest at a party. Neha is suddenly acting all grown up and I am finding it difficult to come to grips with it. But, then, I myself am responsible for it. By abdicating my responsibility as an elder, by forsaking my duty as a daughter, I have allowed Neha to usurp my place. And now she has cut me out, made me a pariah in my own house.

I go to bed with a bruised ego and a nagging conscience. Money can buy you a kidney, but it can't buy you a sister's respect.

Dr Mittal calls me the next day, just when I am busy explaining the unique features of the Sony BX420 series of LED TVs to a customer. 'What happened? I thought you and Neha were to meet me yesterday.' He sounds irate and a little agitated.

'There has been a change of plan,' I inform him. 'We are exploring the possibility of obtaining a kidney under the altruistic-donation category.'

There is silence at the other end. Finally he asks, 'And who is this altruistic donor?'

'A friend of ours,' I lie.

'Then you better bring him in. I need to check him. It's imperative we perform the transplant within the next five to seven days. Your mother's condition is quite serious. She's dying a little every day.'

'I understand, Doctor.' I quickly end the call, feeling drained and shaken.

It is impossible for me to concentrate on work after that, earning a reprimand from the manager, who is already annoyed at my unauthorised absence yesterday.

Two more days pass and all Neha is able to manage is ₹10,000. Apparently, her buddies were not as generous as she thought. Still, she is not willing to concede defeat. 'Some of my friends are out of town. I'm waiting for them to come back. You rest assured, I'll get the full amount.'

The only bit of good news comes from Dr Nath. 'Success!' he exults on the phone to Neha. 'I have found an excellent donor for your mother. She is an extremely young and healthy girl. And all her parameters match your mother's perfectly. So when are you coming to make the payment? We would like the amount in full, and in cash.'

'Soon, Doctor,' Neha assures him. 'I'm working on it.'

Monday, 2 May, opens with the news of Osama bin Laden's death. We are stunned to learn that he has been killed in a firefight with American commandos deep inside Pakistan.

The news of Osama's death does not excite me as much as the news Neha gives me that evening. 'I did it, *didi*! I got the two lakhs.'

'Really?'

She retrieves her handbag, a fake Gucci. 'Ta-*da*!' She imitates a trumpet fanfare as she dumps two thick bundles

of thousand-rupee notes on the bed. 'Each bundle contains a hundred thousand.'

I pat her shoulders. 'I'm proud of you. So who was this
magnanimous friend?'

'I can't tell you his name.'

'His? You mean it's a man?'

Neha suddenly becomes cagey. 'Look, you want to eat
the mangoes or count the trees? What's important is that
we *have* the money, not how I got it or who gave it to
me.'

'You're right,' I say, conceding the point. 'The important thing is that we can get Ma's operation done now.'

I go to bed that night with a warm glow in my heart.
Osama bin Laden was dead. And Ma was going to live.

Dr Nath's chamber reeks of some kind of cloying perfume
when I step into it at 10 a.m. the next day, dressed in a
white salvar kameez.

The specialist greets me with the shameless eagerness of
an adolescent on his first date. 'Where's your sister?' he
asks, gazing hopefully at the door.

'Neha has her exams. She won't be coming to the hospital any more,' I reply, almost involuntarily adjusting my
dupatta over my chest.

'Oh.' Dr Nath tries to hide his disappointment by
becoming officious and businesslike. 'I have reserved the
OT for the day after tomorrow. You need to admit your
mother tomorrow, so that we may monitor her condition.'

'I'll do that.'

'You have the cash?'

'Yes, exactly two lakhs.' I open my purse and start taking the bundles out.

'Wait.' He stops me. 'I don't handle cash. You need to deposit it with the cashier downstairs and bring me the receipt.'

'I have one request.'

'Yes?'

'I would like to meet the donor to personally say thank you. Can you arrange it?'

'Look, in such matters it is best not to know too much. We follow the same policy as in anonymous adoptions.'

'The donor will be fine after the operation, won't she, doctor?'

'Of course she will be. Healthy human beings can live quite easily with one kidney.'

'At least tell me her name.'

'What good will that do? But if you are desperate to know, it is Sita Devi, like the wife of Lord Ram in *Ramayana*. Satisfied? Now go and get me the receipt from the cashier.'

I step out of his office and take the elevator to the ground floor. The payment window is located on the far side of Reception. Just as I have finished paying the money to the cashier, I hear what sounds like an argument coming from the Reception area.

'I've told you before also not to come here. Does nothing enter your brain?' a man's voice hisses harshly.

'What to do, *sahib*? I need the money urgently. My son is very sick,' a woman's plaintive whimper comes in response. I cannot see her because of a pillar blocking my view.

'You will only get the money tomorrow, after the operation. But let me warn you, Sita, if you set foot here one more time, we are going to stop doing business with you. Then don't blame me if your family starves to death. Now go back to the clinic.'

Sita. My ears prick up at the name. Almost instinctively my head swivels in the direction of Reception and I tilt to one side to see behind the pillar. I am expecting a healthy young girl, but the supplicant who turns back dejected from the counter is a middle-aged woman, dressed in a tattered green sari. She looks like a skeleton, with her sunken eyes, gaunt face and thin, chapped lips. Her hair is dirty and unkempt. Her ribcage is clearly visible under her blouse, the skin shrivelled like some old parchment. She drags her feet slowly, as though suffering the aftereffect of a major operation. In the swanky environs of Unity Kidney Institute she looks as out of place as a meat dish in a Jain vegetarian meal.

No, I tell myself. She can't be Ma's donor. But something about the woman piques my interest, like a story that has to be read. Inserting the receipt into my purse, I follow her as she shuffles out of the hospital's revolving door.

With her head hung low, she ambles to a bus stop adjacent to the hospital. A Delhi Transport Corporation bus bound for Gurgaon arrives within ten minutes and she boards it. After a moment's hesitation I clamber in too, taking the seat directly across from her.

Sitting within touching distance of Sita, I examine her closely. There is a bandage peeking out of her back and her arms are riddled with punctures of surgical needles. It makes me even more curious to speak to her, but she barely notices me, a stranger in a bus full of strangers. From time to time her thumb brushes over the bottom of her eyes, wiping away tears.

The bus traverses an unfamiliar route via the Outer Ring Road, which is congested with traffic. Everywhere I look I see people, cars and more people. As I watch the teeming streets and maddening rush of the city, I am overcome with a strange burst of emotion. How vast the city is, and yet how lonely. No one has time for anyone else. Our lives are ruled by the clock, each one of us trapped in its ticking, stuck in the rat race with no end in sight. Perhaps we are no different from cars, each a self-contained cocoon, each travelling apart from the others, hurtling down a highway to nowhere.

Lost in my thoughts I fail to notice the passage of time. The bus is already in Gurgaon and my quarry has risen from her seat, preparing to disembark.

The bus stops in front of a glitzy shopping arcade full of designer brands and stylish cafés. Through the glass façade I catch a glimpse of the sprawling food court on the second floor, teeming with call-centre executives and suburban yuppies soaking in the hip atmosphere. The mall is emblematic of Gurgaon, a *nouveau riche* city bustling with sleek office buildings, multiplexes and plush housing colonies. People say it looks more Dallas than Delhi. Perhaps that is why it has become a preferred hub of many multinational companies.

Sita casts a wistful eye at the mall, mesmerised by the neon ideograms promising pizzas and fried chicken. Then, with the resigned air of a woman who has accepted her lot in life, she turns around and crosses the road.

I follow her down a couple of blocks, making sure she doesn't spot me. Eventually, she enters a side street and I find myself in a leafy residential area. It has large houses, paved walkways and few pedestrians. After the frenetic bustle of the mall, it is a haven of solitude, the torpid calm of noon broken only by the whirring of air-conditioning units, occasional cars passing, and the faint hum of jazz drifting from an open window somewhere.

Sita stops in front of a modest, double-storey house, painted white with green shutters. A wooden nameplate on the wall outside identifies the house simply as '3734'. There is no name of the occupant. The other intriguing thing is that it has a guardhouse, with a uniformed guard.

Sita speaks to the guard and he allows her to enter through the metal gate. I am still debating what to do when I see a familiar face approaching from the other side of the road. It is none other than Tilak Raj, the ward boy from the government hospital, escorting a man who, from the dust and grime on his clothes, looks like a day labourer. I duck behind a tree, waiting for Tilak Raj to pass. But his destination, too, is house number 3734. I watch him exchange a few words with the guard and then enter the building with his companion.

By now my curiosity is killing me. I simply have to find out what's happening inside the house. Fixing up my courage, I approach the guard.

'Yes? What do you want?' He gazes at me suspiciously.

'I have come to meet Tilak Raj,' I reply, nervously clutching my purse. 'He told me he would meet me here.'

'Yes, he's inside.' The guard nods and unlatches the metal gate.

I enter through an open door into what looks like a waiting room. The day labourer is sitting on a plastic chair, together with two other men and Sita. There is no sign of Tilak Raj.

I wander out of the waiting room into a corridor. Inside, the house is quite spacious. There are at least two other rooms on the ground floor.

I peep into the first one and discover a man lying in a metal bed, an IV going into his arm. 'It's paining a lot, Sister,' he groans, thinking me to be a nurse.

I step closer. A clipboard attached to his bed identifies him as Mohammad Idris. His age is listed as twenty-nine, but he looks ten years older with his straggly grey beard and hollow cheeks. 'See here, Sister, this is where it hurts,' he murmurs, lifting up his shirt. I recoil in shock at the sight that meets my eye. There is an ugly, puckered 10-inch wound in his side, bristling with black surgical thread. It looks like a patch-up job by a particularly callous surgeon.

'If I had known it will be so painful, I would have thought twice before agreeing to sell my kidney,' he says before lapsing into a coughing fit.

I enter the next room to find a woman in a similar condition. Sunita, who is thirty-eight, is strung up with IV leads that are tangled around her arms and chest. Her dark skin is stretched tight across her cheekbones, and her eyes are shadowed in dark circles. She also has an incision in exactly the same spot as Idris, the wound still draining liquid despite the surgical thread holding ragged edges of skin together.

Unlike Idris, she has no regrets about the operation. 'Doctor-*babu* said the second kidney is of no use and takes up unnecessary space. Might as well make some money from it.'

'How much did you get?' I ask her.

'They promised me thirty, but gave me twenty thousand. Still, it's enough to live on for six months at least,' she replies.

So both the patients have sold their kidneys and are now in postoperative recovery. But who has performed the operations, and where?

The mystery is solved when I go up the stairs to the first floor. I enter through a set of swinging doors into a hallway. There is a toilet on one side and a metal door with two glass portholes on the other. Just above the door is a red light flashing like a beacon. I peep through the porthole and freeze. Because before my eyes is a scene straight out of a grisly horror film. There is a patient lying on an operating table, surrounded by masked doctors in green scrubs and lab-coated technicians. There are oxygen tanks, anaesthesia machines, and contraptions and devices I have never seen before. Surgical instruments are lined up neatly on tables, and the shelves are stacked with surgical supplies. I am looking at a full-fledged operating theatre. The air inside, though, is far from antiseptic. It reeks of desperation and exploitation.

The setup is becoming clear to me. This is the kidney black market that has led to the phenomenon of 'transplant tourism'. Dr Nath gets poor, indigent people to sell their kidneys, which are extracted at this facility, and then provided to rich Indian patients and medical tourists from abroad who are willing to shell out big bucks for a transplant. MLA Anwar Noorani is the final link in the chain, the kingpin providing political protection to this nefarious racket.

I'm not sure what galls me more, this brazen harvesting of human organs or my own reprehensible attempt to procure a living kidney donor. This nondescript clinic is thirty kilometres away from the swanky Unity Kidney Institute, but the gap between donors and donees is much wider. Mirza Metal Works was a sweatshop run by children. This is worse: a death trap for the poor.

Feeling overwhelmed and nauseated, I turn away from the operating room only to bump into Tilak Raj. 'What are you doing here?' His eyes widen.

'I came to see the donor who is giving her kidney for my mother. I now realise it was a mistake. I should never have come here.'

'That's right. Those who want to enjoy meat shouldn't visit the slaughterhouse.' He grins. His dark smile sickens me. I now realise he is as much a part of this illegal operation as Dr Nath.

'Anyway, Sita's operation will be performed today,' he adds as he escorts me down to the waiting room. 'By tomorrow the kidney for your mother will be delivered.'

'I don't want it any more.'

'What are you saying?' Tilak Raj's jaw slackens. 'You don't want Sita's kidney?' He says it loud enough for everyone in the waiting room to hear.

'Yes. I can't take her kidney. One person's happiness cannot be born of another one's misery.'

Sita springs out of her chair and rushes towards me. 'What did you say?' she demands, a manic gleam in her eyes.

'I don't want your kidney,' I repeat. 'It will be a sin to accept it.'

'No!' She lets out a terrifying shriek. 'My son will die. They promised me thirty thousand. Where will I get so much money? I've already given my liver. A kidney is all I'm left with. Please take it.'

'I'm sorry.'

'Sorry?' She crouches suddenly, and begins circling me like a predatory creature. 'You rich people, you think just by saying sorry you can get away with anything. I'll kill you, *kutiya, saali.*' She lunges at me, scrabbling at my face like a woman possessed.

Taken by surprise, I fall backwards, almost crashing into a chair.

She pins me to the floor and begins raining blows on my shoulders and head, her face a mask of insane fury. I try to defend myself, flailing to get her off me and not succeeding. Her need is greater than mine, and so is her rage.

It is Tilak Raj who comes to my rescue by physically wrenching Sita off me. 'Have you gone mad?' He grabs her by the throat and slaps her twice.

She continues to glare at me sullenly like a reprimanded child, breathing heavily through her nostrils.

Tilak Raj turns to me. 'Can I ask you a question?'

I nod.

'Why won't you take Sita's kidney? I assure you it is perfectly healthy, hundred per cent guaranteed.'

'It is not a question of health, but of morality. I had become weak. That is why I was looking for an easy way out. But I've realised there are no shortcuts to a clean conscience.'

'All this is beyond me.' Tilak Raj waves his hand. 'Just tell me clearly, have you arranged a kidney from some other clinic?'

'No. Not at all.'

'Then how about *his* kidney?' He pats the shoulder of the man he has brought in. 'This is Gyasuddin, a house painter.' He squeezes the man's biceps. 'See, very healthy.'

'No, I don't want his kidney either.'

'Are you worried that he is Muslim? It doesn't say on the kidney that it belongs to a Muslim or a Hindu. It belongs to whoever pays for it.'

'You don't understand,' I say with a trace of irritation. 'I don't want any kidney from this place.'

'Then how will your mother get a new kidney?'

'From me.'

'What? You will donate your own kidney?'

'Yes.' The answer has been staring me in the face right from the beginning. I just didn't have the courage to confront it.

Sita rolls her eyes. 'You were calling me mad,' she smirks at Tilak Raj, 'but this woman is madder than me. *Ab mera kya hoga?* Now what will happen to me?'

'If this one does not take your kidney, someone else will,' Tilak Raj counsels her. 'You will just have to wait a little bit.'

'I can't wait,' she wails. 'My Babloo will die if he doesn't get treatment by tomorrow. Oh, Babloo, Babloo, Babloo.' She starts beating her chest like a mother who has already lost her son.

'What's wrong with Babloo?' I ask Tilak Raj.

'Loo-kee-mia,' Sita interjects, pausing to let it sink in. 'He has loo-kee-mia. The private hospital has asked ten thousand for his treatment. How will I ever get so much money? Who will give it to me?'

'I will,' I say quietly.

Tilak Raj jerks his head at me. 'Do not play with poor people's emotions. Their ill wishes have a habit of coming true.'

I open my purse and pull out the envelope I received three days ago from the store, containing my salary for the month of April. I count out ten thousand, fold the notes into a wad and offer it to Sita.

She looks at me disbelievingly and does not move, like a cautious cat afraid to touch an unknown bowl of milk. Eventually, hope gets the better of her. She grabs the wad and begins counting the notes, licking her thumb intermittently.

'Yes, it is the full ten thousand.' She emits a puzzled grunt. 'Are you really going to give me all this money?'

'Yes.' I try to smile, but what comes out is a skewed grimace. I just stand there, finding it hard to fight back the tears. I am in the world of the wretched, full of misery and poverty. For these people, the kidney is not an organ, but an asset to be sold, to feed their families, to save a sick child. And even ten thousand is but a drop of water in a parched desert.

'It is a miracle,' Sita shrieks, the crazed glint returning to her eyes. 'Today, I have seen a miracle.'

I feel like telling her that the bigger miracle is that I have woken up, come out of the poisonous fog that had enveloped me for the last seven days.

She looks up at me in wary gratitude, as though worried I might still change my mind. Then, stuffing the cash inside her blouse, she dashes out of the building like someone escaping a raging fire.

'You should also leave now,' says Tilak Raj, shaking his head in apparent frustration. 'From where do such people come, gypping me out of my commission?' I hear him mutter under his breath, as he shoos me out of the door. I know it is a reference to me, not Sita.

I walk out of the clinic with my head held high and my shoulders lighter. How exhilarating it is to be free of the crushing burden of guilt! How dazzling life feels when you're part of the healing and not part of the hurting!

I return to the Unity Kidney Institute with a DTC bus of the same number and go straight to the cashier's window. 'I've changed my mind about the transplant. I want my money back.'

The cashier immediately calls Dr Nath, who invites me back to his office. 'What's the matter? I have got you the best possible deal. All arrangements have been made for the transplant.'

'I don't want Sita's kidney. I've just met her.'

'Just met her? Where?'

'I'm coming from your clinic in Gurgaon.'

'You've been to the clinic in Gurgaon?' His brow

contracts in a worried frown. 'Please wait,' he says, and steps out of the room. Through the small glass window I see him make a call on his cell phone.

A little while later MLA Anwar Noorani makes an appearance. 'Yes, what's the problem?' He gives me a faintly patronising smile.

'Nothing. I've changed my mind about getting the transplant done here and I want my money back.'

'Can you show me the receipt?'

I produce the receipt. He examines it and then tucks it into the top pocket of his khadi vest.

'Now why exactly don't you want to get the transplant done here? We have the best facilities in all of Delhi.'

'I've seen the racket you are running, snatching organs from the poor. It's utterly disgraceful.'

'We are simply service providers, helping out people like you,' he says grimly. 'Anyway, it's too late to get a refund, whether you get the transplant done or not.'

'That's ridiculous!'

'No, it's not. Which shop in Delhi gives you your money back, tell me? We are also a commercial establishment. Once you've made a deal, you can't just back out of it without any penalty.'

'I'll file a complaint against you if you don't return the money.'

'We'll deny that we ever received it. In fact, we never did receive it, did we?' He shares a glance with Dr Nath. Then he takes out the receipt from his pocket and proceeds to tear it into bits before my horrified eyes.

'You can't do this. I'm going to the police right now.'

'You are welcome. Who do you think they will choose

to believe, a respectable politician like me or a two-bit sales clerk like you? So take my advice: go bring your mother and we'll resolve this amicably.'

Behind his slick smile, I understand the cold menace in his words. He has drawn a line in the sand and is challenging me to cross it at my own peril. 'I'll think about it,' I say and leave the room, feeling disgusted, cheated, and totally pissed off.

Once outside the hospital I take out my cell and make two phone calls. The first is to Dr Mittal. 'I'm sorry, Doctor, for having misled you. There never was a friend donating his kidney. I will be the living donor. When can you perform the transplant operation?'

'As early as the day after tomorrow,' he replies, clearly pleased at this turn of events.

The second call is to Shalini Grover, the investigative reporter for Sunlight TV. 'I have a story for you,' I begin.

The wall clock shows the time as 4 p.m. I am in the standard hospital garb of shapeless blue gown, about to be wheeled into the operating theatre. Dr Mittal bustles about the preparation room, asking questions of the nurses, checking to see that everything is in order before the anaesthesiologist comes in to inject me. 'It will all be over before you know it.' He pats my shoulder gently. 'You are a really brave girl.'

I feel no anxiety, no fear, just a deep, heightened sense of being alive. Of having purpose. Now is when Ma gets a new lease of life. And I get a new lease of respect, renewing my credentials as the eldest of the family.

Neha is also in the room with me. She has reconciled

herself to the loss of the two lakhs, but she is still not reconciled to the idea of my being a living donor. 'Why do you have to insist on being a martyr?' she cries, clutching my hand.

'I'm not being a martyr,' I reply. 'I'm just being the elder daughter.'

'I wish I had your courage.'

'Dr Mittal assures me the operation is perfectly safe. Think of it as removing a hundred and fifty grams of redundancy from the body.'

'Karan wanted to come, too, but Dr Mittal did not allow him. Only family members are permitted inside the ICU.'

'How's Ma?' I try to sound nonchalant, hoping Neha does not notice the blood rushing to my cheeks at the mention of Karan's name. I haven't seen him in over a week, and I'm suffering from an acute deficiency of Vitamin K.

'Still singing your praises to all and sundry,' says Neha. Ma almost put the entire plan in jeopardy, refusing point blank to accept my kidney donation. Dr Mittal told me she went into the preparation room kicking and screaming. It took all his effort to convince her of the medical miracle of organ transplantation.

'Time to leave now,' Dr Mittal gently reminds Neha.

With a pensive look and a consolatory pat on my arm, she gets up and then quickly exits the room.

A minute later the anaesthetist troops in, a stethoscope dangling from the collar of his white smock. He is a youngish-looking man with thick, dark hair and wandering eyes.

He stretches out my arm and then pricks it with a needle. For a while I drift in and out of consciousness, vaguely aware of sounds within the room, the movement of nurses around me, the antiseptic smell of the hospital, till a comfortable weightlessness envelops me and I finally fall into the synthetic sleep.

When I wake up, the astringent antiseptic smell of the hospital ward is still there, but the numbness in my body has gone. Instead, there is the itchy feeling of ants crawling all over my skin. I open my eyes, groggy with anaesthetic, to discover a man in a white dress leaning over my bed. I imagine him to be Dr Mittal, but, as the image gradually comes into focus I emit a gasp of surprise, immediately recognising the aquiline nose and the mane of silvery hair. It is industrialist Vinay Mohan Acharya, wearing an off-white silk kurta pyjama, with a white pashmina shawl draped across his shoulders. Though he is dressed exactly as he was the day I first met him at the Hanuman Temple, he looks different. His face is gaunter and paler, his eyes hollower and his body appears to have thinned out, lost some of its bulk.

'Congratulations,' he says, smiling, as he eases himself into the chair next to my bed. 'You've just passed the sixth test.'

I groan, cursing the day I accepted his offer. Ever since, my life has become one long exam, with God testing me on one side and the industrialist testing me on the other.

'This was the test of decisiveness,' he continues. 'Decisiveness is the willingness to make decisions, even in the face of complexity or uncertainty. A CEO is required to make tough calls, and then live with the consequences. You showed this ability by your brave decision to donate your kidney. Not only was it a courageous move, it was also the right one. There's nothing more selfless than being a living donor.'

'But how did you come to know about my kidney donation?'

'Through Dr Mittal. He now works for me, you see.'

'He works for you?' The unexpected twist makes me sit up in bed. I look around for a nurse, but there is no one else in the room. 'What about . . . what about the operation to remove my kidney? Did it go well?'

'There was no operation. Both your kidneys are still intact.'

My hand immediately flies to my side, feeling for the dressing covering the sutures, but my fingers encounter only smooth flesh. There is no cut along my abdomen.

'Then what about Ma? How will she get a kidney transplant?'

'Your mother is fine. She never needed a kidney transplant. That's because she doesn't have kidney disease.'

I feel faint, the blackness seeping into my brain again. 'So all this was . . .'

'A setup. I'm surprised you didn't cotton onto it faster.'

'Since when has this been going on?' I demand weakly.

'Ever since the day your uncle Dinesh threatened to evict you from your flat. It was I who asked him to do so. Isn't it amazing what people will do for money?'

My brow wrinkles in confusion.

'I also arranged to get your purse snatched in Connaught Place, the one containing your mother's gold bangles.'

'No!' I gasp. 'I don't believe you! You're just making all this up.'

'Well, then, you might want to take a look at these,' he says and takes out two sets of gold bangles from his kurta pocket. They glint under the tube light, their ornate patterns of embellishment clearly visible. I don't have to handle them to know that they are Ma's.

'This is insane! Why would you do something like that?'

'Because I was desperate for you to participate in my seven tests. I wanted to be sure that you have the mettle to survive in the rough and tumble of the business world.'

'So were *all* the tests fixed?'

'Nothing was fixed. All I did was create the conditions for your natural instincts to come into play. Take the first test, for instance. My task was limited to ensuring your arrival in Chandangarh village, that hotbed of honour killings. Once we knew about Babli and Sunil, it was relatively easy to persuade Kuldip Singh to visit the showroom for his dowry shopping.'

'But what if Babli had not handed me that note?'

'Then I would have found some other way to involve you. I had a five-member team deployed in Chandangarh since September. Though I must say, you surprised everyone by taking on the *khap panchayat* like you did.'

'And the second test? Did you also mastermind Priya Capoorr's visit to the showroom?'

'Well, isn't she an actor for hire? Nevertheless, it took all my persuasive powers to get her to agree to plant her engagement ring on you. She wanted to use a cheap imitation. The one week you did not return the ring was hell for her. She complained bitterly to me every day, convinced she would never get it back.'

'If you could get Priya Capoorr to plant a ring, then it must have been child's play to set up the lock factory and fill it with child labour?'

'No, I had no hand in that factory. I would rather die than exploit innocent children. But, yes, it was Rana who tipped off your friend Lauren Lockwood about Mirza Metal Works.'

'And the goons who threatened me, were they Mirza's men or yours?'

'They were hired by me,' he admits sheepishly. 'Their job was simply to scare you. They wouldn't have hurt you.'

'I suppose being threatened with rape inside the Japanese Park does not fall within your definition of hurt?'

'Rape? Japanese Park? What are you talking about?'

'Don't pretend that you don't know. You did the same with Neha.'

'I had nothing to do with your sister. I simply fixed her entry into that singing contest and arranged for her to be put in Raoji's team. It was common knowledge in the industry that Raoji has a weakness for women, but no one knew that he was pretending to be blind.'

'Do you know Raoji almost succeeded in molesting Neha?'

'You saved her just in time. I concede, though, that on occasion it is difficult to avoid collateral damage.'

'And, if Nirmala Ben had died, that would also have been collateral damage, right?'

'Ah, Nirmala Ben. I must say the Gandhian presented a unique challenge. My role was restricted to planting the seed of the idea in her head, you know, about shaking the world gently. The rest just fell into place beautifully.' He rubs his hands and grins at me. 'You'll have to admit that no real harm has come to anyone as a result of my tests.'

The glib manner in which he dismisses the six tests makes my jaw clench. What a sucker I had been, living in a universe of illusions till now, trapped in a world where everything was smoke and mirrors. Acharya was the puppeteer and I was the puppet, dancing to his strings.

A cold, murderous rage takes hold of me. 'Who do you think you are? God?' I demand.

'I cannot claim to be God,' he says. 'But, like God, I created your world, and then left you to fend for yourself. I engineered the process, not the outcomes. You created them out of your own free will.'

'You're mad, you know that, don't you?'

'I'm not mad, just different.'

'Karan was right about you. I should never have agreed to participate in your twisted plan.'

'Oh, so you did discuss our arrangement with a third party?' He frowns in disapproval. 'You know that was not allowed under the terms of the contract.'

'To hell with you and your contract. I don't want to ever see your face again. You are a sick person who deserves to be locked up in a mental asylum.'

'I expected such a reaction from you. But believe me, everything that I did was necessary.'

'Necessary for what? Your sadistic fantasies?'

'For your apprenticeship. The true test of a CEO is how he or she faces a crisis. It reveals what the CEO is really made of. I created six crises for you and you emerged triumphant from all of them. Through these six tests, you've learnt more in five months than what Harvard Business School couldn't have taught you in five years. And, once you pass the seventh test, you will be ready to take over the CEO-ship of the ABC Group.'

'I have no intention of taking any more tests. I'm quitting right now.'

'Sorry, you can't quit midway under the terms of the contract. Failure is an option, but quitting isn't. And why would you want to quit now, when heading a ten-billion-dollar company is within your grasp?'

'For God's sake stop selling me that line. You've been leading me up the garden path all this while.'

'You are being unfair. The only person who has been leading you up the garden path is Karan Kant, your so-called boyfriend.'

I glance sharply at him. 'And what do you mean by that?'

'Have a look at these,' he says, and produces a brown envelope. He opens it over my bed and six large colour glossies tumble into my lap. I can feel my chest tightening up as I gaze at the photos.

It is said you don't always recognise the moment when love begins, but you always know when it ends. My love for Karan ended at 6.35 a.m. on Friday, 6 May.

Nothing that Acharya could have said or done would have shaken my faith in Karan, but a camera doesn't lie and the half a dozen freeze-frames on my bed are a nauseating documentation of betrayal and duplicity. They show a couple embracing each other in what looks like the bedroom of my Rohini flat. The pictures appear to have been taken during daytime, from a telephoto lens, every frame zooming in closer. My heart sinks with each and is completely crushed by the final one showing a grainy lip lock between my sister and my best friend.

I fall back on the bed, whimpering like a crippled animal. 'Take them, take them away,' I cry. 'I can't bear to look at them.'

'He's a deep one, that Karan,' Acharya says as he gathers the glossies and puts them back in the envelope. 'Something's not right about him. He beat the pulp out of the detective who was tailing him on my instructions.'

I am barely listening, my mind still trying to cope with the shock of discovery. Why is it that those who are closest to us hurt us the most? And, of all the people in the world, why did Karan have to choose Neha? Acharya's deception was minor, compared with Karan's monumental treachery and Neha's sickening disloyalty.

The industrialist puts a hand on my shoulder, and I don't flinch. I need the soothing balm of a human touch, of kind words. 'I am sorry that I was not totally upfront with you,' he says. 'But you must believe me when I tell you that you are just one step away from fulfilling all your dreams.'

'Please . . .' I look into his eyes, trying to read him. 'Don't play games with me any more. Is this another one of your tests?'

'That will come later. The seventh and final test.'

'Why? Why? Why?' I plead with him like an exhausted fox at the end of the hunt. 'Just tell me: why did you choose me as your guinea pig? You could have picked anyone from your company, anyone from this city. There are millions who are more qualified than me to run your business.'

'Qualifications don't matter. Attitude does. I am impressed by your dedication, your willingness and enthusiasm to learn. You've done remarkably well so far, demonstrating qualities of leadership, integrity, courage, foresight, resourcefulness and decisiveness. Now you need to prepare for the final test.'

I shake my head wearily. 'I don't think I have the strength to undergo another test. Please release me from the contract.'

He abruptly gets up from his chair, goes to the rear door and flings it open. The private room I am in connects to the general ward and my nose is assaulted immediately by the smells of disinfectant and disease. I gaze into a long hall, packed with beds and bodies. The air resonates with the lonely moans of sick patients interspersed with the wails of a hungry child.

'Is this how you want to spend the rest of your life' – he waves a hand at the river of misery and woe at my doorstep – 'living amongst the hungry, the wretched and the poor?'

'There's no shame in being poor,' I reply defiantly.

'Spare me this misplaced empathy with the losers of the world,' he sneers. 'Wanting to help them is one thing, wanting to *become* like them quite another. I am prepared to give you a position far above the crippling mediocrity of the masses. But, if you are content to live like them and die like them, then so be it. Just remember, there are three things that wait for no one: time, death and opportunity.

Once you miss this opportunity, it will never come again. Now it's your call.'

I close my eyes, unable to bear his mocking gaze. 'Even assuming I say yes to you,' I respond after a long moment, 'what explanation will I give to Ma and Neha for not donating my kidney?'

'Dr Mittal will handle that part,' he says. 'My only request to you is to keep our arrangement confidential till you pass the seventh test. So you will do it, right?'

The moment for decision has come; I can't evade it any longer. I reflect on the wasteland that my life has become. There is nothing to look forward to, no one to trust, no job to feel good about. I see a future leached of all colour, every pleasure. I have become a loser all over again. And a loser has everything to gain. 'Okay.' I exhale. 'I'm in. Now tell me, what's the last test going to be about?'

'I can't tell you in advance.' He shakes his head. 'That would be cheating. All I can say is that it will be the hardest of them all.'

'At least tell me what to expect.'

He thinks carefully before replying. 'The unexpected.'

The discharge formalities take less than an hour. Dr Mittal calls Neha to his room and gives her some gobbledegook about a new wonder drug called ImmunoglobulinX. 'This miracle drug came on the market just yesterday. If your mother's condition can be corrected with a few pills, why go for a transplant, don't you agree?'

He doesn't have the guts to even meet me. I see him slinking past the door when I'm leaving the hospital with

Ma. At least he has the decency to feel guilty about what he's done to me at Acharya's behest.

Neha, on the other hand, shows no remorse about her actions. In fact, once we are back in the house, she even breaks into a little jig. 'Now this is what I call having your cake and eating it too,' she rejoices. 'We saved your kidney and we saved Ma as well. Hail to ImmunoglobulinX!'

'Is there something you need to tell me?' I fix her with a steely stare.

'What?' She looks back at me, neither dropping her gaze nor looking the least bit ashamed. Her brazenness astounds me.

I cannot bear to stay in the same room with her. Standing facing the window, I wince at the memory of her kissing Karan in this very spot. Even the air around me now seems contaminated with the smell of subterfuge and secrets.

'Nothing,' I reply, forcing an ironic smile.

With Karan there is even greater awkwardness. He, too, acts without a trace of guilt, a backstabber *par excellence*. I begin avoiding him as much as I can. The evening visits to the garden I terminate completely.

Without a sister to speak to, without a friend to turn to, I am enveloped in a thick shroud of melancholy. It is part anger, part frustration, but mostly it is a grim joylessness that haunts me like a shadow.

Work becomes my only refuge. A single-minded focus on my salesgirl's job acts like therapy for me, even earning an encomium from Madan. I spend my days slaving in the showroom and my nights fantasising about the pot of gold promised by Acharya. He seems to be the lone silver lining in the dark clouds that have gathered over my life. So far I had made his tests into an abstraction. Now, with just one more to go, I feel the adrenaline rush of real, tangible reward. Ten billion dollars! The very thought of all that money causes goose pimples on my skin. For the first time I can feel the pull of destiny. So much so that, while returning from work one evening, I impulsively buy a 'business' book from a street hawker for ₹95. It is by an American management expert named Steven Katzenberg, and it is called *How to Become a CEO: Fifty Secrets for Getting to the Top and Staying There.*

The Seventh Test

Acid Rain

The first secret to becoming a CEO is knowing that there are no secrets to success. It is always the result of hard work, concentration, careful planning, and persistence. Success is not a lottery but a system, and this book will teach you fifty secrets gleaned from hours of conversations with the world's greatest CEOs to enable you to implement that system in your daily life, and get to the top.

It is a slow day at the showroom and I am whiling away the time by imbibing wisdom from Mr Steven Katzenberg, the management expert.

Prachi taps the book in my hand. 'Since when have you started reading business guides?'

'It's still better than killing flies, no?' I reply.

'Are you planning to do an MBA or what?' She looks at me suspiciously.

'Who does an MBA at my age?' I sigh and attempt to change the subject. 'So what's up with you? Any fresh advances from our mutual friend Mr Raja Gulati?'

'The creep was here yesterday,' Prachi says, 'and he's promised me a raise. The company has made a record profit this financial year.'

'Well, I hope I get one too.'

'Tell me, has Neelam written to you?'

Neelam who? I am about to ask, before realising she is enquiring about our ex-colleague. It has been almost three months since her wedding. It is amazing how quickly out-of-sight becomes out-of-mind. 'No. Why?'

'Because I received a letter from her yesterday. From Sweden.'

'What did she say? Is she happy with her marriage?'

'Happy? She is going mad with joy. Her house is a five-bedroom mansion in Stockholm. She says it's the cleanest city in the world. She drives around in a Jaguar. And her husband earns the equivalent of six lakh rupees a month. Can you imagine that? Six lakhs per month! That's like twenty thousand rupees a day.'

'Good for Neelam.'

'I keep hoping some tall handsome millionaire will walk into the showroom and sweep me off my feet,' she says wistfully. 'Sometimes I feel so trapped, wondering if I'll be doing this job for the rest of my life. Don't you also dream of becoming rich?'

I imagine the shock on her face if I were to tell her I'm about to become CEO of a ten-billion-dollar company. Instead, I offer her the old cliché, 'Money cannot buy you love.'

'Who says I want love?' Prachi scoffs. 'I want that Bottega Veneta bag I saw in Emporio Mall.'

In the adjacent aisle Madhavan, one of the sales boys, is busy flipping channels on a LG Pen Touch TV hooked to a satellite dish, when I catch a fleeting glimpse of Shalini Grover. 'Stop, stop, stop,' I shout, startling him into almost dropping the remote.

Sure enough Shalini Grover is on Sunlight TV, standing outside a nondescript house, painted white with green shutters. 'Returning back to our top story, this is house number 3734, from where the nefarious kidney trade was being run,' she says. 'In a day of fast-moving developments, Dr J. K. Nath – or should we say "Dr Kidney"? – was arrested by Delhi police. He was responsible for illegally removing the kidneys of more than five hundred people, mostly poor labourers. The Unity Kidney Institute, where these kidneys were sold to rich patients, has been sealed and a warrant has been issued for the arrest of MLA Anwar Noorani, the man who presided over this entire racket.' She pauses and flicks a finger at the camera. 'Remember, you saw it first on Sunlight, the channel that uncovers the truth, insistently, consistently, persistently.'

I cannot resist calling up Shalini during the lunch break. 'Congratulations on the scoop. But what took you so long to break the story?'

'After you told me about the clinic I did a full under-cover operation, including interviews with over two dozen victims. It's taken a while, but now there's no escape for the crooks. They've literally been caught red-handed,' she replies.

'That MLA swindled me out of two lakhs. I hope he rots in jail for twenty years at least.'

'He hasn't been caught yet. Please be careful, Sapna. He knows I got the story from you, and he can be a dangerous man.'

'No worries. If he had Dr Kidney, I have Dr Mirchi to protect me.'

'Dr Mirchi? Who's he?'

'What? You don't know Dr Mirchi? He's a girl's best friend, also known as chilli-pepper spray!'

On returning from lunch I find Raja Gulati hanging outside the rear door, looking like a clownish cad in a half-unbuttoned, purple silk shirt and tight trousers. He bars my way by draping an arm across the doorway.

'Let me go,' I say coldly.

'Why do you remain so aloof from me, Ice Maiden?' He leers lecherously. 'Even ice melts in summer.'

'But a moron remains a moron in every season,' I reply dryly.

'Who are you calling moron, bitch?' he growls, flaring up like a temperamental diva and grabbing my wrist.

'Don't you dare touch me.' I struggle to break free of his grip.

'First say sorry,' he demands.

'You bastard!' I spin on my heels and slap him across the face.

He releases my wrist, mouth open in shock. 'You'll pay for this, bitch,' he hisses as I shove him aside and enter the showroom.

*

Just before closing time, Madan summons me to his cubicle. 'We are doing another round of stocktaking. I need you in the store on Sunday,' he says without looking at me directly.

'That's June the twelfth, isn't it? It's my father's death anniversary,' I reply. 'I can't come.'

'Who do you think you are?' he yells at me. 'Some queen who can decide when to come and when not? I've had enough of your birthdays and death anniversaries. If you don't come to the store on Sunday, you'll be chucked out.'

My mind is already seething from Raja's brazen effrontery. Madan's bullying is sufficient to nudge me into the chasm of joblessness. 'To hell with you and your store,' I scream back at him. 'I'm quitting right this instant.'

'That will be good riddance. And we will also avoid a payout for the notice period,' he responds, trying to hide the sneaky gloating in his voice.

The true worth of a job is revealed by the amount of time it takes you to quit it. I had invested so little in mine, it takes me barely twenty minutes to clear out from Gulati & Sons. Most of the sales staff are happy to see my back. They can now aspire to the position of Salesperson No. 1. Prachi is the only one who is genuinely sad at my departure. 'You shouldn't have reacted in this way,' she says. 'If you want, I can still speak to Madan, sort this out.'

'I'm done with Gulati & Sons,' I tell her. 'Don't worry, I'll find a job faster than Raja Gulati finds a bottle.'

As I walk out of the showroom for the last time at 7.45 p.m. on Wednesday, 8 June, I am clear-headed and calm. I have never felt lighter, freer than I do in that moment. Like a convict freshly released from prison. For that is what Gulati & Sons had become, a prison of the mind. I've hated the treacherous commute to work every day, the push and shove of humanity in the overcrowded metro, the cacophony and din of Connaught Place, the aggravating customers, the insufferable boss, the apathetic coworkers . . . It has been a miserable, never-ending daily grind, and I am glad to be rid of it.

Sitting in the metro going home, I take out the book by Steven Katzenberg and flip open a page at random. A quote by industrialist Ram Mohammad Thomas leaps out at me:

> I have learnt more from life than books, and it has taught me that you need just three things to be truly happy in this world: a person that you love, a job that you like, and a dream that you live for.

I reflect on his wise words. By this yardstick, I will perhaps never be truly happy. I have no one to love, no job to hold, but I do have a dream to live for, the dream of becoming CEO of the ABC Group.

That has now become the consuming passion of my life. Every night I lie in my bed dreaming about the tantalising promise of a seven-figure salary.

There has been no word from the industrialist for over a month now. Perhaps he is still devising the seventh test. The Seventh Test. The moment I think about it, I am gripped by the sudden conviction that it may have already begun. Acharya said it will be the hardest of them all.

What if he stage-managed that confrontation with Raja Gulati, prepared yet another crisis for me?

I feel a cold sweat break out on my forehead. Did I do the right thing in quitting in a huff? The stakes are so high that to fail now would be catastrophic.

In desperation I turn to the Katzenberg guide, quickly flipping open to Chapter 27. It's called, 'Secret Number 25: How to Handle a Crisis.'

Neha is strutting about the drawing room in stiletto heels, hips swinging out like a model on a catwalk, when I reach home.

'What's got into her?' I ask Ma.

'Didn't Neha tell you?' Ma says, handing me an envelope. 'This arrived today.'

The envelope contains a letter from Nova Talent Management, an agency based in Mumbai, offering Neha a modelling contract.

'You know what this means, don't you, *didi*?' Neha drapes her arms around my neck in an overly affectionate gesture. 'It means I've finally found my true calling. Now you'll see how I make my mark in the world.'

'Are you sure this is a reputable agency?' I ask, disengaging her hands.

'One of the best. They even have an arrangement with Ford Models in New York. They say I could be walking the ramp as early as next month for Delhi Couture Week,' she exults. 'And they think I'm a shoo-in for the Miss India contest as well.'

I cannot prevent a look of chagrin from sweeping across my face. I have just lost my job, and Neha has landed an impressive contract. Of late the equation between me and my sister has become a zero-sum game. Every misfortune that befalls me seems to be accompanied by a corresponding bonanza for Neha.

'And what about your studies?' I enquire coldly.

'Who cares about the BA exams?' Neha says dismissively. 'Once I become a model I can always do a correspondence course.'

After dinner, I concentrate on Chapter 27 again, but Neha keeps distracting me, circling around me like a cat eager for my attention, till I can't take it any more. 'What is it now?' I demand, my voice thick with irritation.

She twirls a lock of hair around her finger, her eyes flashing with indolent impertinence. 'How come you don't go down to the garden any more?'

'Why? Is it compulsory to take a stroll after dinner?'

'Karan says you've started acting very coldly towards him.'

'I don't care what he says.'

'He wanted me to tell you he's leaving the colony.'

'That's good riddance.'

'You are being really ungrateful.'

'Ungrateful? You have some nerve calling me ungrateful after what you've been doing with Karan.'

Neha stiffens. 'And what exactly do you mean by that, *didi*?'

'Don't pretend you don't know anything,' I reply, the sarcasm in my voice now turning to anger.

'I really don't understand what you are hinting at,' says Neha, still pretending to be a lost little girl.

All my pent-up hurt and bitterness comes exploding out. 'You have been carrying on with Karan behind my back. Both of you have been taking me for a ride.'

She gapes at me, momentarily stunned. Her shock looks genuine enough, before it is replaced by a determined bellicosity. 'You had better explain yourself, *didi*,' she demands, a classic case of the red-handed thief challenging the inspector.

'I've seen pictures of the two of you in this very room.'

'Pictures? What pictures?'

'Drop the pretence. Did you or did you not kiss Karan right here, standing next to the window?'

'Oh, that!' She looks down, and a tinge of regret crosses her face at last. 'I confess I shouldn't have done it. Don't read too much into it. I'm not in love with Karan or anything like that. He's reserved only for you. It's just that I was so grateful, I did it out of impulse. It was nothing more than a thank-you kiss.'

'A thank-you kiss? Thank-you for what?'

'I shouldn't be telling you this, but it was Karan who lent me those two lakhs for the kidney transplant.'

'What?'

'Yes, it's true. All my friends had failed me. In desperation I turned to Karan for help. He was amazing. First he went to Dr Nath and offered his own kidney for Ma, but his crossmatch came out positive. Then the poor fellow sold off half his belongings and took a loan from his office to put together all that money. I wanted to tell you, but he forbade me. We can never repay the debt we owe him. I tell you, *didi*, you are the luckiest person in the world to have a friend—'

I don't wait for her to finish. I rush out of the apartment and race up the stairs to the third floor, my mind roiling with self-hatred and shame. I have wronged Karan grievously and nothing can ever make it right.

I knock on the door of B–35 like a storm-wrecked traveller seeking refuge for the night. The door does not open for such a long time that I almost lose hope. My heart sinks with the realisation that Karan has gone for ever.

Just as I am about to turn away in abject despair, a latch is pulled and Karan's face peeps out. 'Yes?' He stands with his hands on his hips, looking at me warily, like a stranger meeting another stranger.

'I came to ask your forgiveness,' I murmur.

'Forgiveness for what?'

'For treating you like dirt, after all that you did for us. Neha has told me everything.'

He keeps looking at me in silent judgement. I hold my breath, waiting, steeling myself for an explosion of righteous fury, when suddenly he holds out his right palm.

I gape at him, completely nonplussed.

'Salvation is free, *balika*, but a hundred-rupee donation would help,' he intones with the gravitas of a guru pontificating on Aastha channel. Then he breaks into a loud guffaw and opens his arms to me, like an impenetrable fortress opening its doors.

His laughter is medicine to my heart. I tumble into his waiting embrace. Just feeling his manly chest pressed against me fills me with such joy and peace that I forget everything else. Tears begin flowing from my eyes, melting away the pain, the shame, the frozen icicles of guilt clinging to the jagged edges of my soul.

Karan had forgiven me. Things were going to be right between us. And that was all that mattered to me.

We have a more extended meeting later that night, in the garden. I tell him everything that has transpired between me and Acharya.

'My God!' He listens to me with growing astonishment. 'So it was all a setup, just as I suspected all along.'

'Yes,' I reply with an embarrassed smile. 'I was the heroine of a private soap opera conceived and directed by Acharya.'

'That man deserves to be shot! He had been keeping you and your entire family under surveillance. He even tried to put a detective on my trail but I caught that bastard snooping around and thrashed him so much he dare not come near me again.'

'Acharya mentioned it to me. Anyway, it will all end soon. I have a gut feeling the seventh and final test has begun.'

Karan's eyebrows knit together in a puzzled frown. 'Do you mean to tell me that, after all this, you've still not put an end to Acharya's charade?'

'Now that I've come so far, why not see it through to the end?'

'How could you?' He slaps the wooden bench in frustration. 'You still believe that psycho is serious about making you his CEO?'

'Look, he's not a psycho. He's an old man desperate for a successor. And he feels I have the qualities to lead his company.'

'He's mad!'

'But he's not malicious. He believes in certain values.'

'Then *you're* mad.' He glares balefully at me. 'I didn't know you were so desperate for money.'

'I'm not!' I say forcefully, surprised at my own vehemence. 'Man does not live by bread alone. Ordinary lives, at times, need the spark of the extraordinary. We need awe, we need wonder, we need hope. Even if Acharya's offer remains a dream, I'm happy he showed it to me.'

'Perhaps you are right,' he says slowly. 'We all need that something extra in our lives. Anyway, it's your life and you are the best judge of what to do. I just want you to be happy.'

Our eyes lock and a strange sensation washes over me. I can sense the dawn of a softer understanding between us, a new compact forged in the crucible of heartache and reconciliation.

Maybe it is the full moon, maybe it is something in the air, the cool breeze that has suddenly sucked out the humidity like a blotter, but I am overcome with a desperate, irresistible urge to kiss him. Even though we are sitting a foot apart on the bench, I can feel the heat of his body on my skin, awakening an answering heat in me, a desire so powerful that it is almost lust. My palms become slick with sweat, my breath becomes ragged.

I think Karan senses the feverish signals being emitted by my body, for he changes the subject abruptly. 'Did Neha tell you about my leaving the colony?'

'Yes.' I nod. 'Is it true?'

'It's not the whole truth. I'm not just leaving the colony: I'm leaving the country.'

'Leaving India? But . . . but why?'

'There's no dearth of ambition in India, Sapna,' he says, looking straight ahead. 'What there *is* a shortage of is opportunity. So I've decided to go to the *land* of opportunity. America.'

'America? But this is so sudden!' I respond with the shell-shocked look of someone who has run face first into a wall.

'There's this friend of mine in California who called me up out of the blue with this fantastic job offer. It's too good an opportunity to pass up.'

'You are making a mistake. The whole world is coming to India and you want to go in the opposite direction?'

He gives a bitter laugh. 'Let me tell you something, Sapna. For people like us there's no future in this country. Only the very rich and the very poor know how to survive in India. Nobody cares for the rest. We aren't even needed at voting time.'

I feel as if an icy claw has gripped my heart. My mind screams, Don't go, I love you, I'll die without you. But what actually comes out of my lips is, 'And when exactly do you leave?'

'Tomorrow. I've already got the visa. My flight leaves at eight forty-five a.m.' He pauses and draws a deep breath. 'Now that I'm leaving, I want to tell you something.'

The way he gazes at me with his brown, dreamy eyes, the way his Adam's apple bobs as he swallows, I think he's going to say something special, sentimental even. My cheeks heat up in a blush with the intuitive perception that our courtship is reaching a climactic moment. Karan is finally getting ready to open that black box, reveal his true feelings about me. A million emotions stir inside me.

I wait for him to say those three magical words I've been yearning to hear for so long.

His lips quiver, but the three words that tumble out are very different from what I was hoping for: 'I am gay.'

I'm about to poke him in the ribs for trying to be facetious, when the tortured grimace on his face stills me. It's an instinctive confirmation that he's telling the truth, and I can see how much anguish it has caused him.

In a way it explains everything: his strange reluctance to enter into a serious relationship with me, his inexplicable failure to return my kiss, his secretive lifestyle, his decision to escape India. And yet it is so unexpected that it leaves me reeling.

I have nothing against gays. They are some of the nicest people in the world, wonderfully kind and caring, sensitive, loyal and selfless. But somehow Karan's turning out to be gay seems like a cruel joke on me. I gnash my teeth at the unfairness of it all. It is not the outrage of a bigot, but the frustration of a jilted lover unable to come to terms with reality.

'I hope we can still be friends,' Karan mumbles in a tone of meek disgrace, shrinking into himself. He seems so fragile right now, I fear one wrong word might break him completely.

My heart goes out to him. 'Of course you will always remain my friend, my best friend,' I say, squeezing his hand tightly. But, even as I comfort him, I can sense a new distance between us. It's as if suddenly the earth had parted and put us on different ends. The thought looping like a mantra in my mind is that Karan is no longer mine. Perhaps he never was.

The silence between us lengthens, becomes awkward.

'Well, good luck with your new life,' I say with a forced smile. Then I turn around and head straight back to my apartment.

I enter my bedroom and bury my face in the pillow, muffling the sobs that threaten to engulf me in a tide of sadness. Every dream of mine has had Karan in it, and suddenly all those dreams have been crushed, pulverised to dust. I gained Karan only to lose him for ever.

Karan leaves for the airport promptly at 5.45 a.m. I watch him from the balcony as he lugs a battered suitcase to the gate, dressed in a white T-shirt emblazoned with the Indus logo and scuffed jeans. Dhiman Singh, the colony's guard, has already hailed an auto-rickshaw for him. Karan gets into the back seat without as much as a backward glance. But, just as the auto is about to drive off, he leans out and looks up, searching the second-floor balcony of B-Block. He sees me, and raises his right hand in a tentative gesture of salutation-cum-apology, before he is jerked back by the auto lurching onto the road.

I stand watching the departing auto till it vanishes in the dusty distance. Just as I watched Nirmala Ben leave the colony a month ago. One by one, my friends are deserting me, leaving for greener pastures.

Papa always used to say that life is about letting go and moving on. But I can't just erase Karan from my life like a mistake on paper. Each time I pass by his apartment, memories crowd my mind. The sturdy brass lock on his door mocks me, feels like a splash of dirty water on my face.

Even the weather begins to conspire against me, turning from uncomfortably hot to unbearably muggy. Though the monsoon is more than a month away, the air feels sluggish with the promise of rain. Humidity hangs in the atmosphere like a giant, bloated blimp that refuses to leave.

With no job and no Karan, I am filled with a biting emptiness. The desperate need to fill this sudden void in my life drives me to Neha. Her passionate enthusiasm for modelling is infectious, just the spark I need to prevent myself from spiralling down that dark rabbit hole of memory and regret. I decide to devote myself wholeheartedly to her new career. We spend the entire day poring over fashion magazines and Bollywood journals, planning her outfits and makeup. Neha, however, isn't just content with makeup. She wants a makeover. And it begins with a new hairstyle. '*Didi*, hair is very important for a model,' she declares. 'You need to take me to the best salon in town.'

'There's one right next to our colony,' I offer. 'I can unhesitatingly recommend the Sweety Beauty Parlour.'

'Be serious!' She makes a face at me. 'I need a professional hair stylist, not a roadside barber.'

So it is that at 4 p.m. on Saturday, 11 June, we find ourselves in the newly opened City Centre Mall in Sector 10. I am dressed in a white churidar with a matching chikan-embroidered kurta. Neha is sporting her usual jeans and a pink *Hello Kitty* T-shirt.

The mall is bustling with weekend shoppers splurging on designer brands. Today is Bargain Day, with a 10 per cent discount in most stores.

The City Centre Mall is not normally a place where I go for my shopping. The prices are enough to give anyone a nosebleed. But Neha insisted that she would get her hair done only at the Naved Habib Hair Salon located on the second floor of the mall.

The salon looks impressive, with its contemporary design and trendy decorations, but one look at the charges and I almost choke. A haircut with a blow-dry and style costs a mind-boggling ₹1,500! My haircut at the Sweety Beauty Parlour costs just ₹175. But I don't begrudge forking out the cash. Neha has been given a fantastic opportunity, and she must be equipped to make the best of it.

I browse a high-end boutique while my sister gets the most expensive haircut in town. Looking at the prices of L'Oréal eyeshadow, Revlon lipstick and Max Factor mascara, I begin to dread the prospect of Neha's cosmetic shopping. My cash reserves are dwindling fast, and before long I'll need to shore up my finances by getting a new job.

By 5 p.m. Neha is done. I have to concede the hairdresser has done a good job. Neha looks more glamorous than ever in her new stylish hairdo – short side-swept bangs with a medium layered cut – that flatters her oval face and highlights her beautiful eyes. I can see the men ogling her as we step out of the mall. In their eyes she is already a model.

A gaggle of rickshaw-wallahs surrounds us immediately. 'Come with me, come with me,' each of them crows. I zero in on an oldish man in a vest and a lungi, his bronzed muscles glistening from the sweat running down his body. 'Will you take us to the LIG Colony in Sector 11?'

'It will be thirty rupees, *memsahib*,' he says, wiping his brow with a rag.

'*Arrey*, you think we are outsiders?' I scold him. 'We just paid twenty rupees to come here.'

'It's all right, *didi*,' Neha says expansively and clambers into the rickshaw. After a moment's reflection I get in too, realising the futility of haggling over ten rupees after blowing fifteen hundred on a haircut.

Today being Saturday, there is not much traffic on the roads, and the rickshaw has no difficulty in navigating its way towards Sector 11. As we swing into Rammurti Passi Marg, I hear the sound of a motorcycle revving down the road behind us. A second later it is beside us, ridden by two youths in tight jeans, both wearing helmets with tinted visors covering their faces. They look like street hooligans indulging in their favourite pastime: checking out girls. In fact the driver draws so near to the rickshaw that he is almost within touching distance of Neha. I am about to shout at him, when he pulls away. The motorcycle zooms past us, making Neha's hair fly in my face. The pillion rider raises a clenched fist in celebration, mocking us.

'Dogs!' I mutter under my breath.

A couple of minutes later, when we are adjacent to the Metro Walk Mall complex, I hear yet another motorcycle sound coming from behind. I turn my head to see the same two riders accelerating towards us, the low growl of the engine growing louder.

There is something sinister about their intent. I have a gut feel about it. But, before I can take out my pepper spray, the bike is abreast of us.

Through the corner of my eye, I see the pillion rider unscrew the cap off a bottle in his hand. The warning bell in my head goes off instantly.

'Neha! Watch out!' I cry as the ruffian hurls the bottle in Neha's face. A dark oily liquid sprinkles out, and the next instant Neha's shriek of agony rends the air.

The motorcycle races off into the distance, leaving a writhing and twisting Neha on the rickshaw. 'I'm burning, I'm burning, *didi*,' she screams. 'For God's sake do something! Save me!' Only then do I realise she has been hit by acid.

Her body convulses as the acid sears through her skin. It seeps into her hair, and streams down her face and into her mouth. When she tries to wipe it off, streaks of acid run down her fingers and onto her forearms.

I cradle her in my lap, feeling utterly helpless to prevent the slow disintegration of her face. Her hair is burning away, her skin melting like wax. I shudder to think of the pain she must be in.

'Get an ambulance!' I yell at the top of my voice at the rickshaw puller who stands like a statue, paralysed by fear. Fortuitously a passing police van comes to our rescue, spiriting Neha and me to the Shastri government hospital in Sector 5.

Three hours later I am still at the hospital, maintaining an anxious vigil in front of the operating theatre where surgeons are battling to save my sister.

Inside the theatre, Neha is teetering between life and death; outside, Ma and I are teetering between horror and hysteria.

'What have we done to deserve so much misery, Ishwar?' Ma gazes at the ceiling, interrogating her gods. Then she breaks into racking sobs. 'Why didn't God take me and spare my flowerlike daughter?' she asks, clutching my arm.

I have no answer to her questions. My mind is clouded with fury and malice. I want to go out, find those savage boys who have done this to Neha and destroy them equally savagely. I imagine gouging out their eyes, cutting off their ears, smashing their noses, chopping off their fingers one by one, and, when they are begging me for mercy, crushing their heads with a heavy stone.

How I wish I had Karan by my side. He alone can rescue me from the abyss of hatred that threatens to swallow me whole. But he has gone a million miles away and I have no way of contacting him.

The acid attack on Neha has become a police case, and an overbearing officer by the name of Sub-Inspector S. P. Bhatia from Rohini police station has been assigned to investigate it. His incessant interrogation is causing me a splitting headache.

'Did you recognise the two youths on the motorcycle?'

'No. They were wearing helmets so I couldn't see their faces.'

'Is there someone who wanted revenge on your sister?'

'I don't know. Only a crazed psychopath would do such a thing.'

'Do you know any crazed psychopaths in Delhi?'

'No. Do you?'

'Does your sister have a boyfriend?'

'She might have. I don't really know.'

'Do you think this could be the work of a former boyfriend?'

'I don't know.'

'It seems you don't really know your sister.'

'Perhaps I don't.'

He strokes his chin thoughtfully. 'Is it possible that *you* were the intended victim of the attack?'

The question startles me. 'Me? Why would anyone want to harm me?'

'You tell me. Are there any skeletons in your cupboard?'

'No. None.'

'Don't say none. There are skeletons in everyone's cupboard. Every person is a potential criminal. And there is a thin line between sanity and insanity.'

'I know.' I nod. 'I'm standing on it. If you don't find the person who did this, I'll go mad.'

'The whole city has gone mad,' he sighs. 'MLA Anwar Noorani's supporters ran riot through the Sector 7 market this afternoon, protesting against his arrest.'

'My God!' I exclaim, as the memory of a conversation I had with Shalini Grover comes rushing back to me. Anwar Noorani was a dangerous man, she warned me. And the acid attack fitted perfectly with his vengeful nature and volatile temperament. 'This is the handiwork of Noorani, I'm sure.' I grip the sub-inspector's arm with the instinctive certainty of feminine conviction.

'But he is cooling his heels in Tihar Jail.'

'Tihar Jail did not stop Babloo Tiwari from running his kidnapping and extortion business. You go right now and interrogate Noorani. I'm convinced he organised the attack on Neha, because I helped expose his kidney racket.'

SI Bhatia hears me out patiently, but the look in his eyes suggests a man who believes he is wasting his time. Eventually, he snaps shut his notebook and turns to Ma. 'I'll need to interrogate your daughter if she regains consciousness.'

Ma gapes at him in shock and bursts into tears once again.

The sub-inspector hastily amends his statement. 'I meant *when* she regains consciousness.'

The burns specialist at Shastri Hospital is Dr Atul Bansal, a mild-mannered, bespectacled man in his forties with the weary, stoic look of a death-row convict. I don't blame him. Of all the wings in the hospital, the burns ward is the most melancholy, drenched perpetually in tragedy. Serious-burn victims come in at all hours. The causes differ – some have suffered from gas explosions, some from acid dousing or electrical burns – but the end result is the same: horribly disfigured faces, exposed and hanging flesh, skin covered in blisters and boils. Listening to their screams of agony resonating through the corridors is enough to make anyone wish for temporary deafness.

'Neha is very lucky,' Dr Bansal says as he accompanies Ma and me to the ICU, where Neha has been transferred after her operation. 'She received only forty per cent burns, largely on the right side of her face, neck and chest. She could easily have lost her eyes and ears.'

From the opposite end of the corridor a gurney is being wheeled in. I glance at the patient's face and immediately flinch in shock and horror. It is a middle-aged man, around fifty years old. The entire skin of his face has been stripped out, making it not so much a *de*formed as an *un*formed face. It is as though muscle, bone and tissue were still evolving, still working out the interplay of blood and fibre and nerves and veins that gives the structure strength and vitality. But the process appears to have been stopped midstream, before the final outer layer, the epidermis, could be stretched over the structure. The result is a mass of flesh coated with a peculiar crimson hue. Where a little bit of skin remains, it has formed into transparent little globules, as if the head had been put in boiling water and the face had bubbled over.

'Not a pretty sight, eh?' observes Dr Bansal with the matter-of-factness that comes from being exposed to such gruesomeness on a daily basis.

'Who did this to him?'

'His wife of thirty years.'

My eyebrows arch in astonishment.

'I know you must be surprised. Eighty per cent of burn victims who come here are women. The usual cases of dowry harassment. This one is an exception. The husband was a wife beater who assaulted his wife on a daily basis. Yesterday the wife got her revenge. She doused his face with sulphuric acid as he slept, blinding and disfiguring him for life.'

I can only guess at the inner turmoil that must have led the woman to take such an irrevocable step. 'What will happen to her now?'

'She'll probably spend the rest of her life in prison,' Dr Bansal says, threading his way through the clusters of patients, family members and nurses. The ICU resembles a post-battle scene from a war movie, with mangled and mutilated bodies lying in various states of patch-up. Neha's bed is at the very end of the ward, propped against a whitewashed wall spider-webbed with cracks, where a small, square window looks out on the central courtyard.

A lump of sorrow forms in my throat as I approach Neha. My sister's face is completely swathed in bandages, with just the eyes visible, reminding me of the Invisible Man. I gently take her hand in mine, and give it a consoling squeeze. She quickly pulls away, as one would from a leper's touch, and latches onto Ma's hand. The pain in my heart becomes even sharper.

There is a perceptible coldness in Neha's demeanour towards me, verging on hostility. Perhaps she feels I did not do enough to protect her. Or that what happened to her was somehow my fault.

I take Dr Bansal aside. 'Once the bandages are removed, what should we expect?'

'A face that has been permanently scarred,' he replies. 'It will be a painful experience, both for her and for you.'

A heaving sob escapes my chest. Dr Bansal grimaces sympathetically. 'The Neha that you knew has gone for ever. The sooner you accept that, the better.'

'Can't we do something to restore her face?'

'Of course we can. But it will take years of plastic and reconstructive surgery, and will cost you lakhs.'

'I will get you the money,' I say with a fierce determination and take out my cell phone. Going out into the corridor, I dial Acharya's number.

He answers almost immediately. 'Isn't it a bit late for you to be calling me, Sapna?'

'I have never asked you for anything,' I begin, 'but today I need your help for my sister Neha. I need money for her surgery.'

'What happened?'

'Someone threw acid on her. Now she is in hospital, fighting for her life.'

'Tch, tch.' He makes clicking noises with his tongue. 'That's very sad. Did they arrest the boys who did this?'

'Boys?' I pause suddenly. 'How did you know who did this? And that it was more than one boy? I never mentioned it.'

He doesn't speak for a long moment. 'I . . . I guessed it must have been more than one person.'

'My God! So you were behind the acid attack!' I gasp, a bolt of realisation hitting me like lightning. 'Was this another demented test of yours?'

'Now let's not jump to conclu—'

'What have you done?' I shrill at him, my hands forming into fists. 'You are an insane man who has crossed all limits.'

'I have no idea what you are talking about.'

'Don't lie to me. You were behind the acid attack, weren't you?'

'Of course not. But I did tell you that the last test will be the hardest.'

'Why did you have to bring my sister into it?'

'I didn't. God did. Didn't I also tell you there might be some . . . ah, collateral damage?'

'You call butchering someone's face collateral damage?' I shriek.

'The Japanese have a phrase. It's called "*shikata ga nai*", meaning "it can't be helped". Hardship must be borne.'

His preachy pretentiousness infuriates me further. There is nothing more left to say. Each and every illusion that I have harboured over the last five months has finally been shattered. Karan was right all along. Acharya was a violent sadist and I was a certified lunatic for having willingly become a pawn in his evil scheme.

A volcano of hate erupts in my brain as I storm back into the ward. A tidal wave of raw, seething, primal rage courses through my blood, making my fingers twitch. I want to wrap them around Acharya's throat and squeeze until his eyes pop out of their sockets. 'You are a monster. I will kill you!' I scream into the phone. The other relatives in the burns ward look up sharply. A nurse frowns at me and puts a finger to her lips. 'Silence, please.'

'You are needlessly getting excited,' Acharya says. 'Why don't you come over to Prarthana? I'll explain everything to you.'

'I'm coming there right now. You just wait there, you bastard.' I terminate the call and stride out of the ward.

Outside the hospital, the weather has changed completely. The humid heat has given way to lashing rain. Unseasonal, and therefore all the more frightening. Lightning slices through the pitch-black sky like a great, blue knife, followed by an ominous clap of thunder that rattles the bus shelter on the opposite side of the road. Without an umbrella, I am soaked to the bone within seconds. But it doesn't matter. Just as it doesn't matter that I haven't had a morsel to eat since lunch. Nothing matters except my burning desire for revenge.

It takes me ten minutes to find an auto-rickshaw. I explain Acharya's address in Vasant Vihar to the driver. 'It will cost you two hundred rupees, madam,' he says flatly, quoting double the normal fare.

'I'll give you three hundred. Just take me there quickly.'

We drive through pouring rain and howling wind. Throughout the forty-five-minute journey I maintain a stony silence. My thoughts are trapped in a loop of agonised shrieks and phantom sensations of holding Neha's writhing body. Her bandaged face swims before my eyes, blocking out all thought. My entire world has been torn asunder and nothing can ever piece it together again. Now I am going to end Acharya's world, deliver him my judgement from hell.

As the auto-rickshaw approaches Plot No. 133-C, my heartbeat rises. I clench and unclench my fists.

A pair of security types with earpieces and radios stop me at Prarthana's imposing gates. 'Are you Sapna Sinha?' one of them asks as he shines a flashlight in my face.

'Yes,' I reply.

He waves me through to the guard post, where two uniformed guards begin arguing with each other. '*Jaane de na*. Let her go,' says one. 'Boss had told us to expect her.'

'No,' says the other. 'No one is allowed to go in without double checking with Boss.' He picks up the intercom and presses a button. 'Sir, Miss Sapna Sinha is here.'

'Send her in,' I hear Acharya say gruffly. The guard nods and brings me an umbrella.

I glare at him. 'You expect me to walk to the residence in this rain? Why can't I go in my auto?'

'I'm sorry, ma'am, but auto-rickshaws are not allowed to go inside Prarthana. Mr Acharya has given strict instructions. You'll have to walk. It'll only take you five minutes.'

Shaking my head at this ridiculous rule, I turn to the auto driver. 'Wait here,' I instruct him. 'I won't be long.'

He looks at the sky. The rain shows no sign of relenting. He scours the deserted street. There is hardly any chance of finding a new customer. 'No problem,' he says, inserting a freshly made *paan* into his mouth. 'I'll add another hundred rupees' detention charge.'

I unfurl the umbrella and begin the long walk down the curving driveway. The wind picks up, whistling through the manicured hedges like a haunting lullaby. The rain pelts down on the parasol, cascading off the black vinyl in a steady stream. I plod on towards the house, shoes squishing, my wet churidar suit clinging to my body like a second skin.

Halfway to the house the path curves right and as I turn the bend I find my way barred by a couple of fierce-looking dogs who greet me with low growls. They are the Dobermans, their eyes glowing like fiery embers in the night, their thin black fur glistening like wet rock. Though they are tethered to a tree trunk, I skirt the far edge of the path, putting as much distance as possible between me and them. Another crack of lightning tears through the sky, lighting up the mansion like an exposed negative, and another gust of wind almost twists the umbrella inside out.

Reaching the shelter of the covered portico feels like a major victory. I close the umbrella, shake the rain out of my hair, and press the doorbell.

I wait for almost two minutes but no one opens the door. I press the doorbell a second time. Again no answer. That is when I notice that the door is ajar. I push it open and step onto a designer welcome mat. Almost reflexively I begin wiping my shoes, ridding them of excess moisture. 'Mr Acharya?' I call out, only to hear my own voice echo back in the marbled foyer.

The eerie silence in the house is unnerving. On my last visit the place was crawling with servants. Tonight it resembles a haunted castle. The vast, empty rooms seem secretive and sinister as I walk through them, the shadows on the walls appearing to watch my every move, whispering conspiracies to each other in response to my rubber-soled sneakers squeaking on the hardwood floor.

I cross the drawing and dining rooms and enter the study, only to find that empty as well. I gently open the connecting door to the bedroom, and peer in.

A weak spotlight shines a dim glow over the portrait of Acharya's father. The rest of the room is in complete darkness. 'Mr Acharya?' I call out again, thinking he might be in the bathroom.

Receiving no answer, I enter the bedroom gingerly, feeling around for the light switch. After a bit of fumbling around, my fingers hit a plastic panel, and I flick all the switches. The sudden burst of light that floods the room makes me shield my eyes.

The bedroom is pretty much like the last time I saw it. There's the same mahogany bed with purple bed linen, the black onyx mirror and the side table full of old family photographs. The only change in the room is the 65-inch Sony TV, installed on the wall opposite the bed.

'Mr Acharya? Where are you?' I shout, feeling the waves of frustration and impatience surging within me. It is clear that he is deliberately avoiding me. The bathroom seems like the most likely place he could be in. I begin to move towards the solid-oak bathroom door on the far side of the room, when I hear a squelch. I look down and shrink back in horror. I have stepped into a small red puddle. It becomes quickly evident that what I am seeing is fresh blood, pooling on the floor like an oil stain, now all over the sole of my shoe.

My eyes skim over the floor, frantically tracing the source of blood. The trail goes all around the bed till it ends at something that stops me cold in my tracks. There is a body lying on the floor, on the other side of the bed. It appears to be that of a man dressed in an off-white silk kurta pyjama. From where I am standing, I cannot see the man's face, but he is quite obviously dead, a knife with a wooden handle sticking visibly out of his stomach, like a candle on a birthday cake.

A scream rises and dies in my throat. I have just witnessed the first murder of my life. And it induces in me such nausea that I double over on the floor, nearly regurgitating my lunch. A scenario painted by Karan long ago flashes through my mind. Acharya calls me to his house late at night. I don't find him there, but I discover a dead body – and the murder is pinned on me. In Karan's word picture, the body was that of Acharya's wife. Here, I am looking at the dead face of a man, and it drains both my courage and my curiosity to gaze on it. I know I have walked into a trap set by Acharya. Any minute now the security men will burst through the front door, unleashing their dogs on me. Just the thought of those two fierce hounds leaping at me, tearing apart my flesh with their strong sharp teeth, causes my hair to stand on end. No, I can't risk being found lurking at a crime scene. Which means I must pretend I've seen no crime and leave as quickly as I can.

Without any further thought, I take off my shoes and, holding them in my hand, slip out of the bedroom. I gingerly retrace my steps back to the front door, let myself out, and put the shoes back on. Then I open the umbrella and try to walk as normally as possible towards the gate.

A feral snarl almost makes me jump, reminding me that I am approaching the dogs. They begin barking madly the moment they see me, as if some sixth sense has already told them of the murder in the residence. I creep past them as though walking on eggshells.

The tension inside my body is at fever pitch by the time I turn the bend that puts me out of the Dobermans' line of sight. I try to calm down my breathing with slower breaths as I near the guard post.

'That was a quick meeting,' the duty guard observes when I return his umbrella.

'Yes,' I say, smiling weakly and clambering into the waiting auto-rickshaw. 'Take me back to Rohini.' I have to nudge the driver, who is dozing at the wheel. 'Quickly.'

He peers at me. 'Is everything all right? You look like you've seen a ghost.'

'Don't talk,' I reply through clenched teeth. 'Just drive.'

With an indifferent shrug, he spits out *paan* juice and cranks the engine. The auto refuses to start, further tightening my already fraught nerves. My hands turn cold and clammy, my heart is hammering violently in my chest and my stomach is churning like a cement mixer. Eventually the engine does roar into life, but I cannot hold back any longer. We have gone barely fifty metres when I puke all over the back seat.

The bright lights of the hospital are a welcome refuge from the nightmarish world I have escaped from. Even the mutilated faces in the burns ward seem preferable to the sight of the murdered body in Prarthana.

Though it is past midnight, Ma is still by Neha's bedside. 'Where did you go away so suddenly?' she asks me.

'To consult a plastic surgeon,' I lie blithely.

'And what did he say? Can Neha's face be restored?'

'Yes, but we won't be able to afford it.'

Ma turns away, already expecting this. 'I'll speak to Nirmala Ben. Perhaps she can help us raise the money.'

'Why don't you go back to the apartment?' I lay a hand on her shoulder. 'I'll stay here with Neha.'

'Hospitals have become my home now,' she replies. 'You go back and get some rest.'

I look out of the window. The rain has stopped but the atmosphere is still charged with electricity. The terrible cloud of murder hangs over the city like a shroud.

I sit down in the empty chair by Neha's bedside.

Closing my eyes, I try to order my thoughts, make sense of the jumble in my brain. Acharya hired a couple of youths to throw acid on Neha. Then he had bumped off someone at his own residence. He had done his best to pin the murder on me but I was able to get out just in time. Nevertheless, the police are bound to question me, and I have resolved to tell them everything. I will reveal the perverse nature of his seven tests, expose the true face of Vinay Mohan Acharya to the world. But there are some things I won't tell the police. Such as entering Acharya's bedroom and finding the dead body.

I go to the washroom and check my clothes. There's not a drop of blood on them. I take off my sneakers and wash them thoroughly, removing every trace of blood from the soles. Then I return to the chair and try to sleep, but the dead body floats into my mind like a fever dream. The knife dangles before me like a teasing vision, always just out of reach. It is impossible to sleep, impossible to rest, impossible to pretend that nothing has happened.

Overcome with hunger and exhaustion, I finally fall into a fitful slumber around 4 a.m., only to be woken up half an hour later by a policeman prodding me with his stick.

'Are you Sapna Sinha?' he addresses me. Behind him are half a dozen other constables.

I nod, still groggy with sleep. Ma immediately tenses up, her mother's instinct telegraphing that something bad is about to happen.

'You are under arrest,' he says.

'For what?'

'For the murder of Vinay Mohan Acharya.'

I am jolted out of my half-sleep. 'You must be joking.'

'This seems like a joke to you?' he says, holding up the arrest warrant with my name on it.

'There must be a mist—'

Mother doesn't even let me finish the sentence. She lets out a howl of anguish and promptly faints.

Arrest is easily the most shattering and disorienting experience of life. It cleaves your world into two, before arrest and after. You are suddenly wrenched from your everyday life, from your friends and family, and thrown into an utterly alien environment.

I am transported to Vasant Vihar police station and booked for murder. They take my fingerprints, DNA sample and mugshots. My apartment is raided and my computer taken away together with my personal diary. The clothes I was wearing yesterday as well as my shoes and cell phone are confiscated. I am produced before a magistrate who denies me bail and remands me to police custody for seven days.

Now I am at the mercy of Assistant Commissioner of Police I. Q. Khan. A tall, trim man with a craggy face and a neat moustache, there is something very un–policeman-like about him. He has the military bearing of a soldier and the cultured grace of an old aristocrat.

A female constable called Pushpa Thanvi has been attached to me like a conjoined twin. An overweight, bosomy woman with a bad complexion and a voice like that of a duck with laryngitis, she watches me like a hawk and has the disconcerting habit of habit of poking me whenever she needs my attention.

Even more disconcerting is ACP Khan's unblinking stare as I sit across from him. The fatigue of the previous night, coupled with all the rushing around since the morning, has worn me out. The only thought circulating in my brain is that this is some horrible dream from which I will awaken shortly.

We are meeting in ACP Khan's office, a large, cheer-less room made even more stuffy by heavy velvet drapes. The whitewashed walls are adorned with framed photos of Gandhi, Nehru and Subhash Chandra Bose and moti-vational quotes from Einstein and Kahlil Gibran. A wall-mounted Philips LCD television is switched off, but a wall clock next to it is busily ticking away the seconds to 3.55 p.m.

'Are you prepared to make a confession?' he asks, star-ing me in the eye.

I look away, wilting under his remorseless scrutiny. 'I have nothing to confess.'

'Did you go to Mr Acharya's house last night, or do you want to deny even that?'

'I did go to Acharya's house. But I didn't kill him. To be more precise, I didn't even meet him. I kept pressing the doorbell, but no one responded. So I just came right back to the hospital.'

'So you did not find his dead body inside his bed-room?'

'No. I never entered his bedroom. In fact, I still can't believe that he is dead.'

'Then have a look at this photo,' he says, sliding a glossy print across the table.

It is the 'official photo' of the murdered man taken by

the police photographer. I see a pale, waxen face beneath a mantle of silvery hair. It does look like Vinay Mohan Acharya. He is lying in a pool of blood, dressed in an off-white silk kurta pyjama. His eyes are open, but he is quite dead, his features frozen in an agonised grimace, a knife with a wooden handle jutting out of his bloodstained chest.

An involuntary shudder passes through my body as I gaze at the photo. Even though I have witnessed the murdered body with my own eyes, I cannot shake off the air of unreality about Acharya's death, as though I still expect him to walk into the police station and declare, 'You have failed the seventh test!'

The one thing I don't feel is regret. Acharya had committed a horrific crime and deserved to die. But who had killed him, and why? This was a mystery yet to be solved.

I slide the photo back to ACP Khan. 'Who discovered the body?'

'It was Dr Kabir Seth, Mr Acharya's personal physician. Acharya was in Mumbai the whole of last week, admitted to the Tata Memorial Hospital. He arrived back in Delhi only yesterday. Last night, at twenty-two fifty hours, he telephoned Dr Seth, complaining of feeling uneasy and asking him to come over to Prarthana. When Dr Seth reached the house just before midnight, he found Mr Acharya lying dead in a pool of blood and immediately alerted the security at the gate, something that you should have done, if you did not murder Mr Acharya.'

'What makes you think I murdered Acharya?'

'Well, let's see. At least twenty people in Shastri Hospital heard you screaming on the phone at Mr Acharya at twenty-two hundred hours, threatening to kill him. You arrived at his house in pouring rain at twenty-two fifty-eight hours. The guard at the gate personally spoke to Mr Acharya on the intercom and received instructions to let you in.'

'Yes, I heard him too.'

'Well, then you yourself confirm that he was alive at twenty-three hundred hours. The medical examiner has listed the time of death as being not earlier than twenty-two hundred and not later than twenty-three fifteen. Since Mr Acharya was very much alive at twenty-three hundred hours, it means he was killed between twenty-three hundred and twenty-three fifteen. You were the only one inside the house during that period. So only you could have killed Mr Acharya.'

'How do you know I was the only one inside the house? The real killer must have been hiding there.'

'Prarthana is a fortress. Even a bird cannot dare to fly in without permission. On Saturday, eleventh of June, there were only two visitors who entered the premises. One was Rana, Mr Acharya's aide, who came to the house at nineteen thirty hours, spent an hour with Mr Acharya, and then left at twenty thirty-five hours. The other person was you.' He pauses to consult his notes before resuming. 'After arriving back from Mumbai at ten hundred hours, Mr Acharya did not leave the house the entire day. He had lunch at his usual time of thirteen thirty hours, and dinner at nineteen hundred hours. Then he dismissed all his servants for the night, telling them he did not want to be disturbed under any circumstance. All the servants left at twenty thirty hours. Rana left five minutes later, at twenty thirty-five. After that no one entered the house till your arrival. The security at the gate is absolutely certain of this. Which means, when you entered Prarthana, you and Mr Acharya were the only persons inside the house. Ten minutes later he was dead and you were in an auto, making your getaway.' He pauses and gives me that same fixed-gaze treatment. 'So why did you kill Mr Acharya? From what I know of him, he was a gentle and kind man. A fountain of philanthropic generosity.'

'He was a monster,' I hiss through clenched teeth. 'You don't know anything about him. He destroyed Neha's life. And now he's destroyed mine. All because of those wretched seven tests.'

'What seven tests?'

I take a deep breath and begin. 'It all started when he accosted me in the Hanuman temple that winter afternoon ...'

Speaking continuously for more than an hour, I tell him everything, starting from that fateful meeting in Connaught Place to the acid attack on Neha.

ACP Khan listens to me with utmost attention, taking notes in a slim notebook. When I finish, he lets out a breath of air, rubs the bridge of his nose contemplatively and quotes an Urdu couplet: '*Katl bhi hue hain hum aur kasoorwar bhi hum the/Apne hi katil se ishq me giraftar bhi hum the*' ('I am the murdered man as well as the culprit/ My crime: that I was in love with my own murderer').

'Acharya was not in love with me, and neither was I in love with him,' I correct him.

'We'll see about that,' he says when a sub-inspector enters the room and salutes him smartly. '*Jai Hind*, sir. A lot of media people have gathered outside. What should I tell them, sir?'

ACP Khan sighs in exasperation and nods. 'Tell them I'm coming to brief them.'

He gets up from his chair and turns to Pushpa Thanvi. 'Watch her.' Then, with long strides, he leaves the room.

Now that she is alone in the room with me, Pushpa's face crinkles into a smug grin. She goes to the window, lifts the heavy curtain and peeks out. 'They are all here.' She lets out a little giggle.

'Who all?'

'Aaj Tak, Zee News, Star, IBN-7, NDTV, Sunlight, ITN . . . Looks like finally I'll be able to fulfil my dream of being on TV.' She takes out a compact mirror and quickly checks her teeth.

ACP Khan is gone for over an hour. When he returns, his body language is quite different. 'I hope you used the interval wisely to repent,' he says, standing over me.

I sit staring pensively at the cement floor, picking at the threads of my sky-blue salvar suit. He smiles in a sad sort of way and quotes yet another Urdu couplet: '*Voh kaun hain jinhen tauba ki mil gai fursat/Hamein gunaah bhi karne ko zindagi kam hai*' ('Who are the fortunate ones who have the luxury to repent/I don't have time enough even to commit sin').

He sits down in his chair and resumes briskly. 'We've just located Mr Acharya's will.'

'And?'

'And he's donated his entire personal wealth to charity. So, if you were expecting to inherit a fortune, I'm sorry.'

'Acharya was against the culture of inheritance. He had only promised to make me his CEO, not his heir.'

'I'm afraid I have more bad news for you.'

'What now?'

'Forensics has just confirmed that the blood on your sneakers matches Mr Acharya's. You took the precaution of washing your shoes to rinse off the blood, but in doing so you failed to notice the blood that had seeped into the crack between the upper and the sole. We found it.'

My heart pulses violently and the blood rushes to my head. I am about to say something when he raises his hand. 'Wait. It gets worse. Forensics has also confirmed that the fingerprints on the knife that was used to murder Mr Acharya match yours.'

'That's totally impossible! I never touched the knife.'

'Perhaps this might refresh your memory,' he says, holding up the murder weapon encased in a plastic bag. Now that I see it at close quarters it does seem eerily familiar. I can make out KK Thermoware imprinted on the wooden handle, and a bolt of recognition strikes me like a punch in the gut. It's the same knife I had bought from the street hawker on the night I was attacked by those three hoodlums outside Japanese Park.

'This is what is technically called an open-and-shut case,' ACP Khan observes as he snaps shut his notebook. 'So save yourself a lengthy interrogation and sign a confession statement.' He looks at me hopefully.

I shake my head. 'I did not murder Acharya. But now I have a good idea who killed him.'

'Well, let's hear it.'

'It's Rana. He alone had access to that knife with my fingerprints.'

'How?'

'Don't you see? Acharya had me attacked by those goons outside Japanese Park as part of the third test. They took away my knife and must have returned it to Acharya or Rana. And that same knife has now been used to murder Acharya. Which means only Rana could have done it.'

'But Rana left Prarthana at twenty thirty-five and did not return till midnight.'

As I ponder the problem I am struck by another idea. 'What if this isn't murder, but a suicide?'

He looks at me intently. 'Have you now decided to go in for an insanity plea?'

'What if this is a suicide?' I repeat. 'Remember the seventh test? Acharya said it will be the hardest of them all. Well, this is it.'

'You're not making any sense.'

'Look, Acharya was the one who set those ruffians on me outside the Japanese Park so he could get hold of the knife with my fingerprints. Then he lured me to his house with that acid attack on Neha. The moment I started walking towards the house, he stabbed himself with the same knife, just so that I could be framed for his murder. This is easily the biggest crisis of my life. Hence the final test. QED.'

'You can tell these fanciful theories to your state-appointed lawyer,' ACP Khan laughs, and signals to the lady constable, signifying that the interrogation is over for now. 'Take her to the female lockup.'

'*Jai Hind*, sir-ji.' Pushpa offers Khan a limp salute and pokes me in the forehead. '*Chalo*. Let's go.'

She escorts me down a short corridor. We pass the male lockup, where a couple of unshaven, unkempt men are slumped behind the door. They watch me with dull curiosity. I clamp my nose, unable to bear the strong smell of liquor that radiates from them like incense smoke.

At the other end of the corridor is the female lockup, mercifully empty. Pushpa unlocks the sturdy cell door, allows me to step inside and clangs it shut with such force that the metallic echo rattles in my ears like thunder. I stand for a moment staring at the dim, dirty light filtering through the grille of the iron door, blinking back tears, absorbing the fact that I had finally become a prisoner.

On paper, police custody means that an accused is kept in a police station under police surveillance temporarily till the next judgement. In practice it means being held prisoner in a fetid, oppressive cell that reeks of human misery. The walls of the female lockup are stained with mildew, graffiti and years of dirt. The floor is bare, rough concrete. There is no window and no sunlight, making it a dark, gloomy place even in the middle of the day. The bed is a lumpy, lice-infested cotton mattress. Worse of all, the bathroom is not separated from the rest of the cell. Behind a low wall is an Indian-style toilet with no mug, no toilet paper, no running water. It gives off the rancid stench of excrement and urine of previous occupants. A metal bucket in the corner actually has faeces smeared all over it. The smell is so distinct, so overwhelming, I can taste it.

I have borne the ordeal of arrest and interrogation with

determined fortitude, but I cannot bear to stay in this horrible, stinking cell. It makes me want to die. I know that, if I remain in this hellhole for more than twenty-four hours, I will lose my sanity.

The oppressive drabness of the walls closes in on me. I try so hard but I just can't breathe. I drag myself to the cell door and grip the iron bars. 'Help me!' I scream like a deranged inmate in a mental hospital. 'Get me out of here! Please, for God's sake.'

'*Kya hai*?' Pushpa Thanvi appears momentarily. 'Why are you making such a racket?'

'I can't stay here.'

'What did you expect? The Sheraton?'

'I . . . I have to go to the toilet.'

'So why don't you?' she barks. 'There's one right behind you.'

'I can't go here. Please, can you at least take me to a proper toilet outside?'

'No,' she declares with the finality of a judge delivering a verdict. 'Those in lockup have to use the toilet *inside* the lockup.'

'I'm begging you,' I weep. 'Please show me just this much consideration.'

ACP Khan hears my plaintive cries and comes striding down the corridor. He sees my tear-streaked face and nods in silent understanding. 'Okay, as an exception, I'll allow you to use the toilet that the women constables use. Pushpa,' he says to the lady constable, 'take her, but keep her under lock and key throughout.'

'*Jee* sir-ji,' Pushpa says stiffly, clearly unhappy at being overruled.

She leads me around a rectangular open courtyard with a large guava tree in the middle. The courtyard is ringed by a dozen rooms. I read the wooden nameplates hanging in front of each: Barrack, Computer Room, Interrogation Room, Investigating Officer's Room, Wireless Room, Evidence Room . . .

The ladies' toilet is located at the northwestern end of the courtyard, towards the back of the building, facing the Women's Resting Room, where five women constables are sitting around, watching a serial on TV. Pushpa unlocks the toilet door with a key and rudely shoves me inside. 'Just thump on the door when you are done. I'll be right opposite watching *Ladies Special* with my friends.'

As the key turns in the lock from outside, I am overtaken by a stomach-wrenching wave of shame and degradation. What has my life come to? I ask myself again and again. Now I have to beg someone even to take a pee.

I sit down on the cracked toilet seat, close my eyes and try to imagine myself somewhere else. A sunny Sunday afternoon, with wispy white clouds drifting across a perfect blue sky. In the distance, mist rising from the pine-clad mountains. I'm curled up under an oak tree with a book of poetry. Behind me Ma and Papa are sitting on wicker chairs, laughing and chatting. Alka and Neha are lounging on the grass, soaking up the sunshine. It is a place without fear, without sadness, without the police. I lose myself in this long-lost world till I am jerked out of my fantasy by someone banging loudly at the door. I hear Pushpa Thanvi's grating voice, bringing me back to reality with a thud: '*Arrey*, are you taking a dump or dressing for a party? It's been half an hour!'

When I return to the cell, there is a tiffin waiting for me, containing dinner. It is an unexpected treat, consisting of galouti kebabs and chicken biryani. Pushpa reveals that the food has come from ACP Khan's house. 'What black magic have you done to him that he is being so generous to you?' she asks cattily.

ACP Khan's kindness brings tears to my eyes, makes the lockup slightly more bearable. Still, I spend the night propped up against the wall rather than risk lying on the lice-infested mattress.

Morning brings a new day and a welcome visitor, Ma. We meet in the visitors' room, under Pushpa's eagle-eyed watch.

'How are you, *beti*?' Ma asks with such concern, that I don't have the heart to tell her the truth.

'I am fine, Ma. Everything is fine. How's Neha?'

'She is recovering well. She sends you her love.'

A tear leaks out of my eye and, before I know it, I am sobbing my heart out. Ma draws me to her chest and begins caressing my head, silently pouring in her love and affection. We remain like that for close to ten minutes, a telepathic communion that requires neither words nor unnecessary gestures. And I can sense something pass from her to me, a protective reassurance that I am not alone, a healing, spiritual energy that drains the tension and negativity out of me.

That morning I understand for the first time the true depth of the mother–daughter bond, its fierce intensity, its indestructible nature and, above all, its redemptive power.

*

Just before noon, the state-appointed lawyer also makes a belated appearance. Mr Trilok Chand is a small, scrawny man, dressed in an ill-fitting black coat, who inspires as much confidence as a homemade sanitary napkin.

'I have seen your case file,' he tells me in a conspiratorial whisper, 'and it doesn't look very good.'

'For me or the police?' I am compelled to ask.

'For you. The evidence against you is quite strong. The murdered man's blood was on your shoes, the knife that killed him has your fingerprints. You lied to the police about not entering the house. You had motive, means and opportunity, the three things needed to secure a murder conviction.'

'You sound more like the public prosecutor than my defence lawyer.'

'You don't need a lawyer,' he says, licking his chapped lips. 'You need a crooked judge.'

The most startling development of the day comes at 3 p.m. ACP Khan summons me to his office, where he has one eye on the desk phone and another on the LCD television tuned to Sunlight TV. Shalini Grover is standing in front of Kyoko Chambers, which is ringed with police vehicles.

'This is easily the biggest story of the year,' she intones breathlessly into the mike. 'Two days after the sensational murder of industrialist Vinay Mohan Acharya, when police raided the posh headquarters of the ABC Group to uncover more clues about his grisly death they discovered something completely unexpected. Inside Mr

Acharya's locked safe, which was kept in his private office, investigators stumbled onto a cache of secret documents that make the WikiLeaks revelations seem like a juvenile prank.' The camera cuts to a sound bite by a crime branch sleuth: 'We are still examining all the data recovered from his safe, but preliminary analysis leads us to believe that there is a link between Acharya and Atlas Investments.'

'No!' I gasp.

'Yes,' Shalini contradicts me. 'Sunlight can declare with complete certainty that Vinay Mohan Acharya has been unmasked as the mastermind behind Atlas, the elusive front company that is at the centre of virtually every scam that has happened in recent times.'

ACP Khan uses the remote to switch off the TV. 'Amazing, isn't it?' He turns to me. 'This man donates all his wealth to charity, and then we discover that his wealth was obtained illegally. Acharya pretended to be the epitome of rectitude, but was in actual fact the biggest scamster the country has ever produced.' In a flash he latches onto yet another telling couplet: 'Oh virtuous, how I worshipped thee/But you turned out to be a sinner bigger than even me.'

'Will this have any impact on my case?'

'Murder is murder,' he notes wryly. 'Whether you kill a dacoit or a nun, the punishment remains the same.'

'So what will happen to Acharya's company now?'

'I don't know. It may even go into liquidation if the income-tax authorities levy a hefty penalty on Acharya's black income. Or the board may decide to sell out to another conglomerate. I'm told Ajay Krishna Acharya,

Mr Acharya's twin brother, is keen to buy the ABC Group. He'll probably succeed.'

'That will be the ultimate travesty. Acharya hated his brother like poison. In fact, once he even confided to me that he thought AK was the mastermind behind Atlas.' I look up at ACP Khan with that momentary stopping of the breath which comes with a sudden insight. 'Of course! AK had Acharya bumped off so that he could take over his brother's company.'

ACP Khan shakes his head in slow negation. 'I've already looked into that possibility. AK was in the Grand Regency Hotel the night Acharya was murdered.'

'What was he doing in the Regency?'

'Addressing a healthcare conference in front of a thousand delegates. There's no way he could have murdered Acharya.'

'I still feel Rana is the key to this entire case. Don't you think it's time you interrogated him?'

'I've already summoned him. He should be here in the next five minutes.'

Rana walks into ACP Khan's room looking somewhat different from the last time I saw him. Perhaps it is something to do with his dress of polo shirt, khakis and fancy shoes, lending him a touch of easy prosperity.

'I hope you rot in hell,' he whispers angrily as he sits down next to me.

ACP Khan deals with him with the brusque profi- ciency of a seasoned investigator. 'What was the nature of your relationship with Mr Acharya?'

'I was his chief aide. You could think of me as a kind of confidential secretary.'

'So is it true that Mr Acharya had selected Miss Sapna Sinha for consideration as CEO of the ABC Group of Companies?'

He nods with a grimace. 'It was a mistake. I told Boss so.'

'What made Mr Acharya choose Miss Sapna?'

'I have no idea. Boss did not share everything with me. My own guess is he was attracted to her for some reason. That is why last September he secretly bought Gulati & Sons.'

'But that's before he even met me!' I interject.

'Carry on,' urges ACP Khan. 'So Mr Acharya purchased the company Miss Sapna was working in. Then he met her and told her he wanted to make her the CEO of his group if she passed his seven tests, right?'

Rana nods.

'And you helped Mr Acharya in executing those seven tests?'

'Not seven. Just six.'

'What do you mean?'

'Mr Acharya became quite sick recently and didn't have time to devise the seventh test.'

'That's an utter lie!' I butt in again.

'ACP *sahib*, you can speak to Dr Chitnis at the Tata Memorial Hospital in Mumbai,' Rana says evenly. 'He will show you Mr Acharya's medical records, which will prove that Boss was suffering from pancreatic cancer. Terminal stage. He was going to die pretty soon anyways. But this woman' – he pauses to bestow a look of undisguised contempt on me – 'just couldn't wait that long.'

'He's making this up,' I declare flatly.

ACP Khan shoots me a stern look before resuming his questioning. 'Were you aware that Mr Acharya was the mastermind behind Atlas?'

'I didn't have an inkling. It has come as a huge shock to me.'

'But you were his most trusted aide. How come he didn't trust you with his secret bank accounts?'

'I guess there are some secrets that are never shared. But I'll tell you this: Mr Acharya was a good man, not the monster he's being made out to be by the media.'

I marvel at the act being put on by Rana. He is still wearing that mask of servile blandness, pretending to be the devoted servant, the loyal aide.

'May I ask when was the last time you saw Mr Acharya alive?'

'When I left Prarthana on Sunday, just after eight thirty p.m.'

'And where did you go after you left Mr Acharya's residence?'

'To my house.'

'And where exactly is your house?'

'DDA Flat No. 4245, Sector C-1, Vasant Kunj.'

'Did you remain in your house throughout that night?'

'No. At ten thirty I left for Infra Red, the bar in Basant Lok.'

'And how long did you stay there?'

'Till midnight, when I got a call on my cell from the security at Prarthana informing me of Boss's murder.'

'And what did you do after that?'

'I immediately went to Mr Acharya's residence, where I met Dr Seth. The police also arrived a minute later.'

The interrogation drags on for another fifteen minutes, but it's getting nowhere, and I'm becoming increasingly impatient. 'If Acharya did not organise the acid attack on Neha, who did?' I demand, glowering at Rana.

'How would I know?' Rana responds. 'That's for the police to find out.'

'And find out we will,' says ACP Khan.

Lauren comes to visit me that evening, accompanied by a tall, dark-haired kid.

'Do you remember him?' she asks me.

I glance over at the boy and recognition dawns on me. 'Guddu, right? The expert lock maker.'

A shy smile crosses Guddu's face. 'Yes, madam. I used to work at Mirza Metal Works till you and Lauren Madam rescued me.'

'What are you doing now?'

'I'm learning computer skills at the Foundation.'

'Chin up,' says Lauren. '"If we had no winter, the spring would not be so pleasant; if we did not sometimes taste of adversity, prosperity would not be so welcome".' She is quoting the poet Anne Bradstreet.

So great is my despondency that, in return, I can only quote from Oscar Wilde's 'Ballad of Reading Gaol' on prison life: 'All that we know who lie in gaol/Is that the wall is strong;/And that each day is like a year,/A year whose days are long.'

At 6 p.m. ACP Khan summons me to his office again. He regards me with solemn eyes as I take the seat opposite him. 'It's not looking good for you,' he says. 'I've just spoken to Dr Chitnis at the Tata Memorial Hospital in Mumbai. He has confirmed what Rana told us. Mr Acharya was indeed suffering from metastatic pancreatic cancer. It has a median survival of just three to five months. Mr Acharya's condition had deteriorated to such an extent that Dr Chitnis had told him he had barely two weeks left to live.'

My eyes widen in surprise. 'Acharya never mentioned a word about his cancer to me!'

'I've also seen footage from the security cameras at Infra Red. Rana was indeed there from twenty-two forty-five till twenty-three fifty-five, which means he also has an airtight alibi.'

'Then he's manipulated the cameras somehow. I'm pretty sure he was in Acharya's residence when I entered. He killed Acharya and managed to get out by hood-winking the security at the gate.'

'But why would Rana want to kill his boss?'

'For that most basic of reasons: hate. Rana hated Acharya for not choosing him for the CEO's job. And he hated me for being the chosen one. So he killed Acharya and framed me, getting two birds with one stone.'

'What if you had passed the seventh test? Do you think Acharya would have really made you his CEO?'

'I don't know,' I reply, biting my lip.

'I think he was setting you up as a scapegoat. You would have been the one saddled with the Atlas mess.'

'Yes.' I nod slowly. 'He was much more devious than he looked.'

ACP Khan steeples his fingers and looks me in the eye. 'Are you prepared to make a confession now?'

I look right back at him. 'Do you really believe I murdered Acharya? Is it really that simple?'

He exhales. 'Murder is never simple,' he says. 'But we have to go by facts. And the facts are against you. In any event, I'm no longer in charge of the case. It's become too big for this police station. The Crime Branch has taken over. They will be the ones questioning you from now on.'

I have my first encounter with the Crime Branch at 8 p.m. that day. 'They want you in the Interrogaysun Room,' Pushpa announces, sending a nervous tingle up my spine. I imagine a dim basement room, lit by a lamp suspended over a table, around which grim men sit in shadows, cigarette smoke clouding their faces.

In fact the Interrogation Room turns out to be brightly lit, with the atmosphere of a cosy classroom. There is a wooden table surrounded by sturdy metal chairs and even a blackboard. The three men sitting around the table, however, do not resemble teachers at all. Dressed identically in nondescript safari suits, they have the faceless look of government sleuths.

They tell me to sit down on the lone seat opposite them, making it clear that it was me versus them, one versus three.

Then the interrogation begins. At first they are civil, asking me routine things about my family, my job at Gulati & Sons and my interactions with Acharya. Then, gradually, the tone changes. The questions become pointed, suggestive and downright offensive. 'Did you have a sexual relationship with Acharya?' 'How many times did he call you to his bedroom?' 'Were you aware of Acharya's connection to Atlas?'

For three hours the Crime Branch investigators grill me mercilessly, trying to browbeat me into admitting that I murdered Acharya. When I stand my ground, they yell and scream at me, bully and intimidate me. 'We'll hang you for this murder if you don't confess.'

'Then hang me,' I say defiantly. 'But I won't admit to a crime I did not commit.'

Being enmeshed in a police investigation, I realise, is like stepping into quicksand. No matter how hard you fight to get out, you end up sinking deeper and deeper. Bit by bit, the Crime Branch sleuths gather evidence against me, connecting all the dots, making it a damning indictment. From what I can gather, the police case against me runs as follows: I was Acharya's mistress, having an affair with him; Acharya had promised me the CEO-ship of his company, provided I succeeded in his seven tests; having completed six tests I became impatient, wanting to lay my hands on all his money; along the way a completely unrelated incident, the acid attack on Neha, happened; thinking it to be the handiwork of Acharya, I went to his residence with a knife to blackmail him; Acharya rejected my demands and, in a fit of rage, I attacked him with the knife and murdered him.

I have to admit that the hypothesis sounds quite plausible. In fact, by the end of the third round of coercive interrogation I am almost ready to believe it myself. Perhaps I have indeed killed Acharya, and so traumatic was the experience that I have locked that memory deep inside me and thrown away the key.

As part of their strategy, the Crime Branch people try all kinds of mind games. I am deprived of sleep and food. Instructions are issued to treat me as a maximum-security criminal. A male guard is now posted every night outside my lockup, as though I were some kind of Houdini who can escape from a locked, windowless cell.

Media interest in the case shows no sign of abating. There are more OB vans parked outside Vasant Vihar police station than outside 7 RCR, the Prime Minister's residence. My arrest is the number-one story in India, beating even the soap operas on TV. A famous director announces plans to make a biopic on my life. As he puts it, 'All juicy scandals revolve around money, murder or sex. And, when you have all three present, as in the case of Sapna Sinha, then you have a superhit on your hands!'

Nirmala Ben comes calling on Day 5 of my arrest. News of her impending visit causes a stir in the police station. 'You even know Big Ben?' Pushpa Thanvi asks me with reverential awe, looking at me with new respect.

The Gandhian arrives at 1 p.m., but is not brought to me directly. First, she is taken for a cup of tea in ACP Khan's office. Then he escorts her on an inspection tour of the police station. She peeps into the various rooms around the courtyard, poses for photographs, even signs autographs. 'Big Ben, Big Ben.' I hear chants, cheers, and laughs. My anticipation has reached a crescendo by the time Mrs Nirmala Mukherjee Shah steps into the visitors' room, which has been swept clean and spruced up with a flower arrangement.

She looks comfortably elegant in a simple white sari. A roiling scrum of press photographers and TV cameramen surges behind her like a tsunami. The reporters trip over cords and each other in their desperate attempt to get a sound bite. It is not every day that they get a chance to record an encounter between the most famous anticorruption crusader in India and the country's most famous detainee.

Pushpa preens by my side as flashbulbs go off in my face from all directions. The reporters crowd closer, thrusting their microphones at me like daggers. I hold up my hands before my face, shrinking back from the bright lights and shrill voices, from all these people who want to make a spectacle of my misfortune.

ACP Khan tries to get the journalists and TV crews to leave after the photo op, but no one listens to him. It is left to Nirmala Ben to restore a modicum of order. '*Dekhiye*, this is a private visit,' she says with folded hands. 'Please allow me to meet my goddaughter alone, and then I will come and have an interaction with all of you outside. *Barobar chhe ne?*'

It is like a magician performing mass hypnosis. The hordes depart instantly, leaving the Gandhian alone with me, ACP Khan and Pushpa.

Nirmala Ben looks deep into my eyes, searching them, and finds the truth she is looking for. Like a good doctor who knows what is wrong with a patient simply by reading his pulse, she cognises what I am going through, understands my torment.

'Be brave, my girl,' she says. 'Remember, bravery is not a quality of the body, but of the soul.' Then she wraps her arms around me and pulls me to her shoulder. I cling to her tightly, feeling her warmth, searching for that well-spring of compassion and understanding I found in Ma. Though I try very hard not to cry, that pit of sadness and despair in my soul bubbles over, and I begin sobbing like a lost child. She passes a hand through my hair, soothing me. 'Don't worry, everything will be sorted. I've told Susheela, too, that I'll do my best for Neha.'

Twenty minutes later, Nirmala Ben prepares to leave. 'Close the day with prayer so that you may have a peaceful night free from dreams and nightmares,' she offers as parting advice as she takes my hand in hers. I feel something metallic being slipped into the hollow of my palm and instinctively fold it into a fist. Then she bows her head in *namaste* and walks out of the room.

'What a remarkable woman,' ACP Khan says as he escorts me back to the lockup.

'I got a photo with her, sir,' Pushpa beams, eliciting a frown from her boss.

I open my fist to discover a small key.

Nirmala Ben has gone, leaving behind a mystery for me. What is the key, what does it open, and why did she give it to me?

I turn the key over in my hands. It is an ordinary, stainless-steel key, nothing special. Like the type used to close cupboards and cabinets. But there are no cupboards and cabinets inside the lockup. It is probably Nirmala Ben's kleptomania acting up again, I reckon, as I slip it into the pocket of my kameez.

Later in the day a doctor comes to examine me. The

incessant interrogation by the Crime Branch officials has taken a toll on my health, both mental and physical. A queasy combination of dread, sadness, hopelessness and helplessness has settled permanently in the depths of my stomach. Inevitably it impacts on my bowels, leading to such a severe attack of diarrhoea that it sends me scurrying to the bathroom even at odd hours of the night, much to the annoyance of Pushpa.

It is past midnight, but sleep is far from my eyes. Though despondency buffets me every day, I'm feeling particularly down tonight. There is talk of transferring me to Tihar Jail, where only the most hardened criminals are housed. The prospect of spending my entire life behind bars stretches before me like a Siberian winter, barren, bleak and entirely desolate.

I still have belief in ACP Khan, but he has been reduced to the status of a helpless bystander. The Crime Branch sleuths are a law unto themselves and they will stop at nothing to secure a murder conviction. I can feel all doors closing on me. 'Only a miracle can save you now,' my lawyer says. But even Goddess Durga seems to have deserted me, making my faith wobble.

Lost in my thoughts, I barely hear the cell door being opened. It is Pushpa Thanvi, wearing her usual sour face. 'I am fed up of your friends,' she declares.

'Why?' I ask. 'What happened?'

'Now there's a phone call for you.'

'From where?'

'Kochi.'

'Kochi? I don't know anyone in Kerala.'

'Then you better tell that mad night owl to stop disturbing us at unearthly hours,' she says, and marches me down to the Reporting Room where three constables are huddled around an old rotary phone like dogs around a bone.

I pick up the receiver. 'Hello?'

'Is that you, Sapna?' I hear a voice crackling with long-distance static. It is a voice I would have recognised even from a million light years away.

'Karan?' I ask in astonished delight. 'Where are you calling from?'

'From Coachella in California.'

The sound of his real voice is like a balm to my wounded soul, instantly bridging that great chasm of distance and time between us.

'I'm so sorry,' he continues. 'I just heard the news about Acharya. I'm now scraping together funds to get a flight to Delhi as soon as possible.'

'Don't bother,' I tell him. 'You have more important things—'

'Nothing is more important to me than you,' he says, cutting me off. 'I had just started a new job here, but it can wait. First I have to get you out of this mess.'

'There's nothing you can do, Karan.'

'I'm already doing my bit from here, Sapna. I got my friends in Indus to pass me details of Rana's most recent call record. Guess who Rana has been speaking to every day since Acharya's death.'

'Who?'

'Ajay Krishna Acharya. I'm convinced Acharya's murder was a conspiracy cooked up between Rana and

AK. AK looks and speaks just like his brother. What if he was somehow inside Prarthana that evening?'

'My God!' I whisper. 'I never thought about this possibility.'

'I'll blow the lid off this whole thing. You just wait, Sapna. I'm coming,' he says before another burst of static disconnects the call.

I return to my cage infused with new courage and renewed hope. Karan may be gay and a world away, but he is still my rock, and, with him by my side, I might yet be able to prove my innocence.

At the same time I am seized with the sudden, irresistible conviction that I need to take matters into my own hands, get out of this suffocating lockup.

I keep pacing the cell for the next two hours, racking my brains for an escape plan, when the queasiness in my stomach starts up again. Punishing spasms ripple across my abdomen, making me cry out in pain. I drag myself to the cell door and call out to the guard dozing on a chair. 'I need to go to the toilet. Please call Pushpa.'

A few minutes later Pushpa appears, rubbing sleep from her eyes. 'Even a witch does not stay awake this late at night,' she mutters darkly as she unlocks the cell. 'Oh, the grief you've given me.'

The courtyard is silent as a tomb. I can even hear snores coming from a few rooms. Pushpa shoves me inside the ladies' toilet with a grunt. 'I'll take just a few minutes,' I mumble.

'You can rot here the whole night for all I care,' she responds, fumbling inside her pockets for the toilet key.

Not finding it only adds to her irritation. 'Where the hell is it?' she mutters, digging a hand inside her trouser pocket. 'Sarla has already lost hers. Is some bastard now stealing our toilet keys?'

She eventually succeeds in extracting it from her breast pocket. 'Found it!' she says triumphantly, holding it up like some ancient artefact discovered from an archaeological dig. I gaze at it, mesmerised.

'Now shit all you want. I'm giving you thirty minutes. But you dare not disturb me again tonight after then, you hear me?' She gives me a death glare as she slams shut the door and locks it securely from the outside.

I insert a hand inside my shirt pocket and withdraw the key Nirmala Ben had given me. It looks exactly like the one with Pushpa.

In a sudden flash of clarity I understand the purpose of the key. It unlocks the women's toilet. There are five woman constables in the station and each of them has a key to the toilet. Nirmala Ben must have filched it from one of them.

I begin to tremble at the possibilities that have suddenly opened up. I have with me not just the key to the toilet, but the key to my freedom. An impulsive, wild idea takes hold of me, one that makes me throw all caution to the wind. I wait till I hear the echo of Pushpa's footsteps moving away from the door. Then I count to two hundred, and insert the key into the slot. It fits perfectly. I say a quick prayer and twist it as gently as possible. The sound I hear next is the sweetest a prisoner can ever hear: the click of a door unlocking.

I creep out of the toilet, lock it again, and take a quick look around. There's no sign of Pushpa Thanvi and not a squeak coming out of the Women's Resting Room. The courtyard still looks deserted and silence reigns over the night.

With furtive steps I pad into the western corridor. I have just passed the Wireless Room, when I hear a door slam behind me. It startles me so badly, I almost lose my balance. Somehow I retain enough presence of mind to duck behind a pillar. Peeking backwards, I see a man stumble out of the Investigating Officer's Room, dressed only in a vest and striped underpants. For a moment he stands in sleepy-eyed confusion before letting out a loud fart. Then, scratching his hairy backside, he veers left, undoubtedly heading towards the men's toilet.

I have barely recovered from this shock when another sound drifts across the corridor. It is a soft tapping, like someone hitting a stick against the floor. It can only be the night guard, doing his rounds. I freeze like a thief caught red-handed, certain that he has spotted me. But, miraculously, he pauses, having probably encountered the man in the striped underwear. I hear the muffled sounds of conversation followed by amused laughter. This is my only chance, I realise, and dart inside the partially open door of the Investigating Officer's Room.

I crouch in the semidarkness, waiting for the guard to pass. He walks at the leisurely pace of a man who has all the time in the world. As his footsteps come closer and closer, sweat begins to pour off my forehead. And then he stops, almost directly in front of the door. My breath is caught in my lungs. There's a ceiling fan going full blast inside the room, but the only sound in my ears is the dull, thudding rush of blood surging through my veins. I hear the guard clear his throat and spit something out. Then he walks past me down the corridor, his boots creaking on the stone floor like rusted hinges.

I feel relief flooding through me like morning sunlight. By now my vision has adjusted to the gloom inside the small, dingy room. I notice a table, a cot and a nightstand with a covered water pitcher. Quite clearly the room is being used as a bedroom by one of the sub-inspectors. Just as I am about to sneak out of the door, my attention is drawn to two items. One is a uniform hanging from a bent hanger tacked to the wall behind the bed. And the other is a leather holster lying on the table.

Another audacious idea germinates in my head, one that brings the blood rushing back to my ears. Standing on my toes, I reach out for that hanger.

I step out of the Investigating Officer's Room looking like someone headed for a fancy-dress party. The shirt is two sizes too big for me. The trousers are too long, pooling around my shoes like baggy stockings. But I tell myself that it is preferable to look like a joker than an escaped convict.

I go to the end of the corridor, glancing at each door, but, instead of turning left towards the female lockup and risking an encounter with the guard, I turn right, where the front offices join the courtyard. ACP Khan's room is locked, but there are a bunch of constables on night duty in the Reporting Room. They are so engrossed in play-ing cards they barely notice me as I walk past the open window, heading for the outer gate. 'Hey, Pushpa!' one of them shouts out. 'Is that *chhori* still giving you sleepless nights?' The others laugh raucously.

Every nerve in my body is like a coiled spring as I make my way to the front gate. I am terrified that someone will recognise that I am wearing an ill-fitting man's uniform on top of my lady's salvar suit and raise the alarm. Any second now I expect a siren to be sounded and to be grabbed from behind. But I am not challenged; I am not stopped as I shuffle out of the metal gate.

The police station is a stone's throw from the Priya complex in Vasant Vihar, famous for its cluster of bars and restaurants, and that is where I proceed. I pinch myself from time to time to make sure this is not just a hallucination. It is difficult to believe that I am finally free. My destiny is now in my own hands.

Even at this late hour the complex is buzzing with life. Revellers are still pub-crawling and there is traffic on the streets. I discover an auto-rickshaw disgorging a young couple and clamber into it instantly. 'Take me to Vasant Kunj, Sector C, quickly,' I tell the driver.

'First pay up one hundred fifty,' he responds without even bothering to see who the customer is.

'Since when have drivers started asking for advance?' I bark at him.

He turns his head around and I see a dark face pitted with smallpox scars. It is only now that he notices my uniform, and his entire demeanour changes. 'Sorry, madam. Give according to the meter,' he says meekly and switches on the digital fare display. I smirk with the satisfaction of having achieved that rarest of triumphs: putting a Delhi auto driver in his place.

We have just come onto Nelson Mandela Marg when a police siren sounds, piercing the stillness of the night like a scream. It perks up the driver. 'Looks like some thief has escaped,' he observes.

'Yes.' I nod gravely. 'That appears to be the case. Wonder who could it be.'

Nelson Mandela Marg is empty and desolate as we chug towards Vasant Kunj. This eight-lane highway is the artery that links Vasant Vihar with Vasant Kunj. It hosts a five-star hotel, some top educational institutions and two of the biggest malls in Delhi. But it is also infamous for being one of the most unsafe stretches in the capital after dark, thanks to poor patrolling, inadequate lighting and thick foliage with no habitation on either side, all of which suits me just fine.

The first signs of trouble emerge when we are at the section that straddles the ridge near Jawaharlal Nehru University. In the distance I see metal barricades being moved to the middle of the road, a checkpoint being set up. A pang of fear spasms through me. I didn't imagine news of my escape would get flashed to all police units in the city so quickly.

'Stop! Stop! Stop!' I yank the driver's collar. 'I'll get down here.'

'Here?' He does a double take. 'But there's nothing and no one around for miles.'

'You see that?' I point out an abandoned tin shack by the side of the road that probably once served as a teashop. 'I've been sent to investigate it.'

'As you wish.' He shrugs and stops the engine. 'That will be fifty-two rupees, madam,' he says, reading off a printed chart, basically the meter fare plus 25 per cent night charge.

I step down from the auto and rummage through the pockets of the uniform, hoping to find some cash, but no such luck. 'You are asking money from a police officer on duty?' I demand, trying my best to imitate a policeman's gruff swagger.

'Where does it say police people don't need to pay fares?' he challenges me. 'Last month an inspector tried the same thing and our union went direct to the Commissioner, threatening to go on an instant strike.'

'I can't give you money.' I shake my head. 'But I can give you a bullet in your head.' Simultaneously, I withdraw the revolver from the trouser pocket and aim it in his face with the theatrical flair of a Bollywood villain.

His eyes dilate with horror and a flash of sudden terror and recognition passes through them. '*Arrey baap re!* You're that girl I saw on TV, that killer.'

The revolver feels heavy and awkward in my hand as I wave it at him. 'Yes. And I'll have no compunction in killing you too.'

'No ... no. Please spare my life. I have a wife and three daughters. They'll die without me.'

'Then leave immediately. Go back the same way you came. And don't utter a word to anyone.'

'I won't, I promise. I'm going ... I'm going.' He trembles as he cranks the engine. Reversing the vehicle, he points it in the direction of Vasant Vihar and presses the accelerator all the way down.

I watch the auto till it becomes a speck in the distance. Then I lope to the tin shack and slump down behind it, my body aching with fatigue and insomnia. I need a little rest, time to figure out my next move. Below me the forest looms, dark and forbidding. It is actually the spur of the ancient Aravalli range known as the South-Central Ridge.

I have been sitting for less than ten minutes when the air begins to resonate with the wails of multiple police sirens. I peek out from behind the tin shack to discover half a dozen police vehicles coming towards me from the direction of Vasant Vihar, their top lights flashing like signals to a UFO. I swivel around to find an equal number of cruisers approaching from the direction of Vasant Kunj. They all seem to be converging upon the shack.

The auto driver has blabbed, I realise, and now the police have arrived to capture me. Staying on the road is no longer an option for me. So I turn to my only possible sanctuary: the forest.

I stare down the steep slope in front of me, leading to the ravine below. It looks fearfully precipitous and rocky, but desperate times demand desperate measures. Hitching up my stolen trousers, I begin the perilous descent. Twigs and thorns dig into my ankles, loose dirt falls into my shoes, and sharp, jagged stones indent my knees, but I continue to descend with slow, deliberate movements, till I suddenly lose my footing and hurtle headlong down the rocky slope. Pain shoots through me as I graze my knee. Then my head hits a boulder, causing a momentary blackout.

When I come to, I find myself sprawled on the ground like a rag doll with all limbs splayed akimbo. There's dirt in my mouth and leaves in my hair. I groan, stand up and survey my surroundings.

There are tall trees all around me, forming a dense canopy. The ground is full of thorny scrubs, briars and brambles, all covering a jumble of broken sandstone. The primeval forest is alive with the sounds of its nocturnal dwellers. Owls hoot, insects chirp. Something slithers off to my left and I jump back in alarm, hoping it is not a snake.

And then I hear something that chills me: the shrill barking of dogs, coming from somewhere above me. Pressing myself up against a large tree, I raise my head and stare blindly upwards. I see beams of light probing the sky. The police have not come alone. They have brought searchlights and sniffer dogs.

Now, for the first time, the reality of being a fugitive from justice hits me like a slow bullet. Images of those fierce Dobermans in Acharya's residence fill my mind, and I take flight.

Overhanging branches hit my face like whips; thorny brambles try to trip me up like barbed wire; leathery leaves lash my cheeks like a thousand needles, as I crash blindly through the wild woods. I have no idea where I am headed, but I know I need to keep ahead of the dogs.

I trip and fall a few times, my shirt gets all ripped up and there are numerous cuts and bruises on my face and arms, but I keep running. Every one of my pores is filled with sweat, my muscles stiffen, my breath comes in gasping, ragged sobs every few gulps, my heart pounds wildly in its cage, but I do not slow down. All I am aware of is the crisp scent of the woods, the twigs snapping beneath my feet, and the wind rustling through the leaves. More than panic, more than instinct, it is pure will. There is a voice somewhere in my head impelling me on, giving me that raw determination to ignore all bodily requirements for sleep, food and water and to just carry on. Tonight I am running for my freedom and nothing is going to stop me.

After three hours of intermittent running, the darkness begins to thin, as also do the trees around me. The first rays of dawn pierce the forest canopy like spears, pushing out the gloom. Birds are beginning to chirp and I can hear the soft gurgling of a stream. But overlaying these sounds is another: the discordant din of traffic rushing by on a nearby thoroughfare.

I follow the sound of the road for another few hundred metres and abruptly come to a halt. I have reached the edge of the woods and come out into the open. Instead of verdant forest, I find myself at a gravel pit. Massive concrete pipes are strewn about the ground, doubtless in preparation for the construction of yet another five-star hotel or glitzy mall. Slowly but surely, the green lung of the Ridge is being sacrificed on the altar of commercial development.

Far in the distance I can see the rear end of some kind of complex crowned with a glittering dome, which looks very familiar. I jog my memory and remember having seen it at the DLF Emporio Mall. Which means I have arrived in Vasant Kunj.

This is an area whose geography I know rather well,

mainly because Papa taught briefly at Ryan International School in Sector C.

The horizon becomes a mystical magnet, pulling me in. The adrenaline is still pumping through my veins. My legs are so numb, the pain and fatigue don't even register.

I strip off the police uniform, which is already in tatters, and dump it inside a pipe. I heft the revolver in my hands, before inserting it into the inside pocket of my kameez. I smooth down my salvar suit, scrub my face and tug my hair back with both fists. Then I take in deep gulps of air and begin running for one last time.

I am heading for the road, for Sector C-1, for Rana.

Sector C is the first sector on entering Vasant Kunj from the side of Vasant Vihar. Pocket 1 is bang on the main road and the cacophony of traffic on Abdul Gaffar Khan Marg is a reassuring sign that news of my escape has not yet disrupted the rhythm of the day.

The colony is still waking up when I approach the entry gate. It is manned by a young-looking security guard who glares at me suspiciously. '*Nayi aayi kya?* Are you new here?' He speaks to me in a casual, offhand tone, as though addressing someone of inferior status.

At first I don't understand him. And then I realise he thinks I'm a new maid.

I don't blame him. I am nondescript, featureless. There is nothing in my face that stands out. Plus, with the dust in my hair and the grime on my clothes, he could only think of me as a servant girl. I could be Bela or Champa, Phoolmati or Dharamwati, or any of the thousands of maids who stream through the houses and streets of Delhi every day.

'Yes.' I nod eagerly. 'I'm starting today in the colony.'

'Where?'

'Rana *sahib*, in 4245.'

'But doesn't he already have Putli working for him?'

'She left yesterday, for her village,' I ad lib. 'That is why I am here. To do Putli's work till she returns.'

'Oh, so you are the temporary help. Did you get your police verification done?'

'No. What's that?'

'Ask Rana-*babu*. That's a compulsory requirement introduced by the Residents Association for all domestic helps.'

'You mean I can't work till I get it?'

'Of course you can. We have to help each other, don't we?' He winks and waves me inside the half-opened gate. 'By the way, you didn't tell me your name.'

'Oh, it's Pinky.'

'Good. See you around, Pinky.'

I enter the compound and take in the surroundings. The ground-floor flats have manicured gardens and trimmed hedges. The rooftops glint with dish antennae and water-storage tanks. Almost every house has potted plants and hanging baskets. There are SUVs and luxury sedans parked in the shade. Pocket C-1 has the refined gloss of suburban middle-class prosperity.

Rana's flat is in the very first building to my left, adjacent to the boundary wall. As I climb up the stairs to the fourth floor, a knot of tension forms in my chest. Slowly, inconspicuously, I draw the revolver from my inside pocket and hold it in my right hand. Then I press the doorbell of 4245 and wait.

I imagine the shock on Rana's face when he opens the door and finds himself looking down the barrel of a revolver. I will rudely push him inside, make him kneel on the floor and force him to recount the entire sordid tale of how he murdered Acharya in partnership with AK and implicated me. Then I will phone ACP Khan, make him record Rana's confession and bring an end to the nightmare that has plagued me since my arrest.

There is always the possibility that things may not go according to plan. Rana may choose to bluster again, believing me to be incapable of shooting him. How wrong would he be! The revolver no longer feels awkward in my hands, it feels lethal. And I know deep down that I will pull the trigger if I have to. A murder suspect has nothing to lose.

Almost five minutes pass and no one opens the door. I try the handle and discover it to be securely locked. I press the doorbell repeatedly, but Rana does not respond. After ten minutes of fruitless bell-pushing I come to the conclusion that my quarry is not inside. My heart sinks with the leaden realisation that Rana has also left Delhi, flown the coop. This is one possibility I had simply not considered.

As I turn away in dejection, something catches at the edge of my vision. It is a flash of blue, somewhere on the main road. I look out at Abdul Gaffar Khan Marg. In the short gaps between waves of early-morning traffic, I catch a glimpse of a tight huddle of joggers in tracksuits and tennis shoes, coming towards Sector C. That is where I saw that blur of blue. But it is no longer there. No, wait, it *is* there. It is a runner wearing a deep-blue Reebok tracksuit, moving with fluid grace. As I continue to track him, I feel a prickling sensation in my palms. It is none other than Rana.

The despondency in my heart is replaced with the grim satisfaction of a patient hunter finally sighting his prey. Yes, God is indeed in heaven and justice will finally be done.

The group are now almost directly opposite Gate Number 4, on the other side of the road. I see Rana break out from the pack and wave to the others as they continue on their way. He hunches over his knees at the edge of the road, like an exhausted runner bowing for breath, as he waits for a break in the traffic to cross the road.

Now he straightens himself, and takes out a cell phone from his pocket. He glues the phone to his ear, as though receiving a call, and begins to stride across the road. He has not even reached the divider, when out of nowhere a light goods truck comes up behind him, hurtling down the street at dangerously high speed. Rana is too busy talking on the phone to either see or dodge the truck before it ploughs into him. I hear the sickening impact of metal hitting flesh and bone. The phone flies out of his hands. His body catapults through the air and hits the pavement with a nauseating crack. The truck, having rammed Rana, continues to move down the road. There is no squeal of brakes. On the contrary, the driver picks up even more speed, desperate to get away.

It all happens so quickly that I can only stare in helpless horror. But now my brain is relaying urgent messages, telling me that, if Rana dies, so does my last chance of proving my innocence. '*Noooo!*' I scream, and run blindly down the stairs.

I race out of the gate, risk life and limb while dodging traffic, and somehow manage to get to the other side of the road. When I reach Rana, he is still alive, but only barely. The pavement is splattered with his blood and the right side of his face is a mass of raw flesh and oozing brain tissue. His phone lies shattered in pieces a couple of feet away. I kneel down on the pavement and cradle his head in my lap. 'Rana . . . Rana,' I whisper urgently. 'This is Sapna.'

'Sapna?' he repeats in a hoarse whisper. Then he coughs, spitting out blood. His breath is coming in short gasps. The pulse at his neck is throbbing erratically. I know he does not have much time left.

'What . . . what happened? Who did this to you?'

'He . . . me . . . cheat,' he splutters incoherently.

'Who? Tell me, tell me now,' I say, trying to coax a confession out of him.

'I'm sorry,' he says in a death rasp, gazing at me with a mixture of realisation and regret. He coughs again and his eyes begin to roll upwards. The pulse in his neck slows and then stops completely.

By now a large crowd of onlookers has gathered around me. '*Arrey*, quickly call the ambulance,' someone shouts.

'No need,' says another. '*Khatam ho gaya*. He's dead.'

'Was he your husband?' yet another bystander asks me.

'No,' I shake my head. 'I . . . I just knew him.'

Surprisingly, traffic continues to flow on Abdul Gaffar Khan Marg as though nothing had happened. Rana's death is just another cold statistic of a traffic accident. An anonymous death in a dangerous city.

But the police do have to take note of it. Soon, cutting through the din, comes the sound of a police siren, and I know it is time to leave. I stand up to discover that my salvar suit is stained with blood and even my sneakers have a coating of Rana's viscera. 'I have to go now,' I say, looking for an opening in that tight circle of onlookers.

'My God! Aren't you Sapna Sinha? The girl who murdered Vinay Mohan Acharya?' a voice shrills out of nowhere. The spectators draw back with the abruptness of a shudder.

I freeze like a statue, my entire body numb with panic. Get out! The thought rings in my head with the clarity of a bell. *Get out now!* I charge headlong into the throng, like a bull into the ring, and force my way out. Not knowing which direction to go, I run haphazardly across the road, just about managing to avoid getting run down by a bus.

'Catch her!' a man roars.

That is when I remember the gun. Taking it out of my inner pocket, I stop and whirl around. 'The next man who comes near me gets a bullet in his head,' I snarl at my pursuers. They see the revolver and scatter like a flock of pigeons.

So engrossed am I in watching them flee that I fail to notice the man creeping up behind me, a cricket bat clutched in his right hand. By the time I turn around it is too late. Mouthing an obscenity, he hits out with the bat, catching me full in the stomach. The air gets knocked out of my lungs in a rush, and I crash down on the pavement, staggered and dazed. The revolver goes tumbling out of my hand and ends up in a gutter.

Somehow I pick myself up and begin running again on stumbling feet, feeling sick and nauseous. The man with the bat tries to tackle me from the side, and I slam into him with full force, sending him crashing backwards into the same gutter.

By now the crowd have warmed up to the visceral thrill of a hunt. Over a dozen men begin giving chase. I run blindly now, past neat little houses and a Mother Dairy booth, not daring to look back, but the mob dog me like a shadow.

'Faster!' that voice in my head commands, but my legs just don't have any more strength left in them. My heart is ready to burst and my brain is threatening to split open.

I am almost about to collapse on the pavement when I see a red Maruti Swift pull up to me. The rear passenger side door opens and a woman orders, 'Get in!'

I fling myself at the back seat with the thoughtless obedience of a cultist. The moment I'm in, the car swerves away from the pavement and gathers speed. When I raise my head I discover a woman in a blue T-shirt peering at me from the front passenger seat. She looks like Shalini Grover of Sunlight TV. The driver is a skinny man with dishevelled hair whom I have never seen before.

'Are you all right, Sapna?' the woman asks, and I sag in relief. It is indeed my friend Shalini.

'How . . . how did you find me?'

'I've been staking out Rana's house for the last two days, hoping to prove his link to Acharya's murder. I saw him being run over by that lorry. And a minute later I saw *you*, brandishing a revolver and haring off like P. T. Usha. When I found that mob trying to lynch you, I told D'Souza, my cameraman, to become your getaway vehicle.'

'Hi, I'm D'Souza,' the driver waves at me from the steering wheel.

Shalini lights up a cigarette with a lighter and offers me a drag. Only then do I notice the nicotine embedded in the surfaces inside the car like a tattoo. She must be a chain smoker.

'No, thanks,' I decline, my heart still pounding from that narrow escape.

'I'm assuming you've escaped from the lockup,' Shalini says after a while.

I give a fearful nod. 'Will you hand me back to the police?'

'Am I nuts?' she laughs. 'I have a better plan for my most precious source. I'm taking you to our safe house in Daryaganj.'

'What's the point?' I ask with the bitter taste of bile rising up in my throat. 'Rana's death has dashed all my hopes.'

'On the contrary, it's proof positive that you are just a pawn in a deeper game. The way that truck rammed into Rana looked preplanned. That was not an accident: it was murder,' she says, blowing a smoke ring in my face.

'Somebody called him on his phone just before that lorry hit him.'

'Yes. And I have a very good idea who it was.'

'Who? Was it AK?' I ask.

'No, it was probably the owner of Indus Mobile, Swapan Karak.'

'What makes you say that?'

'Something was cooking between Karak and Rana. I saw him enter Rana's flat yesterday and stay there for over two hours.'

'But what business could the owner of Indus have with Rana?'

'That's what I'm going to be digging into. You relax now, try and get some sleep,' Shalini says and switches on the car stereo.

The serene strains of Raga Khamas sung by Pandit Jasraj ooze out from the speakers, calming the world of chaos that has surrounded me. I close my eyes for the first time in more than twenty-four hours. The reassuring trust of a friend and the smooth motion of the car allow me to drift into a much-needed slumber till a burst of sirens startles me into wakefulness.

'Shit, shit, shit!' I hear D'Souza curse. 'I've got three police cars on my tail.'

'One of the mob must have reported our number,' Shalini mutters, looking at the rear-view mirror.

'You got me into this mess, now you get me out of it,' D'Souza wails.

'Calm down,' Shalini snaps and lights up yet another cigarette.

I blink several times, forcing myself more fully into consciousness as I try to ascertain my bearings. We seem to be near India Gate and approaching a red light.

'What the heck should I do?' D'Souza demands.

'To begin with, jump the red light,' Shalini says calmly.

'What?'

'Jump it!'

Horns honk and vehicles swerve out of the way as D'Souza speeds through the intersection.

'Now you'll really get into trouble,' I fret to Shalini.

'Don't worry,' she says. 'We'll tell the police *you* hijacked *us*.'

Just when I'm beginning to think we've hoodwinked the police, more sirens fill the air, getting shriller and shriller.

Ditching the main road, D'Souza veers the car into a secluded side street. With one hand firmly on the car horn, he zigzags through a maze of small alleyways, changing directions like an indecisive compass. Still we are unable to completely shake off the lone police Gypsy now on our tail. In desperation, D'Souza cuts across three lanes of oncoming traffic and plunges into the chaos of early rush-hour commute on Janpath.

It turns out to be a disastrous move. Once we join the sea of cars gridlocked in the outer circle of Connaught Place, Shalini knows it is impossible to reach the safe house. 'Stop the car,' she instructs her cameraman.

D'Souza nods and brings the Swift to an abrupt halt in front of the Regal Cinema.

'It's best you get out here and look for a hiding place,' Shalini advises me. 'We'll drive for another couple of kilometres till the police catch up with us. At least it will give you a head start.'

I quickly open the door and step out. Shalini instinctively reaches over from her seat and grasps my hand in a gesture of sisterly solidarity. 'Keep fighting, Sapna,' she says. 'Never give up. And here, take this.' She pulls out a brown-leather shoulder bag lying at her feet. 'It's my emergency travel kit. It has some ready cash, a change of clothes, toilet paper, torch, pocket knife and even duct tape.'

I grab the bag and give Shalini a wan smile, hoping she can read the gratitude in my eyes behind that patina of fear and uncertainty. 'How will I ever repay you for all this?'

'Simple. You'll give me an exclusive interview once you've proved your innocence. Now go, go, *go!*' she says as D'Souza eases the car back into traffic.

For a moment I stand still, like someone caught in the disorienting aftermath of a car crash. Shalini wants me to hide out in Connaught Place, but I don't know a single hiding place here. In fact, it would be impossible to hide in the throbbing, hectic heart of the city.

I can sense the panic creeping up my spine when my eyes are drawn to a corner of the pavement where a hawker has spread out religious posters for sale. Goddess Durga beckons me like a lighthouse to a storm-troubled ship. And I know that I do have a place of refuge in Connaught Place.

Pulling my chunni over my head, partially obscuring my face, I join the flow of pedestrians making their way to offices and shops. After turning left onto Baba Kharak Singh Marg, I proceed to the Hanuman Mandir.

Though it is just after 9 a.m., the temple complex is bustling with activity. Tattoo and mehndi artists, bangle sellers and roadside astrologers have already set up their stalls. An elderly 'Spiritual Forehead Reader', offering his services for the auspicious fee of ₹101, accosts me. 'Want to know your future?' he asks. Even God doesn't know my future, I feel like telling him.

Depositing my sneakers with the old lady at the temple entrance I bound up the steps, two at a time. Seconds later I am in the presence of Durga Ma. Just seeing her divine face fills me with such peace that I forget all my travails. There must be some cosmic coincidence that today is Friday, the day of the Goddess. Perhaps Durga Ma had been calling me all this while, and I was meant to be here today.

A group of women dressed in red saris and loaded with offerings of fruit and flowers are already settling down on the marble floor, preparing to listen to bhajans being sung by a middle-aged devotee in a white sari. I unobtrusively take my place in their midst, keeping my head down so that no one can see my face.

The songs work their magic, and the devotees are soon swaying together, swept up in the rising tide of devotional love and the simple truth of the message. I feel a shower of heavenly grace healing me, renewing me. The queasiness in my stomach and the pounding in my head miraculously disappear.

I remain in the temple for close to nine hours. Till the hunger pangs can no longer be ignored.

When I step outside, the grey of dusk is creeping over the city, enveloping the surroundings in a pallid blue haze. Street lamps are beginning to flicker on, casting ominous shadows on the pavements. Shalini's bag contains the healthy sum of ₹3,000 and I grab a plate of puri-aloo from a roadside vendor.

I sit on a bench and watch the tide of humanity pass by. Bank workers and government employees are hurrying to the metro, eager to go home after another hard day. On the adjacent bench a pair of lovers are whispering inconsolable, desolate good-byes. A flute vendor approaches them and begins playing an appropriately tragic song from *Kal Ho Na Ho*. The melody hushes the cacophony that customarily accompanies peak-hour traffic in Connaught Place, till the moment is shattered by the whine of police sirens.

Soon every street corner is bristling with uniformed men, wary and alert. Barricades are being put up at the intersections to intercept cars. Near the parking lot of A-Block I spot an inspector questioning the parking attendant, showing him a photograph. I have no doubt it is mine. My breathing quickens. Sweat slicks my palms. One part of me just wants it to end. I want to surrender. This miserable life of living in constant fear and secrecy is worse than death. But that old tenacity also surges within me, telling me that I have to keep running, if not for my sake then for Ma's sake and Neha's.

For the next two hours I duck and skulk, weaving my way through the crowded bazaar and busy traffic. Just after 9 p.m. I find myself at L-Block in the Outer Circle, in front of 'Jain Travel Agency'. My eyes fall on the display window offering summer specials to Gangotri, Kedarnath, Badrinath, Almora and Nainital.

Nainital. Just seeing that word brings back so many memories that I almost well up with tears. My decision is made then and there.

The night clerk, a jaded old man, is busy flipping

through a TV magazine when I ask for a ticket to Nainital.

'Eight hundred rupees,' he says in the weary tone of someone who would rather be home watching a serial. 'Bus leaves at ten thirty tonight from just in front. No cancellation, no refund.'

When I arrive at the boarding point, I discover my fellow travellers to be a large group of boys and girls from a local college, dressed casually in jeans and T-shirts and armed with suitcases and rucksacks. With my head bowed low, I take a seat at the very back of the bus and bury my face in a magazine.

I am a jittery bundle of nerves as the bus approaches the police checkpoint. By the time a perspiring constable clambers inside, my heart is almost in my mouth. He takes a cursory look at the young, grinning faces before him and, with a bored flick of his wrist, waves us on our way.

There is a massive traffic jam on Ring Road as a result of all the security checks, and the bus takes two hours just to reach National Highway 24. My paranoid tension abates only when we successfully exit the municipal limits of Delhi.

The rest of the journey is a blur of off-key songs, lewd jokes, constant chatter and the juvenile boisterousness of college students on a road trip. I watch everyone, observe everything, but do not utter a word. The students also leave me alone. They are too engrossed in their own carefree world to realise that they are travelling with India's most wanted woman.

The luxurious air conditioning, the steady drone of the motor and the gentle rocking motion of the bus soon lull me to sleep. When I open my eyes, warm sunshine is peeking through the gaps in the curtain. I gaze out of the window to discover that the brown, flat landscape of the dusty plains has given way to the lush, green, undulating Himalayan foothills. That first sight of the shadowy distant mountains, wreathed in mist, mesmerises me.

The route is now more challenging, twisting and winding through narrow hairpin bends. We stop in Haldwani for breakfast at a local *dhaba*. The food is delicious and the cool, crisp air invigorating. The restaurant also has a small shop selling various knick-knacks and I pick up an oversized pair of dark glasses. I observe myself in the mirror and note with satisfaction that the sunglasses cover a good part of my face. But then I happen to glance at the wall-mounted TV and learn the devastating news that Shalini Grover has been arrested by the police for aiding and abetting a fugitive. A wave of sadness washes over me, making me slink into the bus before anyone notices my distraught expression.

The remaining forty kilometres go by in a haze of tears. And at seven o'clock I am back in the city of my childhood and youth.

In the early-morning light of peak summer, Nainital looks like an overcrowded train station. Mall Road is flush with gaudy honeymooners and noisy Punjabis. Cycle rickshaws lurch through the bazaar, tinkling their bells at those in their path to give way.

The lake gleams in front of me, full and inviting. A slow, sensuous roll of water shrugs like a shoulder against the Boat House Club. The seven proud hills surrounding the lake lend a mystic feel to the setting, providing a majestic contrast to the shallow, manufactured prettiness of Delhi. As I take in the full sweep of the panorama in front of me – Flats, Naina Devi Temple, Capitol Cinema, Thandi Road – everything about my old life comes rushing back to me.

Someone taps me on the shoulder. I shrink back in alarm only to discover a South Indian family staring at me – father, mother and two young girls. The father, dressed in spotless white linen, with a yellow caste mark on his forehead, approaches me again. 'Excuse me, madam, could you please be directing us to Rosy Guest House?' He has the hesitant air of a tourist, unsure of a new place, his fingers twisted around the handle of a battered black trunk.

'I'm sorry,' I reply, pushing the large sunglasses further up my face. 'I'm new here myself.'

Turning away from him, I fix my gaze on the Grand Hotel at the opposite end of the lake, the Mallital side. It is a low, colonial-style building with long, open verandahs. Slowly, my gaze travels upwards, tracing a point on the hill behind the hotel, covered in low clouds. That is where the Windsor Academy used to be located.

Almost propelled by an invisible hand, I begin hiking in the direction of the school. The gently winding road takes me past the tacky souvenir shops and the cut-price tour operators, past the Methodist Church and the Inter College. By the time I reach the entrance of the Academy I am wheezing with exertion.

The wrought-iron gate with the blue-and-white school logo invites me. The school must already be closed for the summer holidays, as there is no entry check. I go in through the pedestrian entrance and walk up the paved path bordered by mighty deodars. It forks at the top of the hill, one branch of it going to the principal's office and the main building, the other to the staff residences.

I take the left fork, towards what we used to call the Teachers' Colony. It consists of a grid of whitewashed bungalows laid out in neat rows and separated by wide, cobbled paths. Alka found the housing campus creepy in its extreme orderliness. I always thought of it as a haven, an antidote to the madness wreaked by the disorderly tourists outside.

The colony is eerily quiet. There is not a soul in sight, the residents probably still enjoying their weekend nap. As I pass by the numbered houses, names enter my head automatically. No. 12, Mr Emmanuel; No. 13, Mrs Da Costa; No. 14, Mr Pant; No. 15, Mr Siddiqui; No. 16, Mrs Edwards; and, before I know it, I have come up to my old house.

I stand in front of No. 17 and stare in shock. The house doesn't look like a house at all. It resembles a neglected pigsty. The magnificent lawn, which I had diligently watered, is a wilderness of weeds, rank grass and over-grown bushes. The walls are tinged green and covered with mildew. The front porch, which we used to deco-rate with *diyas* on Diwali, is strewn with windblown trash. The corbelled chimney, jutting out of the low-pitched roof like a turret, now flaunts a bird's nest.

I feel a rush of anger at the current residents who have brought No. 17 to this pitiful state. This was the house I spent my childhood in, the house where I learnt the hard truths of adulthood. The fondest memories of my life were attached to it, memories of Dussehri mangoes and fireside stories, of the happy family that used to live here before tragedy overtook it.

As I continue to gaze at the house I find those memories coming back. Any minute now Neha will step out of the kitchen door practising a raga taught by that cranky old master-ji. I can see Papa sitting in the wicker chair, laying down his newspaper to regard me with stern affection, and Alka, dear sweet Alka, darting out from behind that ancient oak tree in the rear garden, screaming '*Kamaal ho gaya, didi!*'

With every nostalgic recollection comes a wave of unsettling emotions. Familiar voices echo inside my head. It feels as if some fibres in my body are still connected to this house, to this city. I reflect on the balance sheet of my life, what has been gained and lost in the transition to Delhi.

The trilling of a bell brings me out of my reverie. I turn around to find a little boy on a tricycle asking me to give way. He gazes at me with the unabashed curiosity of a four year old.

'Can you tell me who lives in this house?' I smile at him.

'*Bhoot*. Ghost,' he replies laconically.

'I'm sorry?'

'No one lives here, only the ghost of that girl who died here. Don't stay here too long otherwise she will suck your blood. That's what my mother says,' he says in the exaggerated manner of a child sharing a secret. Then he gives me a brief wave and pedals away on his tricycle.

I realise that the house is empty. It has probably remained empty ever since we moved out. Alka's death tarred it with the taint of scandal and suicide. And now no one wants it.

I pick my way through the weeds to the rear of the house and discover the same rotten detritus that mars the front. The back garden has become a dumping ground for neighbours' trash, giving off the fetid stench of a cesspool. A jumble of discarded furniture and broken equipment is piled up right in front of the rear kitchen door. I step around an upturned toilet cistern and peer through the door's glass panels. The feeble light filtering through the dusty, grimy glass bathes the kitchen in a spooky aura, giving it the abandoned look of a ghost ship.

I notice that one of the glass panels on the door is cracked. A little push and it splinters into pieces on the floor. With my right hand I reach inside and undo the latch.

The dark and foreboding house matches my mood as I step inside it. The musty smell of mould and damp assails my senses, making me sneeze. I stumble through to the dining room and open the blinds. A shaft of light pierces the gloom, refracting off the dust molecules dancing in the air. In that soft, ambient glow I see a room coated in a thin layer of grey dust. Cobwebs hang from the high ceiling like stalactites. Rat droppings litter the hardwood floor. But for my sense of familiarity with the place, it would seem positively spectral, straight out of a horror film.

As I venture deeper into the house, whispers of the past

overcome me. With every room I step into, memories and recollections flood my mind. The living room, where we used to watch TV while munching on peanuts; the study, where Alka made her final mutiny; the master bedroom, with that little alcove that Ma had converted into her own private shrine; the bay window in Neha's room, from where we used to spy into No. 18; and finally my bedroom, where, propped up against the pillow, I used to scribble in my secret diary and fantasise about becoming a writer one day. Alka's bedroom is the only room I am unable to gather the courage to enter.

Everything about the place looks different now. This isn't the house of my dreams any more. The vast, empty, furniture-less rooms seem like empty shells without souls. Suddenly I feel like a trespasser in an alien house.

Some memories, I realise, should be allowed to remain memories, lying undisturbed in some deep, dark corner of the mind. Bring them into contact with the open light of reality and they instantly combust, turn to dust.

Having surveyed the entire house, I decide to make it my temporary abode. Its notoriety as a haunted site will keep out the peeping Toms. And holing out here for a few days will enable me to recharge my batteries before going after AK. But first I need to do something about my appearance.

Shalini's emergency kit comes in handy once again, as it contains a pair of scissors. I enter my former bathroom and look at myself in the old, cracked mirror, still splattered with my toothpaste stains. Just the memory of standing before this mirror every morning and brushing my teeth overwhelms me, brings tears to my eyes. I know those halcyon days will never return again.

The thought also makes me inexplicably angry. What have I done to deserve this fate, this life of a hunted animal? Seething with an almost atavistic fury, I attack my hair with the scissors, chopping off a lock.

Every cracked mirror, every shuttered window, every cobweb in these rooms speaks to me of the past. And with every flash of memory I cry some more and snap the scissor blades.

Within a couple of minutes my long locks are gone, to be replaced by a super-short bob. Once my tears subside, I also get rid of the smelly salvar suit and put on the skin-hugging jeans and black T-shirt contained in Shalini's brown bag.

When I put on the sunglasses and observe myself in the mirror again, I see a fashionable stranger staring back at me. Somehow the new look feels appropriate. For this is what I have become: a stranger in my own house.

Fortunately, the water still runs from the taps, and the gas cylinder in the kitchen still contains some gas. So I spend the rest of the day thoroughly cleaning the house, and getting the kitchen ready. I remove the dust from my bedroom, the dirt from my bathroom, and the thin film of grime that has settled over the kitchen counter like moss. This spell of uncustomary domesticity is just what I need to distract me from the increasingly depressing turn my thoughts are taking.

With the first stirrings of darkness comes the confidence to venture out of the campus. Sticking largely to the shadows, I make my way to Thapa's Provision Store situated just outside the school gate.

Thapa, the proprietor, is a wizened old Nepali with close-cropped hair and a smile ruined by bad teeth. He peers at me with his muddy eyes. 'I've never seen you before. Would you be Miss Nancy, the new biology teacher at the school?'

'No,' I reply, trying to keep my voice neutral, casual. 'I'm Mrs Nisha, from Nagpur.'

For more than ten years I bought groceries from Thapa, yet he was unable to recognise me tonight. I chalk it up as a small victory and go on a buying spree.

Half an hour later, when I surreptitiously return to No. 17, I have enough provisions to last me a week. There is tea, milk, sugar and a loaf for my mornings; matchboxes and candles to illuminate my evenings; noodles and ready-to-eat meals for instant lunches and dinners; and sufficient toiletries to stay clean.

After a hasty, unappetising dinner, I wander out of the back door. The night air is chilly, and, even with my kameez draped over my T-shirt, I feel a little shiver.

I sit down by the oak tree, silently watching the lake. Under the star-studded sky, the rippling dark waters are alive with a kaleidoscope of swirling patterns formed by the bright lights of the Boat Club merging with the shimmering neon of downtown Nainital. It looks so beautiful, it is almost melancholic.

My thoughts move seamlessly towards my family and friends. I wonder how Neha is doing, how Ma is coping. I want desperately to speak to Shalini, and I want to believe that Karan is on his way to India. It is heart-breaking to be cut off from the people who matter to me the most.

Finally, exhausted from my own thoughts, I return to the house, lie down on the cold floor of my old bedroom, and go off to sleep.

In Rohini I used to wake up to the high-pitched klaxons of trucks rumbling past the LIG Colony. On the Windsor campus I am woken up by the sound of birdsong. I look out of my bedroom window to find a blue-capped redstart perched on a convenient pine branch. The air is clear as glass and I can see for ever, even to the far horizon, where jagged, snow-covered peaks are staking a bold claim on the nascent sky. Delicate pink clouds float across the hills, looking like balls of candyfloss in the first light of dawn. A gentle breeze whispers through the wild sunflowers, still wet with sparkling dew. I feel blessed, comforted by the aloof, serene grandeur of Nainital. To return to the mountains is to return to a world of softness and colour, after the grey, concrete harshness of the city.

I also notice a rolled-up copy of today's newspaper lying in the porch of No. 16. The newspaper boy must have delivered it quite early. An irresistible urge to check the news makes me creep into my neighbours' front yard and steal their newspaper.

It turns out to be a mistake. The newspaper is full of depressing bits of information about me. The police are calling it the biggest manhunt since the terror attacks of 26/11 and have announced a reward of ₹200,000 for information leading to my arrest. Even though I no longer have the revolver, I am being described as 'armed and dangerous'. There are attempts being made to implicate me in Rana's death as well. The only pieces of good news are that Constable Pushpa Thanvi has been suspended and Shalini Grover has got bail.

I also learn from the business pages that the board of the ABC Group has approved the acquisition of the company by Premier Industries. There's a picture of Ajay Krishna Acharya grinning in front of Kyoko Chambers. With each passing day, the mastermind behind Acharya's murder is strengthening his position, and I am still a suspect on the run.

I tear out the picture and begin gouging out AK's eyes, slashing at his mouth, shredding him into tiny pieces, venting all my fears and frustrations on that bit of cheap newsprint.

Time passes between tedium and terror. My waking hours are spent in paranoid anticipation of a police raid. My sleeping hours are a swirling phantasmagoria of dreams, flashbacks and nightmares. Cooped up in the dark, cold house, I am going stir-crazy. Have I exchanged one prison for another? I wonder.

Every night I make a new plan to unmask AK, only to dismiss it in the cold light of day as impractical, pointless, or just plain dumb. I don't even know where AK lives. And, without a gun, without a partner and without the element of surprise, collaring the industrialist seems as impossible as trying to scale Mount Everest in rubber slippers.

By the end of the fourth day, a paralysing lassitude

descends upon me. I don't feel like eating, I don't feel like sleeping and, most of all, I don't feel like thinking.

Karan is my only hope now. Only he can do the miraculous, locate some clinching piece of evidence that will unravel AK's sinister plot and get me back my freedom.

It is 8 p.m. now and I am sitting in the dining room. A single candle anchored with melted wax on the hardwood floor provides the only light in the room. In its gentle glow I try to psych myself up for the battle with AK. I scour my mind for a new plan, any plan. But, no matter how hard I try, I keep drawing a blank.

Simply to divert myself, I take out my remaining cash and begin counting it. After my grocery shopping, I am left with only ₹1,420. I upturn Shalini's bag to see if I have missed anything, and a five-rupee coin tumbles out. Like a loose hubcap, it goes rolling along the wooden floor. I follow it with my eyes as it briskly traverses the smooth floorboards, but then it curves to the right, and keeps going across the short hallway till it slips under the door of Alka's room and disappears from view.

With a frustrated groan I stand up and pluck the candle from its waxy nest. Then I pad softly out of the dining room.

I hesitate for a moment in front of Alka's door, as though it still contained a malignant spirit that must not be allowed to escape. I think I can hear strange, whispery voices calling out from the room, speaking in an indecipherable tongue. I dismiss them as figments of my imagination from seeing too many ghost movies. But then I detect a low scrabbling sound, as if someone or something is moving across the hardwood floor inside the room. It makes me shrink back in sheer horror.

For a few moments the only sound ringing in my ears is my own shallow breaths and the thudding of my racing heart as I summon the courage to face my demons, both imaginary and real. Taking a deep breath and emptying my mind of all thought, I boldly grab the handle and push the door open. A small rat scurries out with a squeak, making my stomach knot in disgust.

The whispery voices become louder as I step into Alka's room. The flickering candle casts grotesque shadows on the wall, making the surroundings seem even more eerie. The room is completely bare, but in my mind's eye I can see Alka's wooden bed. Almost involuntarily my eyes roam upwards, to the ceiling, and Alka's dead body flashes upon me, like a dark scene lit up for an instant by a sudden crack of lightning. I can see her face clearly as she dangles from the fan, her head hanging to one side, a yellow dupatta knotted around her neck. That grisly memory floods my senses completely, so real that I gasp.

It takes all my willpower to block out the searing image from my mind. I loved this room once, I remind myself, recalling the sunny days I spent within these four walls sharing jokes with my sister, the nights when Alka would snuggle up to me in her pyjamas and I would regale her with instantly made-up stories of wise kings and evil sorcerers.

Having restored my mind to an equilibrium, I try to push Alka out from it completely as I concentrate on the task at hand: finding that five-rupee coin. I cannot see it on the floor. In the smoky light of the candle, I look in every direction, search in every shadowy corner, but fail to locate the coin. It seems to have vanished without a trace.

Since I have never believed in magic, it can only mean one thing: the coin has slipped through a crack between the floorboards. Crouching down, I begin tapping the boards with my knuckles, looking for a loose one. It takes me a while, but I hit pay dirt in the exact centre of the room, where Alka's bed used to be. The wood is pale here, more worn than the rest, and the board emits the hollow sound I am looking for.

I try to pull the board out, but the gap between the edges is not large enough for me to insert my fingers and grip it. Not to be deterred, I retrieve the penknife from Shalini's bag and use it to pry up one end. My hand reaches out, grabs the raised edge in between my fingers and this time the board lifts up.

I remove the floorboard and peer into the hollow cavity. The five-rupee coin glints atop a small mound of accumulated dust. But below the coin there is something else, a narrow cardboard box.

More dismayed than intrigued, I pull out the box. A musty, rancid smell radiates from it, tickling my nose. With trembling fingers I open the box and discover a cache of letters. For a moment I feel guilty, like a voyeur caught looking at something meant to be private or forbidden. Then my curiosity gets the better of me and I begin to thumb through the pile. Full of passionate endearments and manic declarations of love, the letters are all addressed to 'My darling Alka' and signed simply 'Hiren'.

Hiren. That word triggers something within me, but it flickers at the edge of my memory, and slithers away before I can track it down. Disturbingly, some of the letters appear to be written in blood, and some are adorned with Satanic symbols. One declares chillingly, 'You're my light in the darkness. I will seek out and destroy whoever stands in the way of our everlasting love.'

Below the pile of letters is a solitary birthday card, doubtlessly given on the occasion of Alka's fifteenth birthday. As I flip it open, a handful of colour photographs slip out. I take one look at them and feel the world around me beginning to spin, my body turning numb.

The photos are of a handsome boy, tall and well built, with straight, black hair falling over his forehead and a bushy moustache providing a finishing touch of virile masculinity. It is only the eyes that give him away. I would have recognised those eyes anywhere.

No, it can't be him, I try to tell myself, but I know in my heart that he is the one. An inscription behind one of the photos gives me his full name, too. 'ALKA SINHA + HIREN KARAK = WORLD'S GREATEST LOVE STORY'.

So Alka's lover was Hiren Karak. My mind is a raging inferno of conflicting emotions as various scenes flash through it. I remember Shalini's words about Indus owner Swapan Karak's link with Rana. I recall Lauren's boyfriend James telling me at Jantar Mantar that he had seen Karak Junior at Nirmala Ben's fast. And Papa's dying words reverberate in my mind like an echo in a cave. Lauren thought she heard '*hiran*' – 'deer' – but now I know Papa was actually saying 'Hiren'.

My blood runs cold. An inky blackness begins seeping into my consciousness. I have to put a hand against the floor to steady myself.

Suddenly, like death, the truth flashes on me. In that instant I know what I have to do.

I stuff the letters and photos inside the brown shoulder bag, pick up all my money and silently leave the house.

As I step out of Windsor Academy, I am gripped by a powerful sense of purpose. There is no doubt in my mind why I am here, what brought me here. This is the place where it all started, where one traumatic event set off a chain reaction of calculated, wanton destruction. And there would be poetic justice in ending it from here.

I proceed to Rawat's Communication Centre, which used to serve as the local PCO before the era of cell phones, and discover it to be still in operation. I enter the small wooden booth, its interior defaced with countless phone numbers, and dial Lauren's cell.

She answers on the fifth ring. 'Lauren, this is Sapna,' I say, keeping my voice low.

'Sapna, is that really you—' she begins before I cut her off.

'I don't have time, Lauren. Just do me a favour. Tell Guddu to meet me in front of the LIG Colony at six o'clock tomorrow morning.'

'What do you need Guddu for? Where are you calling from?'

'It's best you don't know,' I say and cut the line.

While paying for the call I ask the young attendant, 'Do you know what time the night bus leaves for Delhi?'

'At ten o'clock,' he answers. 'Are you from the Academy, *didi*?'

I nod.

'They say that girl's ghost has returned to haunt Number Seventeen.'

'Really?'

'Yes. The lab assistant saw candlelight flickering inside the house two days ago. And one of the teachers heard strange sounds coming from it.'

'I don't believe in ghosts.' I smile sadly at him. 'And, even if there is one, something tells me it will be exorcised by tomorrow.'

It is the season of water.

The Southwest Monsoon has arrived five days ahead of its normal date, and the entire city is wrapped in its soaking embrace. The thin, intermittent drizzle that started when I reached Delhi from Nainital at 5 a.m. has turned into a fully-fledged thunderstorm. Angry dark clouds rage across the slate-grey sky before bursting balefully over buildings, streets and fields. The rain pounds down in a stinging curtain, punctuated by jagged snakes of lightning.

I stand in front of apartment B–35, where a sturdy brass lock is dangling from the door. 'Come on,' I urge, nudging Guddu. 'You said you could open any lock. So let's see you open this one.'

Guddu gets to work immediately, fiddling around with a fat bunch of keys. He proves that he is indeed a master locksmith, taking less than three minutes to get the lock open. I show my appreciation by giving him five hundred rupees, virtually the last of Shalini's emergency cash. I know I won't need it any more. I have reached the end of my journey.

'Now you can go,' I tell Guddu. 'The next part I can handle myself.'

As Guddu leaves, I turn the latch and step inside the apartment. It looks like a typical bachelor's pad, sparsely furnished, with a big TV, a PS3 console and a kitchen that hasn't been used in days. Crossing the drawing room, I enter the first bedroom. It simply has an almirah, nothing else. The second bedroom is in darkness as I enter it, but it is full of a cloying smell.

I flick on the switch, flooding the small room with sickly yellow light from a naked bulb. As I look around, my eyes dilate in shock. I feel faint. The room is a shrine to Alka. Huge blowups of my sister are plastered all over the walls. There's a yellow scarf draped in a corner like a garland. It looks just like the dupatta with which Alka killed herself. And then there are morbid pictures of blood and death, skulls, serpents and satanic beasts. Proof that I am in the inner sanctum of a criminal psychopath.

I spend the next thirty minutes searching the room, opening drawers, rummaging inside closets, even upturning the mattress. I discover plenty of cash, plenty of cocaine, and a dozen letters from Alka to Hiren.

As I begin reading the letters I am taken back in time, to the idyllic world of an innocent fifteen year old who had stars in her eyes and dreams in her heart. So many of the letters make a mention of me, how Alka doted on me, trusted me with her life, that I cannot contain myself any longer. I sink to the floor clutching these last relics from

Alka. The tears that refused to fall the day she died now come gushing down as I mourn my departed sister.

The crying does me good. I feel cleansed from inside, as if a malignant deposit over my heart had been washed away.

So lost am I in that cloud of grief that I don't even notice when the front door opens and someone tiptoes in. Before I know it, a cold metallic barrel is pressed into the small of my back.

I turn around and gaze at the man wielding the gun. Dressed in a white Adidas tracksuit, he looks unkempt and scruffy. His hair is back to what it was in those old photographs, long and straight. The moustache has also grown back, thicker, even a shade darker.

'Hello, Karan,' I address him, dabbing at my eyes, 'Or should I call you Hiren?'

'Some sixth sense told me you might be coming to the colony. But I didn't expect you inside my house,' he whispers in disbelief. 'I thought I had covered my tracks pretty well.'

'You did, but a lucky five-rupee coin led me to you. Tell me, did you even go to America?'

'I never left Delhi.' He grins.

'And exactly how old are you?'

'I'm twenty. Old enough to know what it means to lose the one person you love the most in the world.'

'I also lost a sister. Alka was—'

'Don't you dare utter Alka's name,' he shrieks in outrage. Bending down, he grabs my hair and yanks me back. Pain spiders through my scalp and down my neck. With his free hand, he pulls at my T-shirt, ripping it, exposing

my bra. 'Just checking to see if you are wired up.' Then he
snatches my leather bag and upturns it. 'Good.' He nods.
'No tape recorders here either.'

'I wasn't sent here by the police.'

'I figured that out. It means no one knows my secret.
Except you.'

'And what do you intend to do with me?' I ask as a bolt
of lightning floods the room, like an enraged eye watching everything.

'Kill you, of course,' he says tonelessly, training the gun
on me, as a loud peal of thunder shakes the walls, fling-
ing open the window. 'No one will hear the gunshot in
this rain. And I can easily take care of the body.'

'Kill me if you have to,' I say calmly, 'but can you at
least tell me why you did all this? And for once can you
speak the truth?'

'The truth, eh?' he sneers. 'You were always a sancti-
monious bitch. Just like your father.'

'You hated him, didn't you?'

'Hate is a mild word. I utterly loathed him for what he
did to Alka, for what all of you did to Alka.'

I point at the corner with the yellow dupatta. 'How
come you have this piece of cloth?'

'It was part of a pact with Alka,' he says, his voice
acquiring the mellow tone of melancholy remembrance.
'The night of her death I came into her room through the
window. We made a vow to run away and get married in
an Arya Samaj Temple. The yellow cloth was to be the
marriage knot, one for her and one for me. She just asked
me for a couple of hours to pack her bags. I kept waiting
at the bus station but Alka did not come. She loved her

family too much, a family that didn't deserve her love at all. Rather than elope with me, she chose to die. Her bridal knot ended up as the noose around her neck.'

He gazes at me with judgemental eyes before resuming. 'You took away the only thing that mattered to me. When Alka died, I died too. The world became a dark place. Studies seemed pointless. I dropped out of school, burning with just one desire: to have my revenge.' He pauses for a breath, and his tone changes. Gone is the grieving lover, to be replaced by the warped psycho. 'I could have wiped out your entire family in a second. But that would have been too easy. I wanted to make you suffer. Like I have suffered since my beloved's death.'

'So you followed us to Delhi?'

'Yes. First I got rid of that vermin Pramod Sinha. I was the one who lured him to Deer Park. Nothing cooled my heart more than seeing him being run over by that truck.'

'And Neha? How did she fit into your sick scheme?'

'Alka never got along with her. Neha was so in love with herself, so obsessed with her beauty. I wouldn't have minded screwing her but she spurned me. Said a kiss was all I would get. So I had to teach her a lesson. It was me on that motorcycle who burned her with acid.' He curls his lips in contempt. 'The bitch had it coming.'

I know I am in the presence of pure evil. The turmoil that has seethed in my brain for so long is close to boiling over, rendering me speechless for an instant. In that eerie hiatus, the only sound in the room is the steady pounding of falling rain.

'But my biggest revenge was reserved for Alka's betrayer – you,' he says, his face contorting into a grotesque visage of wrath and loathing.

'So was it you who got Acharya to propose those seven tests?'

'No. I had nothing to do with that crackpot. In fact, I have still not figured out why he chose you out of the blue to be his CEO.'

'But you certainly had a role in his death, didn't you?'

'Damn right. When I couldn't dissuade you from taking part in Acharya's mind games, I decided to play a few of my own. After the second test I met Rana and made him an offer he couldn't refuse.'

'Was it you who got me attacked by those hoodlums inside the Japanese Park?'

'Who else? I needed that knife with your fingerprints.'

'And then you used the same knife to murder Acharya and frame me.'

'Bingo! The plan was to send you to the slammer for at least twenty years.'

'You might as well tell me what happened the night of the murder.'

'It went exactly as per plan. After taking care of that little business with Neha, I proceeded to Acharya's house, hidden in Rana's car. We let him finish his dinner, and then went up to his bedroom. I waved a gun in his face and told him to keep his mouth shut. The best part was calling those idiot servants pretending to be Acharya and getting rid of them for the night. Rana left five minutes later but I kept Acharya company with the gun at his head. When you called Acharya's phone from the hospital, I answered it. I was always a good mimic, and imitating Acharya's distinctive voice was dead easy.'

'When exactly did you kill Acharya?'

'Immediately after your call. The moment you started for Prarthana, you signed his death warrant. You should have seen the way the old codger squealed when I stabbed him with a knife. Once he dropped dead, I simply replaced the knife with the one carrying your fingerprints. And then I waited for you to walk into the trap.'

'So you were inside Prarthana when I arrived?'

'But of course. I was the one who answered the intercom. And I stayed even after you had left, holed up in the garage. Rana returned just after midnight and I left the way I had come, curled up inside his car. You'll have to admit it was the most ingenious murder plan ever devised.'

I remain silent, still processing what he has just said.

'If you want I can also tell you the Atlas side of the story.'

'I think I already know. The Indus Group was the front for Atlas, wasn't it?'

'Correct. Except my dad, Swapan Karak, revealed the secret to me much later. If I'd known, I'd never have agreed to impersonate Salim Ilyasi.'

'Not only did you kill Acharya, you also framed him.'

'It was a gift for Dad,' he says. 'My father never liked me, always preferring my elder brother Biren over me. After I dropped out of school he virtually disowned me. But, when the noose of Atlas around his neck began tightening, he came to me in a panic. I sorted it out for him. All it took was for Rana to put Dad's secret bank documents into Acharya's safe. So I actually managed to kill two birds with one stone.'

'And then you double-crossed Rana.'

'That skunk got greedy. He began demanding more. So Dad and I had to take care of him. And now I'm going to take care of you.'

It seems inconceivable that I loved this man once. All I feel for him now is an all-consuming hate. And I cannot bear the prospect of his going scot-free. My eyes dart around and settle on a glass paperweight with the Indus logo, just out of arm's reach. Alka's letters are still clutched in my hand. In a daring instant I fling them at him, momentarily startling him. Simultaneously my right hand shoots out, grabs the paperweight and hurls it at him. I aim for his face, but it hits him in the chest, rendering him off balance. I scramble to my feet, but, before I can gain a steady footing, Hiren lashes out with his leg, sending me crashing to the floor. I grunt in pain, only for it to increase as Hiren grinds his heel into my midsection, pinning me down. 'You had the guts, but not the aim,' he whispers, his teeth bared in a wolf's snarl.

'There's just one more question I—'

'No more talking,' he says, interrupting me. 'I'm now skipping straight to the killing.' He raises the revolver and points it directly at my face.

A foreboding sense of *déjà vu* sweeps through me, my senses heightened by the cold adrenaline of physical danger. I look into his stark, uncompromising face, into his eyes shining with a fanatic coldness, and know I can expect no mercy from him.

With the deflating knowledge that I have failed in my

mission comes a more mature realisation. Justice, revenge, retribution are best left to the gods of karma. I am going to join Alka and Papa and I want to go with a peaceful heart. In that moment I empty my mind of everything, even the thought of God. I let go of all resentment, regret, bitterness, unforgiveness, leaving only a lingering residue of sadness that I was not able to do my bit for Ma and Neha.

'Do it,' I say, just as another crack of thunder erupts outside.

Hiren thrusts the revolver inside my mouth. The cold, metallic taste of death is on my lips. It will be quick at least.

The scene unfolds with the punishing clarity of a bad dream. An obscenity slips out of Hiren's lips, his trigger finger twitches, there is the blast of a gunshot and I flinch. But, instead of toppling down, I see Hiren staggering back, incredulity written large on his face. He clutches his left shoulder, where a giant flower of blood is blooming on his tracksuit top.

ACP Khan bursts into the room, his revolver drawn, wisps of smoke curling from the barrel. The acrid smell of cordite fills my senses.

'Arrest him,' he directs the constables who surge behind him. And trailing all of them is Shalini Grover.

She embraces me. 'Thank God you are all right.'

I gaze at her with the bewildered air of a coma patient who has just regained consciousness. 'What's all this? Who tipped off ACP Khan? And what are *you* doing here?'

'It's a long story, but basically you need to thank this.'

She holds up the brown leather bag lying on the floor. 'My emergency travel bag is also a complete spy kit, with a miniature camera in the buckle, a micro audio recorder sewn into the flap and a wireless transmitter in the base. I was tracking your every move as you went from Delhi to Nainital. But, when I discovered that you were back in Delhi, I alerted ACP Khan. We've got every word uttered by Hiren on tape. This is one jam he won't be getting out of.'

The background noise of wailing sirens and the chatter of police radios drifts up into the rain-soaked air as I make my way through the mêlée of patrol cars, policemen and paramedics.

Standing in the front courtyard, I look up at the heavens. The rain has stopped completely and the sky is starting to clear up. It promises to be a gorgeous day. After all I've been through, that simple assurance rekindles something in my heart I haven't felt for a long time. Hope.

I have settled an old score. The past has finally been buried. Over the eastern horizon the future beckons, still hazy, but slowly becoming bright.

Epilogue

It is a dull, overcast day, filled with intermittent rain. I sit by the window of my new house in Saket, sipping coffee and listening to the gentle patter of raindrops cascading from the gulmohar tree that hugs the compound wall. It is in full bloom, the flame-bright flowers providing a stunning slash of colour against the turbulent grey sky.

I took the house only because of the tree. It comforts me, a shaded, scarlet haven in a hectic corner of the city.

Three months have passed since the traumatic events of June. For the first few weeks, the media hounded me relentlessly. I featured on magazine covers, trended on Twitter, became the staple fare of talk-show discussions.

The one positive outcome of my recent notoriety is that I've landed a dream job as fiction editor at Publicon, a small but sought-after imprint. The pay is good, but, more than that, it is so rewarding to be finally able to do something that taps into my passion.

Besides editing other people's stories, I am also writing my own. A top publishing house in Britain has commissioned me to write my debut book, essentially a memoir covering those tumultuous six months of my life.

My British publishers have also given me a not inconsequential advance. The money has enabled me to begin Neha's reconstructive surgery treatment. Every day brings a new cheer to her face, and the doctors say she will be able to resume her former life fairly soon.

Ma has joined Nirmala Ben and now stays with her in Gandhi Niketan. The austere life of faith, simplicity and charity suits her and has already caused a dramatic improvement in her health.

Shalini Grover is on the front page of today's newspaper, receiving the Courageous Journalism Award. As I gaze at her picture, I am filled with vicarious pride. She didn't need that exclusive interview with me after all. The front page also contains a news item that the bail applications of Hiren Karak and Swapan Karak have been denied yet again. DCP Khan (he got promoted to Deputy Commissioner of Police last month) tells me that, even if they manage to avoid the death penalty, father and son are looking at twenty-year spells in jail, at the very minimum. The Indus Group (dubbed 'The Atlas Loot' by the media) has gone into liquidation, its assets attached.

I have just set down the coffee cup when the doorbell rings. A groan escapes my lips. It is bound to be yet another pesky reporter. Rising from my seat, I answer the door with the unwilling air of a government clerk at office closing time, and stumble back in shock. Because standing on my doorstep is a ghost. It is Vinay Mohan Acharya, dressed in an off-white silk kurta pyjama, a white pashmina shawl draped across his shoulders and a vermilion tika raked across his forehead. Looking exactly as he did the day he first met me.

'I . . . I don't believe this,' I gasp, feeling my head spinning violently, my legs buckling underneath me. It is only the quick catching arms of my visitor that prevent me from collapsing in a heap on the floor.

'I'm sorry if I alarmed you,' he says as he helps me back on my feet. 'I'm Ajay Krishna Acharya, owner of the ABC Group.'

'You mean AK? Mr Vinay Mohan Acharya's brother?' I say weakly.

He nods. 'May I come inside?'

I still feel wrapped in a fog of surreality as he sits down on the wicker sofa in the drawing room. 'You look very different from the last time I saw you in Mr Acharya's house,' I observe.

'I have changed,' he replies. 'My brother's death made me take a hard look at myself, at my methods of doing business.'

'Rana was your mole in the ABC Group, wasn't he?'

'Yes,' he sighs. 'Rana was a scoundrel ready to sell his soul to the highest bidder. He was on my payroll since 2009. But when he helped Hiren murder Vinay Mohan for a handful of silver, that is when something woke up inside me. It's sad, but I discovered my brother only after his death. And I also discovered God. It will please you to know that I have just come from giving a cheque for two crores to your friend Lauren's charity.'

'So what do you want from me?'

'I want you to read this,' he says, passing me a folded sheet of paper.

'What is it?'

'A message from my brother addressed to you. I found it only yesterday, while going through Vinay Mohan's old papers. I thought you should see it.'

I open the sheet to discover a letter written on buff handmade paper monogrammed with Acharya's initials. Dated 10 June, a day before he was murdered, this is what it says in his flowing calligraphic handwriting:

My dear Sapna,

If you are reading this then I have already left this world. The pancreatic tumour has claimed me just a little bit earlier than I expected.

I am writing this from my private room in Tata Memorial Hospital, where the doctors are about to operate on me. I may not survive the operation. And, even if I do, the doctors tell me I have less than three more weeks to live. My cancer, which first metastasised to the lymph nodes surrounding the pancreas, has now spread to the liver and lungs. Even with aggressive chemotherapy my chances of survival are less than five per cent. With such odds, I have refused chemotherapy, preferring to die with dignity. As my daughter Maya always used to say, it's the quality of life that's important, not the quantity.

I have had many regrets in the last few years, but none bigger than not being able to spend as much time with you as I had wanted to. You remind me so much of my daughter.

When you met me for the first time on that cold grey afternoon of 10 December, I told you that I had seen a spark in your eyes, but that was not the whole truth. You also have something else, a generosity of spirit that is so rare to find.

I wonder if the date 23 August holds any meaning for you? To you it is probably just another day, but for me it meant a rebirth.

I have one of the rarest blood groups, the Bombay Type. Last 23 August, I had to undergo an emergency surgery. I was in a critical condition, requiring five units of blood, but none of the blood banks in the city had the Bombay Type. The doctors had almost given up on me, till you volunteered to donate your blood.

That day you saved my life. That was the day I decided to make you my CEO. I told you that you were candidate number seven, but that wasn't true. You were always the only one.

You must have thought of me as a heartless sadist when I set you those tests. But inheriting a position is easy; retaining it is the difficult part. Modern business is a dog-eat-dog world, full of risks and falls. I wanted to ensure that you had the necessary qualities not only to take over my company, but also to take it forward. More importantly, I wanted the CEO-ship to be an accomplishment, not a gift.

Through the six tests, I've already taught you the attributes of leadership, integrity, courage, foresight, resourcefulness and decisiveness. The seventh test I will unfortunately not be able to complete. But through this letter I am passing on my final lesson to you.

It is one of the paradoxes of success that the more power you gain, the more you lose control. No amount of foresight, planning or resourcefulness can keep you completely insulated from the vagaries of the outside world.

Past performance is no guarantee of future results. The fact is that nothing remains constant. You might be on top today, but there are always rivals within and without looking to bring you down. And, when that happens, you need that most essential quality in a leader: wisdom.

Many people think that wisdom comes with age, but that's not true. Only white hair and wrinkles come with age. Wisdom comes from a combination of intuition and values, from making choices and learning from them. It comes from the ability to handle failure and rejection. Each of my six tests has taught you a valuable lesson. But the most valuable lesson of life is to trust your own inner voice. Knowing the world is cleverness; knowing yourself is wisdom.

So, whatever you do, be yourself. At all times listen to your heart, do what you think is right, and stand up for the principles you believe in. Everything else will follow.

To show that I practise what I preach, I am hereby nominating you as CEO of the ABC Group. I am leaving my business in the hands of the most deserving candidate: you.

It is now up to you to set the future direction of the company and carry forward my legacy. My best wishes will always be with you.

Good luck and God bless.

Affectionately,
Vinay Mohan Acharya

I close the letter with tears in my eyes. Behind his stern façade, Acharya was a loving father and a dogged teacher, straining to impart his knowledge till his last breath. Even delivering a final lesson from the grave.

'Thank you,' I tell AK, wiping my eyes. 'I'm glad you showed this to me.'

'I didn't come here just to show you the letter,' he replies. 'I've come to make you the same offer my brother would have made you in person had he not been treacherously murdered.'

'I'm sorry, I don't understand.'

'Become CEO of the ABC Group. Only this time there won't be any tests. You've already proved your mettle.'

I remain silent, my eyes half closed, as a menagerie of memories from Acharya's tests flash before them like a newsreel on fast forward.

'How does a salary of one crore per annum sound to you?'

One crore. That's ₹10,000,000. Just the thought of all this money makes my throat run dry.

Once the initial shock subsides, I assess the offer dispassionately. All those zeroes had overwhelmed my mind; now I try to listen to my heart.

The answer comes to me in a heartbeat, and I know it is the only decision to make. 'I don't want it,' I say.

He frowns. 'Pardon me?'

'I don't want to become CEO of the ABC Group. I'm not really suited for the cutthroat world of business.'

'I think you are underestimating yourself,' he says. 'There is a lot you can contribute to the company.'

'I'm trusting my inner voice. Just like Mr Acharya wanted me to. I know that I'll be happier as a struggling writer than a business tycoon.'

'Can nothing change your mind?'

'No,' I say firmly.

'Very well, then. I will respect your wish, Sapna.' He exhales and rises.

As I watch the industrialist get into his chauffeured Bentley, I do not feel any pangs of regret. I have realised it takes more than money to be truly happy in this world. What sustains me is the love and support of my family, the kindness of friends, the compassion of strangers and the little miracles that God blesses us with every day.

One happens right before my eyes. The dark clouds are suddenly torn open, allowing the sun to break through. And then a magnificent rainbow appears, painting the sky with its dreamy, magical colours, suffusing my soul with an overwhelming joy and wonder. It leaves me without a shred of doubt in my mind. I know who I am, what I want to be.

Sometimes it takes a trial by fire to overcome our greatest fears, to find out what we are truly made of. I have passed seven tests, but more will come. And I'll be ready for them. For Acharya has taught me the most important lesson of them all.

I don't believe in lotteries: I believe in myself. Life does not always give us what we desire, but eventually it does give us what we deserve.

Acknowledgements

This book grew out of an image that came unbidden to me several years ago: of an elderly billionaire at the Hanuman Mandir in Connaught Place, searching for someone.

From that seed, a story began to sprout as I tried to figure out how and why he was there. The journey led me eventually to Sapna Sinha. In the eighteen months it took me to chart her path, Sapna became more than a character; she became a voice in her own right, one that I learnt to trust and respect.

I was fortunate in being able to call upon my family and friends for advice in mapping the seven tests. My father helped me out with some of the legal intricacies. Sheel Madhur and Dr Harjender Chaudhary gave vital creative inputs. Dr Kushal Mital and Dr Edmond Ruitenberg chipped in with their extensive medical knowledge. Varuna Srivastava served as my first reader and biggest cheerleader.

One of the verses quoted by ACP Khan is by Markandey Singh, a.k.a. Shayar Aadin.

My wife Aparna generously shared her insights into a

woman's world. My sons Aditya and Varun were both fierce critics and valuable sounding boards.

The book benefited from the suggestions made by my agents Peter and Rosemarie Buckman.

Suzanne Baboneau, Publishing Director at Simon & Schuster UK, earned my gratitude and respect for welcoming this novel with such enthusiasm. I was blessed to have an editor like Clare Hey whose astute perceptions helped sharpen the final text.

This book was written while I was posted in Osaka-Kobe. I have learnt a lot from the kindness, honesty, generosity and courage of the people of Japan. There is an order and a serenity in their country that equally calms the creative mind and excites it.

Lastly, a big thank you to my readers for their patience, loyalty and encouragement. That is the fuel that nourishes me as a writer.